D0571235

Penge Library
020 3915 7066

IE LONDON BOROUGH
ww.bromley.gov.uk

12/18

A Baby for the Billionaire

MAUREEN CHILD
JULES BENNETT
DANI WADE

MILLS & BOON

First Published in Great Britain 2019
by Mills & Boon, an imprint of HarperCollins*Publishers*
1 London Bridge Street, London, SE1 9GF

A BABY FOR THE BILLIONAIRE © 2019 Harlequin Books S. A.

Triple The Fun © 2015 Maureen Child
What The Prince Wants © 2015 Jules Bennett
The Blackstone Heir © 2015 Katherine Worsham

ISBN: 978-0-263-27471-4

0119

MIX
Paper from
responsible sources
FSC® C007454

Printed and bound in Spain
by CPI, Barcelona

TRIPLE THE FUN

MAUREEN CHILD

For all of you reading this book right now! Because of you I'm able to tell the stories I want to tell. I'm incredibly grateful for each of you!

One

"You're *where*?" Connor King didn't bother to hide the laughter in his voice. He kicked back in his office chair, propped his feet on the edge of his desk and stared out the window at his view of the Pacific Ocean. Holding the phone to his left ear, he listened to his twin's grumbling with a widening smile on his face.

"With the twins at the park near the house."

"How the mighty have crashed and burned," Connor chortled, shaking his head. Only two years ago, his identical twin, Colton, had been single, driven, a wild man who chased down every extreme adventure their company offered to other risk takers around the world.

Then Colton had found out that his ex-wife, Penny, had given birth to twins, a boy and a girl. His world had been thrown into turmoil and he'd been forced to make some real changes and face some hard truths. Though he'd nearly blown the whole thing, Colt had wised up in time to build a new life. Now he had a wife and two kids and was happier than ever before.

That didn't mean that Connor wouldn't give him grief at every opportunity, though.

"A *playdate*," he repeated with a laugh. "Man…"

"Yeah, yeah," Colt muttered. "Have your laugh and get it over with. Then we can talk about the Ireland plans. You still flying over there to check things out?"

"That's the idea," Connor said, still chuckling. In the last year, King Extreme Adventures had morphed into King Family Adventures. When Colt had finally realized what was most important in his life, he and Connor had reevaluated their business plan. Extreme adventures were risky and dangerous, and the potential client base very limited. On the other hand, by switching the emphasis of their company to family adventures, they'd opened themselves up to a worldwide audience.

Sure, they still ran the extreme adventures for those that wanted it, but since shifting their business focus, the company had grown exponentially.

"I'll be staying at Ashford Castle and Jefferson's setting me up with a guide to show me around the area."

"Amazing," Colt muttered. "We go from offering black diamond ski runs in the Alps to family tours of Ireland."

"Things change," Connor reminded him. "You should know that better than anyone."

"Not complaining," his twin said, then in a louder voice called out, "Reid, don't throw sand at your sister."

Con chuckled. "Riley can take care of herself."

"Yeah—there she goes. Sand right back at him." Colt laughed a little. "Penny's at home painting their bedroom.

I figured taking the dangerous duo to the park was the easier job. Should've known better."

While his brother talked, Connor looked up as their admin, Linda, walked into his office with the mail. She smiled at him, handed the stack of letters over and left the office. Idly, Con picked out a legal-size manila envelope from the rest and threw the others on his desk. Catching the phone between his ear and his shoulder, he ripped open the flap, pulled out the papers and skimmed them. It only took a second for him to say, "What the hell?"

Colt paused, then asked, "What's wrong?"

"You're not going to believe this," Con muttered, straightening in his desk chair, staring at the papers in his hand. The edges of his vision darkened until he was looking at the typeset words as if through a telescope. Despite the legal language designed to make most people feel inadequate to the task of deciphering it, Connor understood enough to know that his world had just taken a major shift.

"What's going on?"

Colt's voice in his ear sounded far away, as though the phone had become a tunnel miles long. Connor's gaze locked on the phrase that had leaped out at him. A heavy band tightened around his chest until drawing a breath seemed a Herculean feat. A ball of ice dropped into the pit of his stomach.

He swallowed hard and made himself say the words. "Apparently, I'm a *father*."

An hour later, Con was standing on the flagstone patio at Colt's cliff-side home in Dana Point. Staring out at the ocean below them, Con hardly noticed the sailboats, the surfers or the waves pounding against the shore with a regular rhythm that sounded like a heartbeat. If he turned his head to the left, he'd be able to see his own house, not a mile farther down the cliff road.

Colt's house was modern, with lots of glass and chrome, though Penny had made inroads there, infusing the place with warmth and color over the last couple of years. Con's place was more traditional, though it clung to the face of the cliff as well.

But he wasn't thinking about houses, style or the damn sea that relentlessly swept in and out. All he could think was: *triplets*. He'd outdone his brother by one, though he couldn't really take credit for it, could he? Sure, it had been his sperm, but it wasn't as though he'd been involved any further than that.

Hell. He hadn't even known the babies existed until today. Because a woman he'd trusted—a *friend*—had lied to him. And that was almost harder to believe than the fact that he was suddenly the father of three.

He had to get to the bottom of this. Find out everything he could before deciding on a plan of action. But there *would* be a plan. He was sure of that much, at least. What exactly it would entail was still a mystery.

Connor had put the King family lawyers on the case before he left to come to Colt and Penny's house. He was going to be logical. Rational. He wasn't giving in to his instinct to *do* something. Anything. But it wasn't easy.

So far, all he knew was the name of the woman currently suing him for child support. Dina Cortez. Sister of Elena Cortez, wife of Jackie Francis.

Jackie.

Shaking his head, Con gritted his teeth against a wild rush of anger. Jackie had been Con's best friend all through high school and college. When he got burned in love, Jackie was the one he turned to. She was the one woman in his life he'd always trusted—mainly because she'd never wanted anything from him. In fact, the only time they'd ever argued was second year of college when they'd both fallen for the same girl. A faint smile briefly twisted his mouth as he remembered that rather than discover which of them the woman might go for, they'd both chosen their friendship over the redhead.

Three years ago, Con had been Jackie's best man when she married her longtime girlfriend, Elena Cortez. Hell, he'd even taken her to Vegas for a mini bachelorette party before the wedding. He would have bet the King family fortune that Jackie would never lie to him. And yet...

"So stupid," he muttered, stabbing his fingers through his hair as a cold June wind pushed at him.

"How were you supposed to know?" Penny King stepped up alongside him and gave his arm a pat.

As much as he appreciated the support from his sister-in-law, she simply couldn't understand the level of betrayal he was feeling. *He* could hardly grasp it. "I should have checked. When Jackie moved to Northern California, I should have kept in touch. Maybe then..."

"None of this is your fault," Colt said as he walked up beside his wife and stood staring at his twin.

"My sperm. My babies. My fault." Con shook his head and tightened his grip on the bottle of beer he didn't even want. He knew his family was on his side, but the bottom line here was, he hadn't made a move to keep up with Jackie. He'd merely let her slide out of his life. If he'd done things differently, he wouldn't be in a state of shock today.

"You know," Colt murmured sagely, "it's easy to see

where you made a wrong turn when you look back at the road you're on. Not so easy when you're looking ahead."

Frowning, Connor grumbled, "You can spin this any way you want. Fact is, I screwed up."

And nothing his family said could change that. Turning his face back into the wind, gaze fixed on the frothing ocean, memories rose up and nearly choked him.

"Connor, we want to have a baby."

He laughed, dropped one arm around Jackie's shoulder and said, "Congratulations! So it's a trip to the sperm bank for you guys! See? I always told you that you'd need a man eventually."

Jackie grinned and shook her head. "Funny guy."

"I try. Which one of you's getting pregnant?"

She leaned into him and shrugged. "Elena's going to do the heavy lifting. I'm her support system."

"You'll be great parents," he assured her and steered her toward the bar in the corner of his living room. Once there, he dug a couple of beers out of the minifridge and opened them. Handing one to Jackie, he tapped the neck of his bottle against hers. Then, frowning a little, he asked, "How does that work, though? What does the kid call you? Are you both Mommy? Mommy One and Mommy Two?"

"Yeah, I don't know. We'll figure that out when we get there." Jackie took a sip of her beer and said, "There's a lot to take care of before we get to the kid talking. And part of that is, Elena and I, we wanted to ask you something important."

"Okay..." Connor picked up on her sudden nervousness, and it was so unlike Jackie, he was concerned. "What's going on?"

Rather than answer right away, she took another sip

of beer, chewed at her bottom lip and then blew out a long breath. "See, this is why Elena will carry the baby. I don't think I could give up beer for nine months."

"Uh-huh," Connor said with a frown. "Quit stalling. What is it you're trying to say?"

They'd spent the day together, catching a movie, going to check out the Porsche Connor was thinking of buying and ending up back at his house for a quick one-on-one game of basketball. She hadn't said a word about any of this. Suddenly, though, she wasn't being herself, and that was starting to worry him.

"Okay," she repeated, then took a deep breath. Lifting her gaze to his, she said, "The thing is, Elena and I have been talking about this for a long time."

"Yeah? Not surprising. You're both all about hearth and home—"

She snorted. "Yeah, we're practically a '50's sitcom. Anyway, you know how you just said we'd have to head for the sperm bank because, you know, obviously we need a donor, and—" She paused for another sip of beer as if her throat was too dry for her to force the words out. "Okay, I'm just gonna put it out there. We don't want to go with some stranger we picked out of a catalog. We'd like you to be the baby daddy."

Surprise slapped at him. For a second or two, he could only stare at his best friend. Jackie's gaze was sure and steady, but there was also a flicker of understanding there, too, as if she knew exactly what he was feeling. Well, hell. He hadn't really thought about who might be the father of the child his friend wanted so badly—he'd assumed that she and Elena would go to a sperm bank and pick out some genius donor.

But now that she'd asked him, Connor realized it

*made sense. He and Jackie were practically family. Who
the hell else would she ask?*

"Elena wants this, too?"

*"Completely," Jackie assured him, and now that ev-
erything was out in the open, she was clearly more relaxed. "Con, there's no pressure on you, okay? Feel free
to say no, with no hard feelings between us, I swear.
Just...don't say no right away. Think about it, all right?"*

*Connor reached out, grabbed her and pulled her in
for a tight hug. She sighed, wrapped her arms around
his middle and held on. "I know this is big, Con. Seriously big. And I know it's kind of weird, me asking you
for your baby stuff. But—" she tipped her head back and
looked at him "—we really want this and we want that...
connection to the baby's father, you know? You mean a
lot to us. Not just me."*

*He gave her a squeeze. "Yeah, I know. I love you,
too."*

"God, we're mushy all of a sudden."

"Babies'll do that to you, I hear," Con said.

*Her eyes went misty. "A baby. Hard to imagine me
a mom."*

*"No, it's not," he assured her. And seeing that dreamy,
wistful look on her face would have decided him even if
he hadn't already made the choice. They'd been friends
so long, how could he not help her when she needed it?
"I'd have a condition, Jack..."*

She sucked in a breath and held it. "What?"

*"I can't just father a kid and walk away. I'll have to
be a part of my child's life."*

Part-time father, *he told himself.* All of the fun and
little of the hassles.

"Absolutely, Con. Agreed."

"All right then." Connor swung her in a circle and Jackie shrieked with laughter. When he set her on her feet again, he gave her a fast, hard kiss and said, "Let's make a baby."

They'd tried.

But Jackie told him the insemination hadn't taken. When he'd offered to help them try again, she'd turned him down. Said that she and Elena were moving to Northern California to get a fresh start. Then she'd sort of disappeared from his life. No phone calls. No nothing.

He'd allowed it to happen, too, so he couldn't throw all the blame on Jackie for that. "I should have checked," he said again, hating that he hadn't.

"Yeah, well—" Colt leaned back against the low stone wall separating the patio from a wide swath of manicured lawn "—who would have expected Jackie to lie to you?"

That was the hardest part to swallow, Connor admitted silently. He'd always trusted her. Had never doubted what she told him. And all this time, she'd hidden *his children* from him.

Con shook his head and squinted into the wind. His heartbeat raced and the ice in his stomach was colder, deeper somehow than it had been only an hour before. And after all the lies, he couldn't even yell at her. Because she and Elena were dead. He hadn't been able to cut through most of the legalese in the damn letter from the lawyer, but that much he'd caught. Dina Cortez, the babies' guardian, named by the *late* Jackie and Elena Francis, was the one suing him.

How the hell could he mourn his friend when he was so furious with her all he wanted to do was rage at her for what she'd done?

"So who's Dina Cortez?" Colt folded his arms over his chest.

"Elena's sister," Connor told him. "I met her at the wedding. She was Elena's maid of honor and the only one of her family who showed up." He frowned. He still couldn't understand how family didn't support family, no matter what. "Don't remember much about her, really."

"Doesn't matter, I guess," Colt mused. "You'll be getting to know her pretty damn well soon enough."

"True." And he'd have plenty to say once he met up with Dina Cortez again.

"Sure," Dina said into the phone. "We can cater your anniversary party on the twenty-fourth. No problem. If it's all right with you, we can meet later this week to discuss the menu."

Idly tapping her pen against the desktop calendar already filled with doodles, squiggles and notes incomprehensible to anyone but her, Dina listened to her latest client talk with only half an ear.

How could she concentrate when she knew that very soon, she was going to be clashing with one of the Kings of California? Connor King, father of the triplets even now playing on the floor beside her, was a member of a family with more money than God and far more power than she could ever hope to claim.

She'd met him once before, when Dina's sister, Elena, had married her longtime partner, Jackie Francis. Connor had been Jackie's best man and he'd caught Dina's attention from the moment she saw him. Of course, any woman would have been captivated by the man. He was gorgeous and possessed that innate sense of being in charge that was both alluring and irritating to a strong woman.

His easy relationship with Jackie was one of long standing; they'd been best friends since high school. But what was more impressive to Dina at the time was that he had been so focused on being there for his friend. Most single guys used a wedding as an opportunity to pick up women. But Connor hadn't paid attention to anyone but his friend.

Of course, he might be feeling a little differently toward Jackie at the moment. What Jackie and Elena had done to him was unforgivable.

While her client rambled on in her ear, Dina shifted her gaze to the babies behind a series of child gates. When the kids came to live with her, she had cordoned off a section of her work area in the kitchen. Blankets were piled on the floor, toys were scattered everywhere and three beautiful thirteen-month-old babies giggled and squealed and babbled to each other in a language no one but the three of them could possibly understand.

In a few short months, those babies had become Dina's whole world and it terrified her to think of what Connor King might do when he found out about them. Would he fight her for custody? Oh, boy, she hoped not. There was no way she could win in a legal battle with a King.

Her client finally wound down and in the sudden silence, Dina said quickly, "Right. I'll give you a call in a day or two and we'll set up that meeting. Okay, great. Thank you for calling. Goodbye."

She hung up and her fingers rested lightly on the back of the receiver. Naturally, as soon as she was off the phone, the babies got quiet. Smiling, she looked at them, two boys and a girl, and felt a hard, swift tug at her heart. She loved her niece and nephews, but being a single mother wasn't something she had planned for.

But then, Jackie and Elena hadn't *planned* to die, had they? Tears stung the backs of her eyes and she blinked them away. She looked at those shining, smiling faces watching her, and Dina felt such sorrow for her sister. She and Elena had been close, joined together against the chaos their mother had created. With their grandmother, the two sisters had formed a unit that had been shattered when Elena died.

Heart aching, Dina thought about her big sister and wished desperately that things were different. Elena had wanted nothing more, for most of her life, than to be a mother. She'd dreamed of having her own family.

Then she and her wife, Jackie, had finally succeeded in having the children that completed them, only to die before their triplets were a year old. The unfairness of it ripped at Dina and lodged a hard knot of pain in the center of her chest. But crying wouldn't help. She should know. Dina had cried an ocean of tears in the first couple of weeks after her sister and her wife died unexpectedly. So she was done with tears, but not panic.

Panic wasn't going anywhere. It came to haunt her in the middle of the night when she lay awake trying to figure out how to care for three babies all on her own. It walked beside her when she took the kids for a walk in their triple stroller. It whispered in her ear every time she bid on a catering job and didn't get it.

Which was one of the reasons she had decided to sue Connor King. He had money. Besides, he had been a big part of Jackie and Elena's lives. He had been prepared to be a part of the kids' lives. He owed it to his children to help pay for their support. With fewer financial worries, she could hire a part-time nanny to assist her in taking care of the triplets. Not that she was looking to bail out of caring for them—she wasn't. But she had to work and leaving them with a babysitter—even a great one like Jamie, the teenage girl who lived next door—just wasn't a permanent solution.

Sadie, Sage and Sam were all looking to her for protection. For safety. For love. She wouldn't fail them. Smiling down as the boys wrestled and Sadie slapped her teddy bear, Dina promised, "You'll know who your mommies were, sweet babies. I'll make sure of it. They loved you so much."

Sadie chewed on her bear's ear and Dina huffed out a sigh. Raising three babies alone wouldn't be easy, but she would do it. The triplets were what was important now, and Dina would do whatever she had to do to protect them. And on that thought, she stood up and announced, "You guys ready for a treat?"

Three heads spun toward her with identical expressions of eager anticipation. She laughed a little as Sadie pulled herself to her feet and demanded, "Up!"

"After your snack, okay, sweet girl?" The sweet girl in question's bottom lip quivered and Dina had to steel her heart against giving in. If she got Sadie up, then Sage and Sam would want out, too, and instead of a snack, she'd spend the next half hour chasing the three of them through her house. And, since it was closing in on their bedtime, she didn't want them getting all worked up anyway.

Before any of them could start complaining—*loudly*—Dina hustled to the counter to slice up a couple of bananas and pour milk into three sippy cups. Thank heaven Elena and Jackie had weaned them off bottles early. As soon as the kids were settled, gnawing happily on bananas and laughing together, the doorbell rang.

"You guys be good," she said and headed down the hall to the front door. She took a quick peek out the side window at the man on her porch and gasped. *Connor King.* The image of him was so clear and sharp in her memory, it was almost weird to see him standing on her porch.

Panic swam through her veins and she wasn't even surprised. She was becoming used to that out-of-control sensation, and she was pretty sure that wasn't a good thing. Somehow, Dina hadn't expected this meeting to happen so quickly. Maybe she should have. He was a King and he'd just found out he was the father of three children. Of course he would show up. Of course he would start pushing his metaphorical weight around. She knew enough about him and his family to know that he was going to be a formidable opponent, no matter what.

And since there was no ignoring him, she squared her shoulders, lifted her chin and yanked the door open. "Connor King," she said. "I wasn't expecting you."

"You should have been," he ground out tightly, then pushed past her into the house. "Where are my kids?"

Two

Conner had come for his kids, but now couldn't take his eyes off the woman who'd opened the door. Lust surged through him, grabbed him at the base of his throat and held on tight. All he could do was try to breathe through it.

The woman currently glaring at him had huge, chocolate-brown eyes, thick black hair hanging loose around her shoulders and long, gorgeous legs displayed by the white shorts she wore. Her short-sleeved red T-shirt clung to her body, showing off breasts that were just the right size to fill a man's hands.

Con couldn't understand how he hadn't noticed her at Jackie and Elena's wedding two years ago. Or how he'd managed to forget her. This was *not* a forgettable woman.

"Dina Cortez?" he asked, though he knew damn well who she was.

"Yes. And you're Connor King."

He nodded. Lust was still there, clawing at him, but he breathed through it and got back on track. "Now that the formalities are over, where are the kids?"

She folded her arms beneath her breasts, lifted her chin and said, "You shouldn't be here."

"Yeah," Con told her. "That's what my lawyer said, too."

In fact, he hadn't needed his lawyer to tell him to stay clear until they had more answers. Con knew he shouldn't have come, but there was no way he could stay away, either. He was a father. Of triplets. How the hell was a man supposed to ignore that?

He'd had to come, see the kids and find out what he could for himself, minus lawyerspeak. His twin had understood, though Penny had argued against it. But then, a couple of years ago, Colt had barged right in, too, to get a look at his twins and to confront the woman who'd given birth to them and then kept them a secret.

Well, Con couldn't face down Jackie or Elena, but the triplets were here, which explained, at least to him, why he was.

"Lawyers can still do their legal dance," he said, silently congratulating himself on keeping the temper still frothing inside him at a low boil. "For now, I had to come."

"Why?"

"*Why?*" He choked out a short laugh and shook his head. "Because I just found out I'm a father by hearing that I'm being sued for child support."

"Maybe if you had kept in contact with Jackie and Elena you would have known earlier," she pointed out.

"Seriously? You really want to go there? Maybe if

my best friend hadn't *lied* to me about those kids, this wouldn't be an issue," he argued and took a step closer. "And your *sister* was in on those lies," he reminded her tightly.

She blew out a breath and seemed to release some of the anger he could still see churning in her eyes. "Fine. You're right. They didn't tell me, either, you know. About you, I mean. They didn't tell me who the babies' father was."

His breath exploded in a rush. He was angry and had nowhere to focus it. He and Dina had been caught up in a web spun by Jackie and Elena. God, he wanted five minutes with Jackie just to demand some answers. But since he wasn't going to get that time, he said, "How did you find out about me, then?"

Sighing, Dina said, "There was a letter to you in their papers. I read it."

His eyebrows lifted.

She saw it and shrugged. "If you're waiting on an apology, there isn't one coming."

Reluctantly, he felt a flash of admiration for her. She was tough. He could appreciate that. She was gorgeous and he really appreciated *that*. Lust still had him by the throat and it was a wonder he could talk at all. Hard to keep his mind on what was happening when his body was urging him to think about something else entirely.

That compact yet curvy body, her dusky olive-toned skin and the wary glitter in her eyes all came together to make Connor grateful to be a man. She smelled good, too. But none of that was important right now.

"Fine," he finally managed to say. "How about a few answers, then?"

Nodding, she walked into the living room and he followed. The house was small and old, like every other bungalow in this section of Huntington Beach. Yards were narrow, houses were practically on top of each other and parking was hard to come by.

He'd noticed when he arrived that her yard was so ratty it looked like she kept goats. The driveway had more potholes than asphalt and the roof needed replacing. The whole place could use a coat of paint and he'd been half-afraid what the inside might look like.

But here he was surprised. The house was old but clean. Clearly, Dina put whatever time and money she had into maintaining the inside rather than the outside. The hardwood floors were scarred but polished. The walls had been painted a soft gold and boasted framed photographs of family and nature. The furniture looked comfortable and though the house was small, it was welcoming.

A hallway spilled from the living room and led, he guessed, to the bedrooms. There was a small dining room attached to the living area and beyond that, the kitchen. A happy squeal erupted and Con flinched. The triplets were back there. His children.

He scrubbed one hand across his face in a futile attempt to clear his mind. Shaking his head, he ground out, "My lawyer did some checking after I got your lawsuit papers this morning."

She frowned a little, but he didn't care if she was having second thoughts about suing him now.

"He says Jackie and Elena died three months ago?"

All of the air seemed to leave her. Dina slumped and dropped into the closest chair. "Elena was taking flying lessons." A smile curved her mouth briefly. "She wanted to be able to come down here to visit me and our grand-mother whenever she wanted to."

Con's stomach clutched.

"Anyway, she got her license and to celebrate, she and Jackie went on a weekend trip to San Francisco."

"Without the kids?"

She nodded. "Thank God, as it turned out. One of their friends stayed at the house with the triplets. Any-way, on their way home, there was some kind of engine trouble. Elena wasn't experienced enough to compensate for it and they went down in a field."

Pain slapped at him as Connor's mind filled with memories of Jackie. Of the years they'd spent together, of the laughs, of all the good times. He hated knowing she was dead. Hated thinking how scared she must have been at the end. Hated that she wasn't here for him to yell at. Getting past his own racing thoughts, he looked at Dina and saw the misery in her eyes before she could mask it. And he was forced to remember that she'd lost her sister in that crash.

"I'm sorry," he said. "About Elena."

"Thank you," she said, taking a breath as she stood up to face him. "And I'm sorry about suing you without talking to you first."

A snort of laughter shot from his throat. "Aren't we polite all of a sudden."

"Probably won't last," she mused.

Con thought of all that had to be settled between them—of the triplets and their welfare, of his still sim-mering rage at having been lied to for two years—and he had to agree. "Probably not."

Nodding, Dina accepted that and asked, "So where does that put us right now?"

"Opposite sides of a fence," Connor answered.

"That's honest, anyway."

"I prefer honest. Lies always end up getting…messy." He didn't say it, but judging by Dina's expression, she heard the implication. That it was her sister and Jackie's lies that had brought them here, tangling the two of them up in a situation that was only going to get more chaotic.

Connor was here to claim his children. To do the right thing no matter who got in his way. That included Dina Cortez.

His stomach clenched as he heard a squeal of laughter soaring from the other room.

God, he was a father, and the ramifications of *that* hadn't sunk in yet. He'd only had a few hours to try to wrap his head around the fact that everything he knew had changed with the simple act of opening that envelope from Dina's lawyer.

He'd helped Jackie and Elena because he wanted to. And, he remembered, because he thought it might be fun to be on the periphery of a child's life—more as a benevolent uncle than a father. But things were different now and they'd all have to adjust.

"So, is this a truce?"

Con looked at Dina when she spoke and thought about it for a second or two. He was still angry—he didn't think that would be going away any time soon—but he had to at least bury that anger long enough to do the right thing. And that meant making sure his children were cared for. How Dina would fit into the future, he didn't know. But better to keep her close until he figured it all out.

When she shifted under his steady regard, he finally said, "Truce. For now."

A long, high-pitched wail erupted from the other room and in the next couple of seconds, two more voices joined the first until those cries built into a combined sound that ratcheted through Con's head like a hammered spike. "What the—"

Dina was already walking and threw back over her shoulder, "You want to be a father? Now's your chance."

Con swallowed back a quick jolt of nervousness and followed her. Hell, the King family had experienced a population explosion in the last few years. Every time the cousins got together, they passed kids from arm to arm, so he wasn't a stranger to crying babies. The fact that these were *his* children made the situation a little different, naturally. But he could handle it.

His babies. His children. Something visceral swamped him and he could finally understand and sympathize with everything his twin had gone through when he'd discovered his own kids. At the time, Connor had listened, sympathized and commiserated, but now he realized just what a life-altering moment this really was. Looked like he owed Colt an apology.

Yet even though he was twisted up over the circumstances they'd found themselves in, he was male enough to enjoy the view Dina provided as she walked away from him. The woman had a great behind.

Shaking his head fiercely, Connor told himself to get a grip and followed her. It wasn't far and yet it felt to him as if he was taking the longest journey of his life. From bachelor to father. From a single man to a family man.

And he wasn't sure yet just how he felt about it.

In the kitchen, he glanced around quickly, noting white walls, black counters and splashes of red in the curtains hanging over the window and the toaster and blender sitting on the counter. But it wasn't the house he was interested in right now. Instead, everything in him concentrated on the far end of the big, square room. There, behind a series of interlocked child gates, were the triplets.

One of them, a girl, stood up, wobbling a little, clutching the top rail of the gate and howling like a banshee. When she saw Dina, the tiny girl started stamping her feet as if she were marching in place. Dina swept the baby into her arms, then turned to face Connor.

"Sadie, meet your daddy."

Tears tracked along her cheeks. Wispy black curls framed her face and Connor's heart expanded so quickly, so completely, he felt a physical ache. A connection he hadn't really expected leaped to life as he looked at the tiny human being he had helped to create. Her coloring was all King, but the shape of her eyes was just like Elena's. Like Dina's. The baby stopped crying as she looked at Connor, and in a blink, she went from tears to a tiny coy smile that tugged at his heart as surely as her little fingers plucked at Dina's shirt.

Without another word, Dina handed him the baby girl, then turned to gather up the boys. She straightened with a baby on each hip, clinging to her shoulders. "They need to be changed, and since they've already had dinner, it's bath time, followed by story time and bedtime and then the countless middle-of-the-night cry times." She tipped her head and looked at him. "You up for this?"

Sadie slapped both hands against his cheeks, then dropped her head onto his shoulder with a soft sigh. Con was toast and he knew it.

"I'm up for it."

* * *

Dina had to give it to him.

She hadn't expected Connor to know a thing about handling babies. First, because he was a man, and sexist it might be, but in her experience the only thing a man knew about kids was how to hand them off to the nearest woman. Secondly, didn't the rich hire nannies so they didn't *have* to know how to care for a baby?

But he'd surprised her. Again. The first big surprise of the day had come when he'd shown up at her house unannounced and snarly yet still managing to look edible. Through their uncomfortable first meeting, the anger on both sides and the still simmering distrust, Dina had felt the unmistakable sizzle of desire.

Oh, it wasn't a good idea, but what woman wouldn't feel it? Tall, with broad shoulders, narrow hips and long legs, Connor King was the kind of man who captured attention as easily as he breathed. His black hair was a little too long, hanging over the collar of his white shirt while thick hanks of it fell across his forehead. His eyes were an icy blue and his mouth seemed to be frozen in a grim slash that only occasionally twisted into a half smile that should have been reassuring, yet wasn't. He had a right to be angry, she knew.

But he didn't have the right to be mad at *her*. She hadn't known about him until a couple of weeks ago. Okay, maybe she should have contacted him directly rather than going through lawyers, but she hadn't expected him to care. He had been a sperm donor—an untraditional one, yes, but nothing more.

Though her sister had never told Dina who the babies' father was, she had said that he'd made the donation and then disappeared from their lives. That was their story.

Of course Elena hadn't bothered to tell Dina that Connor didn't *know* about the children he'd fathered. She winced and silently acknowledged just how complicated this whole thing really was.

Until she'd read the letter that Jackie left for Connor, Dina had assumed he wasn't interested in a relationship with his kids. Which was why she had been so furious when she discovered who the babies' father really was. Because of the secret kept by Jackie and Elena, Dina had been scrambling to take care of the children when it hadn't been necessary.

Connor King was so wealthy that providing for the triplets would be easy compared to how Dina's life was going at the moment. With all the added expense of caring for the three children she was responsible for, she'd had to push her catering business to the max. She was bidding on everything from a ten-year-old's birthday party to the local bank's grand opening. Some jobs she got, some she lost.

And while getting jobs meant staying alive, she was left with the question of who took care of the kids while she worked. Dina's grandmother was always glad to help out, but the triplets were too much for the older woman to take care of on a regular basis, and paying Jamie to babysit pretty much ate up any profit Dina was lucky enough to make.

It had been a hard three months, adjusting to life as a single mom, so was it any wonder she'd sued for child support the moment she found out who the babies' father was?

A splash of water and a screech of outrage caught her attention. Gladly letting her thoughts slide away to be examined later, Dina stepped over the threshold into the cottage's one bathroom. The triplets were in the tub, Connor hanging over it, his sleeves rolled up to his elbows as he tried to deal with all three wet, slippery babies. Puddles gathered on the floor and under the knees of his slacks.

"Don't take the ducky from your sister," he said and relieved one baby of the duck in question.

A howl of outrage followed and Connor said quickly, "Here, um, which one are you? Sam? Sage? Have a boat."

Dina laughed softly, enjoying seeing someone else fight the battle of the bath for a change. Sadie loved the water, Sage spent bath time trying to escape it and Sam would fall asleep sitting up in the warm water if you weren't careful. Sadie splashed again and laughed in delight when Connor yelped as the water hit his eyes.

"Okay, little girl, no fair splashing when I'm trying to get hold of your brother."

Sadie babbled at him while Sage climbed up Connor's chest, a wet, wriggling mass eager to be out of the tub. Connor grabbed one towel, wrapped it around the tiny boy, and said, "Stay right there."

Then he turned his back on Sage to reach for the next baby. Sadie scooted out of reach, so it was Sam who was the next one out and wrapped like a burrito in a soft, dark blue towel.

Dina just watched. Sure, she could grab the boys and lend Connor a hand, but this was more interesting. She wanted to see how he reacted to the nightly ritual. If he'd fold or rise to the occasion.

While Connor reached out to grab Sadie, Sage dropped his towel and ran past Dina into the hallway, giggling all the way.

"Wait! Come back here!" Connor lifted Sadie,

wrapped her up and swung around. His gaze met Dina's and he said, "Well, thanks for the help." Frowning, he looked past her into the hallway, swinging his hair out of his eyes. "Where'd he go?"

She shrugged and smiled wider. Couldn't help herself. "Where he always goes. To the toy box in their room."

"Great," Connor said, holding onto Sadie while she squirmed, trying to get back into the water. Sweeping Sam up into his arms as well, Connor stood and faced her.

He was dripping wet. His white shirt was soaked through and plastered to what looked like a very impressive chest. Water droplets rolled down his face and clung to his hair. She smiled again. How could she not?

"Did you enjoy the show?"

"Oh, a lot," she assured him, still grinning. "But the show's not over yet. There are still three naked babies to diaper, put into jammies and settle down for bed."

He shifted the two on his hips. "And you think I can't do it?"

"I know you can't," she said, leaning against the door-jamb, folding her arms across her chest. "Not on your own."

Sadie squirmed; Sam grabbed a handful of Connor's hair and tugged. "Wanna bet?"

From the other room came Sage's high-pitched squeals and the sound of a little truck being pushed across the floor. Dina bent down, picked up the discarded towel and tossed it over Connor's shoulder. He'd had a rough go of it, but he was still standing, and she had to admire him for that. Still, she had the feeling he was about done.

"Absolutely," she said, enjoying the harried expression on Connor's face. She'd known him less than four hours, but she knew that harried wasn't a look he often wore. This was a man who ruled his world. He was used to people jumping to do his bidding. Now he had to deal with three babies who were used to calling the shots. He was in so much trouble. "What's the bet?"

A slow, seductive smile curved his mouth and Dina's insides shivered in response. Maybe betting with Connor King wasn't the smartest move she could make.

He hefted both babies a little higher and then said, "When I win, we sit down with a glass of wine and talk about where we go from here."

"And when I win, you write a check and disappear?"

The smile on his face faded away and Dina thought she'd gone too far. But what did he expect? She'd known him just a few hours and he'd crashed into her home, her family and taken over as if he had the right—which he didn't. Not from where she was standing.

He took a step closer and she kept her gaze on his. Still holding the babies close, he said, "It won't be that easy, Dina. I'm not going anywhere, so you'd better get used to it."

"And if I can't?" she asked.

"I'm willing to bet you can."

Three

Dina really didn't want to be impressed, but she was.

When the triplets first came to live with her, she'd been completely lost and practically hopeless at caring for them. She hadn't done much babysitting as a kid and none of her friends had children, so she'd had zero experience. But she'd consoled herself with the fact that most first-time moms were as lost as she herself was. Since she didn't have any choice but to jump in and do the best she could, Dina had learned as she went. She hadn't so much gotten the babies into a routine as she'd gotten herself into one. She'd had to learn from scratch—and fast—how to take care of three babies, and she'd made too many mistakes to count.

Then Connor King arrived, jumped into the fray like a natural and handled it all. He'd seemed so darn sure of himself, she'd stood back, prepared to gleefully watch a disaster unfold. Instead, he'd taken charge, as he probably did in every other aspect of his life, and gotten the job done. Sure, he was a little harried, but he'd done it. Babies were bathed and dressed and tucked into their beds with a story read by Connor, complete with sound effects that had them all giggling.

And honestly, that's what irritated her the most. The babies *liked* him. She was here day in and day out and one visit from a handsome stranger and all three of them were won over. What happened to loyalty to good old Aunt Dina, she wanted to know.

As she watched from the nursery door, she felt a small niggle of worry as Connor moved from crib to crib, smoothing his hand across the babies' heads, each in turn. He was taking a moment—what he probably thought was a private moment—to really look at the children he'd helped to create. She thought she understood what he might be feeling right then, as she'd had a very similar moment herself when the trips had come to live with her. To her, it had felt like a wild mixture of protectiveness and the realization that her life as she had known it was over.

She hadn't planned on having custody, obviously, but now Dina loved those babies with a fierceness she wouldn't have believed possible. They were her family. Her only real family now, except for her grandmother and a handful of distant cousins. She would do whatever was necessary to take care of the trips and to protect them from being hurt. Even if that meant protecting them from the man who had only wanted to be a part-time father.

By the time the evening was over, Connor was wet, exhausted and wanted nothing more than a cold beer, his bed and complete silence for ten or twelve hours. One out of three, he told himself wryly, wasn't too bad.

He took a long drink of the beer Dina'd given him and let the cold froth slide through him, easing away the tension that had had him in its grip for the last couple of hours.

"So," Dina said and he heard the grudging respect beneath her words, "you won the bet."

He managed to turn his head to look at her. "I always do, honey."

Her eyebrows lifted. "Honey?"

His lips quirked. The offhanded *honey* had slipped out, but now that he saw how annoyed she was by it, he pushed it a little further, just for the hell of it. "Babe?"

She inhaled sharply and hissed out a breath. "Dina will do."

"Right." He tipped his head and hid his smile. Connor had only known her for a few hours, but he'd already seen how easy it was to rub her the wrong way. And, for reasons he couldn't quite identify yet, he really enjoyed pushing her buttons. There was just something about this woman that urged him to push against her boundaries. "I'll remember that, Dina. Just as you should remember that when I say I'm going to do something, I do it."

"Noted."

"Good. I'm too tired to say it again." He leaned his head against the back of the couch and thought about plopping his feet on the footstool, but he was too beat to lift his own legs. "Those three are something else. Just keeping them all in the tub wore me out. I don't know how you do the whole bath and changing thing every night all alone."

"I bathe them one at a time."

He looked at her again and noticed a smile tugging at her mouth. Apparently he wasn't the only one enjoying himself. "And you didn't think that worth mentioning?"

"Well, you seemed so confident of your abilities..." She sipped at a glass of wine. "I didn't want to interfere."

"Uh-huh." He shook his head. "Well played."

"Thanks, but you got through it anyway. It was hard, but you did it. I hate to admit it, but I'm sort of impressed." She studied her wine, sliding her fingertips up and down the long, delicate crystal stem until Connor had to look away from her before he embarrassed himself. "You don't strike me as the type to know much about kids."

"I didn't," he acknowledged. "Until two years ago. My brother Colt discovered he was the father of twins. So watching him, I picked up a lot. But *three* seems like a lot more than two. Still, I gave him a lot of grief—made jokes about just how demented his life had become," he mused. "Now I feel bad about that."

"Two years?"

She'd caught that. He looked at her again and sighed. "Yeah. Right after Colt reconnected with his kids, Jackie came to me asking for help." He paused for another drink of his beer. Maybe he'd been delusional, but at the time, he'd thought it could be fun. Help Jackie and give himself a sort-of family like Colt had, only without all the hassles and the interruptions to the way he wanted to live. "Getting to know my niece and nephew is probably what pushed me into agreeing to this whole deal."

"No, that wasn't it."

One eyebrow winged up. "Is that right? Know me so well, do you? After three whole hours?"

"No," she said. "I don't know you. But Jackie did.

And she told me all about how tight you guys were. I heard all sorts of stories about you before the wedding."

That was disconcerting. He knew next to nothing about Dina. Hell, he barely remembered speaking to her at the wedding. And Connor really didn't care for being at a disadvantage.

Warily, he asked, "What kind of stories?"

She laughed a little and he thought that probably wasn't a good sign.

"The one about the redhead comes to mind," she admitted.

Surprised, he choked out a laugh. "She was a beauty," he admitted. "But we made a pact that neither of us would hit on her since we both wanted her."

"You cared more for your friendship."

He frowned. "Yeah. Back then, anyway. Apparently, things changed when I wasn't looking."

"Jackie loved you."

Con snapped her a quick, hard look. He didn't need her to tell him about Jackie. Or maybe he did. Everything he'd known was tossed into a high wind at the moment and he wasn't sure of anything anymore. But he wasn't going to talk about Jackie now. Not while his anger was so fresh and raw.

"Yeah," he muttered instead, "I'm convinced."

"All I'm saying is that you and Jackie were really tight. That's why you helped. For her. It had nothing to do with your niece and nephew. You did it for Jackie."

"Reid and Riley played a part, but yeah," he said, voice cold, "she was my best friend. Or so I thought."

In the flood of information that had hit him today, he'd hardly had time to react to any of it. The triplets had taken first priority in his mind, because they were here and the immediate problem of dealing with them was hanging over his head. But the truth was, Jackie's loss was at the back of his mind at all times.

He hated knowing she was gone. That he'd never see her again. And mostly, he hated the fact that he hadn't kept in touch with her when she and Elena moved. Not just because then he would have known about the babies, but because Jackie had been a huge part of his life from the time they were teenagers and now he just missed her, damn it. She had cut him out, true, but he hadn't called. Hadn't asked what was going on. Why she wasn't calling. Instead, he'd let it go by telling himself that it was *her* doing, and that wasn't true at all.

Over the years, whenever he had gone silent, Jackie had been the one to call and demand to know what was happening in his life. To say, *Hello? You alive?* But when she pulled back, he'd never said a word. He hadn't called. He'd assumed that she was through with him and he let it go.

Granted, friendships didn't always last. Even the best of friends eventually hit a bump too big to navigate around and ended up drifting apart. But he hadn't expected it to happen to him and Jackie. Now she was gone and he would never be able to talk to her again. To tell her he was sorry that he hadn't called to find out what she was going through.

"I don't agree with what they did either," Dina said softly, as if she knew what he was thinking.

He shot her a look, bothered by the fact that she seemed to read him so easily. "They didn't lie to you, though. They didn't deliberately cut you out of their lives."

"No," she said. "They didn't. But Elena kept things from me, too. She never told me your name."

He sat up straighter, rested his forearms on his thighs and cradled his beer bottle between his palms. He'd been a secret all the way around. In spite of what Jackie had said to him in the beginning, they might as well have gone to a sperm bank, because he had become an anonymous donor anyway. He was DNA handily acquired and soon forgotten.

There was a slap in the face as well as the heart. Damn it, why had Jackie done it? And why did he care? Whatever her reasons, they couldn't make up for what his reality was now. Anger churned into a nasty brew inside him until it was hard to draw a breath and impossible to take another swallow of beer without choking on it.

Connor needed some time to think. To plan. To gather the wildly racing thoughts circling his mind. Being here, with the kids, with the woman who was too much a distraction, wasn't helping him lay out the immediate future.

Connor liked knowing how things were going to play out. In the business he shared with Colt, Con was the guy who always thought two steps ahead. He laid out the path for their company to follow. He was the one who always knew what was coming next.

Until now.

Now he could only go with his gut. "I'll be needing a paternity test."

She sucked in a gulp of air. "You really think that's necessary?"

"No," he said shortly. Hell, all it had taken was one look at the triplets to convince him they were his. They weren't identical, of course, but each of them had the distinctive King coloring. It was more than that, though.

He'd felt a connection to those children right from the first and that was something he couldn't deny.

"My lawyers will want it," he said, not liking having to explain himself.

"Fine. Then what?"

"Then," he said, setting the beer onto the closest table before standing up, "we'll do what comes next."

"And what's that?" She stood, too, but kept her distance.

"I'll let you know."

"I think you mean we'll decide what that is together."

He laughed shortly. "I meant what I said. Those triplets in there are mine. They're Kings. I'll do the deciding here."

Her cheeks flushed with color and he knew it wasn't a blush but fury that fed the rosiness blooming across her face. "I'm their legal guardian," she reminded him. "My *sister* and her wife wanted the babies in my care."

Con didn't have the time or the patience to fight this battle right now. "And your sister and her wife *hid* my children's existence from me. For all I know, you were in on it."

"I told you I wasn't."

"And I should believe you."

She gulped in air. "Yeah, you should. Why would I lie?"

"Why would Jackie?" he countered and when she didn't have an answer for that, he nodded sharply. "Right. Anyway. I'll want time with the triplets while things are being settled."

She nodded. "I thought you would."

"And I want the letter Jackie left for me."

Her features went stiff and cool, as if she were deliberately shutting off her emotions. He couldn't blame her, because he wished to hell he could do the same. But everything he was feeling was too close to the surface. Too damn inflamed and sensitive to be buried—so instead he had to fight to push them aside.

Without another word, Dina walked across the room to a small secretary table holding a cobalt-blue bowl of fresh flowers. Connor joined her and waited as she opened the top drawer, withdrew an envelope, then handed it to him. Once she had, she crossed her arms over her chest again in what was obviously a self-protective stance.

Too bad she didn't know that whenever she did it, all she really managed to do was hike her breasts up even higher, demanding his attention. Slowly, he lifted his gaze to meet hers.

"Look," she said, "we didn't get off to the best start, but I think we can both agree that we want what's best for the triplets."

Con looked from her to the envelope for a long minute, then tucked it carefully into his inside jacket pocket. He wasn't going to read it here, with an audience.

"We do agree on that much," he allowed, then added, "but we might have different ideas as to what the *best* actually is."

"I guess we'll have to work on that when the time comes, then."

"Yeah." He had no intention of working things out. Those were *his* children, not hers. *He* would decide what was going to happen from here on out and she could either go along with it or not. Her choice. Still, for now, he would keep communications open between them. No point in making an enemy this early in the game.

"I'm gonna go," he said. "I'll be in touch."

"What's that mean?"

Her question stopped him halfway across the room. He turned back to her. "It means, we're not done. Not by a long shot."

Over the next few days, Dina tried to keep the trips on the already shaky schedule she'd had going for the last three months. But it wasn't easy, considering that Connor dropped in and out of their lives with no warning. He showed up for breakfast one morning, then went with them to a local lab where the tech took cheek swabs of each child to compare their DNA with Connor's. It was ridiculous.

He knew darn well those babies were his, so she wasn't sure what he was up to with the paternity test. The next day, he didn't show up until bath time and left as soon as the babies were put to bed. Today, he'd insisted on going to the park with them. Rather than let him have the triplets all to himself—because, really, he was *very* rich, and how did she know he wouldn't just take them to his house and refuse to give them back—she went with them.

Watching Connor interact with the triplets was endearing and irritating all at once. She had had to do a lot of adjusting when the babies had come into her life. But Connor seemed to be sailing through it. But it wasn't only that she was bothered by. He was ignoring her completely.

Not that she wanted his attention, because at this point it would only add to the confusion of the situation. But it was the principle of the thing, really. She might as well have been the babies' sixty-year-old nanny for all the awareness he showed her. Just as well, she reminded herself sternly. Dina had deliberately kept her distance from men like Connor King for most of her life. She'd seen, up close and personal, just what a strong man could do to a woman.

Her own mother had wasted her life trying to change to be whatever the man she was with at the moment wanted or needed. Helen Cortez had slowly faded away, losing herself in the never-ending quest to please a man. Dina had watched as her mother eventually lost her own identity as she depended on man after man to take care of her. Which they never did. By the time Helen died eight years ago, she was just a shadow of herself.

In response to how her mother had lived and died, Dina had vowed to be independent. To count on no one but herself. Strong men could swallow a woman whole, and she had no intention of being devoured. So it wasn't as though she *wanted* Connor—her pride was wounded, that was all.

Frowning slightly, she shifted her gaze from Connor and the triplets to the tablet on her lap. While he played with the kids, Dina took the opportunity to go over business files. An independent business owner had to stay on top of things, especially when the bottom line was looking less than enthusiastic.

Flipping through her calendar, she made notes on the different jobs listed there. She still had to contact the Johnsons about the menu for their anniversary party and then put in a bid on a big class reunion being held at the Hyatt at the end of the month. She had a wedding reception to cater in two weeks and a sixteenth birthday party three days later. None of the jobs she had lined up were exactly high paying, but she was in no position to turn a job down, either. She just wished she had more time to devote to growing her business. Instead, she spent most of her waking hours trying to get more jobs and handling the millions of details that seemed to crop up with depressing regularity.

She had thought running her own business would give her freedom. Instead, she was being strangled by all the tiny strings that were forever coming undone. She spent more time on bookkeeping and client hunting than she did actually cooking anymore, and she really missed that. But between taking care of the babies, worrying about Connor's new role in their lives and paying the bills that never stopped coming, who had time to cook?

A shriek of pain grabbed her. Dina looked up and saw Connor holding Sage while the baby screamed and cried wildly. Tossing her tablet to the park bench, she raced across the sand, feet sliding on the uneven ground until she reached Connor. When Sage lunged at her, she grabbed him, held him close and instantly began to soothe his tears. The tiny boy's breath shuddered in and out of his lungs as tears streaked his cheeks. Patting his back and rocking side to side, she looked up at Connor. "What happened?"

"He fell. He scooted out of the swing and fell about a foot to the sand." Con lifted Sadie out of the baby swing and set her in the sand beside Sam.

Sage's howls had died down to whimpers now and he snuggled his face into the curve of her neck.

"He was okay, I swear. I don't know how he moved that fast in the first place, but he was okay. In fact, he laughed at first. Then, you'd have thought he'd landed on broken glass," Connor was saying.

Dina shook her head. Finally, a chink in the perfect father armor. "He's not hurt. He's scared." She slid the palm of her hand up and down Sage's back. "He's not used to the swings and he's too small to be in a regular one anyway..."

Connor frowned, muttered, "I should have known that." Then he bent to look at Sage. "Hey, buddy, you okay?"

Sage only burrowed closer to Dina and she gave him an extra squeeze for it. The triplets might be enamored by the new man in their lives, but clearly when they wanted comforting, it was *her* they turned to. Her heart swelled with love for the three tiny people who had brought such contained chaos into her life.

"Is he all right?" Connor asked with a sigh.

"He's fine," she said. "But it's nap time, so I should get them home."

"Right." Connor nodded, his expression thoughtful. "Home."

Still holding Sage tight, Dina turned to pick up their things and head to the car. But first she glanced over her shoulder and said, "You might want to stop Sam from eating sand."

"What?"

She smiled, listening to Connor's frantic yelp as he dealt with his sand-eating son.

Con still hadn't read Jackie's letter.

He'd planned to, that first night, but he'd been too angry at her to read whatever it was she had to say. Too twisted up over his first visit with his kids and too distracted by thoughts of Dina. Besides, how could Jackie possibly explain away lying to him about his own children? There was no reason good enough, he told himself.

No excuse that would take away the pain and the fury of the betrayal still raging inside him.

For years, Jackie was the one woman he'd trusted. The one friend he could count on no matter what. To find out now that she'd used him just as so many other women had tried to tore at him.

Con wandered through his darkened house. He didn't need lights since he knew the position of every stick of furniture in the place. He didn't *want* lights because right now his mood was so dark that light would be offensive. The quiet was overpowering—especially after having been in Dina's tiny, too crowded bungalow only an hour ago. A smile teased his mouth briefly as he remembered the chorus of noises created by the busy triplets and for a second, he tried to imagine those sounds here, in his big, empty house.

"Funny," he murmured, just to shatter the silence, "this place never seemed empty before. Just…roomy."

Sure, he knew a man alone didn't need a huge house. But why buy a small one? Con had always had some vague, nebulous idea of finding a woman at some point, getting married and having kids. But he'd been in no rush for that. Now he had the kids, but no wife—just two women on his mind. The memory of one haunting him and the other, one he couldn't stop wanting.

He walked through the living room, skirted the wide coffee table and stepped through a set of French doors onto the patio. Out here, there were solar lights circling the area, but the illumination was so pale, he didn't really mind it. Barefoot, he felt the cold damp of the flagstones beneath his feet and accepted the chill as part of the June night. Moonlight sifted through a covering bank of clouds and lay across the dark ocean like a pale ribbon tossed on top of black velvet. The pounding waves slamming into the cliffs below were a heartbeat. The wind off the sea was cold and cut right through the fabric of his T-shirt, but he didn't care. He had too much to work out to bother about being cold.

For three days, he'd been the part-time father he'd thought he would be. Coming and going from the lives of the triplets and Dina like a ghost. He could drop in, harass Dina a little, play with the kids, then leave it all behind and go to his office. There, his new responsibilities were buried beneath contracts, dealing with clients, new business ventures and a hundred other things that demanded his attention.

But always, the triplets and their guardian came sliding back into his consciousness. And every time he left that cottage in Huntington Beach, it was harder to go. Con scraped one hand across the back of his neck as that realization sank in. However it had started—outrage, betrayal, duty—it had become something else. What, exactly, he wasn't ready to admit yet. But he knew he was deeper into this situation than he would have thought possible three days ago. He knew that he missed those kids when he wasn't around them.

And yeah, he missed being around Dina, too. Damn, but the woman was fascinating. She was on edge around him most of the time, but that didn't do anything to dull the desire he felt every time he looked at her. She was prickly, defensive and her temper made those dark brown eyes of hers flash. Damned if he didn't enjoy that, too.

Then there was today at the park. When Sage was hurt and scared, he hadn't wanted Con. He'd wanted Dina. Her connection to the babies was deep despite the fact that she'd been their guardian only three months. So

Con had to work with that, as well. Did he take those kids away from her? Or did he try to find a way to work with her?

"Hell, this whole mess could have been avoided if Jackie had just told me the damn truth." He tipped his head back, stared up at the sky and said, "You know you did this, right? You enjoying the show?"

He couldn't get an answer from the night. The only one he might get was in the house, in Jackie's letter. And it was time to finally read it. See what his friend had to say to him.

Whatever it is, it's too little, too late, as his mother used to say.

Shaking his head, Con stalked across the patio to the house, then walked into his bedroom and snatched Jackie's letter off the dresser. He hit the wall switch, flooding the huge room with light from the ironwork chandelier overhead. He took a seat on the edge of his bed and pulled the letter free. His gaze swept over the familiar handwriting and in his head, he heard Jackie's voice...

"Con, if you're reading this, Elena and I are both gone, so no offense, but I hope you never read this. But if you are, I know you're pissed, and I can't blame you. Yes. I lied."

Anger spat at him again.

"I didn't tell you about the pregnancy or the babies because Elena and I wanted them all to ourselves. Yeah, selfish. I can almost hear you thinking it. And maybe it was, I don't even know. But when you said you wanted to be a part of the babies'

*lives, it made both of us realize that you would
only confuse things.*

*"Wasn't it enough that they would have two
mommies? Did they really need an on-again, off-
again daddy, too? Besides, we both know babies
aren't really your thing. Remember how you gave
Colt such a hard time over the twins? We named
Dina guardian because of the usual sexist reasons."*

Connor laughed in spite of himself.

*"She's a girl. Kids need a mommy. Sue me. Give
her a chance. You might like her.*

*"Con, I didn't want you to think you had to sup-
port them. Or had to do a damn thing. You'd already done enough. You gave us our family and
we're grateful. We gave you your freedom because
we thought it was best.*

*"But never doubt that we thought of you every
day. Every time we looked into the triplets' faces,
there you were. So forgive me if you can—and if
you can't, I understand. I still love you—Jackie."*

Pain swamped the anger and for the first time in days,
Con felt calm. She was wrong to do it, but he understood.
He didn't want to forgive her, but how could he not?

Holding the letter, he smoothed his fingertip across
the boldly slanted writing and murmured, "I love you,
too, Jacks."

Four

"Jackie made it clear in her letter that they wanted Dina to have custody," Colt said quietly when he'd finished reading it. He handed the paper over to Con, who stared at it for a long minute.

"They're *my* kids, Colt. My blood."

Con couldn't get past that one truth, which kept repeating over and over in his mind, and honestly, he didn't want to. After reading Jackie's letter the night before, his thoughts hadn't been able to settle. He hadn't slept and he was just killing time here at work. God knew there were details of new contracts to work out, but how the hell could he concentrate on that when the bulk of his life was up in the air?

He hadn't forgiven Jackie for what she'd done. Did he understand why she did it? A part of him did. The cool, rational, logical voice in his mind could even agree with her. But the reality was, emotion was running the show right now. And he couldn't get past the fact that he'd lost more than a year of his children's lives. He'd never get it back. He was a visitor in that house near the beach. A stranger. And that just burned him.

Behind him, there was a wide window, offering a spectacular view of the beach and the ocean, but it might as well have been a blank wall for all the attention he'd paid it that morning. Sunlight streamed through the tinted glass, painting the office a soft gold that glittered in his twin's eyes as Colt stared at Connor, waiting.

Finally, Con spoke again. "You know that Sage hates taking a bath?"

"What?" Colt frowned at him.

"Sage. He hates the water. Why? I should know that, but I don't." He pushed out of his desk chair and stalked around the perimeter of his office. It was a plush room with thick carpeting, framed photographs of their many adventure sites dotting the walls and comfortable furniture for clients. "Sadie loves taking a bath. She splashes and squeals." He smiled to himself, remembering. "Sam couldn't care less either way, but Sage..." He shook his head, then whipped a look at Colt. "Did something happen to him? Did he get scared? Of what? By who?"

"You're overreacting, Con," his twin said. "Kids are wildly unpredictable. Who the hell knows what they're thinking or why they react to things the way they do? Trust me on this. Like, for instance, right now, Reid won't wear shoes." He laughed to himself. "Takes 'em off the minute you put them on him. It's driving Penny nuts. But maybe it's because last week he walked through a deep puddle and his sneakers were squishing. I think he hated the sound so much, it creeped him out."

"See?" Con jabbed a finger toward his twin as fresh fury erupted inside him. "That's what I'm saying. Reid has an issue and you know why! Sage hates water, I don't have a clue." He threw his hands up in frustration. "I've known my own kids for three lousy days. I'm a damn stranger to them, Colt. They're nuts about Dina and they don't even know me."

"That'll change," Colt told him.

"Damn straight it will." Con jammed his hands into his pockets and rocked back on his heels. The wheels were in motion now and things should start happening.

After reading Jackie's letter, he'd been up all night. And this morning, he'd made his decision. He'd called his lawyers, telling them to put together whatever it was they had to do to get him custody of the triplets. But his lawyer had told him that Dina had good ground to stand on, too. She was the legal guardian. The kids' aunt. They were settled with her. But it didn't have to stay that way.

"You've already called Murdoch and Sons in on this, haven't you?"

Con shot his brother a sly smile. "Best team of lawyers in the state."

"Yeah, I know," Colt said, standing up to face his brother. "But think about it for a minute. Remember how mad you were when Dina went through a lawyer and sued you instead of just talking to you?"

"Yeah, I remember." His scowl deepened. "This is different."

"Always is," Colt muttered, then said more loudly, "You can't cut Dina Cortez out of this, Con."

He shot his twin a hard look. "What makes you think I'm considering it?"

Colt laughed shortly. "Because I know you? Because

when I found out about Penny and the twins, that was *my* first thought?"

"Okay." Con rubbed the back of his neck. Maybe he had thought of it, but he was willing to be reasonable about all this. If she fought him on custody, though, he wouldn't make any promises.This would all be a lot easier if he didn't want Dina so much. Every time he saw her it was harder to keep his hands off her—but this was about the kids and he had to keep focused.

"You think you can pull it off." Colt shook his head. "Delusional. That usually doesn't happen until you start losing sleep because of the kids invading your life. But kudos for managing on your own."

"Funny."

"Seriously, Con, she's not just their guardian, she's their *aunt*. You really think she's going to just walk away because it would be easier on you?"

"No." He sat back and shook his head. "The last thing she wants to do is make anything easy on me."

"There you go. This means you're going to have to find a way to work with her—or around her."

Con slanted him a look. "As in…"

Colt shrugged, "As in, you could try buying her off."

Frowning, Connor thought about that for a minute or two.

He'd seen her house. It was too small and gave every indication that money was tight. According to his lawyer, her catering business was barely above water. He knew she couldn't afford to take care of the babies on her own, and he wasn't about to settle for being nothing more than a monthly check in the lives of his kids.

According to the King family lawyer, the best thing for him to do, as far as a custody hearing went, was to become an everyday part of the children's lives. To stake a claim, basically. Well, that worked for Con. He just had to figure out the best way to go about it.

The easiest way, of course, would be to bring the triplets to his place. He already had his housekeeper setting up a temporary nursery in one of the guest rooms. A more permanent room was in the works, too. Their cousins Rafe, Nick and Gavin owned King Construction and Con was going to have them build a full nursery suite for the triplets as soon as possible. Meanwhile, the rest of Con's house was being babyproofed as well. He'd seen what Colt and Penny had gone through at their house, making sure everything was safe for a set of curious twins, so he had a good idea of what was needed.

The obstacle to overcome would be Dina. But he had an idea on that, as well.

"Whose side are you on in this, anyway?"

"Yours." Colt lifted both hands in the classic surrender pose and smiled at his brother. "I'm just saying that if you try to cut Dina out, you're inviting open war, and once that happens, nobody wins."

"I'll win."

"Really?" Colt shook his head and stood up. "She's their aunt, Con. You cut her out, the kids get hurt. You become enemies and this battle will get uglier and uglier."

"That's the thing though," Con said. "It *is* a battle. Or will be as soon as Dina realizes I'm not taking a backseat in all this. Damn it, if Jackie—"

"Let it go already," Colt muttered. "Jackie did what she thought she had to and so will you."

"Damn right I will."

"But you *could* listen to your older and wiser brother."

Con snorted. "Five extra minutes of life makes you the expert?"

"No," Colt corrected. "Going through practically the same thing you are and surviving makes me the expert. Penny and I were able to work things out between us—"

"Yeah, but you were already in love with Penny, you just didn't want to admit it."

"Good point and yeah, I know you don't love Dina." Colt gave him a grin. "But you do *want* her."

Did he ever. The desire he'd felt for her from the start had become a *need* that he really didn't want to admit to, because it just made everything else that much more convoluted. But just thinking about Dina made him hard and hungry.

"Mess this up and you'll never have her."

"Fine, fine." Con waved one hand at his twin. He hated to admit that his brother had a point. "Don't make her an enemy. Go slow." He paused. "I don't like slow."

"You're not used to it, that's for sure."

"True." He pushed one hand through his hair. "I want to get moving on this but I know I've got to make the right steps."

"That's something, anyway," Colt said wryly.

"I got the DNA results," Con said.

"That was fast."

"Money talks." Ordinarily, it would have taken a week, maybe two, to get the results from the private lab. But with the King family fortune pushing buttons, it had only been days. He paused. "The kids are mine."

"You had a doubt?"

"Of course not. But now it's legal. It's ammunition for a custody fight."

"Con…"

"I know, avoid a fight if I can." He held up one hand to stop his brother before he could get going again. "And I will. But I like knowing I've got an ace in the hole."

"Okay, clearly you're going at this full tilt and nothing I say is going to make any difference," Colt said. "So I'm going to say one more thing."

"Naturally."

"Go easy on this or you'll lose."

"You're wrong. I don't lose."

"I'm really sorry, Abuela," Dina said, "but the babysitter canceled on me at the last minute and I have to be at this party." She unloaded all of the supplies she'd brought for the triplets as her grandmother sat on the floor, playing with the babies.

"Dina, you don't have to apologize," she said, throwing her granddaughter a quick glance over her shoulder. "I love having the children here."

"Yeah, but you were going to dinner with your friends."

"Pish. I can eat anytime." She reached out and caught Sage up in a quick hug. "It's not every day I get snuggles from *los niños*."

Dina smiled as the triplets crawled all over the older woman. At seventy-five, Angelica Cortez was trim, with stylishly cut gray hair that swung at her jawline. Her brown eyes were shrewd and her striking face remained remarkably unlined, which gave Dina hope for her own future.

Angelica's English was lightly flavored with her native Mexico; Spanish and English mingled happily in everything she said. She did love seeing the babies and if Dina and the kids were here strictly for a visit, it would be different. Dina would be here, too, taking care of them rather than expecting her grandmother to pick up the slack. But with her babysitter sick, Dina just didn't have a choice. She was catering an anniversary party tonight and if it went well, there was a chance she'd get more jobs out of it.

A headache began to blossom behind her eyes and that didn't bode well for the long night she had ahead of her. Guilt pinged around inside her like a crazed Ping-Pong ball. Guilt for leaving the kids, for making her grandmother change her own plans to watch them—and then there was the guilt for choosing work over the babies. But on the other hand, if she wanted to be able to feed them, she had to get as many jobs as she could.

Her grandmother's duplex in Naples was two blocks from the ocean. It was decorated in a blend of Mexican and American styles and was warm and inviting. Furniture was overstuffed; the walls were painted a rich brick red with white crown molding. It should have been dark and depressing, Dina had thought more than once. Instead, it was like being enveloped in a hug. Angelica owned the building and lived in the front apartment while renting the second to one of her best friends. Between the two women, the gardens were so lush and beautiful, they regularly had tourists stopping out front to take pictures.

Naples was small, and elegant, and there were canals winding through the neighborhood much like its Italian namesake. The Christmas parade through the canals was amazing, with the houses and boats decorated with millions of colored lights. Dina was looking forward to taking the triplets to see the spectacle.

"So what is the job tonight?"

"An anniversary party in Newport Beach."

Which was about a half hour away, and that meant Dina would have to leave soon to get to the site early enough to set up.

Not too long ago, Dina had been the owner of a great little food truck. Business had been good enough that she'd decided to move on and open the catering business she'd always wanted. And it had been doing well, too. She'd had more jobs than she could count, her reputation was growing—and then...

She looked to where the babies were clustered around their great-grandmother. Dina's world had crashed every bit as much as her sister's plane had three months ago. When she had taken custody of the trips, Dina had had to cancel a lot of jobs. She simply hadn't been able to keep up the pace when faced with caring for the three kids. Though her income had been slashed, the bills hadn't stopped coming. Her rent had gone up, her car broke down, and with the triplets, there were *more* bills. Doctors, clothes, diapers—the list was never ending, and it was scary being the sole responsible one.

Now she was having to scramble to get jobs, which meant she was bidding on parties she might have ignored a few months ago. But she needed the work to take care of the babies and make sure they were safe.

"Don't worry so much, *nieta*," her grandmother said, and Dina had to smile in spite of the anxiety that never quite left her. "Things happen whether you're ready or not. You simply have to do what you can to keep up."

"Yeah," Dina said, dropping to her knees to gather Sam up into her arms. The tiny boy sagged into her, wrapping his little arms around her neck and smacking her cheek with an openmouthed kiss that left drool behind on her skin and warmth in her heart. She kissed him back, then set him down on the floor beside his brother and sister.

"You haven't spoken of their father yet."

Dina looked at her grandmother. The unsettled feeling she'd been carrying around for days deepened. Of course, she had told her grandmother about the suit for child support and the letter she'd found in Jackie's things. But she really hadn't had a chance to talk with her about it since.

Mainly because what could she say? That Connor was getting too involved for her peace of mind? That she couldn't seem to think straight when he was near? That she was worried not only about what his presence meant to the triplets—but what it meant to *her*?

He was at the forefront of her mind, always, and she hadn't been prepared for that. It had been a long time since Dina had met a man she was attracted to. And she'd *never* met one who affected her as Connor King did. It was stupid, she knew, to even indulge in idle daydreams about a man who had the power to take her children away from her. Connor made her want all sorts of things, but at the same time, she knew she should be keeping him at a safe distance. It was as if she were waiting for *two* shoes to drop. What were his plans for the kids? What were his plans for *her*?

"I don't know, Abuela," she finally said. "He really enjoys the triplets when he's with them. Naturally, he's angry. With Jackie and Elena. And with me."

Nodding sagely, the older woman said, "I told Elena what she was doing was wrong, but like you, she was *cabeza dura*. A hardhead." She paused, made the sign of the cross and whispered a quick prayer for Elena's soul, then reached out to pat Dina's hand. "His anger will pass."

"I know." Dina sighed. No one could hold on to anger

forever. It would eventually burn itself out, leaving bitterness behind, and it would be up to Connor if he chose to hang on to it or let that go as well. Right now, she thought it was a toss-up as to which way he'd go. "But what then?"

"Well, he has a decision to make, doesn't he?" her grandmother said. "He must decide how involved he wants to be with his children." Her gaze swept over the three babies playing and babbling together. "I've read of the King family. They are not the kind of people to walk away from their children."

Dina's heart sank. Different members of the King family were always in the news or the tabloids or national magazines. And in interview after interview, one thing they all had in common was just how close they were and how important family was. "I know."

Her grandmother heard the disappointment and worry in Dina's voice and laughed. "That's a good thing, *querida*. He's their father. They'll need him."

"And what about me?" She shook her head and watched as Sadie and Sam had a tug-of-war over a stuffed bunny. The thought of losing the triplets made her chest hurt. Yes, they were a lot of work, and yes, her life had been turned upside down at their arrival, but now she couldn't imagine living without them.

"The Kings are also *really* rich," she pointed out, more to herself than to her grandmother. "If he wants to take the babies from me, I won't be able to afford to fight him. He can hire a fleet of lawyers and I'll be down at Legal Aid with my fingers crossed."

Her grandmother laughed, handed a baby doll to Sadie and smiled as she watched Sam chew on the stuffed bunny's ear. "Wealthy doesn't mean evil, Dina."

"No, but it does mean powerful," she argued as worry nibbled at her insides. "No judge is going to pick a struggling caterer over a member of the King family when it comes to custody."

"Worrying won't change that," her grandmother warned.

"No, but I'm so good at it."

The older woman laughed. "Yes, you are. But just this once, you should try not to excel at something."

Dina sighed, shook her head and dropped one arm around her grandmother's shoulders, pulling her close for a brief, hard hug. "I'll try. Really."

Giving Dina another pat, her grandmother said, "This is a good thing, for you and for the babies."

"It doesn't feel that way," she said, though her hormones might have disagreed.

"Dina, you can't care for them on your own. You're making yourself crazy by trying."

"I can do it," she said stubbornly. "I'm getting a routine and—"

"And wearing yourself to the bone trying to be all things to all people," her grandmother told her quietly, almost as though she were hoping to keep the triplets from hearing—though they wouldn't have understood her anyway. "Their father is here now. Share the work as well as the joy."

"It's not that easy, Abuela," Dina said with a sigh. "He's one of the richest men in the country and he's furious at being lied to."

"You didn't lie to him."

"I don't think he cares," she said thoughtfully. "If he decides to, he could take the babies from me and no judge would ever choose me over him."

"It doesn't have to come to that."

"Maybe not, but I think it will," Dina said, remembering the look on his face the night before. He was bonding with his children and digging himself deeper into all of their lives. Connor King wasn't going to back off. It wasn't in his nature.

She'd done some checking on him. Granted, it had been on the internet and she knew you couldn't believe everything you read there. But she had no other options.

He and his twin, Colton, had built their own business outside of the family fortune. They were rich in their own right now, after spending years providing risk to thrill seekers. A little less than two years ago, the twins had shifted their business model to family vacations and hadn't missed a step. According to financial websites, King Family Adventures was even bigger than its precursor, which made sense, since their potential client base was so much bigger.

From everything she'd read, Connor was a hard, cold-eyed negotiator and didn't tolerate mistakes. He was the kind of man who laid down the rules and expected everyone else to fall into line. Since Dina didn't take orders well, she couldn't see any way this situation was going to have a happy ending.

"I see another problem on the horizon as well," Angelica said softly.

"Great. Just what we need." She blew out a breath. "What problem?"

"You like him." Her grandmother smiled knowingly.

"Please." Dina laughed and ducked her head to keep her too-knowing grandmother from reading her eyes. She grabbed Sadie as the baby toddled past and plopped the tiny girl onto her lap. "You're wrong, Abuela. I don't like him."

"So you didn't lie to him, only to me," the older woman said, "and to yourself."

Reluctantly, Dina lifted her gaze to her grandmother's. It was pointless to keep avoiding this particular truth anyway. "Fine. I admit to being…intrigued. He's so different from every other man I know. But—"

"Different is good, *mija*," she said, scooping Sadie off Dina's lap and onto her own. "And who knows? Maybe this man's arrival in your life is a good thing."

Dina wouldn't go that far.

A little after midnight, Dina pulled into her driveway with three sleeping babies in the backseat. Glancing at the house, she muttered a soft curse because she'd forgotten to leave the porch light on.

With a sigh, she climbed out of the car and then as quietly as possible closed the door behind her. The street was silent, houses dark, with families tucked in for the night. It was so quiet, it was as if the whole world had taken a breath and held it.

And then she heard a voice.

"Where the hell have you been?"

Five

Dina jumped, slapped one hand to her chest and spun around all at the same time. Heart in her throat, she watched Connor stalk across the yard toward her.

"You scared me to death," she said, her voice a harsh whisper.

"Welcome to my world," he snapped. "I've been sitting on your front porch for the last three hours, not knowing where the hell you were."

"What? Why?" She looked past him to the porch as if she could see evidence of his vigil.

"I came to see the kids, but you weren't here." He scrubbed both hands across his face, then glared at her. "I didn't know where you'd gone. For all I knew, you were out and trapped somewhere, or maybe one of the kids was sick. I called your cell and you didn't answer. Went straight to voice mail."

One small niggle of guilt wormed its way through her, but Dina dismissed it fast. How was she supposed to know that he would show up? Just because he'd been dropping by on and off for days was no reason to assume he'd keep doing it. Besides, he was overreacting and that she could hardly believe. He sounded like a worried husband, for heaven's sake.

"I always turn my phone off when I'm working," she said, though that wasn't true. She'd kept the phone on in case her grandmother needed to reach her. She simply hadn't answered the phone when she saw it was Connor calling. "And now I'm going to put the triplets to bed. They're sound asleep in their car seats and if you wake them…"

Her threat lay open-ended between them, but it did the trick. He took a breath, made an obvious effort to calm himself and said, "Fine. I'll help. Go unlock the front door."

She did it, but only because that's what she was going to do before he'd ordered her to do it anyway. Muttering under her breath, Dina crossed the yard with hurried strides. It was cold and damp and the moon and stars were blotted out behind a layer of clouds. She opened the door, then turned and headed back to the car, where Con was already unhooking Sam from his car seat. Her heart twisted a bit as the little boy draped himself across Con's shoulder, arms and legs limp in sleep. Connor kept one hand on the boy's back and walked to the house without another word to her.

Good, Dina thought. She was in no mood for his attitude. She was tired, her feet hurt and all she wanted was to sit down, have a glass of wine and then crawl into bed for the few hours' sleep she'd get before the babies woke up.

She freed Sadie from her car seat and soothed the baby girl as she snuffled, whimpered and settled down again.

"I'll take her," Connor whispered when he came up behind her.

"You get Sage," she said, already walking.

In what used to be the bungalow's master bedroom, three cribs were crowded together in the small space. It wouldn't be long before Dina would have to find somewhere else to live. The babies were going to outgrow this house within the next year or so. But that was a worry for another day.

"Why the hell didn't you answer the phone?" Connor's strained whisper sounded overly loud in the quiet.

"I was working," she reminded him. "Then when I wasn't, I turned the phone off to keep from waking up the babies on the way home."

"Okay, then," he ground out, "what kind of job are you working that you've got three babies out until after midnight?"

She frowned at him as she leaned over the crib and patted Sam's back until he settled into deep sleep again. "I was catering an anniversary party, and the babies are fine."

"They should have been home," he said, that strained whisper somehow even more strained now.

Dina swallowed her impatience. "Not that it's any of your business, but my babysitter got sick at the last minute, so my grandmother watched them for me."

While Connor soothed a snuffling, writhing Sadie, he glared at Dina. "Why the hell didn't you call me? I could have been here to watch them. Hell, I *was* here.

On the damn porch, imagining you and the babies dead in a ditch somewhere."

He was serious. She didn't know whether to be touched, amused or angry. Amusement won.

She snorted a laugh and was pleased to see his expression darken even further. "Who're you, my mother?"

"No," he reminded her. "I'm their father, and you should have answered my calls."

Looking into his eyes, she saw beyond his anger to the worry that had been dogging him for hours. If the situation had been turned around and *he* had been off with the triplets and she hadn't been able to reach him, she would have been furious, too. And worried. And scared. And her imagination would have tortured her with images of car accidents, kidnappings—heck, even space invaders!

Maybe she should have answered his calls, but the truth was, she only left her phone turned on while working in case there was an emergency with the babies. Otherwise, she was focused on the task at hand. And frankly, every time her phone rang and she saw Connor's number, she'd enjoyed shifting him to voice mail. He was so...dominant male that being able to thwart him even a little had made her feel better. Now, though, she was rethinking that decision.

"Okay, I'm sorry." Oh, that was bitter. "I should have let you know the kids were all right."

"It wasn't only them I was worried about," he said, voice deeper, lower, more intimate.

She looked at him and in the soft glow of the night-light, his blue eyes seemed fathomless, fixed on her. She felt drawn to him. So much so that she deliberately looked away and took a step back.

The babies were settled and the baby monitor turned

on, so to continue the conversation, Dina led Connor out of the bedroom. She needed some breathing room. Flipping on light switches as she went, to dispel the dark and the accompanying intimacy, she walked straight to the living room with him following close behind. She entered the room, turned to face him and saw that he'd stopped in the open doorway. Taking a breath, she steadied herself. "I'm tired, Connor. Can we do the rest of this another time?"

Rather than answer, he asked a question of his own. "Why didn't you ask me to watch the kids?"

"The simplest answer? It never occurred to me."

A rush of pure frustration swamped Connor as he met her eyes and read the truth there. He read the fatigue in her eyes and noted the defensive posture she always adopted when they began to butt heads, and that was almost enough to defuse the anger churning inside him. The last few hours, he'd felt more helpless than he ever had, and he hadn't enjoyed it. He was used to being in charge, to knowing what was going on at all times. To be in the dark about his own children had been torture.

By the time she had pulled into the driveway, Connor had been tense enough to snap in two. It was only the presence of the sleeping babies that had kept his temper from boiling over. But his frustration continued to bubble and froth in the pit of his stomach.

She hadn't called him because she hadn't given him a thought. She'd needed help and she'd gone to her grandmother instead of him. Because he wasn't a part of her or the kids' lives. He was still on the periphery, and he was the only one who could change that.

"That's got to stop," he said flatly, silently congratulating himself on his rigid control.

"Look, I'm sorry you were worried," she said. "But I'm too tired to do this right now."

He nodded solemnly. "Fine. We'll talk about it in the morning."

"Okay, good." She waved a hand at the hall and the front door behind him. "Now I'm going to bed and you should go home."

"Oh," Connor said, leaning against the doorjamb with a casual ease he wasn't feeling, "I'm not going anywhere."

"What?"

Her chocolate eyes went wide and outraged and Connor smiled. He liked the way she went from cool to hot in a split second and he really wanted to see how hot she'd burn in his bed. For a second or two, *that* image scalded his brain and made speech impossible. When he came back to the moment, she was in the middle of a whispered rant, trying to keep her anger from waking the babies in the other room.

"You think you can just stay uninvited in my house? What gives you the right? Nothing, that's what." She answered her own question before he could say a word. She glanced at the baby monitor she held in her hands as the sounds of restless squirming cut into the room. In another moment or two, they might be awake and crying and this conversation—such as it was—would come to an end.

So he ended it first.

Connor didn't think about it, he simply went on instinct, following the urges that had been clawing at him since the first time he'd seen her. Pushing away from the wall, he grabbed her, pulled her close and kissed her.

The instant his mouth met hers, heat exploded between them. Sensations unlike anything he'd ever known before enveloped him and Connor could only hold onto her, tightening his arms around her until he held her captive, pinned to his body. She went from startled to swept away in a heartbeat. As if she, too, were being consumed by the flames licking at his insides, she hooked her arms around his neck and held on. Mouths taking, giving, tongues twining together in a frantic dance of need. Their breath came in short, hard gasps. The bright living room lights shining around them did nothing to dispel the closeness wrapping itself around them.

His brain racing, heart thundering in his chest and his groin so heavy and hard he ached with it, Connor relished the feel of her mouth under his. The longer he kissed her, the more he felt, those flames burning brighter, hotter, scorching his soul. She sighed and leaned into him, and that soft sound was enough to penetrate his brain, bring him back to himself and the realization that he was only a blink away from pulling Dina down to the damn floor.

No. When this happened, he told himself, they would have a bed. And privacy. And all the time they needed to explore whatever it was burning between them. When that thought registered, he broke the kiss, stepped back and with satisfaction, watched her stagger before finding her balance. Breath ragged in his lungs, his heart hammering against his ribs, Con ground out, "I'm staying here tonight."

She shook her head instantly. "We're not going to—"

"I'll sleep on the couch."

Her gaze met his and she must have seen that he wasn't going to be sent on his way. With tension blistering the air in the room, she only nodded, accepting the inevitable.

"This isn't over," he said.

"It is for tonight," she answered and walked past him, down the short hall to her room. She disappeared inside and closed the door behind her.

Alone, Connor shoved one hand through his hair and barely resisted giving it a hard tug to relieve some of the frustration still holding him in its clutches. Instead, he walked to the too-short couch and eyed it grimly.

It was going to be a miserable night.

During the long, incredibly sleepless night, Connor had had time to do some thinking. And some snooping. Sure, maybe he had crossed a line, when he'd poked around in Dina's laptop, which really should be password protected. But he'd told himself that the triplets gave him all the reason he needed to invade her privacy a little.

Just as his lawyers had informed him, her business was in trouble. She was already in a downward spiral of debt and picking up speed every day. He'd flipped through enough of her records to know that she was using her small savings account to supplement her income and that wasn't going to last for much longer.

Bottom line? Dina Cortez was in no shape to provide for three growing kids. And he could use that information.

He already had the babies changed and dressed when she walked into the nursery bright and early the next morning. One look was all it took to tell him that she'd gotten as little sleep during the night as he had.

"You're awake?"

He shrugged and finished pulling Sam's shirt into place. "Never really went to sleep." He shot her a sly glance. "Too much on my mind."

She inhaled sharply and Connor guessed that she'd

been thinking about that kiss and what should have come next. Hell, thoughts like that had been tormenting him all night. Knowing that she was just down the hall from him. Knowing that she would welcome his touch. It had taken everything he had to keep from going to her.

But the bottom line was that he wasn't here because of this attraction and desire he felt for Dina. He was here for his children, and they had to come first. If he made a play for Dina, it would complicate everything. Better to settle the situation here before moving on what he wanted from her.

He took a long breath himself before quipping, "Plus, that couch qualifies as torture equipment."

"Well it isn't built to sleep on," she admitted, "especially for someone as tall as you."

"That's for sure." He lifted Sam off the table, gave the baby boy a kiss, then set him on the floor with his brother and sister. "So. Kids are changed, dressed and ready for the day. How about we feed them and then we have that talk?"

"I need coffee."

"I'll take that as a yes," he said, scooping up two of the babies and leaving Sam for Dina to get. Then he walked past her, heading for the kitchen.

The room was bright with sunshine and ringing with the happy chatter of three babies. Despite being tired, Connor and Dina worked together to prepare milk, oatmeal and bananas. While they fed the triplets, Connor glanced at her and said, "Last night brought home to me that things have got to change."

"What *things*?"

He would have heard the wariness in her tone even if he hadn't spotted it on her features. "Everything about this whole situation. You. Me. The triplets. As it stands now, none of it is working for me."

She sighed and shook her head. "It's been, like, four days. You could be more patient."

"Not in my nature."

"I'm getting that," she murmured.

"Anyway, it's been long enough to make some decisions," he countered and scooped more oatmeal onto a spoon before offering it to Sadie, who opened her mouth eagerly, like a baby bird. "For instance. Your catering business—why catering?"

"What? Oh. Uh. I used to have a food truck and it did really well." She smiled, remembering. "So well, in fact, that I sold the truck to my cousin Raul. I went into catering thinking I could use that as a stepping-stone to my real goal—opening my own restaurant."

"A good goal, but hard to meet when your catering business is sinking."

"Excuse me?" She stopped moving with a spoonful of cereal halfway to Sage's mouth. The little boy howled and slapped both hands impatiently on his tray table. "Sorry, sorry, baby," she murmured and fed him before turning back to Connor. "How would you know anything about my business?"

He couldn't blame her for being mad, but he wouldn't apologize for doing what he had to do to look out for his kids. If that made the relationship between him and Dina tougher for a while, he could deal with that. Connor had the taste of her inside him now and he wouldn't stop pushing until he got more. Eventually he knew he'd have his kids and Dina, too.

But for now he said only, "First, my lawyers have a private investigator on retainer—"

"You had me investigated?"

He nodded, ignoring the shocked expression on her face because it was just going to get worse in another minute or so. "And for another, I looked through your bills last night."

"You did what?" Her voice dropped to a new level of cold that sliced at him like shards of ice. She shot a glance at her laptop, lying innocently on the counter, then looked back at him. "You went through my records?"

"I did, and if you're waiting for an apology, don't hold your breath." His gaze speared hers and he didn't flinch away from the pure rage spitting back at him. Those dark brown eyes of hers flashed with heat in spite of the cold in her voice. "You're taking care of my kids and I needed to be sure you can do that properly. As it turns out, you can't."

"Is that right? Well, I've been managing all right so far. The babies are *fine* and you know it. They're fed, they're happy, they're *loved*." She stiffened, squared her shoulders and lifted her chin. "The four of us are getting along great. You want to pay child support, I'm happy to take it for them. But I don't need your help to run my business or our lives."

Connor could admire her pride even as he dismissed it. Being proud was one thing. Being too stubborn to see the truth was another. "Of course you do, and you know it. That's why you contacted me in the first place. It's not just the money and you know it, Dina. You're running yourself into the ground trying to do everything by yourself. You're behind on your bills, and you haven't had a good paying job since before the triplets arrived."

She flushed and again, it wasn't embarrassment but anger that flooded her cheeks with color. "I admit, my business suffered some when the babies first came to me. I had to back out of jobs and spend most of my time with them. They were traumatized—not that you'd know anything about that since you weren't here—because they'd lost their parents and their home. It took weeks to get them settled into a routine. Make them feel safe."

She glared at him and those eyes of hers were damned captivating.

"I was the one who held things together. And they were my priority. I'm so very sorry if you think my business isn't doing too well." She took a breath. "Now that the kids are settled in, I'm bidding on jobs again and—"

"Birthday and anniversary parties," he finished for her. "Not exactly big-paying jobs."

Dropping her gaze, she scooped up more oatmeal and spooned it into Sage's waiting mouth. "No job too small," she said tightly. "Besides, one job leads to another. Catering is a lot about word of mouth and—"

"Admit it, Dina. You're in the water, holding onto a lead ball and trying to kick your way to the surface."

"Could you please stop interrupting me?"

"Admit it," he urged again. "At this rate, you will never reach your goal of opening a restaurant. Hell, you'll be lucky if you can keep the catering going through the rest of the year. And once it fails completely? Then what? What's your backup plan? Or do you even have one?"

Con watched her and saw in her eyes that she couldn't argue with him, but that she was going to give it a try anyway.

"These children will never suffer." She swore it, meeting his eyes, willing him to believe her. "It doesn't matter what I have to do, they will never go without."

"I know they won't," he said quietly and set small plastic bowls of sliced bananas onto the triplets' food trays. Connor waited until she turned to face him. When he had her complete attention, he said, "I'll give you two hundred and fifty thousand dollars to sign over custody of the kids to me. Right now. Today."

He saw confusion obliterated by fury in her dark eyes an instant before she exploded in a wild burst of rage. "You would *dare* to offer me *money*? You think you can *buy* me? That I would *sell my family*?"

She stood up slowly, as if every bone ached. The babies watched her with curiosity. They didn't cry, because even in her anger, Dina kept her voice a hushed whisper that somehow made her temper sound even more volatile than if she'd been shouting.

"Do it and open that restaurant you want so badly. Build your dreams. I'm offering you a way out of the financial hole you're sliding into."

"Build my dreams by selling the babies? Do you really think so little of me?"

"Not at all," he countered smoothly, refusing to match her temper. "I think you're smart, clever and wise enough to recognize a real opportunity when it presents itself."

She choked out a laugh. "You think I want your money?"

He shrugged. "You're the one who sued me for child support."

"For *them*," she snapped. "Not for me. My God, you're incredible. Because I asked for child support you believe that means I'd be willing to be bought off?"

He shrugged, not letting her see that he was pleased at her reaction, if surprised. Not many people would have turned down a quarter of a million dollars without at least thinking about it first.

"You rich guys are all alike. The world runs on money. Well, maybe in your universe, but not here in reality. I want nothing from you. I make my own way and I always have. My business is exactly that—*my* business."

"Your business," he argued as he slowly pushed himself to his feet to face her across the kitchen table, "became mine when you became the guardian of *my* children."

He'd let her rant and rage, but she was going to understand this if he had to repeat himself ten times a day. "Those kids are what concern me. *My* children. Not yours."

She snorted. "You were the sperm donor. You're not a father."

Everything in him went still. Her words, practically spat at him, hung in the air between them like an ugly smear. "You don't get to say that to me," he said, his voice low and hard. "You know what Jackie and your sister did to me. You know the truth."

She gritted her teeth, pulling in a breath with a soft hiss. "Fine. You're right. About that. I shouldn't have said it. But you're not right about everything else. I don't want anything from you, Connor."

"Then you're the first woman I've ever met who didn't have an agenda. What're the odds on that?"

"What are you talking about?" Anger shifted to confusion.

"Every woman I've ever known has tried to use me—my name, my money, my family." His ego took a slight beating at the admission, but he was going to let her know from the jump just who was in charge here. "You think you've got issues with rich guys? Well, how would you like it if everyone you've ever known approached you with their hand out at one point or another? Jackie," he continued, "was the only woman who didn't try to use me in some way." A hard lump settled in his throat as he admitted tightly, "And in the end, she—and your sister—used me, too."

He hadn't meant to go that deeply into his own life. This was about Dina, the failing business she depended on and the welfare of the triplets.

It was a second or two before she spoke again. "Well, I'm not them."

"Yeah, you turned down the money. That's something. But," he added, tipping his head to one side as he studied her, "maybe you're just holding out for more." He didn't really believe that, but he felt a small slice of satisfaction when her eyes narrowed.

"I think you should go."

"Not gonna happen," Con told her. He glanced at the babies, who were now staring at the two of them with tiny worried frowns creasing each of their faces. Deliberately, Connor dialed back on the anger churning inside him. He wasn't going to traumatize his kids. "I'll tell you what is going to happen, though. You and the triplets are moving to my house. Starting today."

"You've got to be kidding."

"Nope. Dead serious." He planted both hands on the table and leaned toward her. "I'm not going to disappear from my kids' lives. I'm not going to be the last one you think of when you need backup to take care of them. And most importantly, I'm not going to try to sleep on that torture rack you call a couch again."

"You can't just decide something like this and expect me to go along—"

"Did you or did you not *just* say that the babies would always be taken care of no matter what you had to do?"

"Yes," she snapped. "But I didn't mean *this*."

He held up one hand for silence, and damned if he didn't get it. Con figured she was too surprised to argue. "Your house is too small for all of us and you know it."

"You weren't invited to stay," she pointed out.

"I'm their father. They stay with me."

"I'm their guardian. They stay with me."

"There you go," he said. "Neither one of us is going to give on this, so my solution works best."

"Because you say so."

"Because your whole house is the size of my closet." He pushed off the table and folded his arms across his chest. "You won't be bought off—which I admire, by the way."

"Wow." She tipped her head to one side and gave him a look that should have set fire to his hair. "Thanks."

He ignored the sarcasm. "You want the kids. So do I. The answer is, we both stay with them. We can't do that here, so my house is the logical move."

"Logical. That's all this is about?"

"What else?"

"And this new living situation," she said. "How would it affect us?"

"You're talking about the kiss last night?"

"No, I'm talking about what you might expect after the kiss last night."

A little insulted at the notion that he would maneuver her and the kids to his house as a way of forcing her into his bed, Connor frowned at her. "Relax. You'll have your own suite. I don't need to trick women into my bed. Or force them. They come willingly enough."

If she gritted her teeth any harder, her jaw might snap.

"I won't," she finally said and those two words, along with the situation, tugged a smile at the corner of his mouth.

"Yeah, I seem to remember you kissing me back last night."

"A minor bump in the road."

"Yeah we'll see about that."

"Trust me on this," she said, eyes flashing. "I won't be one of the legions of women who have rolled out of your bed."

"Don't paint yourself into a corner," Connor said. "Or make vows you'll just have to take back later."

"That won't happen."

"But the move will," he told her flatly and waited for her response.

She looked at the kids, each of them with banana smooshed across their tiny features. He could see her heart in her eyes as she looked at those children, and he knew the moment she made the decision to go along with his plan.

"Fine," she said tightly. "We'll come. *Temporarily.*"

"What's your definition of temporary?"

"I guess we'll find out, won't we?"

One eyebrow lifted. Once those triplets were in his house, they wouldn't be leaving again. Whether or not Dina stayed with them would be up to her. But one thing Con was sure of, in spite of her denials, was that before whatever this was between them ended, he would have her in his bed.

Six

"This is a mistake."

Dina's grandmother looked up from packing the babies' clothes and clucked her tongue. "That is not the right attitude to take."

"What other one is there?" Dina's insides were churning and she had a pounding headache. No doubt caused by last night's sleeplessness, the argument with Connor and now this hurried move that she was sure was going to turn into a disaster. "Living with Connor King? Even temporarily? Bad move. I can feel it."

Actually, what she felt was worry. Ever since he'd kissed her, she'd felt herself teetering on a shaky ledge. Moving into his house, onto his turf, sleeping in a room close to his…no way was this going to end well. Especially because as infuriating as the man was, as frustrating to deal with, he was also way too tempting.

And that wasn't even taking the triplets into consideration. He was getting the babies into—for lack of a better phrase—his possession. Surely that was going to mean something if he really did sue for custody. Any judge in the world would leave the babies in a palatial home cared for by a billionaire who could afford an army of nannies rather than with a nearly broke caterer living in a rented bungalow that was too small for one, let alone *four*, people.

"Oh, God."

Her grandmother did the tongue clucking thing again and Dina winced. "This is an opportunity for you to get to know the father of the children you love," the older woman said. "Use it. Learn what you can."

"You mean to use against him later?" She tapped her finger against her chin as she considered it. Dina couldn't risk Connor taking too much of the upper hand. As it was, she'd be living at his house, sharing the kids with him and reluctantly giving him a greater standing in the custody issue. She had to go into this ready to defend herself if need be.

"No," her grandmother said with a sigh. "I mean, get to know him. The two of you are now linked through these children. You will be a part of each other's lives always. Isn't it smart to know the person rather than to assume the worst and act on it?"

Dina groaned and plopped onto the bed, hands in her lap. "I hate it when you're rational."

The older woman chuckled and went back to folding tiny T-shirts and pants. "You don't want to admit he's right, either, do you?"

"He's not right. About what?"

"About this house. It is much too small for you and

three growing babies. You know this, Dina. You just don't want it thrown in your face."

True. The bungalow felt stifling most of the time. She had rented it three years ago for herself as a stepping-stone. A way to save money—since the rent then was reasonable—so she could save to buy her own place. With her business doing well, it wouldn't have taken her long to afford a nice condo somewhere. She'd built up a savings account, opened the catering company and was sure that all of her plans were going to sail on nicely.

But then the babies came, the rent went up, her business went down and she'd been pretty much stuck here. When Connor had said that her business was sinking and taking her dreams of a restaurant along with it, he'd really hit the nail on the head.

Maybe her grandmother was right. She would still have to pay rent on this house while living with Connor, just to keep her own place to run to when his plan was shot out of the sky. But everything else could work in her favor. Bills for diapers, food, babysitting wouldn't mount because she would be at his place. Maybe she could start saving again and begin to rebuild her nearly empty savings account.

"Fine. We'll go. We'll stay. For a while."

"Good. And you'll do this with a positive attitude."

"Oh, I'm positive this is all going to blow up in my face. Does that count?"

"No, it does not," her grandmother said, then asked, "What is this really about, *nieta*?"

Frowning, Dina picked at a splotch of dried baby food on the hem of her white shorts. "Connor King is overpowering," she finally said, her voice little more than a whisper of complaint. "He's gorgeous, he's pushy, he's rich."

"And you worry because of your mother."

Dina looked at her grandmother, apology in her eyes. Whatever kind of mom Helen had been to Dina, she had also been Angelica's daughter, and Dina felt guilty for reminding her grandmother of her loss. "I'm sorry. But you saw what happened to Mom, too. She would get involved with men who were larger-than-life and then she'd slowly crumble to whatever they wanted. She was lost, trying to be something she wasn't."

Sighing heavily, Angelica took a seat beside Dina, reached out and squeezed her hand. "I loved your mother," she said, "but she was not a strong woman. She had doubts about who she was, always. My daughter looked to men for the answer rather than to herself, and that was her mistake. Her fault. It's not yours."

Dina looked into her grandmother's eyes.

"You worry for nothing," her grandmother said softly. "You have a strength she never had, your mother. You are confident where she was hesitant. Strength in a man is not a bad thing. It is only weakness that can be devoured by strength. You have none."

Dina would like to believe that, but her confidence level was at an all-time low at the moment. Living with Connor, being around him nonstop, was going to be the kind of temptation she had always avoided. And that knowledge only made her feel even more uneasy about this whole thing.

"Now," her grandmother said as she stood up, "help me finish packing for the *niños*. It's time to face your fear and conquer it."

"Right. Conquer my fear." Dina stood up, too, and

looked at the pile of baby clothes still waiting to be folded. She had a feeling, though, as she started working again, that Connor King wasn't an easy man to conquer.

Of course his house was amazing. Set amid lush gardens and heavy greenery, it was a ranch-style home built of brick and stone and glass and looked as though it had simply grown organically where it stood.

Dina was speechless from the moment she entered through the double front doors. Polished oak floors, beautiful furnishings from the gleaming tables to the paintings on the taupe-painted walls to the gray marble fireplace that dominated one wall of the massive great room. It was there they settled the kids down to play and that Dina could take a moment to admire the room. Overstuffed furniture stood in silent invitation to curl up and relax. Books and magazines were stacked on the oak tables and a set of French doors opened onto a stone patio that fed down into a green lawn overlooking the ocean. One entire wall was glass, providing a view that was simply breathtaking, especially at the moment, with sunset spilling across the sea in a path of gold and red and staining the sky in shades of rose and gold and violet.

She did a slow turn, taking it all in and silently wishing she didn't feel like a peasant invited to the castle. The whole house smelled like fresh flowers and lemon polish. And though she hated to admit it, her entire bungalow would fit nicely into the great room.

The kids were at her feet, spread out on a wide rug that probably cost more than her car, with toys that were so new, she and Connor had had to pry them out of their packaging. Two nut-brown leather couches faced each other across a wide coffee table of distressed wood. Club chairs in varying shades of green and blue were scattered around the wide room in conversational groups and the wall of glass seemed to bring the outside in.

A housekeeper named Louise, a woman of about fifty, with graying dark hair and bright, curious blue eyes, had brought out tall glasses of iced tea along with a plate of cookies and three sippy cups of milk for the triplets. It was perfect, damn it.

"Think you'll be able to tough it out here?"

She turned to look at Connor, sprawled on one of the couches, looking exactly what he was...lord of the manor.

"Enjoying this, are you?"

"Being comfortable?" he asked. "After time spent on your couch? Oh, yeah."

She sighed because she couldn't really blame him. "Your house is beautiful."

He laughed shortly. "How much did that hurt?"

"A lot," Dina admitted. "I admit, I was hoping to find that you lived in some soulless, white everywhere modern nightmare—"

"Ooh, careful there. You just described my brother Colt's house."

"Really?"

He shrugged. "I never liked it. Felt cold to me, but he thought it looked clean. His wife and kids are currently dirtying it up for him."

"Right. Well, anyway. This house is beautiful, but you have to know that I feel like you maneuvered me into this move, and I don't like it."

"I did, and you don't have to." Connor straightened up in the chair, braced his elbows on his knees and slapped his hands together. "I want my kids, Dina. You come with them."

"For now," she said.

He lifted one shoulder. "Now's what we're dealing with, right?"

Yes, but what happened later? A week, two weeks, three? The longer they stayed in this house, the more solid footing Connor would have for a custody suit. And Dina wasn't an idiot. She knew he expected to take the kids from her. That thought made her heart ache, but a split second later, something clicked in her brain.

All along, she'd been thinking that Connor had the upper hand. And in a lot of ways, he did. But the reality of actually *living* with three babies who demanded plenty of attention was something he hadn't experienced yet. She smiled as she realized that staying here might actually work in her favor after all.

She knew that Connor had only been interested in being a part-time father before Elena and Jackie were killed. Now, it was his own sense of duty and honor—and the realization that he'd been lied to—that had him scrambling to take charge of the triplets.

But what if once he had what he wanted he didn't want it anymore? What if the day-to-day dealings with three babies showed him that he wasn't ready for fatherhood? This could turn out to be the best thing she could have done. Living here, letting him take charge of the kids, might just prove to him once and for all that the trips were better off with her.

She smiled to herself at the thought and relaxed for the first time since their kiss the night before.

"Why are you smiling?" he asked, voice colored with suspicion.

"No reason," she said. Meeting his gaze, she felt something inside her tremble and felt suddenly uncomfortable. But then, she wasn't comfortable with a lot lately. That kiss they'd shared had been overwhelming and the feelings it engendered were still with her. Along with anxiety. She'd never let a man get close enough to her to make her anxious about her feelings.

Looking across the room at Connor, she stared into his ice-blue eyes and knew that *this* man was dangerous. Not just to her guardianship of the babies, but to *her*.

"Louise has your room ready," he was saying. "It's upstairs, next to the babies' room. Mine's across the hall."

"Handy," she murmured.

"Isn't it?" He smiled and her stomach spun unsteadily.

"What's the matter, Dina?" he asked. "Don't trust yourself with me?"

Exactly, but she couldn't really admit to that.

"I think I can manage to restrain myself," she said, scooping Sadie off the floor and onto her hip.

"Wanna bet?" Connor stood up, grabbed the other two kids and held them while he looked into her eyes. A smile curved his mouth and something inside her flipped over in response.

Oh, yeah. This was not good.

A week later, Connor was a man on the edge.

Who would have guessed that three babies could take over a house in so little time? There were toys everywhere, forgotten sippy cups under the couch, and stains on half of his shirts. The three of them were a force of nature.

Connor was exhausted.

And it wasn't just the triplets wearing him down, either. It was the knowledge that Dina was just across the hall from him, every night. It was imagining her showering, naked and wet, with water streaming along her honey-colored skin. It was the images of her floating through his mind, stretched out on the four-poster bed in her room, wearing nothing more than a welcoming smile as she held her arms out to him. It was remembering the taste of her so well he still held her scent inside him.

The way she laughed, the way she smiled at the babies or the way she held them, loved them. She was sparking too many thoughts in his already tired brain and Connor was sure that she somehow knew he was suffering—and she was enjoying it.

Hell, Dina'd hardly lifted a finger for the kids since they moved in. She'd taken a giant step back, telling him that she was sure he wanted to get to know his children. She left the bathing and feeding to him. She watched as he chased them down every morning just to get them dressed. And she laughed whenever one escaped him.

So Connor knew that she was expecting him to fail. To surrender and say that he wasn't interested in full custody, that it was too much work or some other nonsense. But she was going to be disappointed. He hadn't changed his mind. If anything, his resolve had only strengthened over the last week. His children belonged with him and he was going to do whatever he had to do to make sure that happened.

The question was, how to deal with Dina.

"She said no, didn't she?"

"What? Who? Oh. Yeah." Connor shook his head and looked at Colt. Smoke from the barbecue on his patio lifted into the sea wind and twisted into knots before dissipating. The scent of cooking burgers filled the air.

A family barbecue had been Penny's idea. Colt's wife had wanted to meet Dina and the kids.

"You mean to my offer of buying her off?" Grimly, he smiled at the memory of her outraged expression. "Yeah, she said no. And a few other things as well."

"Told you it wouldn't work," Colt said and took a drink of his beer.

"Thanks. *I told you so* is always so helpful to hear."

Colt ignored that. "So any ideas on where you go from here?"

"Plenty." He nodded, picked up the spatula and flipped the burgers on the grill. Grease dropped onto the coals and flames erupted.

"You should get a gas grill," Colt mused.

"I like charcoal," Con told him. "Anyway, Rafe and his crew are coming out next week to sketch out plans for the new nursery suite."

"And Dina knows you're doing this?"

"Not yet, but why should she care?"

"Oh, I don't know, because she thought moving in here was temporary and now you're making it permanent?" Colt's eyes narrowed on his twin. "What's going on in your head?"

"Plans. Okay," Con said, "I admit, it's a little tougher than I thought it would be, taking care of so many babies at once."

"As I remember it, you laughed your head off when it happened to me."

Connor ignored that. "My plans right now are to get to know my kids, to have the lawyer looking into custody and to get to Ireland."

"You taking Dina and the kids with you?"

"Why not?" He made it sound casual but the truth was, he had to go on this trip and didn't much care for the idea of being away from Dina and the babies for a week. He refused to look at *why*. "Dina's got a passport and I had the family lawyers arrange them for the babies. We'll go. Say hi to cousin Jefferson and his family and check out Ashford Castle. Three, four days tops and we're back in California." When his brother gave him a knowing look, Con shook his head. "Don't make more of this than there is. I'm taking the kids and Dina's part of the package. That's all."

"Uh-huh." Colt took another drink of his beer, nodded to where the women and kids were and said, "If you ask me, she's quite a package all on her own."

"Nobody asked you," Connor snapped. Then he took the burgers off the grill. "Time to eat."

"You didn't tell me you and your brother were identical twins," Dina said later after everyone had gone home again.

"There are some differences," Connor said. "I'm the good-looking one."

She laughed and realized that over the last week, she'd become less anxious around him. Less wary. And that should probably worry her. But at the moment she felt too good to ruin her mood with anxiety.

With the triplets tucked into bed and the housekeeper in her suite at the rear of the house, Connor and Dina were alone. The patio was quiet and cool and the sound of the ocean slamming into the cliffs below was rhythmic, soothing. They sat on Adirondack chairs, each of them holding a glass of wine.

"Colt's wife is great," she said. "Did you know she's having the whole house redone?"

"Yeah. Our cousin Rafe at King Construction is madly in love with her," Con said with a chuckle. "She's changing so much it's turned into a huge project that'll keep Rafe's crew busy for months."

"She pointed the house out to me earlier. The big white one that looks like a box with windows?" Dina had taken one look at the place and hated it. Penny had told her she'd felt much the same way when she first saw it. But she was having Spanish revival style added to the basic box and by the time she was finished, Dina was willing to bet that the house would be beautiful. "Penny also told me that Rafe was going to be taking a break from working on her house long enough to do a job for you."

"Told you that, did she?" He turned his head and looked at her, and in the moonlight, his blue eyes shone.

"You're building a suite for the babies but you didn't tell me?" When Penny brought it up, Dina had felt a quick jolt of panic. Adding onto a home was a permanent thing. To Connor's mind, this wasn't temporary at all.

"I was going to," he said, voice quiet and almost lost in the sigh of the waves below.

"You're really going to sue for custody, aren't you?"

He sat forward. "I never made a secret of the fact that I want my kids, Dina."

"I know," she said, shifting her gaze to where a full moon hung in a black sky and slanted silver light on the sea. "The problem is, I want them, too, Connor."

He stood up and pulled her to her feet. She was barefoot and the stone patio was damp and cold, seeping into her bones. With his hands on her upper arms, holding her in place, he looked down into her eyes and Dina felt that tremble of something wild and dangerous rise up inside her again.

"You don't want to fight me for them, Dina," he said. "You would lose."

"If I don't fight, I've lost already," she pointed out and congratulated herself on keeping her voice steady and even despite the insistent tremble she felt within.

The wind sighed past them, briefly enfolding them in a chilly embrace. Dina's hair flew across her eyes and Connor tugged it free, rubbing the silky strands between his thumb and fingers.

"We don't have to be enemies," he whispered. "We can find a way to work together on this."

"I don't see how," she said, staring into those blue eyes that only seemed to shine more brightly in the darkness.

"This is a start," he murmured and kissed her again.

Dina melted against him, plying her body along his as he pulled her in more tightly, pressing her to him closely enough that she felt the hard proof of what he wanted. Her insides churned, her heartbeat quickened and her mind went blessedly blank.

Her entire life had been spent trying to avoid the kind of feelings she was right now surrendering to. If she thought about what she was doing, she'd have to stop. Have to be rational. Logical. Clearheaded.

So she didn't think.

Dina gave her emotions free rein and let herself wallow in the amazing sensation of being held and kissed by a man who could turn her knees to water with a single look. She had known that one kiss would never be enough.

And when Connor pulled back, breaking contact, she knew that two kisses wouldn't be enough, either.

She was heading down a road she'd never intended to travel. But turning back simply wasn't an option now.

He cupped her cheek in his palm and smiled down at her. Dina's only consolation in all of this was that he looked as shaken as she felt. "What're we doing, Connor?"

"Right now?" He grinned, lifted her chin and planted a quick, hard kiss on her mouth. "We're saying goodnight while I'm still enough of a gentleman to let you walk away from me."

"That's not what I meant."

"I know," he said and stepped back and away from her. "Dina, I want you more than I've ever wanted anyone before, so I'm giving you fair warning. Leave now, or wake up in my bed."

Heat pooled in her center and her breath came just a little bit quicker. "I'm not sleeping with you, Connor."

"You're right about that, anyway," he said wryly. "Sleeping wasn't what I had in mind."

More heat flared until Dina felt as if she might simply spontaneously combust right there on the patio. Funny, all it took was warning her away from him to make her want him even more. How twisted was that?

"Connor—"

"Do us both a favor and go to bed, okay?" He scrubbed one hand across the back of his neck, then let his hand fall to his side.

"Fine. I'm going." She hadn't taken more than a few steps, though, when his voice stopped her.

"Oh, yeah. We'll be going to Ireland in a few days, if there's anything you need to take care of before we go."

"Ireland?"

Seven

Dina was being treated like a princess.

And she felt like a fraud.

For heaven's sake, she'd been whooshed through security, bypassing the thousands of people lined up at the other terminals, in favor of the charter jet area that was practically empty in comparison. That's when she discovered that flying on a KingJet was a far different experience than flying coach on a regular airliner.

The KingJet boasted comfy leather seats, a full bar and three cribs bolted to the floor to accommodate sleeping triplets. There was room to wander around and a bathroom—complete with shower—that was as luxurious as the rest of the plane. During the long flight to Ireland she'd relaxed by watching movies on a big-screen TV while Connor buried himself in work.

Once they landed, they were all once again hustled

through customs without having to wait like every other human being on the planet and ushered to a limousine complete with a liveried driver. The ride from Shannon airport to Ashford Castle took an hour and a half, but Dina was so busy with the triplets and admiring the view out the windows, she hardly noticed time passing.

Just the day before, she had been at home, scrambling for work—and now she was in Europe. Sadly, she hadn't had to do much in preparation for this trip. She had no immediate jobs lined up and so no reason to tell Connor she couldn't go with him. And now, as the beautiful countryside streamed past the car windows, she was glad for that.

Connor had been in Ireland before and enjoyed playing tour guide. "In a day or two, we'll drive over to Cong and take the kids for a walk through the village."

"Okay," she said, smiling. "What's Cong?"

He laughed. "Just a really beautiful village in Ireland, but they filmed *The Quiet Man* there. You know, the John Wayne movie?"

"I love that old movie," Dina said.

"Yeah, me, too. They've got a statue in the village commemorating the film, too. Plus, you can visit a perfect replica of the cottage they used. There's nice shops, some good restaurants and great pubs. You'll like it."

She was sure she would. What she wasn't sure of was why Connor cared if she was having a good time or not. But that question went unanswered as the limousine turned in to a long, graveled drive at the end of which the castle waited.

Once the car stopped, Dina stepped out and right into a fairy tale.

The castle was amazing. Weathered gray stone, trail-

ing ivy, glorious flower beds in vivid colors, forests and
a long, winding drive. There was a fountain in the center of the yard and a lake spread out in front of the castle, where sunlight glinted off the surface like handfuls
of diamonds.

Dina stood in one spot and did a slow turn, trying to
take everything in and failing. It would take months to
appreciate the whole picture. She had never seen so many
different shades of green, though. Standing there, it was
like being inside an emerald and watching sunlight play
among the shadows—cool and warm at the same time.

"It's a rare day for Ireland in June," Connor was saying. "Usually the skies are gray and the wind is cold and
generally it's raining. The sun must be shining today
just for you."

She laughed, delighted at the thought, even though it
was ridiculous. Then she shook her head and, speechless,
stared at the castle itself, from the ground all the way up
to the battlements, where she guessed ghosts still walked.

"You like it?"

"Oh, I really do," she admitted.

"It's the oldest castle in Ireland," he said, "and that's
saying something. I think it dates back to twelve hundred something."

"And it's still here," she mused, and her fingers itched
to touch the gray stone, to feel it hum with history and the
memories of everyone who'd ever been here. Smiling to
herself at the silly thought, she turned to look at Connor.
"It's incredible. I've never seen anything so beautiful."

He stared at her for a second or two then said, "Yeah.
Just what I was thinking."

Dina didn't even know how to respond to that and
thankfully, she didn't have to. A small crowd of peo-

ple rushed from the castle down the drive to the car. A short man in a sharp black suit and carefully tended hair walked directly to Connor and held his hand out.

"Mr. King," he said, in a voice brushed with a lovely accent. "So good to have you back again. We've your usual suite prepared for you."

"Thank you, Sean," Connor said, shaking the man's hand. "Dina, this is Sean Flannery, the castle manager."

"Nice to meet you."

"And you, madam," Sean said, taking her hand in a firm grip before turning back to Connor. "We've also taken care of your special requirements. The extra bedroom is equipped for your triplets, and may I add my congratulations to you and your lovely wife."

Dina blinked, surprised. Then she realized she shouldn't have been. Why wouldn't the hotel staff assume she and Connor were married? They were traveling with triplets, after all.

"Oh, thank you, but—"

Connor dropped one arm around her shoulders. "My wife's tired from the flight, Sean, so if you don't mind, I'd like to get us checked in right away."

"Certainly." He waved a hand and suddenly the throng of hotel employees with him descended on the limo, taking luggage out of the trunk and hurrying toward the arched stone doorway.

Dina gave Connor a look, but he shook his head as if to say *later*, so she let it go. Instead, she turned back to the limo and leaned inside. She unhooked the babies from their car seats and one at a time, she handed the kids out to Connor, who corralled them on the pristine lawn. But the triplets had been trapped for too long and refused to stand still. The three of them took off in different directions, toddling unsteadily across the grass, squealing and babbling as they went.

"We should catch them before they ruin the flower beds or fall into the fountain—"

"They're fine," Connor said, watching the three of them with a soft smile on his face. "Just exploring."

"Uh-huh." She glanced back at the noble facade of the castle and could only imagine the luxurious furnishings inside. With that thought came the worry of just what three curious babies could do to elegant accommodations. "Maybe we should have found a smaller hotel. Triplets? Here?"

"If you'll pardon me, Mrs. King," Sean said with a smile and a wink, "you're not to worry about a thing. This is Ireland. Children are welcome everywhere."

With those words, she felt more than welcome, and nearly relaxed. Until she saw Sadie pulling flowers up and had to run to catch the little girl before she did too much damage. Connor ran after the boys at the same time and while the Irish wind blew all around them, they worked as a team to gather the babies.

By the time they were settled in their palatial suite and had ordered room service dinner, the trips were ready for bed. Using teamwork, Connor and Dina got all three of them bathed and tucked in, then Connor poured two glasses of wine and they collapsed into lush green velvet wing-back chairs in the luxurious living room.

Through the wide windows that overlooked what she'd learned was Lough Corrib, Dina saw the twilight sky and the tips of the trees guarding the castle dancing in the wind. Still watching the magical scene outside, she took a sip of her wine and said, "The manager seems to know you very well. You even have your usual suite."

"I stay here when I visit my cousin Jefferson and his family." He eased back into the cushy armchair. "Maura's sheep farm is only a half hour away, and the castle is comfortable."

She laughed a little. "Comfortable? It's…I don't even have a word for it." Shaking her head, Dina said, "I've never been anywhere even remotely like it."

He stretched his legs out in front of him and crossed his feet at the ankles. "Wait until you see it at night with the moonlight on the lake. Pretty spectacular. Tomorrow, we can take the triplets down to the lake, let them throw rocks…"

"Or fall in and go swimming?"

"We'll be with them. But that's a good question. Have they taken swimming lessons yet?" he asked.

"No," she said, studying the gold-colored wine in her glass. "Elena was going to take them this summer, but—"

He frowned, took a small sip of his own wine and said, "We'll have to do it instead. My cousin Rafe is going to install a fence around my pool, but swimming lessons are pretty much life or death for kids, don't you think?"

"I agree."

"Good." He gave her a fast smile that resonated inside her with a heat she really didn't want to acknowledge. "I'll arrange for a private instructor to come to the house starting next month."

"I don't know that we'll still be at your house next month," she said.

"Oh, I think we can count on it." He tipped his head to one side and stared at her for a long moment or two.

"Connor…" He wasn't treating their move to his house as if it were temporary, but that was how she *had* to think of it. No matter what it felt like occasionally, she and

Connor and the trips weren't a family. They were…more like survivors of a shipwreck huddled together in what, at the moment, was a pretty fabulous lifeboat.

She had to make him see that she couldn't stay indefinitely at his house. But what could she say? She was too nervous to stay at his place? She didn't trust herself around him? Oh, a man that sure of himself really didn't need to hear anything like that. Muttering under her breath, she took a sip of her wine.

"What was that?"

"Nothing," she said. "So what are we doing here in Ireland, exactly?"

His mouth quirked as if he knew she was desperately trying to change the subject. "Well, I told you I've stayed here at the castle before, but this time I'll be talking with management, gathering information about what kind of activities they offer families and in general seeing if Ashford Castle would be a good fit for our family adventure company."

"I can't imagine anyone *not* enjoying staying here."

"Oh, it's beautiful," he agreed, shifting his gaze around the room, "but will it be enough to qualify as a family adventure? We'll see."

"Maybe it doesn't have to be so much about adventure as it does a family spending time together in an amazing place," she said. "I know the castle itself would be enough to capture the imagination of any child. They'd picture themselves as knights and princesses…"

He nodded. "You might be right about that. My brothers and I would have loved this place when we were kids."

Several seconds of silence passed before he asked,

"Did you see much of the triplets before they came to live with you?"

"What?" The change of subject threw her for a moment.

He stared into his wine, then slowly lifted his gaze to hers. "The babies. Did you see much of them before Jackie and Elena died?"

"Not a lot, because they were living in San Francisco," she said quietly, sensing the shift in his mood to contemplative, "but they came to visit and I went to see them a few times."

"What were they like?" His voice was so soft, it was almost as if he regretted asking the question at all. "The babies, I mean."

Looking at him, Dina felt a twist of sympathy. Over the last week or so, he'd become so involved with the triplets. She'd stopped expecting him to give up and walk away. The man would never turn his back on those children and he was doing more and more to convince Dina that he was actually *enjoying* being a father.

Bottom line was, Connor was changing his home, his world, to accommodate them and he had been cheated out of knowing them for the first year of their lives. Yes, cheated, she thought and sent a disgusted thought toward her sister, wherever she might be. Jackie and Elena had been wrong to keep the kids from him. Wrong to leave town and run rather than share the children with the man who had helped to create them. And if Dina had known the truth, she would have told Connor herself.

So maybe, she thought, she was wrong to fight him so hard on the kids now. But what choice did she have, really? She couldn't lose the triplets. Not even to their father. It would be like tearing her own heart out. He was watching her, waiting for to speak, to tell him about the children he hardly knew. She took a breath and said, "The babies were always so cute. But oh, boy, were they tiny when they were born."

A wistful smile curved his mouth as he tried to picture it. "I bet Jackie was afraid to pick them up."

"She was," Dina said with a laugh. "For a while, but she got over it because Elena insisted."

"What kind of mom was she? Jackie?"

"A little crazy. Fun." Dina smiled at the memories and tried to make them feel real for Connor. "Elena was the one with the schedule. She wrote everything down. What time the trips ate, napped, play time, bath time. My sister loved schedules." Now it was her turn to be wistful. Only three months since she'd lost her big sister and Dina missed her. "But Jackie was fun. As the kids got older, she would dress up to read them bedtime stories. She bought them all miniature baseball bats so they'd be ready to play as soon as they could walk..."

"Sounds like Jacks. She used to play shortstop. She was really good, too." His smile faded into a thoughtful frown.

Twilight crept into the luxuriously appointed room, and shadows lengthened. It felt intimate, sitting here in the half light with Connor, sharing memories with him so that he could hold the images in his mind. But, she realized suddenly, she could do better.

Reaching to the table beside her, she turned on a lamp that sent shards of light glancing off its carved crystal base. He scowled a little at the sudden brightness, but Dina ignored that and picked up her purse. Pulling her phone free, she turned it on, went to the gallery and asked, "Would you like to see pictures?"

His eyes flashed with interest and a warm smile curved his mouth. "Are you serious?"

She answered the smile with one of her own, then held her phone out to him. "I never delete anything," she said wryly, "so there are photos of them from newborn on."

He was already looking at the pictures, swiping his finger across the screen to look at more.

"Some of them I took, others Elena emailed to me."

He laughed.

"What?"

Connor looked up at her, a mixture of amusement and regret in his eyes. "This picture. Last Christmas, I guess."

Dina knew which photo he was talking about, but she went to him anyway, knelt at his side on the thick rug and looked at the phone screen. Three babies, dressed in candy-cane-striped footie jammies, each of them with a Santa hat on their heads and tiny white beards on their faces.

Still laughing, Connor asked, "Even Sadie had a beard?"

Dina smiled at the memory. She'd been at her sister's house when the two women took that picture to use as their Christmas card. "Jackie didn't want Sadie to feel left out," she said quietly.

"Sounds like her," he agreed. Slowly, he flipped through the rest of the pictures, not speaking again.

Dina stayed where she was, watching—his expressions, not the phone screen. Every emotion he felt flickered over his face, shining in his eyes, curving his mouth. On a too-small screen, he watched his children change and grow and it was clear that those pictures touched something inside him. When he'd finally come to the end—she really did need to delete at least some of those pictures—he handed her the phone.

"I missed so much already."

"You didn't know, Connor."

"Doesn't change anything." He turned his head to look at her. His eyes shone with sadness, but a glint of determination was there, too, and Dina braced herself for what he might say next.

"I won't miss any more time with my children, Dina."

Her hand closed around her phone and held it tightly. Wow, just a couple of minutes ago, she'd been feeling bad for him, taking his side against the memory of her own sister. But looking into his eyes now, she saw that *this* man didn't need her sympathy. "Meaning?"

"Meaning," he said quietly, "I'll never get back their first Christmas. They got their first teeth, took their first steps, all without me even knowing of their existence."

"I know, Connor and it's terrible, but—"

He shifted in his chair, cupped her chin in his palm and lifted her face to his. "You and me, Dina, we're going to have to come to an understanding."

"What kind of understanding?"

"Well, that's the question, isn't it?" he whispered. "I know what kind I'm interested in. I guess all we need is for you to decide for yourself what it is you want here."

Oh, she knew what she *wanted*. Dina just didn't know if getting what she wanted would make things better... or worse.

Watching Connor with his family was a revelation. Oh, she knew he was close to his twin—why wouldn't he be? But Jefferson King was a cousin and yet he and Connor seemed as close as brothers. Obviously, family was vastly important not only to Connor but to the Kings in general. That acknowledgement underscored what she'd felt only the night before. As his children, the triplets weren't something Connor would risk losing.

"Lovely, aren't they?"

Dina glanced at Maura King. The woman was short and gorgeous, in spite of her heavy rubber boots, and the oversize jacket she wore over a thick red knit sweater. June in Ireland, just as Connor had told her, meant clouds, wind, cold and spatters of rain.

They'd gone shopping in the village of Craic only that morning, buying the triplets warmer clothing, since a California wardrobe didn't prepare anyone for the damp chill. Ireland was beautiful and wild in a way that California never could be, and Dina loved it already.

Maura King had been a sheep farmer when Jefferson, scouting a location for one of the movies King Studios made, met her for the first time. Since she still ran her farm and Jefferson worked from the manor house, Dina assumed that marrying one of the wealthiest men in the world hadn't changed Maura Donohue King much.

"Lovely?" Dina repeated, glancing back to where Connor, Jefferson and six children—Maura and Jefferson had three of their own and another on the way—raced madly around the yard alongside a galloping black-and-gray Irish wolfhound named King. Dina had thought his name to be an odd choice, but Maura had explained that she'd gotten the wolfhound when she and Jefferson were on the outs and that she had named the dog after him because, she said, like Jefferson, the dog was a "son of a bitch."

The sheer size of the dog had intimidated Dina at first. She'd never seen such a big animal. But as Maura promised, a wolfhound was the original gentle giant. In no time at all, the triplets were crawling across the big dog, pulling his ears and stepping on his huge feet, and King never made a sound. Rather, he acted like a nanny, herding the kids back into the center of things when they wandered too far on their own.

"Yeah," Dina said, smiling at Connor's hoot of laughter as Jefferson's oldest son, Jensen, sneaked up behind his father and gave him a swat. "I guess they are lovely. So's your home, by the way," she added, turning her face to look out across the pewter-colored waters of Lough Mask, spread out beneath gray skies.

Trees bent in the ever-present wind and tiny whitecaps formed on the lake's surface. Narrow roads lined with gorse bushes boasting tiny yellow flowers spilled through green fields dotted with rock walls like thread loosed from a spool. The farmhouse itself was big and old and behind it rose the Partry Mountains, looking like a purple smudge on the horizon.

"Thank you," Maura said, giving her house a quick glance over her shoulder. "I like it, too, just as it is, but Jefferson is forever adding this or changing that, until I'm never sure what I'll find when I come in from the fields."

"But you don't really mind."

"Not a'tall, but don't tell him I said that." She winked and smiled. "The man is too sure of himself already."

Dina laughed. "I think that's a King thing."

"Perhaps," Maura said, leaning on the fence that surrounded the front yard. "Since all of his brothers are exactly the same and the few cousins I've met as well. Still, I wouldn't change him for the world. I find I like a man who angers me as often as he attracts me."

"In that, Connor and Jefferson are alike," Dina mused,

thinking of the many arguments she and Connor had had in the short time they'd known each other. And yes, like Maura, Dina was attracted even when she was furious with the man.

"I've seen the way he looks at you and you at him." Maura smiled and tapped her fingers against the top rail on the fence.

Dina didn't even comment on that—what could she say? That it wasn't true? Hardly.

"And the children are sweet."

"They are. But so are yours," Dina said, turning to look at the kids as they raced around the yard in the sharp, cold wind.

Maura chuckled. "Wild heathens they are, and treasures, each and every one of them. Jensen was the first—he's four now—and then Julie came along a year or so later and then James."

Dina watched the kids playing and laughing and felt her heart turn over at the sight. How would it be, she wondered, to actually be a part of that group? Oh, she belonged, through the triplets. She was their aunt as well as their guardian and that would never end. But Maura, Jefferson and their children and Connor and the triplets were *family*, and that connection continued to elude Dina. It was simply ridiculous to wish to be more deeply involved with Connor when at the same time she was trying desperately to stay out of his bed just to protect her own heart.

Even more ridiculous to admit that up until she'd met Connor, she had instinctively avoided anything remotely resembling a real relationship. Memories of her mother's tumultuous life were too clear in Dina's mind to allow for anything else. And yet, somehow Connor had slipped past her defenses.

"And with three children, you're pregnant again," Dina said with a glance toward Maura's rounded belly.

"My Jefferson is mad for children, wants as many as we can handle." Maura ran one hand over her belly as if soothing the restive child within. "And as I agree and find I love being a mother more every day, I'm thrilled to be having another. Even if it does mean Jefferson is adding another wing onto the house, crazy man that he is."

Dina laughed but felt a tug of envy for the relationship Maura and Jefferson shared. He ran his movie studio from right here with the occasional trip to the States. Maura remained her own person and operated her sheep farm just as she always had, and yet the two of them together were a team that was only enhanced by the kids they shared. Who wouldn't be envious?

Dina's gaze locked on Connor, pretend wrestling with Jefferson and the kids. Squeals of laughter from the children were swept up by the cold Irish wind and carried away like dreams. She smiled to herself and if that smile was a little wistful, who could blame her?

"King men are difficult even at the best of times," Maura told her suddenly, as if deciding to skip the polite niceties and just get to the meat of the matter. "But I can tell you from personal experience that they're worth the trouble."

"It's not like that with us, Maura," Dina said quickly.

Maura laughed. "Ah, yes. I remember fighting it myself. Jefferson was forever tossing his money about, waving it in my face. Did you know that he actually bought me a lorry without even speaking to me about it?" Shaking her head as she remembered, she continued. "Red it was, and as shiny as a promise, and though I shouted and raged at him for buying the bloody thing, I fell in love with it the moment I saw it. I still drive it now and it's as lovely as ever it was."

Dina laughed and shook her head. "He bought you a truck."

"Aye. Because he said I needed it whether I wanted to admit it or not. And he was right, though I was loath to admit to it. My old beast was on its last wheels, so to speak. But that's who the Kings are, you see. They make a decision they feel is right and good luck to you trying to convince them otherwise."

"I don't like being managed," Dina said.

"And who does? But that's not saying you can't do some managing of your own, is it?"

Dina smiled at the other woman. "You know, I think you and I are going to be great friends."

"I feel it already," Maura said with a matching grin. "And, as Jefferson has decided that we must all fly to California next month to take the heathens to Disneyland before this one is born, I'll be seeing you again soon. You can tell me all about how the managing of Connor King is coming along."

Next month. Dina didn't even know if she'd still be at Connor's house in a month.

"Maybe we could all go to the amusement park together. That would be lovely." Maura turned her face into the wind. "I'll call my sister, Cara, and make sure she's available for it as well. As busy as she is, she does love to see the children when we're in the States."

"Cara." Dina thought about that for a moment. The sign at the front of Maura's farm still read Donohue

Sheep Farm, despite the fact that the owner was a King now. So...Cara Donohue. "Your sister is Cara Donohue?"

Maura's features lit up. "You've seen her films then?"

"I have. She's wonderful." And she'd had no idea that Hollywood's favorite young actress was related to the King family.

"She is that," Maura said proudly. "It was the film Jefferson shot here on the farm that gave her the big break. She'd done some soaps in London, but after this small film here, Jefferson signed her to do—"

"O'Malley's Bride," Dina finished for her.

"The very one." Maura practically beamed with pride. "She was nominated for best actress for the role. She didn't win, of course, but the nomination itself was a wonder."

This whole trip was a wonder, Dina told herself. Maura was kind and friendly, Jefferson was warm and funny, and Connor...she looked at him, and as if he felt her watching him, he caught her gaze and gave her the smile that made her knees weak and her insides nearly purr.

"Oh, yes," Maura whispered, giving her a little elbow nudge. "There's plenty there to be managed, Dina. Up to you, of course, but a King, as I said, is more than worth the trouble."

Whatever the two women had been talking about earlier had put Dina in an odd mood. Though she'd been patient with the triplets as always, it was as if her body was there, but her mind somewhere else. Back at the castle, with the babies asleep, Connor joined Dina at the open window in the living room. A cold wind rushed inside, but she made no move to shut it. Her long black hair lifted and twisted in that breeze and flew about her face in a dark halo. Her hands gripped the windowsill and her face was turned into the wind, the night.

"Are you all right?"

"I don't know," she said softly.

He took her arm and pulled her around to face him. Studying her eyes, he tried to read what she was thinking, feeling, but though those chocolate depths called to him as always, he couldn't make out what she was hiding from him. The only way to find out was to dig beneath the surface.

Exactly what he'd been aching to do for too long.

He'd never known this kind of overpowering desire. Usually when he wanted a woman, he had her. But for too long all he'd been able to do was ache for Dina. Most of the women he'd come across in his life had leapt at the chance to climb into his bed. The problem had always been getting them to leave again.

Naturally, Dina was different. And he liked that. In fact, everything about her appealed to him. Her gentleness with the babies, her willingness to stand up to him for what she believed was right—the fact that she didn't want anything from him except what he owed the babies. She had even been insulted at the thought of him buying her off. She was damned fascinating in every way and he hadn't expected that. Con wasn't interested in feeling anything other than the desire that pounded inside him. He wasn't interested in *depth*. Wasn't looking for forever. What he wanted was *her*.

"You're thinking," he said, in a quiet, teasing tone. "That can't be good for me."

Reluctantly, she smiled. "Might not be good for me, either," she admitted. "Look, Connor, I think we have to figure out what we're doing here. I can't continue to stay at your house with the trips indefinitely. I have a life and a business to run. I can't just walk away from that."

"Who's stopping you from running your business from my house?"

"That only solves one issue," she said, clearly frustrated. "I can't stay with you, Connor, just because you think it's more convenient."

"You'll be with me, Dina," he said, "because you won't lose the triplets and I'm not giving them up."

"So where does that leave us, exactly?" She shook her hair back from her face and looked up into his eyes. "Neither one of us is willing to give in, so we just live with a stalemate?"

He couldn't give her an answer because he didn't have one. On this trip, it had felt almost as if they were a family. He'd allowed the castle manager, Sean, to assume Con and Dina were married—he'd considered it expedient earlier, but maybe the truth was that he hadn't minded the assumption as much as he would have expected.

And that realization was staggering, so he put it aside to look at later. Maybe. Right now there was only one thing he was interested in and he was done waiting.

"Why worry about any of this tonight, Dina?"

"We have to—"

"Right now, all we have to do is this." He cupped her face in his palms, bent his head and touched his mouth to hers. Soft, gentle, barely a brush of lips to lips before he pulled back and looked down into her eyes.

"I want you, Dina," he said, his voice as quiet as his kiss. "I have from the first moment I saw you."

"I know," she whispered. "Me, too."

He smiled and bent his forehead to hers. The knots inside him loosened and his body went hard and ready in a heartbeat. "Then what're we waiting for?"

Eight

Taking her hand, Connor grabbed the baby monitor from a nearby table before stalking to his bedroom while Dina hurried to keep up. Once inside, he closed the door, set the monitor down and drew Dina into the circle of his arms. He indulged himself with a long, deep kiss, savoring the taste of her, the feel of her, the sweet surrender she offered to the fires burning between them.

Moonlight slanted through the windows and lay across her face and hair like molten silver. She shimmered with beauty that had haunted him from the first. His mouth went dry as he pulled back to fill his gaze with her.

The room was dark but for that pale wash of moonlight. A four-poster spindle bed took up most of the space but there were tables, chairs and a blue tiled hearth that lay dark and cold.

"This is probably a mistake," she said and Connor's heart stopped for a second.

"That mean you want to stop?" He'd stop if she'd changed her mind, but he was pretty sure it would kill him.

"No," she said with a small shake of her head.

"Thank God." They'd waited long enough. Too long. This tension between them had been building since that first day when she'd faced him down in her tiny kitchen. They'd been headed here, to this moment, ever since. Con knew she was right—this probably was a mistake—they still had so much to work out between them, sex would only complicate things. But he'd figure that out later. Right now, they'd waited long enough.

He backed her up to the bed, lifting the hem of her sweater to help her tug it off. Connor couldn't wait to get his hands on her. He wanted to feel her skin beneath his hands. Wanted to touch and explore every tempting curve he'd been dreaming about for days.

Her hands worked at his sweater just as feverishly, her eagerness feeding his own. And yet, even in the rush to get her naked, Connor felt a driving need to take his time, to savor this moment that had been so long coming.

Deliberately, he slowed things down, forcing himself to strangle the urge to toss her onto the bed and bury himself inside her. He unbuttoned her shirt and carefully slid it down her arms to drop to the floor. She shivered as she stood before him wearing only her bra and a pair of blue jeans.

"Are you cold?"

"No," she said. "The way I feel right now, I may never be cold again."

One corner of his mouth lifted. "Good. That's good."

He trailed his fingers down her sides, sliding over her rib cage, down to her abdomen and up again to the front clasp of the black bra that looked devastatingly sexy against her smooth, honey-colored skin.

He thumbed the clasp open and let her breasts spill into his hands. He cupped their weight and rubbed his thumbs across the tips of her hardened nipples. In response, she sucked in a gulp of air and swayed unsteadily. Connor knew how she felt. His insides were twisted together in heavy, hungry knots. He'd never known such overpowering desire for anyone. Never experienced such pleasure from a simple touch. Maybe it was because of the growing connection they shared because of the triplets. Maybe, he told himself, it was because they'd waited so long to satisfy their shared hunger. Maybe his own dreams were feeding the reactions scuttling through his body like skyrockets.

But the why didn't really matter. All that did matter now was her and the smooth, silky feel of her.

He bent his head to taste her, taking first one nipple, then the other into his mouth. Her breath raced in and out of her lungs. She arched into him, silently asking for more. His heartbeat galloped when she responded by lifting her hands to his shoulders and holding him to her with a nearly desperate grip.

But she couldn't keep him still, not when he wanted to explore all of her. He was a man on a mission now, with nothing more on his mind than fulfilling all of the fantasies he'd indulged in over the last week or more. He slid down her length, his hands moving to release the snap of her jeans and then the zipper. Slowly, he pushed the denim, along with the black panties they'd been hiding, down her legs, following their trail with his mouth.

Her legs went weak until she locked them in place. He pulled her jeans off, stroking every inch of her skin as he did, then he stood up again slowly, sliding his hands over her body, reveling in the sweet feel of her. This was so much more than he'd imagined it would be. Her desire fed his, fanning the flames within until he was a walking inferno, ready to combust.

When he straightened again, Con took her mouth in a hungry kiss while allowing his right hand to shift to the sweet spot between her thighs. A muffled groan tore from her throat when he touched her so intimately for the first time. Then she pulled him closer as their mouths fused and their tongues tangled in nearly frantic desperation.

She was hot and slick and so ready for him, Connor could hardly breathe. He tore his mouth from hers so he could look down into her passion-glazed eyes as he worked her body into a frenzy. His fingers stroked and delved deep. His thumb slid across that hard nubbin of sensation at her core until she whimpered with the crashing need consuming her.

His hand cupped the back of her neck, holding her steady as their gazes locked. She was helpless to hide her response from him and didn't try. Her hips rocked into his hand as he pushed her higher, faster. Caressing her inside and out, he drove her to the edge of completion then pulled her back, refusing to allow her to find release too quickly. He wanted…needed to keep touching her. To hear her sighs, her whispered pleas. He wanted to stare into her eyes and watch as passion flared.

Her hands curled into his upper arms and even through the fabric of his shirt, he felt that contact like match points, burning into his skin.

"Let go, Dina," he told her softly, unable to look away from her amazing eyes. Such fire. Such passion. All for him. "Stop fighting it and let go."

"Connor—" She gasped for breath, his name barely more than a strained whisper shuddering from her throat.

"Do it, Dina," he demanded and plunged two fingers into her heat.

She exploded. Her body shook, her hips pumped wildly against him, and she tossed her head back, crying out his name in a strangled gasp.

Before she had even stopped trembling, Connor reached down and threw back the dark red duvet, exposing crisp white sheets. He laid her down, stripped out of his own clothes and paused only long enough to grab a condom from the bedside table, rip open the package and sheathe himself before he joined her on the massive bed. She lifted her arms in welcome and he slid into the circle of her heat, her warmth, like a man who had been freezing for far too long.

She parted her thighs and took him inside her. He entered her in one long stroke, feeling her silky heat surround and envelop him. For one long, heart-stopping moment, he held perfectly still, savoring the sensations of finally being where he most wanted to be. Then her legs came up to wrap around his hips, pulling him deeper, closer. He moved within her, slowly at first, setting a rhythm she matched, even as her hands moved up and down his back, her short, trim nails scoring his skin, driving him on. His hips pistoned, his body claiming hers in an ancient blending of selves.

They moved as one, pushing each other toward a release that hung just out of reach. He kissed her again and again, their mouths taking and giving as their bodies raced to completion. He felt the tremors of her release take her and when she tightened her grip on him and shouted his name, he let go and joined her, submitting to the inevitable as his soul shattered.

Dina held him long after the last aftershocks of what could only be called a nine-point-five on the Richter scale slowly faded away. She'd never known anything like that. Hadn't even guessed that her body was capable of feeling so much. Oh, she wasn't a virgin, reacting to the first experience of a male-driven orgasm. But in a weird way, the fact that she'd had three previous lovers only underlined the extraordinary truth of what had just happened.

Until tonight, she would have said that sex was good and orgasms were pretty nice. But those pitiful words didn't come close to defining what had just happened to her. With his every touch, Connor had set her body and soul on fire. She'd felt him right down to her bones and even they had trembled under his sensual onslaught. Now, with his weight pressing down on her, she felt… complete somehow, in a way she never had before.

And that's when it hit her. She loved Connor King. Dina didn't know when it had started, or when she had taken that last slippery slide into love, but it was here now. She was sure of it. Oh, God, how clichéd was that? Have incredible sex and assume you're in love?

She squeezed her eyes shut as her brain raced. This wasn't just about the sex, her brain argued. It was about everything else—the way he handled the triplets, his loyalty to family, his willingness to include her, even his stubbornness—and the amazing orgasms were pretty much just the icing on an incredible cake. Yet another part of her mind demanded to know how this was even possible. She'd known him about two weeks. It shouldn't have been feasible to love someone after such a short period of time. It was nuts to even think it, but this feeling she had was undeniable.

Opening her eyes again, she stared up at the ceiling as the irony of her situation sank in. For most of her life, Dina had avoided situations that could lead to love, and here she found herself loving the very man she'd been at odds with from the beginning. It had to be a cosmic joke at her expense.

But while she worried over the implications, she also couldn't help relishing the moment. Love. Whether it would eventually bring her joy or pain, she didn't know. Sliding her hands up and down Connor's back, she relished this moment, this realization, even though it terrified her. For right now, she was at an Irish castle, in bed with the man she loved, and she wasn't going to waste another second worrying about what tomorrow would bring.

There would be time enough to tangle her thoughts around trying to trust that a man could accept her as she was without expecting her to change and be what he preferred. Plus, there was the fact that the only thing holding her and Connor together was the triplets. If he got custody of those babies, he wouldn't need her anymore and she'd be gone. She knew that and hated it.

Oh, loving him was a tremendous blunder, but God help her, she didn't know how to correct that error now, when it was too late to turn back.

"Are you okay?" he asked, lifting his head to look down at her.

Could he sense what she was thinking? Feeling? No,

she told herself firmly. If he could he would be leaping off the bed and putting some distance between them. So she buried her newly realized emotions deep and kept her response light. "I'm *great*," she said, smiling into those ice-blue eyes.

He gave her a brief, hard kiss. "Me, too." He skimmed one hand over to cup her breast and she gulped. Amazingly enough, her body, hardly recovered from that first incredible round, was clearly ready to go again.

She felt him pulse inside her and knew he felt the same. "Connor—"

He shook his head, his smile gone, replaced by the stamp of fresh need on his features. "I want you again. And again. And again."

"We should probably talk about this—"

"Yeah, not really interested in talking." He eased away and off the bed. "Don't move," he ordered.

She didn't think she could move if she had to. Besides he was back a moment later. He grabbed a fresh condom, slid it on and was joining her in the bed an instant later.

"No more talk," he whispered, sitting on his heels, drawing her with him until she straddled his lap, holding his hard length deep inside her. Dina shook her hair back from her face, looked into his eyes as his hands settled on her hips and dismissed the notion of some awkward conversation. There would be plenty of time for that later.

She squirmed on top of him, twisting her hips, creating a delicious sort of friction that rekindled the fire still licking at them.

"Ride me, Dina. Take me to the edge and then jump off with me."

She nodded, breathless at the explosion of sensation rocketing through her. Moving on him, she set a blistering pace, helped along by his strong hands at her hips. The only sound in the room was their eager gasps and the good, healthy slap of skin on skin.

She took him deeper, higher than she would have thought possible, until Dina was convinced he was actually touching the tip of her heart. She moved her hands from his broad shoulders to cup his face and then she kissed him, parting his lips with her tongue, demanding entry. Demanding he give her all that he had and then just a little more.

He threaded the fingers of one hand through her long, thick hair and held her head in place while he gave her just what she needed. And this time, when their shared release crashed down on them, their mouths were fused and each swallowed the other's moans of indescribable pleasure.

When it was over, they stared at each other and Dina wished she could read what was in his mind, his heart. Did he feel anything for her beyond desire? Was there caring and affection, too? Could that turn to love if given enough time?

And would they have that time? This move to his house was temporary and she knew it. Now, especially, she couldn't continue to live with a man she loved knowing he didn't love her in return. Could she?

He bent his forehead to hers and fought to steady his breathing. Their eyes met and he smiled. "Give me a half hour and we can go again."

Since her body was still buzzing with the kind of pleasure she'd never known before, she liked that idea. "It's a deal," she said, still willing to put aside all of her recent revelations until she could be alone with the craziness now settling in to stay in her mind.

"You are definitely my kind of woman," Connor said, grinning now as he rubbed her nipples with his thumbs.

She sighed, loving that near electrical charge zipping through her system. "Keep that up and we'll never make your half-hour timeline," she warned.

"I'm willing to risk it," he said, dipping his head to plant his mouth at the pulse point at the base of her throat.

Dina tipped her head back to give him access and felt the deliciously slow build of excitement stirring in her again. "You're not playing fair."

He smiled against her skin and whispered, "I'm a King, honey. We always get what we want."

Her heart turned over. He wanted her. But for how long?

From across the room, the baby monitor erupted with a half cry that splintered the haze of passion as surely as hitting a light switch chased away darkness.

Sighing, Connor pulled back and looked at her. Smoothing her hair from her face with his fingertips, he said, "Duty calls."

Duty. Why had he chosen that word in particular? Were the triplets merely duty, in spite of the way he treated them? The way he acted when he was with them? Was *she* a duty? Or was she simply handy?

"Yeah," she said, shifting to move off of him as her thoughts darkened and doubts spilled through her veins like tar. "I should go take care of that before whoever it is wakes up the other two."

"No," he said, catching her hand as she moved to grab her clothes. "I'll take care of it. You don't have to do it all anymore, Dina. You've got me."

He pushed off the edge of the bed, pulled on his jeans but didn't bother buttoning the fly. He cupped her chin in his palm, tipped her face up and gave her a quick kiss followed by that half smile that always tugged at her heart. "I'll be back. Don't go anywhere."

She didn't. Dina sat on the edge of the rumpled bed and thought back to what he'd said before. *She had him.* Did she really?

A week later, they were back in Dana Point and Ireland was nothing but a great memory.

Connor grinned to himself as he walked up to the front door of his house. He'd never enjoyed a business trip more. Sure, he'd secured a new adventure for his and Colt's business, but it was more than that. It was spending time with his family—the triplets, Maura and Jefferson and their brood—and it was discovering just how good he and Dina were together.

He hadn't expected it, but maybe he should have. She was nothing like any other woman he'd ever known, so why would *sex* with her be ordinary? Instantly, his body went tight and hard and he wasn't even surprised. Simply the thought of Dina stirred the hunger that was always close at hand.

Connor opened the front door of his house and was hit by a wave of delicious scents pouring down the hall from the kitchen. Mexican food. And since his housekeeper, Louise, had never once cooked Mexican for him, he knew exactly who was at the stove. Smiling to himself, he followed the amazing aromas and pushed the kitchen door open. He stopped in the doorway, fixed his gaze on her and just enjoyed the show.

Dina's long black hair was pulled into a high ponytail at the back of her head. She was barefoot and wore a dark red T-shirt with faded, skintight cutoff denim shorts. Music drifted from the speakers overhead and she moved to the rhythm, dancing across the white and gray marble floor tiles. His gaze fixed on the sway of her hips and his mouth went dry.

They'd been back from Ireland for two days and she hadn't been in his bed since they left the castle. The hell of it was, he missed her. He couldn't remember a time when a woman had made such an impact on him that he actively missed being with her. Until Dina, women had been fleeting distractions.

She was different. He wanted her here. Now. Teeth clenched, he got a grip on his needs and took a single step into the room. "Smells great in here."

Dina shrieked, spun around and slapped one hand to the base of her throat. "You scared me."

"Sorry." He shrugged. "You didn't hear me come in." Glancing around the kitchen, his gaze swept across the familiar pale gray walls, red and white marble counter-tops and white cabinets. The room was big and he'd prob-ably only seen it a handful of times since he'd moved into the house four years ago. This was Louise's territory and he didn't intrude on it.

"So where are the kids?"

"Louise is watching them upstairs," Dina said. "I had to make the appetizers for a cocktail party and she vol-unteered to babysit so I could work faster."

"So we don't get to eat any of this stuff?" His gaze slid across the trays stacked on the end of the counter and the big round table set against a bay window. Late-afternoon sun streamed through that window in golden shafts that cut through the room and sparkled off the stainless steel fridge.

"We get to eat this." She turned back to the stove and

lifted the lid off a tall soup pot to allow a cloud of steam to lift from the surface.

Connor took a deep breath and sighed. "That smells amazing. What is it?"

"Chicken tortilla soup," she said and let him peek into the pot before she slapped the lid back down on it. Her gaze met his and just for a second, he saw the same kind of desire he was feeling. And, as if she sensed what he was thinking, she cleared her throat, stepped back from him and busied herself with the trays of goodies she had prepared.

He walked over and stopped beside her, close enough that their arms brushed together. Connor heard her quick intake of breath and smiled to himself.

"So, what else do you have here?"

As she snapped the clear plastic lids on the trays, she said, "Mini chicken chimichangas, red-pepper-and-spinach quesadillas, shredded beef taquitos, cheese-stuffed jalapenos, and pulled pork miniburritos."

He snagged one of those before she put on the lid and he'd taken a bite before she had time to whirl on him and say, "Hey! That's for my client."

Connor groaned as flavors exploded in his mouth. Everything had looked great on the trays, but one taste told him that she was a damn artist with a stove. He could understand now why she wanted to open a restaurant. The woman was a *chef*.

Chewing slowly, he shook his head and looked at the half a burrito he still held. "That," he said with reverence in his tone, "is incredible."

She smiled, pleased at the compliment. "Thank you." Sighing, she said, "I've been cooking since early this morning and now that everything's done I've got to shower and change so I can deliver the food to my client."

Connor ate the last of his burrito and tried not to send a greedy glance at the covered trays. "Where's the cocktail party?"

"Long Beach," she said, turning away to stack the trays neatly. "So I've got to run. Now that you're back, you can take over for Louise. I'm sure she's more than ready for a break by now."

"Long Beach is, like, an hour from here," he said, not liking the thought of her having to drive alone all the way back after the party. It would probably be after midnight and if she drove down Pacific Coast Highway, there were plenty of dark stretches she'd have to pass through.

Frowning, he realized he was *worried* about her.

"Do you have someone working the party with you?" he asked.

"No," she said. "This is a small affair. I can handle it on my own."

"Maybe I should go with you," he blurted out, almost as surprised by the offer as she appeared to be.

Dina looked at him. "Why?"

Shrugging, he said, "I can help you carry those trays, for one. Help set up, drive you to and from…"

"What's going on with you?" Her dark brown eyes were fixed on his, gleaming with curiosity.

Good question, he thought. Even Connor wasn't sure why he was so drawn to her. Why being around her made him feel more alive. More…hell. Just *more*. After that week in Ireland with her, he'd found that he wanted to be around her all the damn time. To hear her laugh. To watch her with the kids. To have her turn to him with those big dark eyes open and shining with pleasure.

To reach across his bed and have her turn in to his arms. But he wasn't about to say all of that to her, so he went with the most immediate reason.

"I don't like the idea of you driving around so late by yourself, is all."

A slow, pleased smile curved her mouth just before she went up on her toes and planted a soft, quick kiss on his lips. "That is very sweet."

Now Connor frowned. He wasn't sweet. Ask anybody.

"Dina," he said, catching her hand in his as she started to walk past him. His insides were tangled up in a mess of sensations, emotions and thoughts he didn't want to explore. But there was one thing he had to say to her before she walked out of the room. One thing he wanted straightened out.

She looked down to where their hands were joined, then lifted her gaze to his again. "I can't talk now, Connor. I've got a job and I have to go do it."

He didn't let her go. Instead, he gave her hand a squeeze and held on. "Yeah. Another minute's not going to make that much difference."

"Okay. What is it?"

"Since we got back from Ireland, you've been staying in your own room."

"Yeah," she said, inhaling sharply, "I thought it would be best if we got back to reality."

"Reality sucks," he said, giving her hand a tug hard enough to pull her into him. He looked down into her eyes, let her see the need, the hunger in his. He lifted his free hand to cup her breast and smiled when she closed her eyes and sighed in response. Dragging his thumb across her nipple, he felt it harden even through her bra and the thin fabric of her shirt. "I want you, Dina. Right now, but I'll settle for tonight."

"Connor…" Whatever she was going to say changed as seconds ticked past with their gazes locked, their bodies pinned tightly together. She licked her lips, sending a zip of heat sliding through him.

"Okay," she said at last, reaching to cover his hand on her breast with her own. "Tonight."

"And then every night after," he said, knowing he was pushing and not giving a good damn. Having his hands on her again was both torture and delight.

"And every night after," she said softly, shaking her head as if she knew she was making a mistake but was determined to do it anyway. "This is crazy, you know that, right?"

"No. What's crazy is knowing what we have together and not having it."

She laughed shortly. "Still, not a good idea."

"Best idea since pizza," he countered.

"I guess we'll see." Reluctantly, she pulled away from him and moved away. "But for now, I've got to run. I should be back by one or so…"

"I'll be waiting," he said as his body tightened painfully, throbbing and aching with each hard slam of his heartbeat.

"Great. Good." Nodding, she backed away from him and Connor's gaze swept down, loving the look of her long, toned legs in those very tiny shorts.

She made it to the doorway and paused. Turning back to him, she gave him a warning stare. "No more sampling the goodies."

Nine

By the time she got back to the mansion on the cliff, Dina was exhausted and triumphant. She'd picked up two more jobs just on the strength of her appetizers. It really was amazing what you could get done when you had a little help. With Louise watching the triplets all day, Dina had been able to get everything done in half the time it usually took her when she also had to care for the babies.

She let herself in and paused long enough to listen to the silence in the big house. Then she took the stairs in the darkness; the only lights burning were night-lights plugged into wall sockets and gleaming like fallen stars in the shadows. Dina looked at Connor's door, then at her own, and hesitated.

In that moment, his door opened and a slice of light spilled out. He leaned one hand high on the doorjamb and cocked his head as he looked at her. "You weren't going to back out, were you?"

"I was thinking about it," she admitted, giving a quick glance at the triplets' room, its door cracked open just a bit.

"I've got the monitor in here, so," Connor said, with a sly smile, "if you want to be able to hear them tonight, you'll have to be with me."

Dina had thought about nothing but this moment on the long drive back. There hadn't been much traffic and so she'd let her mind wander a little. Of course, it wandered right to Connor and the situation she found herself in.

Ireland had altered everything between them. She'd allowed her relationship with Connor to fundamentally change. She'd slept with him, realized she was in love with him, and still she had no answers to how they would solve the issue of the triplets' custody. She knew he wanted the babies and so did she. Neither of them was willing to give an inch about that, so sleeping together had only confused an already chaotic situation.

But she couldn't regret it, either. Couldn't wish that she'd stayed away from him. These last two days, sleeping alone in her own room had been difficult. She'd wanted to be with him but hadn't wanted to assume that he meant to keep their intimate relationship alive.

Now she knew he did want what she did and it changed…nothing. There were still too many questions. Too many possible pitfalls to count.

"So," he asked, pushing away from the doorjamb and standing straight. The light from the bedroom behind him made the edges of his silhouette gleam brightly. "I can see you thinking from here. Hell, I can almost hear your thoughts crashing through your mind."

Good thing he couldn't tell *what* she was thinking, Dina told herself.

"There's a lot to consider," she said.

"Not really." He walked toward her, taking long, slow steps. His bare feet made no sound on the carpeted hall floor. When he reached her side, he laid his hands on her shoulders and the heat of him slid through her system, chasing away all of her doubts. Questions. At least for the moment.

"We already crossed this bridge, Dina," he said softly, gaze locked with hers. "It would be crazy to try to go backward now and pretend it didn't happen."

"Or was it crazy to cross the bridge in the first place?"

One corner of his mouth tipped up. "Too late to wonder about that, too. Come with me, Dina," he said. "Be with me."

There never had been a real choice for her, she acknowledged silently. It didn't seem to matter that this could all blow up in her face. For now, she could have what she wanted and needed. She could have Connor. However this ended between them, what she could have *now* was too tempting to ignore.

"Yes," she said and walked beside him to his room.

A couple of hours later, she lay curled up against him, listening to the thundering beat of his heart beneath her ear. Her body was still trembling, her blood still buzzing with the force of the release she'd found only moments earlier.

The night was quiet but for the soft, snuffling sounds coming from the baby monitor on Connor's dresser.

Moonlight streamed through the windows as a soft breeze carried the scent of the ocean.

Her gaze swept what she could see of his room from her position. The bed was as big as a lake, and there was a bay window, with a cushioned window seat, inviting a person to curl up, relax and enjoy the view of the ocean and the beach below. There were tables, chairs, a black marble fireplace against one wall and a door she supposed led to a private bath. It was plush, luxurious and comfy all at once.

And yet, she couldn't relax. Now that her body was replete, her mind was busy, racing with thoughts that jumbled together as if they'd been thrown into the air and allowed to drop into a heap.

"You're thinking again."

"Guilty," she murmured on a soft laugh.

"Well," Connor whispered, "I've been thinking, too."

She tipped her head back on his chest to look up at him and met his gaze warily. "About?"

"This. Us. Where we are and what we want."

"That's a lot of thoughts," she said and didn't know whether to be relieved or concerned that he was spending time worrying over the same things she was.

"Things between us are different now than they were in the beginning," he said.

"That's fair." It was a giant understatement, like saying the ocean was big and wet, but okay. She waited, wondering where he was going with this.

He went up on one elbow and looked down at her. He dropped his left arm across her middle as if trying to keep her at her side, even though she had no intention of moving.

"The custody issue is still staring at us."

"Yeah…" Wary now, every cell in her body went on red alert, prepared for anything.

"We should get married."

"What?" Okay, not prepared for *everything.* For one brief, shining moment, she thought—was he in love with her, too? Was this some magical happy ending to a fairy tale she hadn't even realized she was living? For that moment, her heart lifted, worries sailed away and in seconds, fantasies spun in her head like crystallized sugar—and then shattered just as easily.

"It's the only logical solution."

Logic. She actually heard her fantasies pop like soap bubbles.

"In what universe?" Why were they having this conversation *naked*?

Dina scooted up into a sitting position, drawing the edge of his midnight-blue duvet with her, holding it up to cover herself. She'd gone from blissful to dreamy to completely lost in about ten seconds flat.

He grinned and her heart jolted. This would be so much easier on her if she just didn't love him.

"We both want the kids," he said. "We want each other. This could work."

She couldn't believe he was even suggesting it. Married? They couldn't get married.

"Before you say no," he said as if he could read her mind, "think about this. We each get something out of this marriage."

"This is crazy."

He shook his head. "Not crazy. Brilliant."

She choked back a laugh. Honestly, she still didn't know what to say to him. A simple *no* didn't seem wise. He was still in a position of power when it came to the triplets. It all came down to a custody suit and Dina knew there wasn't a judge in California who would choose her—a woman with a failing business and too many bills—over a rich father willing to do anything to keep the babies. Yet at the same time, how could she say yes?

"This way, I get total access to my kids."

"And I get…?"

"You get the kids, too, and the help you need when you need it," he said. "Look at how much cooking you did yesterday. With Louise to watch the babies, you were able to work without interruption."

"True," she acknowledged, "but that's hardly a reason to get *married*."

"But there's more," he continued. "My house has more than enough room for all of us. You and the triplets would have outgrown that tiny cottage in six months."

"Yes, but—"

He kept talking, plowing right over her as if she hadn't said a word. "You and I wouldn't have to go to war over them."

"True, but—"

"And," he added with a wicked grin that sent shards of light glinting in his eyes, "you have to admit, the sex is great."

"Sure, but—"

"Then there's your dream of opening a restaurant. I can help with that. I'll back you."

Something cold settled in the middle of her chest. Suspicion trickled through her bloodstream. "Why would you do that?"

He shrugged. "Hey, I had that soup you made for dinner. Incredible. Tasted that burrito—were there any of those left over, by the way?"

"No." One word, forced through gritted teeth. She didn't know where he was going with this, but she didn't have a good feeling.

"Too bad." He shifted position on the bed so that he was sitting opposite her. Unlike Dina, who continued to clutch the duvet to hide her nudity from a man who already knew every inch of her body, Connor had no qualms about having this conversation naked.

She told herself not to let her gaze drop below his neck. She was going to need focus and concentration to keep on top of this little chat. And being distracted by his muscled, tanned body wasn't going to help her with that.

"Anyway, to answer your question, I'm willing to back you in a restaurant because you're a talented chef."

"Uh-huh." Her breath was coming fast and shallow.

"Then you won't have to worry about the catering business failing. You can just end it."

"Is that right?" Suddenly, that sexual heat they shared wasn't as much of an issue. God, she was an idiot. She was feeling all warm and fuzzy and he was thinking strategies. "I can quit. Let you buy me a restaurant."

"Yeah." He looked so pleased with himself, she wanted to shake him.

Instead, she got a grip on her rising temper and sense of outrage and ground out, "So rather than letting you pay me for the babies, I let you pay me to marry you."

A couple of seconds passed before he said, "What?"

"Unbelievable." She slid off the bed and tugged on the duvet until he lifted himself off it so she could wrap the damn thing around her like a puffy toga. "I told you I wouldn't sell my *family*. What makes you think I would sell *myself*?"

"Whoa, whoa," he said, holding up both hands in a

placating gesture. "Who said anything about you selling yourself?"

"You did. Just now. 'The sex is great. Marry me and
I'll buy you a restaurant.'" She pushed her tangled hair
back from her face with an impatient gesture. "Seemed
pretty clear to me. All I have to do is have sex with you
and I get to keep the kids I love and, oh, boy, have my
dreams fulfilled."

"That's insulting."

"You're right about that."

"To *both* of us," he clarified. Shaking his head, he
jumped off his side of the bed and came around the end
of it to stop right in front of her. "It amazes me. Why is
it that people with no money are so damned defensive?"

She gasped. "Seriously? You think the problem here
is *me*? Why is it that people with too *much* money are
so damned arrogant?"

"I'm not being arrogant, I'm being helpful," he argued.

"Not what it sounds like on *this* side of the checkbook."

"You're taking this all wrong."

"Must be because I'm so defensive," she muttered
and kicked the duvet away from her feet so she could
pace. She couldn't stand still another minute. Her insides were jumping, her blood felt as if it were boiling
and Dina could have sworn that the edges of her vision
really were red.

"Not exactly the response I was expecting from a
proposal."

"Not exactly the kind of proposal every girl dreams
of hearing."

"Hold on here," he said. "I'm not talking about love.
I'm talking about a business deal, via marriage."

She stopped at the bay window and whipped her head around to shoot him a glare that should have frozen him on the spot. "Oh, you've made that perfectly clear."

"Why the hell are you acting like this?"

"Amazing that you can't figure it out."

He huffed out a breath and set both hands at his naked hips. "I'm not trying to buy you, Dina."

"Really? Then why do you keep throwing your money at me?"

"What am I supposed to do," he demanded, tossing his hands high, "pretend I don't have any?"

"You'd never be able to pull it off anyway," she grumbled. Dina stared out the window at the night. Stars studded the sky and the moonlit ocean frothed and churned like the emotions inside her.

"You know, this backward snob thing is getting old."

"Excuse me?" She turned around to look at him through narrowed eyes.

He laughed a little, but the sound held no humor. "You know just what I'm saying. You're threatened by my bank account."

That was true. With money came power, and no one knew that better than those who didn't have any. "Well, who wouldn't be?"

"I'm offering to marry you, share the kids with you and help you make your restaurant dream come true." He shook his head. "How does that make me the bad guy?"

"Not bad…" she said, "just dictatorial, and overbearing." Dina's hair was really bugging her. She stabbed her fingers through the heavy mass and pushed it back and away from her face. "I don't need you to tell me when to end my business or to buy me a restaurant. I can make my own dreams come true."

"And I can help. What's wrong with that?"

"Because you want me to do something because you think it's the right thing to do and I should just fall in line."

"Where the hell did that come from?" he demanded.

Dina knew where it came from. Years of watching her mother change her life, her hair, her personality, her laugh, all to please the man she was with at the time. She did it for so long, the woman she was at the heart of her had faded and blurred like a photo left in the sun. Finally, it was as if she'd disappeared completely, dissolving into one of the faux women she'd pretended to be.

Dina wouldn't do that. Wouldn't allow her attraction to Connor to morph into the identity-crushing thing her mother had lived through.

"You don't have to open a damn restaurant," he argued. "Keep the catering business…"

"Thanks so much." She folded her arms under her breasts and tapped the toes of one bare foot against the rug. "Are you sure a *caterer* is good enough to marry one of the Kings of California?"

"Good enough?"

"Can't have one of you married to some lowly caterer, can we?"

"You're nuts. I've got a cousin married to the cookie queen, another one's wife owns a Christmas tree farm and I could go on, but what's the point? This isn't about *me*. This is about you and whatever the hell's going on inside your head." Shaking his head he added, "Hell, make tacos and sell 'em at a stand in front of the house. I don't care."

"Wow, thank you again." Dina didn't believe him. He was maneuvering her until she was in just the spot he wanted her to be. Her heart hurt and yet in spite of this awful argument, she still loved him. She probably always would. Which was just so depressing.

"So I'm damned if I want to help and damned if I don't?"

She clutched the duvet even more tightly to her, fisting one hand in the silky fabric. Making sure her voice was steady, she took a breath and said, "You want too much."

"I want my family," he corrected, "and I'm willing to include you in that. What's the problem?"

She couldn't tell him that. Couldn't tell him that she loved him, because he didn't want to hear it. Couldn't say that a business proposal broke her heart even while it tempted her to accept. Because he wanted too much and didn't give enough.

"Connor, you can't marry someone just to solve a custody dispute."

"Why the hell not?" He waved one hand at the rumpled bed behind him. "Tell me that what we have together is not the best sex of your life."

She couldn't. Frowning at the bed, she tried not to think about what they'd been doing there so amazingly just a little while ago. "Sex isn't a reason for people to be together, either."

"Sure it is. And a damn good one." He blew out a breath, folded his arms across his chest and braced his bare feet wide apart.

She was still deliberately not looking at his body.

"Dina, you're reacting emotionally."

"Well, yeah."

"If you look at it rationally instead, you'll see this makes perfect sense. We get along fine. This house is perfect for kids and will be even better after my cousin Rafe builds out a triplet suite—"

She rolled her eyes. There went his checkbook again, waving back and forth in front of her face.

"—we have great sex. I like you. You like me."

Not right now, she didn't. Love, yes. Like? Not so much.

Outside the windows, surf pounded against the rocks at the base of the cliffs and sounded like the universe sighing. He kept talking and his voice, low and persuasive, meshed with the sighs of the sea.

"We'll never have to fight over the kids, Dina," he said in a near-seductive tone. "We can share them. Share everything."

Her gaze flicked up to his. Ice-blue eyes stared at her and she felt herself falling into those alluring depths. She loved him. She couldn't tell him that because he wouldn't want to hear it and she didn't want to give him that much power over her anyway. But was one-sided love enough to make a marriage any damn good? Even a marriage of convenience?

"Think about it," he said, skimming the fingers of his right hand along her cheek before pulling her up against his body and holding her there. He held her head to his chest, and she heard his heartbeat again. Steady, regular, calm. "Just think about it, okay?"

That was the problem. Dina was pretty sure she wouldn't be able to think of anything else.

"Say yes." The very next morning, Angelica Cortez smiled at her granddaughter from across the table at a local coffee bar. "Why wouldn't you say yes?"

"Because he doesn't love me," Dina answered, stirring cream into her coffee and watching the clouds of white dissolve into the darkness.

"But you love him."

Her head jerked up and her gaze fixed on her grandmother. "I never said that."

"I'm not blind, *nieta*," the older woman said softly.

The coffee bar was crowded, mostly with people coming or going from the beach. In late June it was still cool, but not cold enough to keep the surfers at bay. There was a thin coating of gritty sand on the floor and every time someone opened the front door, a brisk wind entered, reminding everyone that it wasn't the heart of summer yet.

Dina had slipped out of the house early, thanking heaven that Louise was willing and eager to spend time with the triplets. Dina needed some time with her grandmother, the most rational human being on the planet, and she knew she wouldn't get much talking done if she had to chase the babies around.

Connor was meeting his cousin Rafe at the house to start the renovations. And things seemed to be rolling along whether or not Dina was ready to accept them. Once he had the triplets' suite completed, he would go for full custody—she knew it. The only way to forestall that was to marry him. But how could she do that knowing the marriage would never be what she might want it to be?

Now, looking into her grandmother's understanding eyes, Dina sighed. "Fine. I love him. But isn't that one more reason to *not* marry him?"

Her grandmother laughed, clearly amused. "Love is the only reason to marry," the older woman told her with a shake of her head. "You and he, you love the children. You are living together now anyway…"

Amazing that having her grandmother know that she was sleeping with someone could make Dina blush, but there it was.

"Why not be married?"

"Because it would be a contract," Dina said, taking a sip of her coffee. "A business agreement."

"An arranged marriage," Angelica said, nodding. "Your grandfather and I, ours was an arranged marriage also. That worked out well for both of us for forty-seven years."

Dina sighed. "Abuela, that's different."

"How? You already love him, *nieta*. This is not a bad thing."

"It could be."

"And it could be wonderful. You won't know until you try."

"And if we try and fail, the babies suffer."

"Then don't fail." Angelica reached across the table and took Dina's hand in hers. "Many arranged marriages become unions of love. Why shouldn't yours?"

Because Connor didn't want a wife. He wanted a bed partner. A co-parent. And because even loving him, there was a part of Dina waiting for Connor to turn on her. To insist she be other than what she was.

"You're not your mother," Angelica said quietly, and still her voice carried over the clash and clang of coffee cups, the espresso machine and the muted conversations going on all around them. "Trust him. Better still, trust yourself."

Two weeks later, Dina's new last name was King.

The wedding was small, only family and a few friends. Connor's backyard was transformed with white ribbon, summer flowers and tables and chairs clustered across the wide, manicured expanse of lawn. The sun was out, music soared from outdoor speakers and their guests were helping themselves to the buffet table that Dina had prepared.

"Your new wife is a hell of a cook."

Connor glanced at Colt, then shifted his gaze back to where Dina, in a long strapless cream-colored dress, danced with Sage clutched tightly to her. The other two kids were being passed around the family while his cousins' kids raced through the crowd, laughing.

"She really is," Connor said, not taking his gaze off of Dina. Her dress clung lovingly to the lush curves he couldn't wait to get his hands on again. Her long dark brown hair flowed and swayed around her shoulders as she danced with the tiny boy in her arms. When she tipped her head back to laugh, the line of her throat was an elegant column that made him want to lick the length of it.

His body went tight and hard and he was forced to tear his gaze from her before it became impossible to hide his reaction to her.

"Couldn't talk her into hiring a caterer," Connor told his twin. "She insisted on doing it all herself."

"And I for one, am grateful." Colton picked up another miniburrito and popped it into his mouth. Grinning around it, he said, "She's also gorgeous."

"Yeah, she is."

"Never thought I'd see you get married, though."

"It's business, Colt," Connor told him, looking back at Dina because he just couldn't help himself. "I explained it to you."

"Right. Business." Colt elbowed his twin. "That's why you're drooling."

"I'm not—" Connor broke off, took a sip of a cold beer and then said, "I never wanted to get married because I'd never be able to trust a woman enough. But if this is business, then I risk nothing." He shrugged, looked at Dina as she handed Sage off to Louise and swung Sam into the dance. Tenderness ached in his heart, but he ignored it and said, "If Dina screws up, I'll divorce her and keep the kids. If everything goes right, we have great sex with no messy emotions. It's a win-win."

The idea of divorcing his brand-new bride gave Con a cold feeling in the center of his gut, but he ignored it. He still wasn't sure what had finally convinced Dina to marry him, but he suspected he had Angelica Cortez to thank for that. And now that they were married, he'd make sure divorce didn't come into the picture. He watched Dina and felt the cold ease away into heat that seemed to be with him all the damn time now. It wasn't just desire, it was more. It went deeper than want, richer than like, but trying to pin a name to what he was feeling only made him more uncomfortable, so he let that go, too.

Colt just stared at him for a long minute, then shook his head and scooped up a tortilla chip loaded with seven-layer dip. Taking a bite, he said, "You're an idiot. Marriage is about more than sex, Connor. It's about talking together, laughing together and *trust*. You're already talking about divorce."

"No, I'm not," he argued, though a slight ping of guilt jabbed at him. "I'm just saying, I can't lose here."

"Sure you can." Colt finished off the last of his food,

shrugged and said, "But you'll figure it out. I have faith. Right now, though, I'm going to go dance with my wife. Maybe you should think about doing the same."

Ten

Dina's life changed almost instantly.

Being married to a King opened doors that she hadn't even known about. Suddenly, her catering business was busier than ever. She wanted to be annoyed that it was the King name, not her own cooking abilities that were getting attention. But she was too happy with the results.

Catering her own wedding hadn't been easy, but how could she call herself a caterer and then hire someone else for her big day? So she'd worked for two days and with Louise's help had pulled it off. Not only had everyone at the wedding loved the food, but two of the guests had called a few days later to hire her for their own parties.

But as much as her business was already looking healthier after a month of marriage, she was still on edge, worried about whether or not she'd done the right thing. Loving Connor was a part of her now. Something that had worked its way into every cell of her body, and there was no denying or ignoring it. But being in love didn't make her blind, either.

Connor wasn't interested in love. He'd made that plain enough. And since the wedding, she'd sometimes caught him looking at her in such a thoughtful way that she wondered what the heck he was thinking. But he remained the same man he was before. Irritating. Charming. Seductive. And when he took her to bed every night in the room they shared, he managed to banish the doubts that nibbled at her during the day.

Sitting on a quilt spread under a tree in the backyard, she watched as the trips ran in circles, laughing and babbling at each other. The three babies were happy and healthy and they loved Connor and their new home. The five of them were meshing into a unit and while she loved it, Dina worried about what would happen if it all fell apart. Still, it was moments like these when she told herself that marrying Connor had been a good decision.

From the house came thundering crashes, the high-pitched whine of saws and shouts from the crew of workmen. King Construction was busily tearing out walls and expanding the triplets' bedroom into what would be a suite that would grow with them. The noise was deafening, but they were working at top speed and would probably be finished in another couple of weeks.

Everything in Dina's world had changed.

And while it was exciting, it also made her feel vulnerable.

Maybe it hadn't been the brightest move, to marry knowing her husband didn't love her, but she couldn't regret it. She had the triplets. She had Connor. And she had a business that was booming. She'd be crazy to complain.

Surrounded by sippy cups, cookies and bowls of sliced bananas, Dina picked up her legal-size pad of paper and her favorite pen. She loved her laptop and her tablet, but when she really wanted to feel creative and let her mind flow, she needed pen and paper.

Idly, she started sketching out menu ideas for the start-of-summer open house party at a local realty office. Glancing from the pad to the kids, she smiled as she began listing ingredients she'd need.

When she heard the heart-wrenching scream, Dina dropped everything and ran.

Connor had a stack of files to go through and sign and a lunch meeting in less than a half hour. Once that meeting was over, though, he was thinking about blowing off the rest of the day and skipping out early. He smiled at the thought, since he was always the responsible one around here. Come in early, stay late, build the business. He hadn't really had a *life* until the triplets and Dina had shaken up his world. And now that he had them, he resented being away from them.

Two days ago, they'd all gone down to the beach and Connor smiled to himself, remembering. The triplets had loved the sand, the water, the seagulls. He could still hear Sadie giggling as he held her toes into the frigid ocean. Sage had been more interested in eating the sand, but Sam had loved knocking down every castle Connor and Dina had built for them.

His smile softened, deepened as he remembered Dina in her oh so tiny electric blue bikini. Oh yeah, maybe he'd leave early and they could all make another trip to the beach.

He'd never even considered getting married in the

past, but so far, it wasn't bad. Except, of course, for the growing feeling that he was becoming more and more deeply attached to his wife. Just the thought of her made him smile, and wasn't that another worry? He'd never had a woman in his life that he not only liked but couldn't wait to see. He'd never before felt that quick rush of excitement when she walked into a room.

It was a little unnerving to admit, even to himself, just how much her presence in his life affected him.

"Con."

He looked up to see Colt, grim faced and steely eyed, standing in the open doorway of his office. Instantly, fear slithered down Connor's spine like drops of ice water rolling along his skin. Pushing up out of his chair, he demanded, "What's wrong?"

"Louise called." Colt winced as he added, "Sam got hurt and Dina took him to the emergency room."

Cold grabbed Connor and filled him, head to toe. He felt bathed in icy water and struggled to draw a breath. Fear. So rich, so raw, it closed his throat. An image of the tiny boy filled his mind. So easygoing. So happy. So dangerously vulnerable. Con forced his legs to work, walking around his desk, headed for the door. "How bad is he hurt? What the hell happened? Why didn't Dina call me?"

"She tried—" Colt followed him as Con walked through the front office. "You were on the phone with a client and Linda didn't put her through."

"I'm so sorry," their admin said from her desk, tears pooling in her eyes. "She didn't tell me—"

"It's okay." Con didn't have time to soothe Linda. He looked at his twin. "I'm headed to the hospital."

"I know." Colt slapped his shoulder. "Call me when you know something."

"Right." He was out the door and across the parking lot in seconds. Less than a minute later, he was on Pacific Coast Highway headed south. Thankfully, their office was in Laguna Beach, only a few short miles from the local hospital. Every one of those miles felt like a hundred to Con.

His mind filled with images designed to torture him. Sam bleeding. Dina sobbing, all alone in a sterile room, hovering over the baby boy they both loved so much. In his mind, Con heard Sam screaming and the sympathetic wails from his brother and sister.

Con's heart jackhammered in his chest and his fists flexed convulsively on the wheel as he tore in and out of traffic, ignoring yellow lights, punching the accelerator when he had a chance for more speed. Fear snapped at the edges of his heart.

He whipped into the parking lot, parked outside the emergency room and didn't give a damn if they towed his car. He had to get to Dina. To Sam. He hit the automatic double doors at a run, sprinted to the reception desk with a quick look in the waiting area. No Dina. No Sam. Just kids and adults, crying, worried. He knew how they felt. He slammed both hands on the desk and barked, "Sam King. Cortez. Where is he?"

The older woman took one look at him and her eyebrows lifted. "Which is it? Cortez or King?"

He took a breath, summoned a semblance of calm and said, "Cortez. Soon to be King. And why does this matter? He's a baby. He's hurt. I'm his father."

For a second or two it looked as though she might argue with him, but she must have seen the desperation in his eyes and taken pity. Whatever worked, Con thought wildly. Hell, if he'd had to, he'd have offered to build a wing to the damn place if it meant they'd get him to Sam.

"Exam room two. On the left."

He spun away from the desk, ignored the stench of misery and antiseptic and headed for the designated room. He burst inside and Dina whirled around to face him, Sam clutched in her arms. The baby's face was red and streaked with tears, his breath hitching in and out of his little chest. His black hair stood up on end and the moment he saw Connor, he reached out both chubby arms. "Da!"

Con's already unsteady heart lurched, but he snatched the little boy from Dina and cuddled him close. *Da.* Sam had just said his first word and the magic of that briefly swamped the building fear. For one moment Con inhaled the soft, clean scent of Sam and let his own heart drop to a more normal rhythm as he felt the little boy's warm, solid weight. Sam laid his head on Con's shoulder with a breathy sigh and Con looked to Dina.

"What happened?"

Tears had left their mark behind on her face as well. Her big brown eyes were still wet with them. Her bottom lip trembled. "They were playing in the backyard. I was right there, Con. Everything was fine, then Sam screamed and when I went to pick him up, his leg was bleeding and—"

Connor shifted his grip on the baby and for the first time noticed a hastily wrapped, bloodstained bandage. Sam sniffled and Connor patted his back gently, hoping to soothe.

Shaking his head, Connor asked, "How did it happen? What cut him? Did you see it?"

She nodded. "A nail in the grass. A big one, like a roofing nail," she said. "It must have come from the construction on the house." Shaking her head furiously, she said, "I should have thought of that. Been more careful. Realized that this was a possibility."

She was beating herself up so badly, Connor's heart hurt for her. Without even thinking about it, he snaked his free arm out and drew her into his chest, holding her tight alongside Sam. "Not your fault. I didn't think of it, either. But I'm going to talk to Rafe. Tell him I want one of his guys running a damn metal detector across the grass every night when they're done for the day."

She shook her head against him. "They're not going to want to do that."

"I'll pay extra."

She laughed a little and looked up at him. "Okay, sometimes your checkbook comes in handy."

He smiled and kissed the top of her head. "Accidents happen." With the two of them held tightly to him, Connor said, "Remind me sometime to tell you about all the times Colt and I ended up in the emergency ward. Our mom used to say they were going to give us our own rooms."

He felt her relax a little and smiled in spite of everything. Sam was hurt, but he wasn't in danger. He would heal. And Dina was here in Connor's arms, and for the first time since his brother had walked into the office with grim eyes, Con took an easy breath.

"So what's the doctor say?" he asked.

"Nothing." She tipped her head back to look at him. "We haven't seen anyone yet."

"That's unacceptable," he said. "You take Sam. I'll find a doctor and get him in here—"

The door opened and a young woman with a warm smile, copper-colored hair and a teddy bear on her stethoscope walked in. "Hi, I'm Dr. Lamb." She checked the chart in her hands, then looked at the baby. "This must be Sam."

The little boy lifted his head, glanced at her, then buried his face in Connor's shoulder again.

Every protective instinct he possessed rose to the surface. Sam expected Con to take care of him, keep him safe. Hating to let go of the boy at all, especially when tiny hands fisted in his shirt and hung on, Con had to force himself to sit Sam down on the examining table.

Dr. Lamb dug into a nearby drawer and pulled out a tiny stuffed animal still in protective plastic wrap. She freed the elephant, then bent down to look Sam in the eye as she handed it to him. "Why don't you hold onto this while I look at your leg, okay?"

Warily, Sam took the stuffed animal and held it tightly in both hands. Connor gave Dina's hand a squeeze, then reluctantly released her so they could each take up a post on either side of the young doctor. Connor felt helpless and he hated it. He couldn't *do* anything and that tore at him. He scrubbed one hand across the back of his neck and watched the doctor examine Sam with gentle fingers.

When she was finished, she said, "Well, looks like we're going to need a few stitches."

"Oh, no," Dina whispered.

"No worries," the doctor said, smiling for Sam's benefit. "We've got a numbing spray. He won't feel a thing, I promise. Are his immunizations up-to-date?"

Connor blanked. "I have no idea." He turned to Dina.

"Yes," she said. "He's had the usual shots and vaccines. I didn't bring his records with me, but if I can use your computer, I can get them for you."

"That's all right. I think we'll give him a small-dose tetanus booster, just to be on the safe side."

While the doctor got busy and Dina kept Sam distracted, Connor watched and realized that if Dina hadn't been there, he wouldn't have had a clue about Sam's medical history. There was still so much he had to learn. Discover. And he had to arrange to legally adopt his kids, make sure they carried his name.

He looked at Dina as she comforted Sam and played with the stuffed elephant. She was a wonderful mother to the triplets and she was a hell of a woman. And they were married now, so she should probably adopt the three of them, too. Make it official. All of them Kings. A family.

He was grateful Dina was here with him, sharing the worry, the anxiety. He'd always been the kind of man to stand on his own. To take care of business and to never allow panic to creep in and get a grip on him. But he'd never had kids before, either, and now that he did, Connor knew that fear would always be his closest companion. Having Dina there eased something in him that he hadn't even known existed, though. She had, in the short time he'd known her, dug deeper inside Connor than anyone else ever had.

Just then, as if she'd sensed him watching her, Dina looked over at him and smiled, and in response, Connor's heart did a hard, irrevocable tumble. She quickly turned her attention back to Sam, but the damage had been done. That smile of hers, those open, beautiful dark eyes, the easy warmth that surrounded her had finally pushed past Connor's last line of defense.

And it was there, in that small, crowded room rich

with the scent of antiseptic, that he realized he couldn't ignore the terrifying truth any longer.

He was a man in love with his wife.

A fact that shook him to his bones.

All right. Since that moment in the emergency room two weeks before, Connor had been able to admit—at least to himself—that he loved Dina. He could accept that. But he still didn't trust her, so he kept his feelings to himself. He kept waiting for her to make a mistake. To prove to him that she was just like every other female he'd known in his life.

Yet so far…she hadn't.

Instead, she continued to show him that she was just who she claimed to be. Strong. Independent. Loving. So why couldn't he relax his guard?

He couldn't love her without being at risk—and as long as she didn't know how he felt, that risk was mitigated. *Cowardly?* his mind whispered. *No. Smart*, he argued sternly. He'd been used too many times to let down his defenses, even if Dina was like no one else. She wasn't interested in his money. Had been insulted any time he'd tried to help her financially.

But how did he know if that was for real? Maybe it was a well-performed act and she was just lulling him into complacency. Okay, that sounded stupid even to him. But he still couldn't bring himself to trust her completely. How could he be expected to? He hadn't even known her until a little more than a month ago. So he'd bide his time. Give it a few months. Maybe a year. If she really was who she claimed to be, then he'd tell her he loved her. He just needed to be sure.

He'd had Dina cater the party for fifty of his most

important business associates and he'd had nothing but compliments all night—not just on the food but on his good fortune in marrying her. Between Dina and the event planner she'd worked with, the party had been a huge success.

Most of the guests were gone now, and as two men left, Connor overheard their low-pitched conversation.

"Yeah, who knew Connor King would ever get married?"

"And to a woman with kids," his friend said. "You really think they're his?"

"Who knows?" the first man said, and Connor stepped deeper into the shadows so he could listen without being seen. "I'll tell you what, though, if I could get a woman like that in my bed, I'd take her even if she was lying to my face. Wouldn't be the first time a woman with nothing married a man with money just to make life easier."

The second guy said, "If you're gonna get used, get used by a woman who can cook like *this* and looks like she does."

They were gone a moment later and Connor stepped out to say goodbye to the rest of his guests. But that conversation kept echoing in his mind. People were talking. He'd expected that. They were saying he was being used. Was he?

"It was a wonderful party, Connor. Thanks for having us."

"My pleasure," he said, shaking hands with David Halliwell, one of his clients.

The August night was warm, but the ocean breeze kept it comfortable. There were white fairy lights strung through the trees and strings and piano music still soaring from the speakers. Guests were beginning to leave and frankly, he was ready to be alone with his wife. Maybe he was wrong. Maybe it was time he told her that he loved her. Take that risk.

"Your wife is a genius," Marian Halliwell was saying. "In fact, I've hired her to do our anniversary party next month and my sister is going to call her in for the grand opening of her boutique in September."

He felt a swift flash of pride. "I'm sure she's looking forward to it."

"Oh, she is," Marian practically cooed. "I told her now that she's a King, the world is going to open up for her."

"Is that right?" He flicked a glance across the yard to where Dina was supervising the cleanup.

"Well, she already knew that, of course," Marian continued. "She said herself that becoming a King was the best business decision she'd ever made."

He looked back at the middle-aged woman. "Did she?" A slender thread of suspicion began to uncoil inside Connor. *Business decision.* She'd married him, gotten his name, and now was building her business into the kind of success she'd only dreamed about before. He had offered her a straight business deal proposal and she'd turned that down, insulted. Now it seemed she was okay with the business aspect and he was the one who wanted this marriage to be about more.

"Come on, Marian," her husband said, steering her toward the door. "Time to go."

"Of course," his wife agreed, looking back over her shoulder as she walked away. "Tell Dina I'll be calling her to go over details."

He nodded and waved, but wasn't really paying attention anymore. Doubts assailed him, and though he didn't want to admit to it, Connor realized that Marian's throwaway comment had shaken him. His go-to emotion of cautious mistrust rose to the surface and neatly displaced the whole notion of telling Dina about how he felt.

Across the yard, she moved through the moonlight, the tiny, flickering white lights above her, and she looked like a dream. The kind of dream a man might convince himself to believe in even if it wasn't real.

As he watched, a man approached her and steered her toward the shadows. Instinct drove Connor across the yard, ignoring the two or three caterer's helpers stacking chairs and carrying dishes into the kitchen. His gaze fixed solely on the bushes and the man trying to tug Dina farther into them, Connor hurried forward. But what would he find? Was Dina in on this little rendezvous?

"Nice party."

Dina cringed, but forced a brittle smile as she turned to face the man who'd spoken. For the last half hour, everywhere she went, there he was. He was about forty, wearing a suit that probably cost more than the rent on her old bungalow. He also, thanks to too many trips to the margarita bar, seemed to think he was irresistible.

"Thanks," she said, "I'm glad you're having a good time."

"Connor always did have all the luck with women," the man said, moving in closer and reaching out to stroke her arm.

Dina stepped back, but he moved with her and she realized that they were alone in this shadow-filled corner of the yard. "Thanks, but if you'll excuse me—"

"You don't have to run away," the man said, reaching out to take her arm in a firm grip. "I've got as much money as ol' Connor. You and me could have some fun."

"Excuse me?" She tried to yank her arm free, but he was strong in spite of being drunk. This was a fine line to walk, she thought. She didn't want to cause a scene, but she also didn't like being manhandled.

"Come on, just give me a little kiss and I'll leave you alone."

"You can leave me alone without the kiss," she told him. Honestly, she just wanted him gone and this night over. It was an important party for Connor's clients and she didn't want to ruin it by creating a scene. But if this man didn't let her go, she was going to start kicking and screaming.

"One kiss. What's the big deal?"

"Get off of me," she said, trying to pull free.

"But you're so pretty," he was saying and maneuvered her around until his back was to the party and hiding her from sight. "One kiss. You'll like it."

"No, I—" He bent his head and Dina jerked back, but before the man's mouth met hers, he was yanked away and tossed to one side.

She looked up into Connor's furious features and her heart swelled. Feminism be damned, there was something to be said for having a white knight of your very own ride to your rescue. It was over quickly, with the drunk already scrambling to his feet, mumbling apologies and escaping. Thank heaven that most of the guests had already left. She glanced around the yard and realized that she and Connor were alone. Most of the cleanup was finished and the crew would leave right after.

"Thank you," she said, shifting her gaze back to Connor's. "He was just drunk, but—"

Then she noticed the harsh light in Connor's eyes and

the grim slash of his mouth. He was still furious. But not at the guy he'd already vanquished…at *her*.

"Connor?"

His features went even colder. "We'll talk about this later. When everyone's gone. Meet me in the great room."

She watched him stalk across the yard, never once looking back at her. A yawning emptiness opened up inside her and still, she had to breathe. Had to move, had to help finish the cleanup. But she felt as if her feet were encased in cement. She was hurt and confused and working slowly toward the anger that Con obviously had already carefully banked inside him. What the heck was going on?

By the time the servers were gone, it was late. The triplets were upstairs asleep, Louise was tucked up in her own suite and the entire house felt dark and silent. Dina put the last of the dishes into the dishwasher, set it to run and only then did she allow herself to even think again about what had happened earlier.

The hurt was still with her, but her anger was now free to build and quickly outpaced the ache in her heart. She had done nothing wrong, yet he was clearly mad at her. Well, she could match him in that at the moment. In the quiet house, the hum of the dishwasher was overly loud and chased her out of the kitchen. Her steps clicked quietly against the hardwood floor as she walked along the hall to the great room at the front of the house, where Connor had asked her to meet him.

He was standing in front of the wide windows, staring out at the night beyond the glass. His hands were tucked into his slacks and if she hadn't known him well enough to see the tension radiating off him, she might have thought him relaxed.

"Connor?"

Slowly, he swiveled his head to look over his shoulder at her and his expression looked as if it had been carved in stone. His handsome features were tight and hard and there was no welcome in those ice-blue eyes.

"If you're going to cheat on me," he said, keeping his voice a tight, low hiss, "at least be discreet."

"Cheat?" Stunned surprise rocked her back on her heels, but she recovered quickly. "That's what you thought you saw? Are you crazy?" She took a step forward and stopped again. "The man was drunk and annoying me. There was no *cheating* going on. I was trying to get him off me without creating a huge scene. Couldn't you tell that when you made your grand entrance?"

"What I saw was the two of you headed for the shadows."

"He was pulling me into the bushes."

"And I should believe you."

"Why wouldn't you?" She wouldn't have thought she could be more surprised than she had been earlier by his unjustified anger, but she would have been wrong. "I don't cheat, Connor. And I don't lie."

"Right. You just use people to get what you want."

"What are you talking about?"

He walked toward her. Every step was slow and measured, sounding like a heartbeat in the quiet.

"I thought you were different," he said, moving in on her. "You almost had me fooled. But it was all a setup, wasn't it? You get me to marry you—"

A short, sharp laugh shot from her throat. "Get you to marry me?" she repeated, shocked both at what he was saying and at the cold, dispassionate set of his features. "You're the one who talked me into marrying you—"

"Oh, yeah." He nodded. "You worked that well. Tangle me up in my own sheets, make me want you so bad I can't think straight. Move in here and make yourself a part of my life." He scrubbed one hand across the back of his neck. "You were probably the start of all of it. Why wouldn't you be? You made me so nuts it was easy to maneuver me into proposing—"

"Maneuver you?" Fury didn't even cover what she was feeling. Dina could hardly draw a breath, her chest felt so tight. "You arrogant, conceited…"

"You know what the best part was?" Connor asked with a shake of his head. "Every time I tried to help you financially, your insulted act was impressive."

"Act? I wasn't acting. I didn't want your money then and I don't want it now."

"No, you just wanted my name. That was it all along, wasn't it?" He came even closer but Dina didn't back up. She stood her ground, tipping her chin up so that she could look into the eyes she had thought she knew so well. There was nothing familiar there now. Just suspicion and regret and anger.

She could meet fury with fury or she could dig deep and come up with some sort of calm. Try to make sense of this. Hurt tangled with temper and won. The cold went deep into her bones and she thought she might never be warm again. "I don't know what you're talking about."

"You told Marian Halliwell that marrying me was the best business decision you ever made."

Had she? She didn't remember. She'd talked to so many people at the party, they all sort of blended together. But in a way, that was true. Being married to Connor *had* helped her business grow, even though she hadn't taken Connor's offer of an investment. She'd done the work herself. Being a King wouldn't continue getting her jobs if she couldn't pull them off.

"Using the King name's getting you a lot of new clients lately, isn't it?"

"You've gotten me two of them," she pointed out.

He waved that away. "You're using me, Dina."

"You actually believe that, don't you?" She just stared up at him, her own eyes blurred with a sheen of tears that she refused to let fall. Dina was shaken, disheartened but somehow not disappointed.

"Yeah," he said simply. "I do. You know, when I offered to use my name and contacts to give your business a boost, I meant the offer. But I was actually impressed when you said no." He shook his head slowly. "Turns out though, you just wanted to do the boosting yourself. Did you really think I wouldn't find out how you were milking your new last name for business? Did you think I wouldn't care?"

"I wasn't doing that, Connor." Silently she congratulated herself on keeping her voice quiet and even in spite of how she was trembling. Pain shimmered brightly as her heart simply broke.

A part of Dina had been waiting for the fairy tale to shatter. For Connor to let her down and for reality to come crashing in on her. She loved him, but that wasn't enough. He didn't even know her, she thought sadly. If he did, he never would have believed the worst of her so easily. So she couldn't trust him. And love without trust didn't stand a chance.

"I don't cheat, Connor. I don't lie," she repeated. "And I don't use people." Her gaze locked on his, she tamped down the anger churning within and let the pain color her words as she said, "But you can't see that because you're too busy waiting for people to fail you. You actually went out of your way to twist things around to make me look as guilty as you're afraid I am."

"Afraid?" He scoffed at that.

"Yeah. Afraid." She reached up, but instead of slapping him, she cupped his cheek in her palm. "I recognize the signs because I was scared, too, and tonight, it looks like I was right to be. I didn't use you, Connor. I didn't marry you to help my business or for the sake of the triplets—no matter what you originally offered me. See, the only reason I married you was because I loved you."

He blinked and then his eyes narrowed.

She let her hand drop. "And that disbelieving look in your eye is why I never bothered to tell you."

"What do you want me to say?" he ground out.

"Nothing. You've already said too much," she told him. "It's late. I'm tired. I'm going to bed. In my old room."

She took a couple of steps and stopped when he asked, "Did he hurt you?"

Dina looked over her shoulder at him. "Who?"

"John Ballas. The guy who was bothering you." Connor's face was hard and still. "Did he hurt you?"

Shaking her head, Dina said, "He was just being drunk and foolish. If you hadn't shown up, I could have handled him." She paused and said, "But to answer your question…no. He's not the one who hurt me, Connor."

Eleven

Connor spent the night at the office. It wasn't the first time he'd slept on the wide leather couch. But this time was a misery.

All night he'd lain awake, replaying that scene with Dina, and no matter how many different ways he tried to examine it, he still looked like an idiot. Even if he was right—he'd handled it all wrong.

He didn't even know what had set him off. Con only knew that the last couple of weeks he'd been tense. To be honest, he'd been tense ever since that afternoon when he'd realized he loved her. That had thrown him. Hard. Still, he'd been working through it, pretending that everything was fine. Then his guests had started complimenting him on Dina's talents and saying how they were going to be hiring her for upcoming events. He'd watched her, smiling, happy, connecting with people, and a voice in the back of his mind whispered that she was just using his name to promote herself. That she was no different from any of the other women who had tried to use him in the past.

Pushing up off the couch, he stumbled into the front office and made coffee. But while he performed the familiar task, his mind was dredging up images of Dina. The smile on her face when he'd pulled John Ballas off her and the way that smile had died away because of *Connor*. God.

He leaned both hands on the tabletop and listened with half an ear to the hiss and bubble of the coffeemaker. He'd saved his wife from a jerk and then turned on her. "Who does that?"

"Does what?"

Connor didn't bother to muffle the groan as he looked over at Colt, standing in the doorway. No one would ever think them identical today, he thought in disgust. Colt had clearly slept well. He'd shaved and wasn't still wearing the clothes he'd had on the night before. Plus, his life wasn't currently in the toilet.

"What did you do?"

"What didn't I do?" Connor answered, turning back to watch the rich black liquid drip all too slowly into the waiting pot.

"Seriously, Con. I saw you at the party last night. You were wired so tight I half expected you to give off sparks."

"I know."

"So. I repeat. What did you do?"

"Made an ass of myself, apparently," he muttered, not happy about sharing this moment with his twin.

"Yeah, I guessed that, since Penny talked to Dina this morning."

His head snapped up. He looked at his twin and squinted against the morning sunlight streaming in through the front windows. "Is she okay?"

"Is there some reason she wouldn't be?"

Plenty, he thought but didn't say. There were some things he wasn't going to talk about, even with his twin. "Give me a break, will ya?"

"Sure," Colt agreed quickly. "Arm? Leg? Thick head?"

"Don't be funny," Con muttered. "Not in the mood for funny—thank God. Coffee's done." He grabbed the pot, poured a cup and took that first hesitant yet blissful sip. The heat and caffeine didn't help, though. There was still a black hole of misery in the center of his chest. And being completely awake only made him more aware of it.

"What the hell happened?"

"I don't even know," Con said before he could measure his words. Hell, he'd been going over all of this since the night before and he still couldn't have said exactly why he'd snapped. Shaking his head, he took another sip of coffee before asking, "Penny talked to Dina. How is she?"

"Hurt. Confused. Mad."

He wiped his face with his palm and blew out a breath. "Sure she is. Why wouldn't she be?"

"What's the deal, Connor?"

"I don't know." Colt followed when Connor walked back to his office. Dropping back down onto the couch, he braced his elbows on his knees. "Something had been building up in me for days. Maybe weeks. Last night, I don't know. I just…snapped." He looked up at his twin. "I love her."

"News flash," Colt said wryly.

Scowling, Connor said, "Well, it was news to me. And not happy news." He leaned back on the couch and threw one arm across his eyes. "I didn't want to love her. Too risky. Too messy. So, I don't know, maybe I was looking for reasons to *not* care."

"Why?"

"You can ask me that?" Connor's gaze snapped to his twin's and there was heat in it. "How the hell did you react when you found out Penny had been lying to you? That she'd had your children and never bothered to tell you?"

Colt shifted, clearly uncomfortable. "Different situation."

"No, it isn't. I had three kids out there that I never knew about." Connor set his coffee cup on the low table in front of him with a slap and stood up. "Jackie, my *best friend*, lied to me and disappeared out of my life to hide the lie. She *used* me. If Jackie could do it, why not Dina?"

"So you judge everybody based on Jackie?"

"Not just her." Connor started pacing and while he talked, his anger spiked again and he told himself that maybe he hadn't been wrong at all the night before. "How many women have tried to get their hooks in us? For the money? For our name? For what we can do for them? Hell, have you forgotten how fast you ran from Penny? Didn't your original marriage last a whopping twenty-four hours before you bolted?" Connor stabbed his index finger toward his brother. "You told me that you loved Penny even then, but you didn't trust it. Didn't trust *her*. So you ran."

"This isn't about me," Colt said, mouth grim, eyes hard.

"Sure it is. We're identical twins. Why is it so hard to see that I'm doing the same thing you did?"

"Exactly." Colt stomped across the room toward him and stopped. "Why can't you see it? Hell, maybe learn from my mistakes? You're doing the same damn thing I did, and I was wrong. If I remember right, it was you who called me an idiot over it."

Connor grimaced.

"Yeah. I ran from Penny. Doesn't make me proud to admit that. Makes me a damn coward."

"No, I was wrong back then. You were smart to trust your instincts."

Colt snorted a laugh. "If I'd done that, I would have stayed with her, because every instinct I had was telling me she was the real deal. The once in a lifetime. But I let my fear rule me. Just like you are."

Connor laughed and the sound scraped over his dry throat. He walked to the windows that overlooked the beach and the ocean below. The sun stained the morning sky rose and gold and there were whitecaps frothing on the water. Surfers were already out there, bobbing like corks in a bucket as they sat on their boards waiting for just the right wave. What should have been a soothing view did nothing to ease the knots inside him, though.

"I'm not afraid of anything." Then he heard Dina's voice in his head. *You're afraid, Connor. I know because I was scared, too.* Deliberately, he pushed it out.

"You think I don't know you?" Colt countered. "Think I can't see it? You're quaking in your boots, man."

"Go away."

Colt snorted. "No. I'm gonna save you from yourself."

"Just butt out, Colt. Do us both a favor."

"You can try to blow this off, but it's not working."

Colt walked up and stood beside his brother, both of them looking out over the water. "I tried the same damn thing. Told myself Penny was just in it to use me. Thought she wanted money, or whatever, but all she wanted was *me*." He shook his head slowly as if he still could hardly believe his good fortune.

"No accounting for taste," Connor mused, and felt the knots inside him tighten.

"Right," Colt said, nodding sagely. "Easier to make jokes than to face what's right in front of you. I tried that, too. Didn't work for me, either."

Con remembered what Colt had gone through when he and Penny were trying to work out what had brought them together. He remembered finding it damned amusing too. Wasn't so funny when he was in the hot seat. "John Ballas grabbed Dina at the party last night."

Colt stiffened instantly. "Bastard. Tried that with Penny, too. She dumped her drink on his head. The man thinks he can get away with anything."

"Yeah, well, we're done with him. I don't care how much business we lose."

"Agreed. How'd Dina handle him?"

Connor shoved his hands into his slacks pockets and fisted them there where his brother couldn't see them. "She didn't. I saw them moving off toward the bushes and I intercepted them. Tossed Ballas aside."

"Good for you. Wish I'd had the chance."

"Then later," Connor added, "I accused Dina of cheating on me with him." God, just saying the words out loud shamed him. He knew damn well what John Ballas was like. Hell, he knew Dina wasn't cheating. His *wife* had been accosted and he'd turned on *her*.

Stunned, Colt stared at him, openmouthed. "Are you out of your mind?"

"I don't know," Connor admitted. "Maybe."

A low whistle slipped from Colt. "No wonder Dina was so mad this morning."

"That wasn't the only reason."

"Connor..."

"You know what?" He glanced at his twin. "I don't need to hear any more from you."

Colt studied him. "No, you need to hear it from Dina. But that's gonna be tough, since she's gone."

"Gone?" His heart stopped. Hell, a part of him felt like the *world* had stopped. "What do you mean gone?"

"What do you think it means? She left. She told Penny this morning that she was leaving."

"And you didn't mention it until *now*?" Connor turned and headed for the door.

"I wanted to hear your side and now that I have, I don't blame her."

"Thanks for the support."

"When you do something right, I'll support you. In this?" Colt shook his head. "You're on your own."

On his own. It was the way he'd lived his entire adult life, Connor thought as he left the office, his brother's words still ringing in his ears. Connor had never let anyone close—at least, no one outside the family—except Jackie and even she had turned on him, so didn't that justify his actions now? Didn't that explain why the hell he'd snapped? Didn't that prove him right to be suspicious of everyone?

But those suspicions had brought him here. In the car, heading south, Connor fought down the panic that began to race through him. It didn't matter what she'd told Penny. Dina wouldn't leave. She'd stay and fight through this. He thought of all the times she had gone toe to toe with him, standing her ground, arguing her position and not giving way even when he tried to throw his weight around.

He kept telling himself that she was too stubborn, too unwilling to give an inch to ever run from an argument. But then he remembered the look on her face the night before. The touch of her hand on his cheek and the regret in her eyes when he tossed her confession of love back at her.

He slammed the heel of his hand against the steering wheel and flipped the visor down to block the morning sunlight. If she had left, he'd just follow her and get this settled, one way or another. If she had left, he told himself, he'd find her at her bungalow. He knew she'd kept it, so where else would she run?

Settle it. How would he settle it? Could he let go of years of self-protection and let himself trust a woman? If he couldn't, was he really willing to lose Dina?

No. That he wouldn't do. Just the thought of never seeing her again made his breath lock in his chest. What was it Colt had said? That he'd known Penny was the once-in-a-lifetime woman.

Well, for Connor, Dina was that woman. That one in a million he hadn't believed existed. The woman he'd been too stupid to appreciate until it was too late. No. It wasn't too late. He'd figure this out. Despite what his brother might think, Connor was a smart guy. There was an answer. He just had to find it.

At his house, he parked, jumped out of the car and hit the front door running. He took the stairs two at a time, his own footsteps thundering through the quiet house.

Too quiet, his mind warned. The kids should be up and playing, squealing. There should be the scent of scrambled eggs and coffee in the air, but there was nothing.

The house, like Connor, felt abandoned.

At the landing, he walked down the hall, turned into the triplets' suite and stopped dead. The beautiful room was empty. He forced himself over the threshold and looked around, as if he were expecting to find the kids and Dina hiding behind the furniture. But there was no one and his footsteps echoed eerily in the quiet.

His gaze swept the completed room. Rafe had outdone himself. The suite was huge, with a bay window complete with child safety rails and a bathroom designed for small children, with counters and even the tub shorter than normal. There were three matching white cribs that would become daybeds as the kids grew and bookshelves filled with storybooks and toys. Dressers in a walk-in closet held their clothes and soft rugs covered the wood floor. The walls were dotted with framed images from children's stories along with pictures of family.

Almost without knowing where he was headed, Connor moved to the photo of Jackie and Elena. He met his old friend's eyes and felt the anger finally fade. She'd hurt him. Lied to him. But because of her and Elena, he had the triplets in his life. And up until last night, he'd had Dina.

Now all he had to do was get her back.

He ran out of the room, down the stairs and skidded to a stop before slamming into his housekeeper. "Louise. When did they leave?"

The older woman frowned at him, folded her arms over her chest and tapped the toe of one sturdy black shoe against the floor. She sniffed. "Before breakfast. They were crying. *All* of them."

He caught the glimmer of tears in Louise's eyes as well and guilt took a bite out of him, but he swallowed down the pain.

"I'm going to get them now," he told her and started for the door.

"You'd better bring Dina and those children home where they belong," she called out and had him stopping in surprise.

When he looked back at her, she hadn't changed position but managed to look even more disappointed in him.

"Until they come home, I'm on strike. You can cook and clean for yourself, Connor King."

"You can't go on strike," he argued.

"Watch me," she said shortly, then whirled around and quick marched down the hall to the kitchen.

Yeah, looked like he had a *lot* of things to straighten out.

Dina was done crying.

She hadn't slept the night before and most of today had been spent soothing the triplets, who were too young to know why their daddy wasn't with them. Thank heaven they were also too young to know what a jackass he was.

"You know you're welcome to stay with me as long as you like."

"Thank you, Abuela," Dina said and curled her feet up under her on her grandmother's couch. "But I'll start looking for a place for the four of us tomorrow."

She sent a look at the three babies on her grandmother's living room floor. Hopefully, they would get accustomed quickly to not having Connor around all the time.

"You're not going back to the bungalow?"

"It's too small," she said. And crowded with memories. Connor had spent too much time there. She would see him in every room and be haunted by images of what might have been if he hadn't been so stupid.

"Ah. Well, if it is only size that concerns you, maybe you should go back to the home you left this morning."

Dina looked at her grandmother, surprised. "How can I go back there? After everything Connor said to me... no, I don't belong with him. Not anymore. And he doesn't want me, either."

"*Nieta*, you love the man."

"I'll get over it." In forty or fifty years.

"He loves you as well," her grandmother said and Dina laughed shortly. "I know what I saw. And on your wedding day, I saw a man in love."

"You're wrong." She wished her grandmother was right, but if she were, how could Connor have said all of those things to her?

"I am never wrong, *nieta*." A warm smile softened that statement. "You should know that by now."

"I'm sorry, Abuela," Dina said. "I know you mean well, but this is one story that won't have a happy ending. Even if Connor showed up right this minute and apologized, how could I ever forgive him for thinking so little of me?"

From her end of the couch, Angelica leaned forward, caught Dina's hand in hers and said, "For love, we do many things. We forgive thoughtlessness, carelessly given pain and the mistakes that all people make. And you must take pity on a man as well," her grandmother added, sitting back again. "They do not adapt to deep emotions as well as women do. They fight against love as if feeling deeply somehow weakens them." She shrugged. "They're foolish, because loving makes you strong. Strong enough even to forgive."

Dina watched her grandmother and wished she were half as nice a person as Angelica Cortez. She didn't know if she would be able to forgive Connor, but thought it probably didn't matter since he would never come around to apologize. When the doorbell rang, the older woman said, "Ah. It is time."

Suspicion awakened inside Dina. "Time for what?"

Her grandmother smiled and walked to answer the door. "Time to see how strong your love is, *nieta*."

"Is she here?"

Connor's voice pulled Dina to her feet. Her heart leapt, her stomach did a quick tumble, but she was standing when he rushed into the living room, followed more slowly by her grandmother. "Traitor," she murmured.

"I love you as well," Angelica said with a smile. Then she added, "I will be in the kitchen making some tea."

Connor didn't hear her leave. He hardly saw the elegant older woman. All he could see was Dina. All he was aware of was that his heart was beating again. He hadn't been sure it ever would when he drove to Dina's old bungalow and found it as empty as his own house was.

That's when he remembered her grandmother. One call to the older woman had assured him that Dina and the kids were safe, and as Angelica had told him, the rest was up to him.

"Dina—"

"Da!" Sam called out and then all three of the babies were hurrying toward him and greeting him as if he'd been gone a year. And really, that's what it felt like. He hugged, he kissed, he patted and when the trips had gone back to playing, he stood up and faced the woman watching him through dark eyes shadowed with wary caution.

He couldn't blame her.

"Connor, I don't want to talk to you anymore."

"You don't have to," he said, taking a half step toward her. "Just listen. *Please.*"

She took a deep breath and then slowly nodded.

His gaze locked on her, Connor felt his world fall back into place. She stood in a slant of sunlight that shone in her hair and sparked in her eyes. Her features were closed, but she wasn't throwing him out, so he called that a win. He had one chance to make this count. To convince her that she was the most important thing in his life.

"Everything I said last night was wrong," he blurted and watched surprise flicker in her eyes. "I didn't even believe it when I was saying it. Oh, and as for John Ballas, he's done. We're through working with him and if I ever see him again, I'll punch him just for the hell of it."

She laughed a little at the image and he smiled too before he said, "The truth is, Dina, I'm out of my depth here. I didn't expect you. Didn't expect to *care* for you—"

"I know that," she said softly. "You made it clear when we got married that you weren't looking for a wife so much as a bed partner and a mom for the kids."

Connor winced and if he could have, he would have found a way to kick himself. "Yeah. I did. And I was wrong about that, too."

"Is that right?"

One corner of her mouth lifted briefly and Connor took that as a good sign. "I let my own past color how I treated you. In a way, I was holding you responsible for everyone who had ever tried to use me or my family."

"I wasn't—"

He held up one hand to stop her right there. "I know you weren't using me. I know you didn't lie or cheat or do any other damn thing wrong. That was all on me, Dina. I kept watching, waiting, sure that you'd betray me, and when you didn't, I panicked, because if you really were as wonderful as I thought, then I was in big trouble. Jackie was the last straw, you know? She was family and she turned on me and that hit me hard."

"Elena was my family and she lied to me about you, too," Dina pointed out.

"I know." He moved a little closer, sending a quick glance at the babies gathered on the floor. "And we let them get in the way. Me, more than you." Closer, one step, then another. She wasn't backing up. "Dina, when I went to the house and found it empty, something in me died. Without you and the kids there, it was emptier than anything I've ever known."

"I couldn't stay," she told him. "Not after last night."

"I know. I hurt you and I'm sorry. So damn sorry."

"Connor—"

"No," he interrupted quickly, feeling his heart begin to beat normally again at the shine in her eyes and the softening of her features. "Don't talk yet. Let me finish. Let me say that I do trust you, Dina. I want you to come home. I want all of us to live together. To build a real life."

She shook her head and he worried.

"Trusting me is good, Connor, but it's not enough," she said softly. "I told you last night that the reason I married you was because I love you. Well, I do. I love you so much that I can't live with you knowing you don't feel the same way."

A slow smile curved his mouth. "That's where *you're* wrong. I do love you, Dina. I love you more than I ever thought it possible to love anyone. You're the first thing I think of in the morning and the last thing I think of at night. I want to spend the rest of my life with you in my arms."

"You do?" Her mouth curved into a dreamy smile and Connor's heart filled.

"I do." Then he grinned. "It's like taking that vow all over again. I will love you forever, Dina. I want to take you and the kids home. I want us to build a life there. Have more babies there."

"God, Connor. I want to believe. I really do."

Dipping into his inside coat pocket, he pulled out a sheaf of papers and handed them to her. "I couldn't get here earlier today because I was at my lawyer's, having him draw up these papers for us."

She opened them, but frowned. "What is it?"

"It's the first of the steps we have to take to legally adopt the triplets."

She inhaled sharply. "Oh, Connor…"

He moved in closer and cupped her face in his palms. The warmth of her skin, the love in her eyes, chased away the last of the cold that had been smothering him since the night before. "We'll all be Kings, legally. We'll be a real family. We'll have each other. We'll have love. And if you can trust me, Dina, we'll be happy."

She stared into his eyes. "I didn't want to love you, Connor, because I was afraid that somehow I would lose myself in that love."

She went up on her toes and planted a quick kiss on his mouth, and that one small taste of her wasn't going to be nearly enough. But he kept quiet, needing to hear what she had to say, hoping it was what he needed to hear.

"But I'm not lost. I'm more found than I've ever been," she said, with a quick look at the babies, babbling and laughing. "You have my heart and I'm trusting you with it. Trusting you with all of our hearts."

The bands around his chest loosened and he drew his first easy breath in nearly twenty-four hours. Pulling her in close, he kissed her almost reverently. "I'll never let you down again, I swear it," he said. "And I will love you for the rest of my life and beyond."

"You'd better," she warned, then smiled as he bent his head to seal his promise with a kiss.

When they broke apart, he rested his forehead against hers. "Louise went on strike."

"What?" Her laugh made him feel warm right down to his bones.

"Yep. Threatened to make me eat my own cooking until I brought you and the kids home where you belong."

"Well," Dina said with a grin, "no wonder you hurried over here."

"Exactly," he said and kissed her again.

"This is wonderful."

They broke apart to look at Angelica as she walked into the room carrying a tray of cookies. Taking a seat on the couch, she set the tray onto the table and began dispensing cookies to the babies, who crowded eagerly around her.

"Now," the older woman said with a wink, "*nieta*, if your husband would bring in the tea and cups, we'll have a celebration before you all go home."

"Abuela," Connor said, bending to kiss the woman's cheek, "that's a great idea."

"We'll go together," Dina said, threading her fingers through his.

"Even better," Connor told her and kissed her again, knowing he was the luckiest man in the world.

* * * * *

WHAT THE
PRINCE WANTS

JULES BENNETT

To the Gems for Jules Street Team!
Thank you for the encouragement, advice and
most of all for the support.
I love you all!

One

The curves, the expressive green eyes, rich brown hair the color of his favorite scotch—all made for a punch of primal lust Mikos Colin Alexander hadn't experienced in years. This sure as hell was not the woman he'd expected to see on his doorstep.

Woman? No, she couldn't be more than twenty years old. She looked as if she'd just stepped out of a photo shoot for some popular American teen magazine. With her pink T-shirt, body-hugging jeans and little white sandals, this was not the image he'd had in mind when he'd gone on-line seeking a nanny.

Iris's angry cry drew his attention back to the point of this meeting. The lady at his door immediately shifted her gaze from him to the child on his hip.

"Aww, it's okay, sweetheart." Her voice, so soft, so gentle, got Iris's attention. "What's a beautiful princess like you crying about?"

Princess. He cringed at the term, hating how dead-on

this stranger was. But he was in LA now, not Galini Isle, a country so small that nobody here knew who he was. Which was just how he preferred it.

His wish to be free from his royal heritage had carried him through life, but the urge had never been stronger than after the accident that nearly took his life. Between that, his failed marriage, Karina's death and his being a widowed prince, the media was all over him. There wasn't a moment's peace back home and he needed to get away, to regroup…and maybe to never return.

Now more than ever he wanted independence—for him and his daughter.

"I'm sorry." Extending her hand, the lady offered him a wide, radiant smile. "I'm Darcy Cooper. You must be Mr. Alexander."

Darcy. The woman he'd emailed, the woman he'd spoken to on the phone. The woman he'd all but hired sight unseen to be his live-in nanny because of her impressive references and the number of years the agency had been in business.

Na pari i eychi. Damn it.

What happened to the short, round, bun-wearing grandmother type he'd seen pictured on the website? He'd been assured the woman coming to care for his daughter was the owner. No way could this curvaceous beauty be in charge of Loving Hands Childcare Agency. Perhaps they'd sent someone else at the last minute.

Colin shifted his irate daughter to his good hip. Damn accident still had him fighting to get back to normal… whatever normal was after nearly dying and then losing your wife. "You're not what I expected."

Quirking a brow, she tipped her head as a smile spread across her face. Her eyes ran over him, no doubt taking in his running shorts, T-shirt and bedhead.

"That would make two of us."

Her sparkling eyes held his. Was she mocking him? Of course she was. She had no idea who she was speaking to…not that anybody here knew of his royal status, but still. Nobody mocked him except his brother.

Iris's piercing wails grew louder, more shrill in his ear. Between lack of sleep and the constant pain in his back and hip, he was done trying to be Father of the Year. The fact that he'd had no choice but to find assistance still angered him. Iris was the only reason he was giving in. Her needs had to come before his pride—which is why he now found himself staring down at the petite, yet very shapely, nanny.

This is what he'd wanted, right? To be free from all the servants, the media, the people ready to step in and practically raise his child for him while thrusting her into the limelight? Hell, he'd even been running his own vacuum here. Among other domestic tasks like dusting and putting the trash out at the end of the driveway. His brother would die laughing if he saw Mikos wielding a dust mop.

Colin. He had to keep thinking of himself as Colin now that he was in the United States. His middle name would help him blend in so much better. He was here to see who he was as a man, not a prince. To rediscover a piece of himself he was afraid he'd lost.

He just wanted these next six months to be free of all things involving his royal status. He was tired of being home where pity shrouded the faces of everyone he came in contact with. Yes, he was a widower, but so many people didn't know he and his wife had been separated for months before her death. They'd had to keep putting up a good front for the sake of their reputations.

Pretenses. That word pretty much summed him up. He wanted this freedom, wanted to see how he and Iris could live without being waited on hand and foot. He'd promised his brother, King Stefan, that he would only be in the United States for six months, the maximum time a member of the royal family could be away from the island for personal reasons. Then Colin would have to decide whether to renounce his title of Prince Mikos Colin Alexander of Galini Isle or return to the island and resume his royal duties.

Colin was first in line to take over the throne if something ever happened to his brother. If he gave up his position, the crown would be passed to their oldest cousin, who'd rather chase skirts and make scandalous headlines than run a country. That fact had guilt coursing through Colin every time he thought about the situation.

He'd temporarily lost his title when he'd married Karina because she had been divorced once. Their land had archaic rules, but that was one he hadn't been about to fight.

Now that his wife had passed on, he was thrust back into the royal limelight whether he wanted to be there or not. And with his daughter being the next generation of royalty, that automatically made her a duchess. The entire situation was a complicated mess. Added to that, he faced years of ramifications if he chose to walk away from his title.

Colin was determined to be a hands-on father. Being in a new country, still adjusting to this lifestyle and trying to cope with this damn inconvenient handicap forced him to admit he might need just a bit of help. This short-term arrangement would give him good insight into whether or not he could fully care for Iris on his own and if he and his baby should stay here.

When Iris arched her back, screaming as if someone had taken her most prized possession, Darcy instantly reached for the girl.

Without asking, the woman swiped away Iris's tears and gently lifted her from his arms.

"Now, now," Darcy said, patting Iris's back and lightly bouncing his eighteen-month-old. "I'm not a fan of Monday mornings, either."

Colin crossed his arms over his chest as Darcy continued to speak in a calm, relaxing tone. Yeah, like that was going to work. Iris couldn't hear this woman for all the screaming. No way would Darcy's sweet, soft voice penetrate the power of a toddler's lungs.

Darcy stroked a finger across Iris's damp cheeks again. Little by little she started to calm as this virtual stranger kept talking in the same soothing tone, never raising her voice to be louder than Iris. Colin watched as his daughter stared at the stranger.

Within a minute or two, Iris had stopped fussing and was pulling Darcy's ponytail around. Strands of rich, silky hair instantly went to Iris's mouth as she sniffed, hiccupped and finally settled herself.

"Oh, no." He reached for the clump of hair that was serving as Iris's pacifier, but Darcy shifted her body away.

"She's fine," Darcy assured him in the same delicate voice she'd used moments ago to get Iris under control. "Babies put everything in their mouths. I promise it's clean."

Colin watched as Iris gripped the strands in her tight fist and gave a swift yank. Darcy only laughed and reached up to pat the baby's pudgy little hand. "Not so hard, little one. That's attached."

Colin couldn't believe this. Iris had cried off and on all night—more on than off—and had been quite angry all morning. How the hell did this woman calm his child in the span of a few minutes? With a ponytail?

Darcy tapped a fingertip to Iris's nose before turning her attention to him. "May I come in?"

Feeling like a jerk for leaving her on his porch, Colin stepped back and opened the door wider. As Darcy passed by him, some fruity scent trailed her, tickling his nose in a teasing manner.

If he thought she looked good from the front, the view from behind was even more impressive. The woman knew how to wear a pair of jeans.

Perhaps she was older than he'd first thought, because only a woman would be this shapely, this comfortable with her body. He'd assumed all women in LA wanted that waiflike build, enhanced with silicone as the perfect accessory.

Darcy Cooper was anything but waiflike and her curves were all natural.

Colin gritted his teeth and took a mental step back. He needed to focus. The last thing he needed was to be visually sampling a potential nanny. He had to blame his wayward thoughts on sleep deprivation. Nothing else could explain this sudden onset of lust. His wife was the last woman he'd slept with and that was before his near-fatal rock climbing accident two years ago. Between the accident, the baby, the separation from his wife and then her death…yeah, sex hadn't been a priority in his life.

Years ago he'd been the Playboy Prince of Galini Isle and now his life revolved around diapers, baby dolls and trying to walk without this damn limp. Oh, and his glamorous life now included housework.

Yet a beautiful stranger had showed up in his house only moments ago and he was already experiencing a lustful tug. He wasn't sure if he should be elated by the fact he wasn't dead and actually had hormones still ready to stand up and take notice, or if he should be angry because sex was the last thing he had time for.

He and Darcy had agreed on the phone two days ago that today would be a mostly hands-on type of interview. It was important that Iris connect with her potential caregiver. However, he had nobody else lined up because there wasn't another agency that had measured up to this one.

Darcy had been here for all of five minutes. How the hell did he expect her to live here for six months if his attraction had already taken such control of his thoughts? His life was already a jumbled mess without a steamy affair to complicate things further.

Colin watched Darcy as she walked around the open-concept living area, bouncing the baby on one hip as if they'd known each other for some time. Iris started fussing a bit, but just like moments ago, Darcy patted her back and spoke in those hushed tones.

He'd never seen anything like this. He'd tried all damn night to calm his daughter.

Karina would've known what to do. Even though he and Karina had been separated for nearly a year before she died of a sudden aneurism, he still mourned the loss. The rock-climbing accident had changed him, had him pushing her away due to his stubborn pride and fear of not being the perfect husband and father, but a part of him would still always love her. She'd been a loyal wife and an amazing mother.

When Darcy bent over the sofa and picked up a stuffed lamb, Colin clenched his fists at how the denim pulled across her backside. Why couldn't he tear his eyes away? Why couldn't he concentrate on something other than her tempting shape? No, she couldn't stay.

What he needed was someone old enough to be his grandmother, with many years of experience, a woman with silver hair in a bun and ill-fitting clothing. What he did *not* need was a woman who could kick-start his libido without even trying. But, damn it, she'd calmed Iris and had done so with the ease of an expert.

"What is her daily routine?"

Colin blinked as he stared back at the woman who

was trying to be professional when his thoughts had been anything but.

"Routine?"

Dancing the lamb toward Iris's nose and then pulling it back, Darcy simply nodded without even looking at him. "Yes. Naps, eating schedule, bedtime."

Since coming to LA only days ago, he did what worked best for them and he was still adjusting. As hard as this change was, he wasn't sorry he'd made the move.

Colin glanced at Iris's smile, the prominent dimple in her cheek that matched his own. Sure, she'd smile for the stranger, but not for him? He loved his little girl with every bit of his soul. He'd give anything to be able to care for her on his own without the fear of his handicap harming her, but he had to face his own limitations to keep her safe.

"Mr. Alexander?"

Colin returned his gaze to Darcy who was actually staring at him. Oh, yeah, she'd asked him a question. Unfortunately, he was going to have to end this trial before it started. Having someone like Darcy here would be a colossal mistake.

Holding those bright green eyes with his, Colin took a deep breath and said, "I'm afraid I can't use your services."

Darcy swallowed her shock. What had he just said? The very survival of Loving Hands was contingent on her landing this job. She refused to take no for an answer. She couldn't afford to.

She also couldn't afford to keep making eye contact with Mr. Alexander's baby blues. No, *blue* wasn't the right word. What was the proper description for a set of eyes that were so mesmerizing they nearly made her forget all her troubles? The power he possessed when he held her gaze was unlike anything she'd ever experienced, so she kept her focus on the sweet little girl in her arms.

Holding onto a squirming Iris was difficult enough without the added impact of desire. Though she'd certainly take a dose of lust over the ache in her heart from holding such a precious child. She'd avoided working with babies for years, giving those jobs to her employees. Unfortunately, the entire staff of Loving Hands had been let go and Darcy had to face her demons head-on if she wanted to save her grandmother's company. So, his "no" wasn't an option.

This would be the first job caring for a young child she'd taken on since having been told at the age of twenty-one she couldn't have kids due to severe endometriosis. She could do this…she had to do this. No matter the heartache, Darcy had to pull through.

But first she had to convince Mr. Alexander she was the one for the job.

Turning to fully face the sexy father, Darcy kept her hold on Iris, who was nearly chewing the ear off the poor lamb. A sweet smell wafted up from the child's hair, no doubt from whatever shampoo her father used for her.

Darcy had learned from the emails and phone conversations that Mr. Alexander was a single father and new to the area. She also knew his wife had died suddenly just a few months ago. What she didn't know was what he did for a living or where he was from. The sexy, exotic accent that made her toes curl in her secondhand sandals clearly implied that he wasn't American.

Honestly she didn't care where he was from as long as he was here legally and the job posting was legit. He'd offered her a ridiculous sum to live here for the next six months and care for his daughter, and that money would help her save her grandmother's dying agency…the agency

Darcy's ex had pilfered money from, nearly leaving Darcy on the street. Oh, wait, he *had* left her on the street.

Darcy didn't know what happened at the end of the six months, and with the amount of money he'd offered, she didn't need to know.

"You can't use me?" she asked, not ready to admit defeat. "Do you have another nanny service lined up?"

"No."

Shoulders back and chin up, Darcy used all of the courage she wished she possessed to cross the room. Closing the gap between them only made her heart pound even more. She would do whatever it took to pay tribute to the grandmother who'd given up everything to raise her.

Darcy's nerves had kicked into high gear before she'd even arrived here because so much was riding on this one job. Being turned away by the client hadn't been her biggest concern, either. Darcy had truly feared she'd take one look at the child and freeze…or worse, break down and start sobbing.

Yet here she was, holding it together and ready to fight for what her ex had stolen from her. Darcy had already given up her apartment and had slept in her car those first two nights until her best friend discovered what happened. Now Darcy found herself spending nights on the sofa in her bestie's overpriced, undersized studio apartment. This live-in nanny position would secure a roof over her head and a steady income to help get Loving Hands back up and running.

As if all of that weren't stressful enough, her would-be employer had opened his door and all coherent thoughts had completely left her mind. A handsome man holding a baby was sexy, no doubt about it. But this man with his disheveled hair and piercing eyes had epitomized sexy single dad. Those tanned muscles stretched his T-shirt in ways that should be illegal. Not to mention the flash of ink peeking from beneath his sleeve.

The man who all but had her knees trembling and her stomach in knots was trying to send her on her way. Not going to happen.

"So you have nobody else lined up," she repeated, praying she came across as professional and not pushy. "I'm here, your sweet little girl is much happier than when you answered the door, and you're ready to usher me back out."

When he continued to stare as if trying to somehow dissuade her, Darcy continued.

"May I ask why you're opting to not even give me a chance?"

His intriguing set of eyes roamed over her face, sending spears of tingles through her body just as powerfully as if he'd touched her. It was as though he was looking straight into her soul.

Iris squealed and smacked Darcy on the cheek with the wet, slobbery stuffed lamb's ear that had been in her mouth. Still, nothing could stop Darcy from trying to maintain some sort of control over this situation…if she'd ever had any to begin with. She had a feeling Mr. Alexander was a man who was used to being in charge. That thought alone had arousal hitting hard.

Focus, Darcy.

"Mr. Alexander?"

"Colin." That husky voice slid over her. "Call me Colin."

A thread of hope started working its way through her. "That would imply I'll be here long enough to call you by your first name."

The muscle clenched in his jaw, the pulse in his neck seemed to be keeping that same frantic pace as hers.

Before he could comment, she kept going, more than

ready to plead her case. "We discussed a trial period over the phone. Why don't we agree on a set time? That way if this arrangement doesn't work for either of us, we have a way out."

She'd care for Lucifer's kids to get the amount of money she and Colin had agreed upon.

"May I be honest?" he asked, taking a step back as if he'd just realized how close they were.

"Please."

Iris wiggled in Darcy's arms. Darcy set the toddler on the floor to play then straightened to see Colin's eyes still fixed on her.

"I wasn't expecting someone so young."

She was always mistaken for someone younger, which was normally a lovely compliment. "I turned thirty two weeks ago."

His eyes widened as he raked that gaze over her body once more. At one time she'd been self-conscious of her slightly fuller frame. Being surrounded by so much surgically enhanced beauty in Hollywood would wreak havoc with anybody's self-esteem.

She could still hear her grandmother's words on the subject: *Be proud of who you are, your body and your spirit. Nobody can make you feel inferior without you allowing it.* So Darcy had embraced her curves and her size twelve wardrobe, meager as it may be. Besides, who was in charge of dictating what was and wasn't socially acceptable?

Her ass of an ex had mentioned her weight. She should've known then he wasn't The One.

When Colin was done taking his visual journey, he rested his hands on his hips and shifted his stance. With a slight wince, he moved in the other direction. That was the second time she'd caught him moving as if he couldn't stand on one leg for too long.

"Are you okay?" she asked before she could stop herself.

"Fine," he bit off. "You don't look more than twenty-one."

With a smile, she shrugged. "It's hereditary and I'll take that as a compliment."

His eyes narrowed as he tilted his head. "It wasn't meant to be one."

Crossing her arms, Darcy glanced down just as Iris gripped Darcy's jeans and pulled herself up. The little girl with bouncy dark curls started toward the other side of the living area, which was immaculate.

Where were the toys? The random blanket or sippy cup? Other than that stuffed lamb, there were no signs a child even lived here. Even if they had moved in just a few days ago, wouldn't the place be littered with baby items?

Beyond that, from what she could see, the house was perfectly furnished, complete with fresh flowers on the entryway table and the large kitchen island she could see across the open floor plan.

"Perhaps you have an older, more experienced worker?"

The man was testing her patience. Withholding a sigh, Darcy focused her attention back on the sexy, albeit frustrating, guy. "I'm the only one available for the job at this time."

Not a lie. She was the only one—period. Just last month she'd had to lay off her final employee. Letting her grandmother's staff go had been heartbreaking, but the money simply hadn't been there after several of her clients had changed agencies. They had been like family and had all worked so well together. Fortunately, everyone understood Darcy's predicament and Darcy happily gave each of them glowing recommendations for other jobs. Hopefully she'd be able to get Loving Hands back on its feet and slowly bring her workers back.

"Listen," she told him, steeling herself against any

worry or doubt. She wasn't going to borrow trouble yet. "I realize I look young. I understand how you only want the best for your daughter. However, everything I do will be monitored by you since I'd be staying here. You see something you don't like or you believe her care is not up to par, let me know. That's what the trial period is for."

Colin glanced from her to Iris, who was now smacking her hands on the coffee table as if playing the drums. Darcy wasn't about to give him a chance to answer, because she might not like the one he gave.

"I'm here now and from the dark circles under your eyes, you need to rest." Darcy smiled, hoping he was not going to put up a fight. "I can take over while you take some time for yourself."

She waited a beat, her heart pounding. Would he send her away simply because she wasn't an old lady wearing an apron and sensible shoes?

Colin rubbed his eyes then raked a hand over his face, the stubble on his jaw bristling beneath his palm. Why was that sound so…erotic? His eyes settled on her again and she refused to look away, refused to step back or show any fear. This was her livelihood, her only option of getting out of the depths of hell she'd fallen into. Though being thrust into a lifestyle she'd dreamed about for years, a lifestyle that was completely impossible for her to have, was a whole other layer of hell.

When the silence stretched between them, hovering in the air like an unwelcome guest, Darcy was convinced he was going to show her the door. After what seemed like forever, Colin nodded.

"I'll give you today to prove yourself."

Two

Never before had he allowed someone to steamroll him into going against his instincts. Yet a determined woman with enough killer curves to fuel any man's fantasy for every lonely night had done just that.

Perhaps it had been her sensual body that had him caving and ignoring common sense. But Darcy had something else he admired—tenacity. She wasn't giving in and she made very valid points as to why he should keep her around.

Such as the fact that he would be monitoring her every move while she was here. Perfect, just what he needed. Watching her every move might very well be his undoing. He'd wanted to figure out who he was as a man while he was here in LA, but this unexpected lust was an angle he hadn't considered.

Colin clasped his hands behind his head and continued staring up at the vaulted ceiling in his master suite. Sunlight spilled in through the sliver of an opening in his blackout blinds. He hadn't even bothered getting beneath his navy duvet because he knew his mind simply wouldn't shut down, and getting too comfortable didn't really matter. Napping in the middle of the day really wasn't something he did, but he was exhausted.

Rest wouldn't be his friend for some time, he feared. He'd needed a nanny fast. Based on previous families his assistants had interviewed, Darcy was the best option. Unfortunately he hadn't had time to do a full background check on individual people, so he'd just placed a quick call to one of his assistants. Hopefully more information would come back within a few hours, but his gut said he could trust her.

When he told her she'd gotten the job, at least provisionally, she'd returned carrying one tattered old duffel bag. Didn't women have two bags just for makeup alone and another two for shoes? How the hell did she fit everything into one bag that looked as if it would fall apart if accidentally bumped the wrong way or dropped too hard onto the floor?

Before he'd come up to his room, Colin had offered to help her inside with her things, but she'd dismissed him. When she came in with so little, he'd assumed she had more in the car. She assured him she had it all under control and she only had the one bag. There was a story there, and if she was staying around he'd get to the bottom of it. Money was apparently an issue, so he'd be interested what her background check showed.

The cell on his nightstand vibrated. Glancing over he saw his brother's name lighting up the screen. Not what he needed right now.

With a grunt, he rolled to his side and reached for the device. "Yeah," he answered.

"I assume by your chipper greeting you're still on the nanny hunt and not resting?"

"I may have found someone," he replied, not adding that this someone would most likely keep him awake at night.

Stefan laughed. "As usual you're not going into details. Fine. I figured you'd have given up by now and be ready to return home."

"I've only been gone a few days. I think you know I wouldn't give up on anything that soon."

Returning home only meant going back to the life of status he'd never wanted, raising his daughter in a setting that would consume her and stifle her growth. As the current duchess, she'd be in the spotlight at all times. He remembered how irritated he'd been growing up when he couldn't just go out and spend a day at the beach. He'd always been escorted by bodyguards, which seriously put a damper on his teen years and his ability to sneak out to have some alone time with friends—not that he didn't invent some pretty creative ways to lose the guards.

His parents had been wonderful, but still they'd had duties to fulfill, which often kept them away for weeks at a time. Then his mother had passed away from a tragic car accident and his father had been even busier, pouring himself into work and serving the people of the island in an attempt to fill the void.

Colin wanted to be there fully for his daughter. He wanted to form a bond that was so strong she would know just how much he loved her and that he would always put her needs first. Even before the crown. Which reminded him, his brother was still on the phone.

"I know you've never wanted this title," Stefan continued. "You do realize that no matter where you live, you're still a prince, but if I die and you've renounced the title, our cousin will assume the position? He's the last person Galini Isle deserves."

Why couldn't he just have a simple life? A life without

the worry of an entire country on his shoulders? A small country, but still.

Again, it was times like this that he wished Karina were still alive. Colin knew his daughter needed a woman's guidance through life and he needed assistance with these major decisions.

"Listen, if an emergency arises, you know I wouldn't turn my back on you or Galini Isle. But I may have to renounce my title if I think that's the best decision for Iris." Colin sat up and swung his legs over the side of the bed. "Maybe I am making a mistake, but for now I need the distance. I need to figure out what the best plan is for Iris and for me. I'm all she has right now."

Stefan sighed. "If you came home, she'd have many people to love and care for her."

"I really need this time. Iris and I don't need to be surrounded by servants who look at us with pity. That's not what I want for myself or her."

"What about Victoria and me? We miss you guys."

Guilt had already eaten away at Colin's conscience, so Stefan adding another layer was pointless. He missed his brother, but they had their own schedules, their own lives. Years ago the two had been inseparable, often rock climbing or kayaking together. Stefan had stepped up when their father had passed from a heart attack and had scaled back his need for adrenaline rushes.

"When are you coming to the States for a visit?" Colin asked. "Isn't it time for Victoria to see her family?"

Colin's sister-in-law was from LA and was a member of the prestigious Dane family of Hollywood.

Stefan chuckled. "I knew you'd say that. Actually we're not coming for several months, but the annual royal celebration ball is in just over two months and we'd really like you here for that. No pressure, just throwing that out there."

Coming to his feet, Colin twisted from his waist in an attempt to loosen his back, which had wanted to tighten up and spasm a bit more lately. He'd slowed down on the therapy he was supposed to be doing at home. After this long he figured the prescribed exercises were a waste of time. Apparently not.

"I haven't even thought about the ball," Colin told his brother.

"The media will not be allowed inside the palace," Stefan assured him. "I can always smuggle you in via one of the underground entrances, just like when we were teens."

Colin laughed, remembering the numerous times they'd covered for each other so they could sneak out and meet up with their girlfriends at the time.

"Will you at least think about this?" Stefan asked. Colin knew he wasn't just referring to the ball. "Think about how hard life will be for you with no family and no one to help you with Iris."

Colin's mind flashed to the woman who had shown up earlier full of confidence and curves. She was helping his daughter, no doubt. It was what she was doing to Colin that had him questioning his judgment.

"I've got everything under control," Colin assured him. "I need to go check on Iris."

He disconnected the call and slid the phone into the pocket of his shorts. Stefan had wanted Colin to think about this decision to leave the royal title behind, as if Colin had thought of anything else. The moment he'd discovered his wife was pregnant he'd done nothing but try to get out of that damn wheelchair in order to live for his child and be the sole supporter and provider—not in the monetary way, but in the fatherly bonding way.

Growing up with maids, butlers, personal assistants and even people who picked out your daily wardrobe was a bit ridiculous. Just because his family happened to be titled, because they had a certain last name and were wealthy, they had every single material thing at their disposal.

But money could only do so much. Colin still worried about the pressure and responsibility that came with being a member of the royal family. He knew he was projecting his fears onto his daughter, but he was her main source of stability now and he'd rather be overprotective than to pass along something that would overwhelm her.

Raking a hand through his hair, Colin opened his door and stepped out into the hallway. The twelve thousand square foot home was large, not as large as the palace by any means, but big enough that he'd had video monitors installed in most rooms so he could watch the feeds from his bedroom. He'd also had sound monitors wired throughout the house so he could hear Iris no matter where he was. There were alarms on the doors and windows, so he definitely would've heard had Darcy tried to take Iris from the house. He might be paranoid, but he would never take a chance with the safety of his child.

Colin was headed for the steps when his back started twitching.

Damn it. He gripped the railing as he stood on the landing and breathed deeply, waiting for the crippling pain to pass. Total agony he could tolerate, but being in a wheelchair and rendered helpless he could not.

Immediately following the accident, the doctors had indicated he might not ever be able to walk again, but the moment he'd heard those words he'd made it his mission to prove them wrong. Granted, he was walking, but the spasms in his back and piercing pain in his hip and down through his leg would blast him at the most inopportune times. Another reason he needed a nanny. Back home he had a driver, but he needed someone for that task here, too. Damn it, he hated being dependent on others for help, but he couldn't risk his daughter's safety if his pain hit while he was behind the wheel.

Colin needed to start making use of that home gym he'd had put in before arriving. He couldn't put off the physical therapy any longer, because he refused to be at the mercy of this injury.

Once the pain ceased, Colin headed down the steps carefully, in case the sensations returned.

Just as he reached the last step, squeals carried through the foyer. Colin followed the sound and stopped short when he spotted the carnage that used to be his spotless living room. He'd seen Darcy and Iris on the screen in his bedroom just before Stefan had called, but he sure as hell hadn't see this disaster.

"What the—"

Darcy sat on the floor surrounded by toys. Her hair, which had been pulled back earlier, was now down and in complete disarray, as if her hands—or the hands of a lover—had been running through it. Dry cereal was strewn across his coffee table and had trickled down to the rug beneath. From the looks of things some of the pieces had been trampled on and ground into the carpeting. A sippy cup sat on its side, but, fortunately, no liquid appeared to puddle beneath due to the spill-proof lid. There was one blessing in this chaos.

While Darcy was smiling, her eyes on his, Iris was playing with the hair on a doll. Doll? That wasn't one of her dolls. Colin had only shipped her favorite things and this wasn't part of Iris's collection.

"Did we wake you?" Darcy asked, smiling as if this scene were absolutely normal. "We were trying to be quiet."

He'd turned the sound down in his bedroom, hoping sleep would come.

"You didn't wake me." He took a cautious step into the room, almost afraid to look for any more destruction. "Is this typically how you watch children? You let them destroy a house?"

Shoving her hair back, Darcy pulled a band from her wrist and secured the dark mass into a low, messy style. As she came to her feet, she wiped her hands on her pants.

"This is far from destroyed, Colin."

The second his name slid through her lips, his eyes locked onto that unpainted mouth. He'd been told numerous times how intimidating his stare could be, yet she hadn't blinked or even shied away from him. Granted, he didn't want to intimidate her, but he was pretty impressed by how strong she seemed to be. One more aspect of American women he found intriguing. So independent, so strong-willed. As if he needed another reason to be drawn to Darcy.

"Iris and I are playing, and when we're done we'll pick it up." Her arms crossed over her chest, sending the swell of her breasts up to the opening of her V-neck. "There were no toys in here at all so we quietly snuck to her room and I grabbed a few things. Then I wasn't sure what her eating schedule was and she was hungry. Took me a second to figure out what nack-nack was, but I figured it meant snacks when she tugged me toward the kitchen."

As she defended herself, Colin couldn't help but slide his gaze to the way the V of her shirt twisted toward one side, showcasing the swell of her breasts, all but mocking him. Then there was the way her rounded hips filled out her jeans in such a way that would make any man beg.

Prince Mikos Colin Alexander had never begged for anything in his life and he sure as hell wasn't about to start now because of some punch of lust to his gut that he couldn't get under control.

Darcy was quite a captivating woman. He still couldn't get over the fact she wore no jewelry or makeup whatsoever. The woman oozed simplicity and for some reason he found that to be utterly sexy and ridiculously arousing. She wasn't out to impress him in any way other than relating to the care of his daughter.

Iris squealed when she spotted him. With her little arms out wide, she ran across the hardwood, over the rug, crushing even more cereal pieces beneath her bare feet before she collided with his legs. Colin cringed when she reached for him. He wanted to scoop her up, but with his back just coming off a muscle seizure, he opted to take a seat in the closest armchair and pull her into his lap instead.

Iris's little hands smacked up and down his arm and he placed a kiss on top of her head, where her wayward curls always tickled his nose. The smile she offered him had him returning her five-toothed grin. How could he look at her and not smile instantly? She was his every reason for being, the motivation behind all decisions he made.

"How long will the living room be a war zone?" he asked, turning his attention back to Darcy.

She glanced around then back to him with a laugh. "You do realize you're raising a toddler, right? They will make messes, they will make memories and they will learn to clean up later. I assure you this area will be spotless once she lays down for a nap."

Iris wiggled right off his lap and headed toward the coffee table covered in a buffet of snacks. Weren't kids supposed to eat in high chairs? Had his assistants at the palace let Iris be so carefree when he hadn't been around?

"She's been playing in her room," Colin informed Darcy when she continued to stare at him. "That's why the toys are kept there."

A wide smile spread across Darcy's face, making her look even younger. "You really are a stickler for rules, huh? Children need room to grow, to flourish. Yes, they need schedules, but they also need to learn to be flexible."

Even though she stood above him, Colin met and held her stare. There was no way this nanny was going to come in here and wreck everything just for the sake of making memories or whatever the hell else she'd babbled about.

Colin wasn't stupid. He knew he owed his not-so-sunny disposition to the fact that he couldn't get a grip on his attraction. Why this woman? Why now? And why the hell were her breasts right at eye level?

"By flourish do you mean grinding cereal into the floor?" he asked, focusing on the mess. "Or maybe you mean throwing toys around the room without a care of what may break?"

"That was another point I was going to bring up." Darcy stepped over a stuffed animal and sank down on the edge of the sofa. Lacing her fingers over the arm, she brought her eyes back to his. "All of these breakables should probably be put away for now, or at least placed higher where she can't pull them down. She'll get used to what she can and can't touch, but for now I'd try to avoid unnecessary injuries."

The home had come fully furnished. Colin had simply paid a designer to get everything set up so he only had to bring their clothes and personal belongings. All the breakables and any other knickknacks sitting around meant nothing to him. He'd replace whatever was broken, if need be.

Colin glanced across the mayhem on the floor. Iris sat on her beloved lamb while playing with the new doll.

"Where did that come from?"

Darcy glanced over as Iris gripped the doll's long, dark hair and started swinging it around. "I brought it for her."

So in the single bag she'd brought, Darcy had managed to squeeze a doll in among her belongings?

"Is that something you normally do? Bribe potential clients?"

Darcy's eyes widened. "I've never had to bribe anybody. Your daughter was being introduced to a stranger and I used the doll as a way to talk to her and make her comfortable. I can take it back if it offends you."

Colin gritted his teeth. In the span of a few hours his house had been taken over by this free spirit who seemed oblivious to the mess surrounding them and was trying to tell him how to raise his child. She'd calmed Iris in a way he'd never seen and now his new nanny was stomping all over his libido. And he was paying her for every bit of this torture.

Iris started whimpering as she rubbed her eyes.

"Is this nap time?" Darcy asked.

"She tends to nap once a day." He smoothed a wayward curl from Iris's forehead and slid his finger down her silky cheek. "There's no set time. I just lay her down when she seems ready."

Darcy came to her feet, crossed the room and lifted Iris into her arms. "Come on, sweetheart. Let's get you down for a nap. I'll clean the mess today and you can help tomorrow."

Colin rose. Now that he didn't have to bend over and pick Iris up, he figured he could carry her to her bedroom. He hadn't felt even a twinge in his back since he'd been downstairs.

"I'll take her up." Colin took Iris from Darcy's arms, careful not to brush against any part of her tempting body. "You can work on this."

Holding his daughter tight, he headed up to the nursery. With her little arms around his neck, she still clutched the new doll and with each step he took it slapped against his back. Iris had taken to Darcy exactly the way Colin hoped his little girl would take to a new nanny. Yet some things about Darcy didn't add up. He'd picked her agency because of its reputation and level of experience. Okay, so she was older than he'd first thought. But why did she have so few belongings and why were her clothes a bit on the cheap, hand-me-down side?

With Iris nuzzling his neck, Colin stepped into the pale green and pink nursery. This was the one room he'd had painted before they'd moved in. Every other room had just been furnished as he'd requested. He'd wanted something special for Iris and the designer really went all out with the round crib in the middle of the spacious room, sheer draping suspended from the ceiling that flowed down over the bed and classic white furniture complete with all things girly, pink and just a touch of sparkle. The floor-to-ceiling window also had sheer curtains that were tied back with some pink, shimmery material, and toy bins were stacked neatly against the far wall.

A room fit for a princess...or duchess, as the case may be.

When he sat Iris in her bed, she quickly grabbed her little heart pillow, hugged her new doll to her chest and lay down. Colin watched until her eyes closed, her breathing slowed.

Darcy might be a bit of a mystery, but with his status, he had to be extremely watchful. She seemed trustworthy so far. If she just wanted privacy that was one thing. Who was he to judge? Wasn't he lying and pretending to be someone else right now?

The fact that there was more to figure out with the alluring, frustrating nanny left him no choice but to head back downstairs and talk with her now that they were alone.

Of course, he was hiding the fact that he was a prince, one who found her to be sexy as hell. Still, he needed help with Iris. For now he'd have to keep Darcy around, but that didn't mean she'd be here for the full six months. They needed to pin down a suitable trial period. In the meantime, he could be researching a backup in case Darcy didn't work out.

Regardless of the end result, he had to ignore how enticing she was. Romance, whether short- or long-term, was not on his agenda, and he sure as hell wouldn't be so trite as to fall into bed with his baby's nanny.

Three

Darcy had picked up the living room, piling all the toys and infant blankets neatly in the corner. The rogue cereal pieces were in the trash, except for the crushed bits. She'd have to ask Colin where the vacuum was kept to get the rug back in order. She'd work with Iris and her cleaning skills next time. The girl needed a nap more than she needed a lesson.

Playing with Iris, truly feeling a bond starting to form, was both a blessing and an ache she couldn't begin to put into words. For so long she'd had that little-girl dream of having her own family, but such things were not meant to be. Darcy hadn't thought this job would be so intense, yet maybe it was the combination of the baby and the man that had her stomach in knots. As grouchy as he was, Colin was still very sexy, there was no denying the obvious.

At first, the instant attraction to Colin had layered over her anxiety of working with an infant. The man was hot, hot, hot, and that was just the physical packaging. When he spoke with that accent he only rose another notch on the sexy scale. But there was nothing like seeing him holding his beautiful daughter, the way he looked at her with all the love in the world. Something about watching him with his guard down had Darcy melting even more.

As Colin's footsteps pounded down the steps, she stood at the kitchen sink rinsing the sippy cup. Quickly placing it on the drying mat, she wiped her hands on her jeans. She had no clue what mood Colin would be in or how he might react once they were alone.

Would he ask her to leave simply because of the mess? A good first impression was everything and she'd probably blown it. He'd told her she had until the end of the day to prove herself, but she may not make it that far. She stood to lose her pride and her grandmother's legacy. There was no plan B, there was no knight who would ride to her rescue. So if Colin was angry enough to ask her to go, she wouldn't have much choice.

Darcy couldn't get a good read on him. When he looked at her she couldn't tell if he was angry or turned on. Ridiculous to think a piece of eye candy like Colin Alexander would find her attractive, but he volleyed between being pissed and raking his eyes over her.

No way would she bring up the fact he turned her inside out. She'd always been a professional and this job was no different…except for the fact she needed this one more than any other.

Just as Darcy turned, Colin was rounding the large center island. Even in the openness of the kitchen, the man seemed to dominate the room. She stepped back, the edge of the counter biting into the small of her back.

"Is she asleep?" Darcy asked, trying to keep her voice steady, though she felt anything but.

"Yes." His eyes pinned her in place as he rested one

hand on the granite counter. "We need to talk while she's down."

Swallowing, Darcy nodded. This was like the equivalent of the breakup in a business setting. Still, she wouldn't go down without a fight.

"I need to clean the rug first," she told him, knowing he probably recognized the stalling tactic. "I wasn't sure where you kept your vacuum."

"There's a handheld one in the utility room. I'll get it later."

Oh, this wasn't good. An image of her grandmother flashed through her mind. Darcy had promised Gram before she passed that Loving Hands would stay up and running. Then love had entered the picture...or what Darcy had thought was love. How could she have been so naive as to trust a man with her life and her family business, and not see that he was a lying, greedy user?

Colin leaned against the island and crossed his arms over his broad chest. "Why only one bag?"

His question jerked her from her thoughts. That's what he'd initially wanted to talk about? Her luggage?

"How many bags do I need?" she countered.

A sliver of a tattoo peeked out from beneath the hem of his T-shirt sleeve. Darcy's belly clenched. She'd always been a sucker for ink. But shallow lust is what got her into a mess of trouble the last time. A sexy, smooth-talking man and tats over solid muscles...she refused to go down the same path again, when all she'd met at the end of her journey was a broken heart. Not that Colin was a smooth talker. He was more of a blunt, grumpy, irritable talker.

"Will you be sending for more belongings?" he asked.

Still stunned that this was what he'd wanted to discuss, she shook her head. "I have all I need. Does this mean I'm staying?"

When he raked a hand through his tousled hair, a masculine, woodsy scent slid across the gap and straight to her. How did the man positively reek of sex appeal when he looked like he'd spent days without sleep?

"I want to discuss the trial period," he told her, shifting his weight with a slight wince. "The contract we mentioned on the phone was for six months. I'll give you one month to prove that you're the right fit for the job. Anytime in that month we can decide to terminate the agreement."

Relief spread through her in waves. She would definitely win him over in a month. She was good at her job, she'd been raised helping her grandmother care for children and, honestly, raising kids was all she knew. The irony of the situation as it related to her personal struggles was not lost on her.

And, actually, caring for kids wasn't all she knew, just all she knew to pay her bills. Cooking was her hobby, her therapy, really, but it wouldn't keep her afloat financially no matter how much she enjoyed it.

"That sounds fair." She rested her hands on either side of her hips, gripping the edge of the counter with her palms.

"I know we agreed on compensation," he went on as if conducting a business meeting and not standing in his kitchen with sexual tension vibrating between them. "I'll give you half now and the other half at the end of the six months, if you stay. Between now and the sixth month, there may be incentives along the way. Bonuses, if you will."

"And if I leave at the end of this month?"

Colin's bright eyes held hers as he lifted a shoulder. "Then take the first half of the money and go. No incentives."

Half the money was better than no money. Still, she

needed the full amount to pay off Thad's debt and jump-start the agency again. This job would save her business and get her back where she needed to be so she would make sure she impressed him with her skills.

She was an excellent cook, if she did say so herself. Surely that would be another check in her favor. What single man wouldn't want someone who had hot meals ready for him every single night?

"I expect you to care for Iris during my working hours which I already went over with you on the phone," he went on. "I don't expect you to cook every meal, that's a duty we can share. I do need you to drive if we go out, as I'm still recovering from an accident that has limited my activities. If all of this is fine with you, then you can stay."

Darcy nodded, though she wanted to ask about his injury. But now wasn't the time and if she stayed on as nanny, she'd most likely discover what had happened to him.

"I'm fine with that deal."

She held out a hand to shake. He darted his gaze down to her hand, then back up to her face. With an emotion-less expression, Colin slid his warm, strong hand into hers and an electric sensation shot straight up her arm. His eyes widened for the briefest of moments. The grip on her hand tightened.

This wasn't happening. No way could an attraction form so quickly, be so intense. She'd been convinced the tension and fascination was one-sided. Apparently not.

Darcy swallowed, wondering what he was thinking, feeling. She didn't want the awkwardness to settle between them. This was only day one, though, so she'd chalk it up to them getting a feel for each other...not the chemistry that was growing and already causing problems.

"Do you want to give me a tour of the house?" Darcy asked, needing to remove herself from temptation.

Colin blinked, dropped her hand and nodded. "Of course. I also wanted to let you know that if you need an evening off to go out or have some personal time, just give me notice. I don't expect you to put your life on hold and work twenty-four hours a day."

Laughter bubbled up and Darcy couldn't keep it contained. Colin's brows drew together.

"You find that funny?"

Waving a hand in the air, Darcy shook her head. "I have no social life. I won't require any time off."

He tipped his chin down slightly, causing a longer strand of dark hair to fall over his eye as he studied her. "You keep surprising me."

Besides his striking looks, Colin had a voice that would make any woman tremble with need. She didn't want to tremble, didn't want to have any type of unexpected attraction toward this man or any other. From here on out, until her agency was back in business, Darcy vowed to stay focused. No men, regardless of how lonely she was. She didn't need someone to complete her, not by any means. But there were those nights she missed being held, missed the powerful touch only a man could provide.

"I'm really pretty simple," she told him. "My work keeps me happy so I don't need anything else."

"What about friends? Boyfriends?"

Okay, that wasn't subtle. Was he asking as an employer or as a man?

Pulling her self-control up front and center, Darcy stepped away from him and headed out of the kitchen. "How about that tour while Iris is sleeping?"

Two weeks and a great deal of sexual tension later, Colin led Darcy down the hall toward the back of the house, well aware of her closeness behind him and even more aware of the unspoken attraction that seemed to be hovering between them. He'd been struggling to keep any emotions hidden. He didn't want her to look at him and see any sign of lust. Colin had no room for such things, not when he and his daughter were desperate for help.

But each time he'd seen Darcy with Iris, something had moved in him. Something he couldn't identify. He assumed at this point she had no boyfriend. She'd made no mention of one even though she'd never come out and answered him when he'd grilled her on the subject her first day.

She'd managed to put him in his place without a word. Fine. He didn't have time to get involved in her personal life and he sure as hell shouldn't want to.

Earlier today, when he'd mentioned working out, he'd seen a brief interest pass over her face. He figured if he showed her the gym and they both made use of it, maybe they could work through…whatever this was brewing between them. He couldn't speak for Darcy, but fourteen days of strain and sexual tension was taking its toll on him.

Colin headed toward the back of the house where the first floor bedroom had been turned into a gym. He'd specified to his designer all the equipment he'd need to continue his therapy on his own and to keep in shape. He had to keep his workouts inside now since his injuries prevented him from going out for a run or rock climbing. He'd never rock climb again. His one main passion in life had been stolen from him.

Shoving aside unwanted anger and frustration, Colin eased the French doors open and stepped inside.

"I know you're busy with Iris, but I wanted you to know this is available to you any time you want to use it. I have weights, a treadmill, elliptical, bike, all top of the line."

"Wow, you certainly take the meaning of home gym

to a whole new level." Darcy glanced through the room and smiled. "I've never had much time to devote to a workout before."

Colin didn't think she needed to work out at all, but he wanted to extend the offer since he'd been using the gym and he hadn't invited her to make use of the space yet. Darcy's shapely body was perfect from every angle… and he'd studied it at every opportunity since the moment she moved in.

"You're more than welcome to everything in here if you decide you'd like to try," he told her.

"I've never used any of these machines before," she muttered. "But I'm sure I could muddle my way through."

Or he could offer to show her.

Colin cursed himself. If they were both going to use this space, he knew they had to do so at different times. The last thing he needed to see was a sweaty, flushed Darcy because that would conjure up a whole host of other images and fantasies.

At this point, he had to get something out in the open. They'd gone two weeks with passing glances and innocent touching as they worked with Iris. Each day he found it more difficult to quash his desires. And Darcy was a damn good nanny, so getting rid of her was not an option.

"I need to be honest with you," he told her.

Tucking her long hair behind her ears, Darcy nodded. "Okay."

"You're a beautiful woman," he began, hoping he wasn't making a mistake. "There's a pull between us and I don't think I'm being presumptuous when I say that. However, I plan to remain single and I have every intention of keeping our relationship professional."

Darcy's mouth had dropped open. For a moment he wondered if he'd gone too far or if his imagination had taken over.

Upfront and honest was how he preferred everything. Okay, obviously there were exceptions since he was keeping a colossal truth from her. But his royal status wouldn't affect her life. She was a nanny, she'd get paid, they would part ways in less than six months and their personal lives could remain private, for the most part.

"Then I'll be honest, too." She laced her fingers in front of her and lifted her chin. "I won't deny the attraction. I mean, you have to know what you look like, but that's just superficial. I still don't know you very well because you're so quiet and brooding, but my main focus is Iris. I promise I'm not here looking for anything other than a job. I've had enough difficulties in my life the past few years. Does that help ease your mind?"

Part of him wanted to know what she'd been through, but the other part told him to shut up and deal with his own issues. Had she just called him brooding? He suppressed the urge to smile at her bluntness. Admiration for this woman who wasn't afraid to speak her mind mixed right along with his arousal where she was concerned. The combination of the two could prove to be crippling if he didn't keep a tight rein on his emotions.

Still, Darcy wasn't like any woman he'd ever known. She wasn't blatantly sexual, she wasn't throwing herself at him even though she'd admitted to being attracted, and she'd been in his house ample time to try her hand at seduction. Not once had she come out with skimpy pajamas or purposely been provocative to try to capture his attention. Perhaps that was just another reason he found her so intriguing and refreshing.

Would she be so controlled if she knew who he really was, how much he was worth?

Being a member of royalty had always made him an instant magnet for women. His late wife hadn't cared about his status, which was one of the things that had initially drawn him to her. But then reality had hit, and the accident that nearly claimed his life wedged between them at the same time she'd discovered her pregnancy. Months of stress and worry had torn them apart and for once in his life, money couldn't fix his problems.

"You okay?" Darcy asked.

Her delicate hand rested on his bare arm and Colin clenched his teeth, fighting away the memories. He couldn't live in the past, trying to pinpoint the exact moment his marriage went wrong. Like everything else, little things started adding up to bigger things and, slowly, the marriage had just dissolved.

Iris was his main concern now. He needed to relax, work on being a regular father giving his daughter the best life possible.

And to decide whether to renounce his title. The pressure of knowing that their wayward cousin, who didn't deserve the title, would have it if something happened to Stefan was overwhelming. He hated being in this position, but ignoring it wouldn't make the situation go away.

"Colin?"

Nodding, he let out a sigh. "I'm fine," he assured her, hating when her hand slid away. Those gentle fingertips trailed down his arm before leaving him wanting more than just an innocent touch. "Anything you want to ask about the equipment while I'm here with you?"

Her eyes roamed over the apparatus in the workout room. An image of her sweating with him flashed through his mind which led to other images of them sweating and he cursed himself. If he didn't get control over his libido he'd have more trouble on his hands than he could possibly handle.

"If I wanted to start working out, what would you recommend? The treadmill? I'm pretty out of shape."

Out of shape? Everything about her shape screamed

perfection. He never was one of those guys who needed his woman to be supermodel thin. He preferred having plenty of curves to explore.

When her eyes came back to his, he fought the urge to pull her inside and get that sweat going. He'd bet his royal, jeweled crown she would look even sexier all flushed, with a sheen of perspiration across her body.

"Do you really want to work out?" he asked. "I don't want you to feel pressured. I'm just offering the room to you."

Darcy shrugged. "I could stand to lose a few pounds."

Anger simmered beneath the surface. "Who told you that?"

Darcy entered the room and checked out the elliptical, the treadmill, the free weights. "He's no longer in the picture, but that's not what matters. What matters is that I've let myself go, and with all of this at my fingertips I don't see why I shouldn't take advantage of it while I'm here."

Colin stepped in and came up behind her, close enough to touch. He clenched his hands at his sides. "If you want to feel better about yourself, that's one thing. If you're doing this because some bastard told you you're overweight, then I have a problem."

Her shoulders stiffened as she turned. The second she realized how close they were, her eyes widened, but she didn't step back. Their bodies were only a breath apart and with each inhale, the tips of her breasts brushed against his chest. He was playing with fire and damn if he could stop himself. He'd always lived for the adrenaline rush and Darcy got his blood pumping.

Being this close he noticed a sprinkling of freckles across her nose. There was so much innocence in this woman, yet in some ways she seemed too tough to be innocent. She'd gone through hard times, according to her. Even if she hadn't said so, he could tell by the way she was headstrong, determined and focused. How the hell could he not find that completely sexy?

"My weight may have been mentioned in my last relationship," she told him, keeping her eyes on his. "But he's history and I want to do this for me. Will you help me or not?"

Would he help her? Close quarters, alone without Iris as a buffer and having Darcy's body as his sole focus for hours? He may not want this attraction, but it was there nonetheless and only an idiot would turn her down.

"I'll help you," he told her. "We'll start tonight after Iris goes to bed. That work for you?"

Her smile spread across her face, lighting up those expressive eyes. "It works if you take it easy on me."

Oiktirmon. Mercy.

"Oh, I plan on giving you just what you need."

Four

What had she been thinking? Darcy had been so impressed by the gym she'd opened her mouth before she could even think about what she was saying. Now she'd committed to exercising with someone who should be posing for calendars sans shirt, while she looked like the before picture on a Weight Watcher's ad.

She'd been taken with Colin and his blunt declaration of attraction. Apparently a lust-filled haze had clouded her mind and hindered her common sense. He'd called out the obvious and now they both had to deal with the tension that would no doubt envelop them every time they were together.

Dinner had been comfortable, though. Iris as the focal point certainly helped. Now she was bathed and in bed, and Darcy had pulled on her favorite yoga pants and an old Loving Hands T-shirt. After pulling on her worn tennis shoes, she headed toward the gym.

The whirring of the treadmill filtered out of the partially open doors and into the hallway. When Darcy peeked around the corner, she was so, so glad she had the advantage of being behind him. Obvious eye-candy images aside, she was thankful no one could see her because there was no way she could take in this male form, all sweaty, shirtless and in action, and not stand here with her mouth open, eyes wide.

The full view of his tattoo caught her attention. A dragon started over one shoulder blade, swirled down one biceps and disappeared over his shoulder to the front. Her fingers itched to trace the pattern, to feel all that taut skin beneath her fingertips. Surely there was some meaning behind the image. Most people had tattoos based on something personal in their lives. She couldn't help but wonder if she'd ever uncover anything beneath the surface with him.

Just as Darcy eased the door open, Colin stumbled, shouted a curse and smacked the red emergency button on the treadmill. Gripping the sides of the machine, he panted, head hanging between his shoulders.

"Are you all right?" she asked, crossing to the piece of equipment in case he needed help.

Colin jerked his head around, wincing as he caught sight of her. "I thought you'd be longer with putting Iris down."

As he turned completely and started to step down, his leg went out from under him and he collapsed, landing hard on the belt of the machine.

Darcy squatted beside him, her hands resting on his bare knee. "Colin, are you okay?" she repeated.

Stupid question, as he'd obviously hurt himself and was trying to hide the fact. Still, she couldn't just stand here and not do or say something.

"Fine," he bit out through gritted teeth. "I'm supposed

to walk every day, but the doctor says if I feel like it I can try jogging."

"Is that why you were running full speed on an incline when I came in?"

His eyes met hers. There went that click once again when this man stared at her. The intensity of his gaze couldn't even be put into words because she'd never experienced such a force in her life.

"I'm not going to be held prisoner by this injury." His tone left no room for argument. "And I don't want your pity."

Colin's eyes held hers another second before they dropped to her hands on his knee. The dark hair on his leg slid beneath her palms as she started to remove her hands. Instantly, his hand covered hers, holding her in place.

"I wasn't feeling pity," she whispered. "Attracted, intrigued, yes. Not pity."

His thumb stroked the back of her hand. "This can't be an issue."

She knew he wasn't referring to his injury or the fact that she'd found him in a state of pain.

"It's already an issue," she retorted, not even trying to pretend she had no idea what he was referring to. "We just have to take control of the tension instead of it controlling us."

His eyes held hers, the muscle ticked in his jaw. "Are you ready to get sweaty?"

Darcy swallowed, then took her own advice and tried to get a grip. Offering a smile, she said, "If you're trying to keep this attraction on the backburner, I think you probably shouldn't ask questions like that."

Laughing, Colin started to rise. "Just wanted to see the look on your face."

The man actually laughed. And there went that zing of desire shooting through her again, because a brooding Colin was sexy, but a smiling Colin was flat-out irresistible.

Darcy came to her feet. "I'm sure I didn't disappoint," she joked.

As Colin got his feet beneath him, Darcy took a step back. "So what are you recovering from?"

Raking a hand through his hair, Colin sighed and shook his head. "A life I've left behind," he muttered.

Curiosity heightened, she wanted to know more about this mysterious man who'd so easily and swiftly captured her attention.

"Tell me what your goal is," he said, resting a hand on the rail of the treadmill. "Are you wanting to lose weight, tone up or just work on feeling better about yourself?"

"All of the above."

A wide smile stretched across his face. The combination of those bright blue eyes and that knee-weakening smile could have any woman throwing all morals and professional behavior out the window.

"Let's get started," he said, clasping his hands together.

An hour later, Darcy was questioning her sanity and wondering why she'd let those sexy, dark-skinned muscles sway her judgment. How in the world did she think she could keep up? This man was obviously in shape and she was obviously...not.

She resisted the urge to bend over and pull in much-needed air to her overexerted lungs.

"Ready for more?" he asked, hands on his hips, devastatingly handsome smile on his face.

She sent him a glare. "I'm not a masochist."

"You're honest," he replied, using his T-shirt to wipe the sweat off his brow. "I prefer honesty."

"That makes two of us."

He moved over to the small refrigerator in the corner of the room and pulled out two bottles of water. After handing her one, they both uncapped the drinks and took long pulls. Water had never tasted so good.

"So why the nanny business?" he asked, propping his foot upon a workout bench. His elbow rested on his knee, the bottle of water hung between two fingers. "Because you're an amazing cook. Dinner was pretty damn delicious. All of the meals have been great, but tonight's was my favorite."

Stunned and flattered at the compliment and his openness, Darcy screwed the lid back on her bottle. "I've never known anything other than taking care of children. I went to work with my grandmother every single day and fell in love. Cooking is a fun hobby and I love trying out new things. I guess if I weren't a nanny, I'd like to be a chef or a caterer."

She'd quickly steered the conversation to cooking. Anything to avoid talking too much about babies. The facts that children of her own weren't in her future and that anything she'd saved toward adoption had disappeared with Thad cut deep. Still, taking care of others was what she was meant to be doing, of that she was sure.

"Hey." Colin tipped his head to the side, searching her face. "You all right?"

"Oh, yeah." Darcy pushed a sweaty strand of hair that had escaped her ponytail behind her ear. "Just tired."

Pushing off the bench, Colin stalked closer, his focus solely on her. "Tomorrow we'll do weights and skip cardio."

"Tomorrow?" she asked. "You mean we're going to do this every day?"

The corner of his mouth twitched. "Only if you want to. I'm here every night after Iris goes to bed. If you want to join me, you are more than welcome. If you don't want to, no pressure. Personally, I think you're perfect the way you are."

"You haven't seen me naked," she muttered, realizing her mistake the second the words were out of her mouth. "Sorry. I'm—forget I said that."

"When a woman as sultry as you says the word *naked* it's impossible to keep certain images from flooding my mind."

Darcy held onto her bottle, thankful for the prop because her hands were shaking, as were her knees, and her entire body was responding to that low, sexy, heavily accented voice.

"Where are you from?" she asked.

"Greece."

Of course he was. Someplace beautiful and exotic, much like the man himself.

"So, dinner requests for tomorrow?" she asked. "I'll probably need to run to the store at some point, if that's okay."

"Not a problem." He turned toward the doorway, motioning her to exit ahead of him. "I have no requests. You obviously know what you're doing in the kitchen, which is more than I can say for myself."

Stepping into the hallway, she waited until Colin reached in and turned off the light. Darkness enveloped them, save for the slash of light at the end of the hallway shining down from the chandelier in the foyer.

"What's your favorite food?" she asked, trying to focus on his face in the dark, though neither of them had made a move to walk into the light.

"I haven't had too many American dishes," he replied. "I normally eat a lot of fish and vegetables."

Which would further explain why he was so buff and polished, and she had more dimples than a newborn baby's backside.

"I know just what to serve," she replied.

Her vision had adjusted to the darkness enough to see

the flare of heat in his baby blues just as he stepped in closer. "You claim I can't deliver loaded statements." His rich, low voice washed over her already heated body, ironically sending shivers all through her. "I'd say that goes both ways."

Before she could respond, Colin trailed a fingertip along the side of her face.

"Wh—what are you doing?" she asked, cursing her stammer, knowing it was a sign of weakness.

"Putting my curiosity to rest."

"Curiosity?"

That finger kept stroking, causing every pleasure point in her body to tingle.

"I needed to know if you are as silky as you appear," he murmured.

Warmth radiated from his broad body as he leaned in even closer, close enough to brush against hers and have her backing up into the wall.

Her gaze held his. "Am I?"

"Here you are," he whispered. "I wonder about here."

His lips covered hers in an instant, leaving her no choice but to reply to his demands. Okay, she could've chosen to push him away, but…why?

His tongue swept inside her mouth just as his hand curved around her chin, his thumb and forefinger on either side of her face as if to hold her in place. Darcy arched into him, wanting more and taking all he delivered. So many promises wrapped in that one kiss and all she had to do was let go.

Hadn't they both agreed to keep this professional? There was nothing professional about the spiral of arousal coursing through her or the need she so desperately wanted to cave in to.

Colin lifted only to shift his stance, pressing her further against the wall and his very hard, impressive body.

Whoever Colin Alexander was, the man possessed power and control. He demanded so much without words and his actions proved he was used to getting what he wanted.

Just like Thad.

Darcy jerked her head to the side, causing Colin's lips to slide against her jaw, his hand falling away.

She closed her eyes, trying to ignore the devil on her shoulder telling her to turn back and let Colin continue whatever it was he had in mind.

"Colin…"

He dropped his forehead to her shoulder, sighed, then took a step back. "Darcy, that was inexcusable."

Holding her hand to her moist lips, Darcy risked glancing back to Colin. "No, no. We're both to blame."

He propped his hands on his narrow hips and stared up at the ceiling. Darcy had no idea what to say, what to do.

"I've never been in this position before," she told him, clutching her water and wrapping her arms around her waist. "You need to know that I don't kiss employers and I've never, ever had a relationship with any of them beyond a professional one."

"I believe you."

When he offered no further comment, Darcy couldn't take the uncomfortable silence any longer. She turned and started walking down the hallway, when he called her name. She froze, but didn't look back.

"You need to know the last person I had a relationship with was my wife." His soft words floated down the wide hall, enveloping her. "I know we aren't taking this any further, but I didn't want you to think I made a habit of coming on to beautiful women."

Beautiful women.

Darcy threw him a look over her shoulder, nodded and carried on. She didn't stop, didn't slow down until she was in her room with the door shut behind her. Her heart still pounded just as fiercely as it had when she'd been in the darkened hall with Colin, the same as when she'd been sweating in the gym with him and the same as when he'd opened the door first thing that morning looking all rumpled and sexy.

With baby monitors in every room, there was no way she'd miss it if Iris needed something. Which was a very good thing because when Colin had been kissing her, for the briefest of moments, she'd forgotten her sole purpose for even being here. Her mind had traveled to a selfish place and all she wanted was more of that talented, demanding mouth on hers.

Dropping her head back against the door, Darcy groaned. This was the last thing she needed. If she didn't straighten up and focus, she'd have to resign and she needed the full amount of money Colin was paying her if she wanted to keep the agency afloat in any way. Not to mention if she wanted to ever get an apartment or a reliable vehicle.

The video monitor on the white nightstand showed a very peaceful Iris hugging her new doll to her chest. It was in the quiet, serene moments like this that Darcy truly felt that void in her heart. Growing up around other children and loving families, Darcy had always assumed she'd have a family of her own one day.

With the way she worked herself now, though, she didn't even have time for a date, much less a husband. Losing her entire savings had only pushed her dream of adopting further back, making her wonder if she just wasn't meant to be a mother.

There were worse things in the world than not having children…though from her perspective not many. She truly wished with all her heart that she had the ability to conceive like nearly every other woman, but that wasn't meant to be and she had to quit dwelling on it and move on. She wanted to be happy, so she had to focus on happy things and things that were in her control…infertility was certainly not one of them.

Tomorrow, she vowed, she would be one hundred percent professional. She just had to figure out a way to become immune to those striking blue eyes, that sultry accent and forget the way his lips basically assaulted hers in the best, most arousing way possible.

Hysterical laughter escaped her. Sure. No problem.

Five

The alarm chimed throughout the house, indicating that someone had triggered the gate and was coming up the drive. Colin lifted Iris in his arms and headed to the door to help Darcy with her grocery bags. She'd been gone for quite a while and he wondered if she'd run away or if she was stockpiling for the next month.

He'd just gotten off the phone with his assistant who informed Colin of some rather interesting information regarding Darcy and her financial situation. Apparently she was much worse off than he'd first thought. He wasn't sure whether to bring it up or let it slide. The last thing he wanted to do was make her uncomfortable or embarrassed, but at the same time, he wanted to do…something.

He was definitely going to have to bring up the fact her business was basically failing, but he needed to figure out the delicate matter.

Colin didn't know her personal issues, and he had no doubt she had them with her financial situation. All he knew right now was that her business had hit hard times in the last year and had fallen from one of the most sought out to an agency with only Darcy as the worker. There was definitely a story there.

When he opened the door, he didn't see her car. Instead, Darcy was walking up the drive, her arms weighted down with reusable grocery sacks bulging with food.

He sat Iris on the stoop. "Stay here, baby. Daddy needs to help Darcy."

With the gated property, Colin wasn't concerned about Iris wandering off. Worst-case scenario, she'd pluck all the vibrant flowers in the beds before he could get back to her. There was a pool around back, but he'd watch her and make sure she didn't toddle around the house.

Quickly moving toward Darcy, Colin felt his blood pressure rising. "What the hell are you doing?" he asked once he'd closed the gap. "Where's your car?"

"Broke down about a half mile back."

He pulled several bags off each arm, narrowing his eyes at the red creases on her delicate skin caused by all the weight. She wasn't some damn pack mule.

"Why didn't you call me?" he demanded as he curled his hands around the straining handles. "I would've come to get you."

Left with only two lighter bags, Darcy smiled and started up the drive. "By the time you could've gotten Iris in the car seat and gotten to me, I would've been here. Plus I didn't want to bother you guys in case you were playing or she was getting fussy and ready to lie down for a nap."

Even though Darcy's hair was pulled up into a high ponytail, Colin noted the damp tendrils clinging to her neck. The heat of the California sun could be relentless.

"Where exactly is your car?" he asked, trying to keep his voice controlled.

She explained what street she'd left it on, which really

didn't mean much to him since he knew little about the area or the street names. He'd call to have it towed and then he'd work on getting her proper transportation. No way was any employee of his going to be stranded again.

What if Iris had been with Darcy? Then what would she have done? The mishap was frustrating on so many levels.

Not only was she his employee, he refused to see any woman working herself to the point of sweaty exhaustion and that's exactly where Darcy was at. A sheen of perspiration glistened across her forehead and upper lip, her cheeks were red and she had circles beneath her eyes.

Where he was from the women would never leave their homes without full makeup, perfectly styled hair and flashy clothes...much like LA. Still, Darcy didn't seem to care that she wasn't completely made up for an outing. He actually found the quality quite refreshing and incredibly hot.

As if he needed another reason to be aroused by her. He needed to nip this sexual urge in the bud and stay focused.

Once they reached the stoop, Iris had indeed plucked up a variety of flowers, clutching them in her tight little hand.

"Pitty," she exclaimed, thrusting them toward Darcy. "You pitty."

Darcy laughed. "Oh, honey. You're so sweet."

Colin looked at Darcy and saw an alluring, determined and resilient woman. How could any man not be attracted to those qualities? And her sexuality was stealthy. You didn't see the impact coming until it hit you hard. Each day that passed made him realize just how much power she was beginning to have over him.

By the time they got all the bags inside and onto the wide center island in the kitchen, Colin had worked up quite a sweat of his own.

"I'll put these away," Darcy told him as she opened the pantry. "I need to walk back to my car after and see if it's the transmission. I've been having issues with that thing, but a transmission would cost more than the old car is worth."

Colin stood amazed. "*You* plan on looking to see if the transmission is shot?"

Over the stacks of bags, Darcy met his gaze. "Yeah, why? Who else is going to look at it?"

Iris patted his leg and Colin leaned down to lift her up. She still clutched those colorful flowers in her hand so he moved to the cabinet to get down a small glass to use as a vase.

"I'd call a mechanic," he replied, filling the glass with water.

With a soft laugh and shake of her head, Darcy turned her attention back to pulling the groceries from the sacks. "Well, mechanics charge just to come look at the car, then there's the labor to fix the problem, plus the part."

As she listed all the costs associated with getting the vehicle fixed, Colin had to remind himself he wasn't back at the palace. He wasn't talking to someone who would just pay someone else to take care of the issue and move on. Darcy was obviously a hard worker and she didn't need to tell him her funds were lacking.

Taking the flowers from Iris's hand, he sat them in the glass. "There, sweetheart."

She clapped her hands together and wiggled in an attempt to get away. Carefully, he put her back down and watched her move to Darcy. The easy way Iris had taken to the new nanny made him happy he'd allowed her to stay. The incident in the hall last night, though, had kept him up questioning his decision. They were still on a trial and he really didn't want to start the process of finding someone else. That was one thing he wouldn't do to Iris.

Even though they'd moved across the globe, he wanted Iris to have as much stability in her life as possible until he was absolutely certain of their future.

"Hey, cutie." Darcy pulled out a bag of flour and glanced down to her side, a wide smile stretching across her face. "I'm almost done and then you and I can play a little game."

"I'll take care of getting your car picked up."

Darcy's eyes flashed back to his. "That's not your job."

Crossing his arms over his chest, ready for the battle she so obviously thought was coming, Colin replied, "Cooking every single meal and going to the store isn't your job, either. I'm trying to help. We agreed on sharing these responsibilities."

"You can help by letting me do what works for me with my personal circumstances. Fixing my car wasn't included in our agreement."

As Darcy ignored him to focus on putting the last of the groceries away, Colin didn't know if he was pissed to be dismissed so easily or if he was elated that she wasn't walking on eggshells around him because he was a prince. How would she react if she knew just how wealthy he was? Would she even care about his royal status? Darcy didn't seem the type to be attracted to money or power. She seemed to be doing just fine on her own.

And that was the main problem he was having. She shouldn't have to do everything on her own.

"How about I fix lunch and you can make dinner?" he suggested.

Bundling all the reusable sacks into one neatly folded pile, Darcy raised a brow and grinned. "And what are you making for lunch, oh great chef?"

"You're mocking me," he laughed. "I know I'm not as good as you in the kitchen, but I think I can give you a run for your money. Isn't that the expression you Americans have?"

Her lips pursed as she continued to stare. "It is, but I don't think you can hold your own against me."

"Challenge accepted," he told her, ready to prove her wrong.

Damn it. Now he needed to search on the internet for something easy, quick and delicious. He'd been thinking of throwing sandwich stuff together for lunch, but given her instant doubt, Colin had to raise his game. And he would, just as soon as he took care of the car. She was getting his assistance whether she liked it or not.

The shrill alarm had Darcy jumping to her feet and pulling Iris with her. They'd been coloring on the floor in the living room when the ear-piercing noise came out of nowhere.

Darcy knew that sound and it was all she could do not to laugh. Calmly, though, she rested Iris on her hip and headed toward the kitchen where lunch was probably not going to be happening anytime soon.

Standing in the wide, arched doorway, Darcy took in the scene and had to literally bite her lips to keep from laughing.

There were dirty bowls littering the island, opened packages of random ingredients spread about and Colin was currently slapping a kitchen towel at the small flame coming from the burner. Smoke billowed through the open space as Darcy moved into the kitchen. She eased Iris into her high chair and wheeled it over near the patio door, which Darcy opened to let some fresh air in. She made her way down the wall, opening each window as she passed.

Colin turned, still holding the charred dishtowel, and shrugged. "I'm not admitting defeat."

"Of course not," she replied, not even bothering to hide her smile. "Why would you?"

"Lunch will be just a few more minutes."

"I'm sure it will be wonderful." Darcy shrugged. "No rush."

Poor guy was still trying to save his pride. She wasn't about to say more. Their easy banter seriously helped take the edge off the sexual tension. Playfulness, even a little flirting she could handle. Anything beyond that… she glanced to the tiny flame Colin was smacking. Yeah, that flame signified her life right now. If she got too close to Colin she'd get burned. The signs were literally in front of her face.

Darcy had just grabbed a handful of puffed snacks to hold Iris over until lunch was ready when another alarm sounded through the house. This one was announcing a visitor.

The darn house was wired so tight with security and monitors and alarms, Darcy's head had practically spun in circles when Colin had explained the entire system to her. Who was this man that he needed so much security?

"Are you expecting company?" she asked, laying the snacks across the highchair tray for Iris.

"Actually, I am." Colin turned off the burner, sat the pan on a cooler one and turned to her. "Don't touch anything. I've got it under control. This won't take long."

He rushed from the room and out the front door.

"Your father is one mysterious man," Darcy muttered to Iris. "And apparently not a chef."

Smoothing the dark curls away from the baby's face, Darcy really studied how much Iris looked like Colin. All bronzed skin, dark molasses eyes and striking features. Iris would be an absolute bombshell when she grew up. Darcy couldn't help but wonder if Iris's mother had been a Greek beauty as well. Most likely Colin wouldn't have married someone who was an ogre.

Moments later, Colin breezed back into the house.

"Sorry about that. Lunch will be ready in five minutes if you'd like to get some plates out."

"Are you going to tell me what we're having now?"

"You'll see," he told her before he went back into the foyer.

On a sigh, she crossed the room and pulled out two plates and one smaller plate for Iris. She resisted the urge to stroke the beautiful cabinets and the quartz counter-tops. This kitchen alone cost more money than she made in a year...during the good times. Having a home and a gourmet kitchen with a family to cook for was a dream she honestly didn't see coming true. That was okay, though. For now she was here, working and making money to save her agency, and in the end that's all that truly mattered. And the fact she was caring for a baby was a great form of forced therapy she'd desperately needed to face her fears.

Moments later, Colin came back into the kitchen wearing a mischievous grin, but he said nothing as he dished out whatever he'd managed to salvage from the burning pan. Apparently he'd removed the pot before the flames consumed their entire meal.

"I admit, after the fanfare with the smoke alarm, this actually smells delicious."

He threw her a glance over his shoulder. "I have a whole host of surprises for you."

Those words held a plethora of meanings, but when said while holding her gaze beneath heavy lids, her mind instantly traveled to the darkened hallway last night and how her body still ached after such a gloriously arousing kiss.

Could such an experience be labeled by one simple word? A kiss was something that could be given from a parent to a child, from a child to a pet, from a peasant to the hand of a diplomat. The word *kiss* blanketed a lot of ground.

"Ready?"

Darcy blinked, realizing Colin stood in front of her with two plates of…

"You made shrimp Alfredo?" she asked, more than amazed.

"You think I can't boil noodles and melt some butter?" he asked, feigning shock.

Taking her plate, inhaling the garlicky goodness, she laughed. "I had my doubts."

Darcy sat her plate on the table and went to move Iris's highchair over.

"I've got her," Colin said, holding his hand up. "You eat while it's hot."

Darcy stared as Colin wheeled Iris closer to the table. She then sat in amazement as he cut up the noodles, blew on them and offered small bites to his daughter.

"You're not eating," he commented without turning his head in her direction.

"I'm surprised." Darcy slid onto the built-in bench beneath the wide window. Grabbing her fork, she started pushing the noodles and shrimp around on her plate. "I'm the nanny, so eating a hot meal isn't something I'm used to. I'm also not used to the parent doing my job while I'm sitting right here."

He tossed her a glance. "I'm not like most parents. She's my daughter and I'm not paying you to raise her so I can prop my feet up and watch her life go by. I'm paying you to help for a few months. There's a huge difference."

Darcy swallowed, hating how her observation instantly made him defensive and how she was reminded again how little time she would actually have here.

"I apologize," she said, stabbing a plump shrimp coated in Alfredo sauce. "I should know by now that every family, every circumstance is different."

"Don't apologize," he replied. "Actually, as soon as you're finished eating, I have something for you."

Intrigued, Darcy stared across the table. "You made lunch, you're forcing me to eat instead of feeding Iris and you have something else up your sleeve? You've got to be kidding."

The muscle in his jaw ticked, his eyes held hers. "I don't joke too often."

The man was intense, she'd give him that. He went from super dad to sexy employer in the span of one quick blink. Regardless of his demeanor, Colin Alexander exuded sex appeal.

Darcy didn't ask any more questions. She didn't know Colin well, but she was positive anything she'd ask would be dodged or ignored. He was a man of absolute control, absolute power. She had no clue what he did for a living, she only knew he worked from home. However Colin made his money, Darcy was positive he dominated every facet of his life, and was even more controlled and possibly ruthless in whatever business he was in.

They finished lunch in silence, except for the cute noises and random words coming from Iris. When Darcy was finished, she took the plates to the sink, rinsed them and put them in the dishwasher.

"This is a really nice dishwasher."

Inwardly she groaned. What sane person coveted someone else's kitchen appliances? Talk about pathetic. She was showing her lower-class side...which was the only side she knew lately.

Pulling the tray out, Colin lifted Iris and carefully set her on the tile. In an instant she darted off toward the living room. Thanks to the mostly open-concept design of the house, they could still keep an eye on her through the wide, arched doorway.

The little girl picked up the doll Darcy had given her,

sat on the floor and started rocking her. That familiar ache spread through Darcy. But there were plenty more blessings in her life to count. Each day with Iris was a blessing. The child was sweet, always happy and fun-loving, when she got her naps in, and Darcy was lucky to be working under such amazing circumstances.

"Get Iris and meet me out front."

Darcy glanced back to Colin. "You're making me nervous."

One corner of his mouth kicked up. "Baby, that's the best compliment anyone has ever given me."

He strode away without another word and Darcy had a gut feeling she'd just stirred the hornet's nest of hormones.

Darcy crossed into the living room and slid her hands beneath Iris's little arms. "Come on, sweetheart. Bring your dolly and let's go see what your daddy is up to."

"Doll," Iris repeated. "Pitty."

Laughing, Darcy kissed the dark head of curls. "Yes, baby. Your dolly is pretty."

Stepping outside, Darcy immediately spotted Colin with a wide grin on his face.

"What is that?" she asked, glancing over his shoulder at the big, black SUV, all shiny and brand-new.

"Yours."

Six

Colin watched Darcy as her eyes widened, her face paled.

"You—what…"

Her stuttering and the fact she was rendered speechless had him confused. "Your car isn't worth fixing and you need viable transportation. Consider this a very late birthday present."

Her eyes darted to his and instead of gratitude he saw… anger? Seriously? He didn't know a woman that didn't fawn all over gifts, especially a new car. He didn't know where he'd gone wrong here, but he'd seriously miscalculated her response.

"You said you'd call someone about my car," she explained.

"I did. I had it removed from the road and now you have a new vehicle that you won't have to worry about."

Darcy didn't look nearly as excited as he'd figured she would. In fact, she looked downright angry.

"I can't accept this," she stated, still remaining on the

concrete stoop holding onto Iris. "I want my own car fixed, not a replacement that cost more than I could ever afford. And I don't need a birthday present from you."

"If you don't want it as a late present, then just use the vehicle while you work for me," he said slowly, moving toward her as he made sure she understood this wasn't any form of bribery or something more. "Consider it one of the incentives I mentioned on your first day. The vehicle is not up for debate. You need to have reliable transportation because you're watching my daughter and had she been in your car earlier, you both would've been stranded."

Darcy rolled her eyes. "Don't be so dramatic. I wasn't stranded. I walked here. Had Iris been with me, I would've called for help and you could've been there in no time. I was only a half mile away."

"What happens when you're ten miles away?" he countered, slipping Iris from Darcy's arms. "You can't walk that far with a toddler and you can't stay in the car in this heat."

Darcy crossed her arms over her chest and glanced away. "I can handle myself."

"Do you even want to go look at the car?" he asked.

"I can see it just fine." She brought her eyes back up to meet his. "I would like to know where my car is and I want it back."

Spinning on her heel, she went back inside, slamming the door. Colin glanced to Iris who was now chewing on the small stuffed doll's hair.

"Where did I go wrong?" he asked.

Colin knew whatever had just happened had little to do with the vehicle in his drive and everything to do with something that was personal to her. Did her old broken car hold some sentimental value?

"We better go see if she's sticking around," he told Iris as he headed toward the door.

By the time he found Darcy, she was in her room, standing at the floor-to-ceiling window looking out onto the backyard. Her room was neat and tidy. She'd plumped the pillows on her perfectly made bed and her single piece of luggage sat on the floor at the foot of it. Other than a small pair of flip-flops, there was no sign she'd even made herself at home. He knew she was orderly around the house, but he assumed in her own room, she'd be a little more laid back.

"Are you quitting?" he asked from the doorway. Even though this was his house, the bedroom was Darcy's for as long as she was here and he wasn't about to infringe on her territory.

Without turning around, Darcy let out a laugh that held no humor. "I have nowhere else to go and I need this job. I'll use the car while I'm here, but I really just want mine back. I have my reasons."

"Down," Iris said, squirming against him.

"Can we come in?" he asked.

Darcy glanced over her shoulder. "It's your house, Colin."

He stepped into the room and closed the door, confining Iris to an area where he could still watch her and talk to Darcy at the same time.

"Listen, I had no idea getting you a car would set off so much emotion." Slowly closing the space between them, he came to stand in front of her. "I'll get your car fixed and have it delivered back here. But you will still be using the new one. No arguments."

She eyed him for another minute before tipping her head to the side. "One of these days someone is going to tell you no."

"No, no, no, no," Iris chanted as she toddled around the room waving her doll in the air.

Darcy laughed and Colin couldn't stop himself from smiling. "She's the only one who can get away with it," he informed Darcy.

Truly focusing on Darcy, he crossed the room. As he neared, her eyes widened. He liked to think it was from the attraction, but that was his arrogance talking. More than likely she was trying to figure him out, same as he was doing with her.

But he would get through her defenses. He knew without a doubt her secret had everything to do with the fact that she had nowhere else to go.

As the space between them minimized, Colin kept his gaze locked on hers. The closer he got, the more she had to tip her head back to hold his stare.

"I can't help but feel you're hiding something," he started. "Your background check told me your business has hit a rough patch and you are on your own now."

Darcy nodded, her lips thinning. "There are challenges I'm facing privately, but nothing that will affect my job with you. I promise. I just don't want to be indebted to you for fixing my car."

Money wasn't the root of all evil as the old saying went. The evil was the person holding the purse strings who did nothing to help others.

"I think I'll take Iris outside for a walk." Darcy skirted around him, careful to shift her body so she didn't even brush against him. "Feel free to join us if you want."

Colin laughed as he turned to face her. "Not very subtle, the way you dodged my question."

"Subtlety wasn't what I was going for." She lifted Iris in her arms and smiled. The way she headed straight out the door as if she hadn't just put him in his place really annoyed and amused him at the same time. Damn, she was fun, yet prickly.

Darcy was perfect with Iris, independent and she turned him inside out at every move.

When his marriage had started failing, Colin blamed himself. He'd put Karina through hell with his injury, his surgeries, not being there for her as a husband should be. He'd never imagined he'd feel a desire for another woman again, but here he was, pining after his temporary nanny, of all people.

If he didn't keep his head on straight, he'd be losing focus on why he was in LA to begin with. He was no closer to deciding if staying away from Galini Isle was best for him and Iris or if returning to the secure, enclosed, yet exposed, lifestyle of the royals was the way he should go.

Here he had more freedom to take her out in public. They'd walked to the park last week and it had been so refreshing not to have guards hovering nearby. The longer he stayed in the United States, the more he worried he'd never want to leave.

There was only one right decision…he only wished he knew which one it was.

Playing outside in the yard was always so much fun for Darcy. She loved hearing Iris's squeals of delight and seeing her little carefree spirit. Darcy had been here for a full month now and had easily passed the trial period. Each second she spent with Iris only had Darcy more thankful she'd fought for this position. Holding onto Iris's tiny little hand just felt right. Everything about being with this sweet child felt right.

Not to mention that working for a man who oozed sexiness, power and control was one giant glob of icing on the proverbial cake.

Talk about landing the job of a lifetime. Still, Darcy couldn't help but wonder what happened to Colin's late wife. He didn't mention her, didn't even have any photos around the house. The man seemed as if he was running away or hiding from something, but she truly had no clue what. She could easily research him online, but she wasn't going to snoop into his life. That would be sneaky and Darcy prided herself on honesty. If he wanted to discuss his life, he would when the time was right.

Iris pulled away from Darcy and started running toward the landscaping framing the patio. Shielding her eyes with her hand, Darcy stared ahead as the little girl ran after a butterfly that had landed on one of the vibrant flowers. By the time Iris got there, the butterfly had flown away.

Iris looked around and when she realized the insect was no longer nearby, her chin started quivering. Closing the space between them, Darcy knelt down in front of the toddler and smoothed the curls away from her forehead, making a mental note to pick up some hair accessories for Iris.

"It's okay, sweetheart," Darcy consoled. "Miss Butterfly had to go home for a nap. I bet she'll be back another time. Would you like to go in and lie down? I saw a butterfly book in your room. How about we read that?"

"No," Iris cried, shaking her head. "No, no, no."

The one word kids learned early and used for nearly every reply, especially when they were in need of a nap. Darcy may have been working with older children these past several years, but certain things she would never forget.

When Darcy scooped her up and headed toward the house, the tears instantly transformed from sad to angry, and Iris's arms started flying as the instant tantrum went into full swing. Maybe Darcy shouldn't have taken Iris on that walk. Apparently the window of opportunity was missed and the nap should've come first.

Patting her back and trying to dodge the whirlwind arms, Darcy took Iris into the house. Of course, inside, the cries seemed to echo into surround sound. Colin came running from the office off the kitchen, his cell to his ear, worry etched across his face.

"What happened?" he said, holding the device away from his mouth.

"She's just tired," Darcy explained. "Sorry we disturbed you."

Colin didn't resume his call as Darcy walked by. Maybe he was waiting for them to pass because of Iris's ear-splitting screams, but the way he studied them, Darcy worried he was wondering why his daughter was so unhappy. This was the first time Iris had truly thrown a fit around Darcy, but every kid had their moments and as a nanny, one just had to learn how to adjust to that child's needs accordingly.

And right now, little Miss Iris needed her bed and a couple of hours of peace and quiet.

As she reached the top of the stairs, Darcy didn't have to glance over her shoulder to know that Colin was staring at her.

"Come on, little one," Darcy cooed.

After walking around the room, shutting the blinds, turning on the small fan for white noise and grabbing Iris's blanket and doll, Darcy settled into the cushy rocking chair and began to hum, occasionally adding in a few lyrics to "You Are My Sunshine." Iris's eyes started to grow heavy. Darcy knew the rule of thumb was to lay young children down while they were still awake, but holding and rocking a baby was a temptation she couldn't avoid. Today Darcy justified it by telling herself she was just waiting for Iris to calm down.

Darcy held onto the precious bundle in her arms and

came to her feet. Iris still clutched the silky blanket and stuffed doll as Darcy eased the sleeping beauty into her bed.

With her hands resting on the rail, Darcy stared at the spiky, damp lashes resting on Iris's reddened cheeks. Moments ago this child was throwing a fit and now she slept peacefully. When she woke she wouldn't remember she'd been upset, and that was how Darcy wanted to live her life.

Moving forward was the only way to prove there was life after the death of a dream. She couldn't allow endometriosis to define her. Discovering that the family she'd dreamed of having one day wouldn't happen had been a crushing blow, but Darcy had persevered, forcing herself to become stronger than her disappointments.

Swallowing the lump in her throat, Darcy turned from the bed and headed into the hall. She'd just pulled the door closed when she turned and ran straight into Colin's hard chest.

The instant force of colliding with him threw her off balance. Colin's hands immediately gripped her bare arms to steady her. Breath caught in her throat, her heart beat a fast, bruising rhythm against her chest. An instant flash of their heated kiss flooded her mind and all Darcy could think of was how perfectly they fit together.

Down girl.

Colin's eyes studied her face, her mouth. Tingles shot through her...tingles she shouldn't be feeling for her boss.

"We need to talk."

The statement, laced with such authority, delivered a punch to her stomach. Were they going to talk professionally? Personally? Was he upset with her for something she'd done?

Or did he want her alone for purely selfish, carnal reasons?

The second he turned and walked away, Darcy followed.

Seven

Fisting his hands at his sides, Colin cursed himself as he went downstairs and into his office. He had to keep reminding himself that the woman he'd hired to care for Iris was an employee, not an object to be lusting after. He'd never been sexually attracted to an employee—before, during or after his marriage.

Not once had his professional and personal needs ever crossed paths, but every single time he looked at Darcy he felt that kick to the gut that demanded he take notice of the all-American beauty.

Added to that, she was the only woman since Karina to have any connection to Iris. Colin would be lying to himself if he didn't admit that seeing Darcy around his daughter in all her youthful, vibrant glory had something tugging on his heart.

Damn it, he didn't want his heart tugged. He had too much on his plate right now and craving a woman, his nanny, for pity's sake, was not an option.

"You wanted me?"

Grinding his teeth to keep from saying what he really wanted, Colin turned to face Darcy. He'd assumed coming to his office would make this conversation easier, less personal.

"I want you to stop rocking Iris before you lay her down to sleep."

Darcy blanched and Colin cursed himself for the rough tone he'd taken.

"She was always used to just being laid down," he went on, trying to lighten his voice. It wasn't Darcy's fault he was fighting a losing battle with his attraction for her.

Darcy straightened her shoulders, tipped her chin and gave a quick nod. "I apologize. I'll be sure to lay her down right away next time."

Stiffly, she turned toward the door and Colin hated himself for making her feel bad about herself. Damn it. He didn't want this. He didn't want the chemistry or the awkward sexual tension, and he sure as hell didn't want to have to mask his arousal by being snippy and gruff with her. He wanted Iris to have that loving touch, to be wrapped in the arms of someone who cared for her, and it was obvious Darcy cared for his little girl.

Maybe he wasn't capable of being happy anywhere if this was any indication. He'd taken out his frustrations with himself on Darcy. If he wasn't happy here, though, did that mean he wasn't happy stepping away from his duty? Is that what all of this boiled down to?

Colin had been in a great mood moments ago as he'd been talking on the phone with his best friend, Prince Luc Silva. He hadn't spoken to him in months, other than texts or emails. As soon as they'd hung up, Darcy's soft voice had filtered through the monitor system in the home and damn if hearing all of that softness wasn't like being wrapped in her sweet embrace.

He couldn't afford to be wrapped up in anything that didn't involve his country, his loyalty and the decision he needed to make regarding his and Iris's future in the kingdom.

"Darcy," he called out before she could clear the doorway.

She froze, but didn't turn around. "Yes?"

Anything he wanted to say would be a bad idea, rocking their already shaky relationship. "Nothing," he said, shaking his head.

Regardless of the attraction, Colin was glad he'd decided to let Darcy stay on after they'd verbally battled that first day. He couldn't imagine anyone else with Iris.

Each day brought them closer to the six-month mark, closer to his staying or going. And, to be honest, he was growing too fond of having her here, in his life. He was finding an inner peace he hadn't expected. He was almost angry at himself for allowing his emotions to get the better of him, but where Darcy was concerned, he was finding he had little say in the matter.

Stefan was putting the pressure on, but Colin couldn't deal with Galini Isle and Darcy simultaneously. Both issues were overwhelming and threatened to take over his life. Right now, though, he wanted to concentrate on Darcy. Even though he knew Galini Isle should come first, he needed to see if there was more to their attraction than pure lust.

After dinner, Colin wanted to give Iris her bath so Darcy took the opportunity to sew a button back on her only dress shirt. The button right at the breast had popped off after a big inhale. In order for this top to fit properly, she either needed to lose a few pounds or stop breathing. She was thankful Colin had been nowhere around to witness the mishap.

Threading the needle, Darcy quickly fixed the shirt and was putting her small sewing kit away when a knock sounded at her door.

"Come in," she called as she wound the unused thread back around the spool.

Colin stepped in, holding Iris who was wrapped in her thick terrycloth monogrammed towel. Darcy didn't even want to know how much that plush towel cost…she'd seen the designer label.

"I need to make a phone call," Colin told her, taking in the shirt in her lap and the supplies spread over the bed. "Am I interrupting something?"

"Oh, no." Darcy scooted everything out of the way and came to her feet, smoothing down her pink T-shirt. "I was just sewing a button back on my shirt."

Colin's brows drew together. "Just buy a new shirt."

Yeah, why didn't she think of that? Between being technically homeless, nearly ready to shut the doors on the business barely keeping food in her mouth and trying to keep her car running, why hadn't she just hit the mall in her spare time for a new wardrobe?

But he didn't need her sarcasm. A man like Colin wouldn't understand because if anything in his life was broken, he could just pay to have it fixed or snap his fingers and have people at his beck and call.

Another layer of division between them, showing her just how vast their differences were.

Ignoring his question, because anything she would reply with would most definitely be snarky, she came to her feet, crossed the room and reached for Iris.

"Go on and make your call." The sweet scent of freshly bathed baby always made her heart weep just a little. "I'll take care of this sweet princess."

"Don't call her that."

Jerking her attention from the wrapped, squirming

bundle in her arms to Colin, Darcy jerked. "Call her what? Princess?"

"I don't like that term," he stated, crossing his arms and leveling her gaze.

"It's a simple term of endearment," Darcy defended herself, shifting Iris to settle her more comfortably on her hip. "I'm not sure what you think I'm implying when I say it, but—"

"No more. I don't want her to be a spoiled child and that term suggests too much."

"Colin—"

He held up a hand, cutting her off once more. "She's my daughter. She will not be called princess."

Feeling her blood pressure rise through the onslaught of confusion, Darcy took a step forward. "Yes, sir. If you'll excuse me, I need to get Iris ready for bed."

She pushed by him and exited her room, headed into the nursery next door and closed the door. What on earth had gotten into him? He was still in a mood and Darcy had no clue why. Darcy quickly dressed Iris in a pair of yellow footed pajamas with little bunnies on each of the toes. Every single baby item the toddler possessed was adorable. Darcy was getting more and more used to being surrounded by everything baby. The only thing she worried about now was how she'd leave at the end of the term they'd agreed upon. Staying away from babies for years had helped to soothe her ache somewhat, but being thrust into the world of all things tiny and pink brought Darcy's wishes back to the surface. To think all of that would be taken from her again in a few months.

She had no clue what he'd do when her term was up. Perhaps he just wanted to get his feet back on solid ground since he was a widower with a baby. Maybe he thought he could take it from there. Darcy had learned long ago not to question her clients' intentions.

She couldn't get too used to the weight of Iris in her arms, or the way Iris would clutch that ugly old doll Darcy had given her or the way she had started to reach for Darcy. But such simple things had already infiltrated Darcy's heart.

And Colin, as grouchy and moody as he'd been, had also managed to capture her attention in a way she hadn't expected. She couldn't get the image of him dominating her, kissing her, demanding more, from her mind.

As Darcy turned off the lights and clicked on the projector that danced stars across the ceiling, she knew she needed to find him and figure out what was going on. The man was a walking mystery, and if she was going to stay, and she really had no choice, she needed to clear the air. He obviously had something on his mind. Now all she had to do was let him know she was here if he wanted to talk and try to prevent anymore kissing episodes from happening.

Because kissing Colin had turned into another one of those fantasies leaving her wanting more. But Darcy was a realist by default. She may want a man to love her and a family to go right along with him in her perfect world, or the image she had of perfection, but the truth was Colin and Iris were out of reach.

Darcy had to keep reminding herself of that or she'd be severely crushed when time came to leave…alone.

Oh. My.

There was a reason Darcy had made her way through the house searching for Colin, but right at this moment she had no clue what it was. In fact, she had no thoughts whatsoever because her mind and her sight were filled with a glorious image of Colin doing one-armed pull-ups, shirtless, displaying that tattoo in a sweaty way that had her all but panting.

Dark skin wrapped around taut muscles flexing with each movement had Darcy gripping the doorframe. She wasn't about to interrupt this free show. There was no way she could miss the chance to see her boss in all his sexy glory. She wasn't dead, after all. She just couldn't think clearly when he was around…an issue she'd never had with any other man.

With a grunt, he pulled himself up one last time before dropping back to the floor. Hands resting on his hips just above his low-slung shorts, Colin's shoulders shifted up and down as he pulled in deep breaths. Then he stilled, turned his head over his shoulder and spotted her.

Busted.

He held her gaze. It was now or never.

"We need to talk," she informed him, bolstering her courage by tamping down her girlie parts and stepping into the gym.

"If you want to work out, fine. I'm not in the mood to talk."

Darcy crossed her arms over her chest. "Seems like your mood is flat-out grouchy."

Colin turned fully to face her, but continued to stare. Darcy wondered if she'd crossed a line. But, boss or not, he shouldn't take his attitude out on her.

"I came to see if you wanted to talk about whatever has you brooding," she went on, trying her hardest to keep her eyes on his and not on the sweaty pecs and the ink that had her heart racing. "This tension is something I prefer not to work around and it's not good for a child because they can sense such things even at an early age."

Colin took a step forward, eyes locked on hers. "Is that right?"

Swallowing, Darcy nodded. "Yes."

He took another step, then another, eventually closing the gap between them. Darcy inhaled that musky, male scent, took in those muscles that were within striking distance and blinked up at Colin.

"If you're trying to intimidate me, you'll have to try harder." She had to keep the upper hand here because her control was slowly slipping and she had to at least put up a strong front. "If you don't want to talk, I'll leave you to your workout so you can take out your frustrations that way."

His stunning blue eyes traveled over her face. "Go change and join me."

"I don't think that's a good idea."

"Because of my mood?"

Darcy took in a deep breath. "Among other things."

"Like the pull between us?"

Why deny the obvious? She'd never been one to play games, though she did do her best to avoid uncomfortable situations. So how did she find herself here?

"Whatever has made you all surly is the main issue," she stated. "But the attraction is something we already discussed and agreed to ignore."

The muscle in Colin's jaw ticked, his nostrils flared. "Discussing and ignoring our chemistry isn't going to make it go away. As far as my mood goes, I had a disagreement with my brother on the phone and I'm dealing with some family things. That's all you need to know and more than you're entitled to."

Shaking her head, Darcy took a step back. "Obviously it was a mistake to come down here."

She turned, set on heading up to her room and figuring out new recipes for the coming week. She'd barely taken a step out the door before one strong hand wrapped around her arm and pulled her to a stop.

"The mistake would be leaving."

His words washed over her, his breath tickled the side

of her neck, the heat from his body enveloped her. Darcy closed her eyes.

"Colin," she whispered. "I can only be here for Iris. Nothing more."

"You deny yourself too much." His thumb stroked over her bare arm. "The car, new clothes…my touch. I've tried to ignore the power you have over me. I've tried, but there's only so much a man can take. You're driving me crazy and I'm taking my frustrations out on you when it's my fault I can't deal with how much you get under my skin. I snapped at you earlier because I'm angry with myself."

Darcy gasped at his raw honesty.

"Tell me you don't want me to touch you," he whispered.

"I'm not a liar," she informed him. "But I can't let you. There's a difference."

Colin turned her around so fast she fell against him. Instantly, her hands came up to settle on that hard chest she'd been lusting after. Why did she have to have such strong feelings for this man? And why was he so forceful, so dominating and constantly arousing at every single moment of the day?

"Being alone with you is not a good idea." Her defense came out weak, and the smirk on his face told her he wasn't buying it, either. "I need this job, Colin. I can't afford to…well…whatever you have in mind."

With a low growl from deep in his throat, Colin framed her face with both hands, forcing her to look only at him.

"*Moro*, you have no idea what I have in mind."

Moro. What did that even mean? Something Greek, she assumed. Coming from his lips, though, it sounded sexy, naughty.

No, she didn't want to appreciate the seductive terms rolling off his tongue, dripping with a toe-curling accent.

With taut skin beneath her palms, Darcy was fighting the urge to dig her fingers into his heated skin, rise on her toes and take what he was so blatantly offering.

"This isn't professional." She focused on his face, wondering if he was having doubts, but all she saw staring back at her was desire.

Had a man ever looked at her in such an arousing way before? If she had to ask herself the question, the obvious answer was no.

"No, it's not," he agreed, still holding her face in his hands. "But damn it, the more I fight this, the more I crave it. Do you want to quit working for me?"

"No."

"I'm not about to fire you." His thumb stroked over her bottom lip, back and forth. "So that leaves us here, fighting an urge that's only gaining momentum. What do you want?"

Was he mocking her? What did he think she wanted to do? She wanted this ache to cease, but she didn't want to be so clichéd as to sleep with her boss.

"I think you need to keep your hands off me," she whispered. "I think we need to focus on Iris and I think we need to be adult enough to have self-control."

Colin slid his hands back through her hair, tipped her head up and inched even closer, leaving only a breath between their mouths.

"I didn't ask what you thought. I asked what you want."

With her hands trapped between their bodies, his firm grip on her and air barely passing between them, Darcy did the only thing she could think to do…she kissed him.

Instantly Colin took control, pushing her back against the wall. Her hands fell away and just as she tried to grip his shoulders, he grabbed her wrists, jerked them away from his body and had both arms pinned up over her head. She was at his total mercy, at his command. His mouth covered hers, dominated, possessed and every part of her wanted more, wanted him.

Her body arched into his. The sensation of those hard planes against her had any feeling of self-consciousness disappearing. Apparently Colin didn't seem to mind his woman a little on the curvy side. If his arousal was any indication, he actually preferred a little extra flesh.

With one hand gripping her wrists, Colin's other hand found the hem of her shirt. His fingers slid beneath the cotton and found her waist. His palm flattened against her heated skin as he brushed his thumb along the satiny barrier of her bra. Such a thin layer, yet it proved to be quite a hindrance. She wanted his hands on her, all over her.

Darcy groaned as his hips pushed against hers; his thumb glided back and forth over her breast. He utterly consumed her with the simplest yet most demanding of touches and she still burned for more.

Wait. What was she saying? He was a widower. He'd been married and his wife had passed not too long ago. So, what did that make Darcy? The rebound? A fling to help him recover from a broken heart?

Wasn't that precisely what Colin was to her? Hadn't her own heart—and apparently her common sense, too— taken a hit from her failed relationship? Were they using each other as stepping-stones to get beyond the hurt?

With her arms still locked above her head by Colin's firm grip, Darcy tore her mouth away, causing his lips to land on her jawline.

"Colin," she panted. "Wait…just…this is…stop. Please."

He froze. His hand fell from her shirt as he slowly backed away. The second he released her arms, Darcy pulled some much needed air into her lungs.

With a curse, Colin raked a hand through his damp hair and turned away. Darcy watched as he walked over and sank onto the weight bench, rested his elbows on his knees and dropped his head between his shoulders. Apparently he was at war with himself.

Unsure of what to do next, Darcy remained still, hoping he'd say something to cut through this instant strain that settled between them. "Go upstairs, Darcy."

The angst in his tone had her glued to the spot. He may want to be alone, but she didn't think he should be. How could she just walk out after what they'd experienced? Ignoring it would only create more friction.

"I'll go," she informed him, smoothing her hair away from her face. "But you need to know something first."

Darcy risked walking toward him and rounding the bench to talk face-to-face, even though he still kept his focus on the ground between his legs.

"I won't be used as someone to pass the time and I won't be anyone's rebound. Yes, I'm attracted to you, but I can work and put that aside." Pulling in a deep breath of air and straightening her shoulders, she pushed forward. "What I can't do is get wrapped up in an affair that will leave me wanting more because I've been hurt before. I'm not going to lie, I'm still recovering from that betrayal. Right now I have to look out for myself because I have no one else. And as much as I'd like to take you up on what you were offering, I can't sacrifice my heart. I'm not a fling type of girl and I know what might be temporary pleasure to you would be much more than I can handle."

Slowly, Colin lifted his head, sought her gaze and nodded. "I won't touch you again. I won't kiss you and I'll make sure not to put you in a position where we're alone. Iris will be our focus. I have enough going on in my life without adding more complications."

Darcy fisted her hands at her sides. This is what she wanted him to say, right? She wanted him to treat her as a professional and not make her choose between her morals and her desires.

Yet now that he'd pulled up this invisible wall between them, Darcy couldn't help but wonder if she'd just be on the outside looking in at what she could've had. And this incident confirmed he was looking for an emotional crutch. Trouble was, she was, too, and hadn't even realized it.

Colin came to his feet, keeping his intense gaze on her. "You need to know that I never meant to make you feel like you were passing my time. I haven't been this attracted to a woman in years and damn if this timing isn't inconvenient. You're my nanny, for pity's sake. But I need to clarify one thing before you go upstairs and we table this discussion."

Darcy swallowed. "What?"

Softly, gently, Colin eased forward and touched his lips to hers for the briefest of moments before easing back. He touched her nowhere else, but just that simple kiss packed as much of a punch as when he'd practically taken her standing up.

"You deserve more than a fling, more than a quickie against the wall." His whispered tone washed over her. "There are just some promises I can't make."

Sliding her tongue over her bottom lip, she savored him. "Why did you kiss me again?"

Bright cobalt eyes locked her in place. "Because I'm selfish and I wanted one last taste."

Heart in her throat, Darcy resisted the urge to reach up and touch her tingling lips. He'd told her he had nothing else to give but a fling and she refused to settle for a few moments of pleasure. She was worth more than that and she'd promised herself after Thad left her with nothing that she wouldn't succumb to passion and charming men again.

On shaky legs, Darcy skirted around Colin and headed out of the gym. By the time she hit the steps, she was nearly running.

What would tomorrow bring, she wondered as she closed herself into her suite. Could they truly put every kiss, every touch behind them? Could she forget the fact she'd felt proof of his desire for her? That he'd touched her breast? They'd crossed into another level of intimacy and that wasn't something Darcy took lightly.

She was just about to change into her pajamas when a piercing cry came from the monitor.

Duty called. She only hoped duty wasn't calling up Colin, as well.

Eight

"How's the nanny working out?"

Colin cringed at his brother's question. For the past three days he'd managed to keep his promise to always have Iris present if he was in the room with Darcy. On the night he'd all but consumed Darcy, right after she had left the gym and Iris had started to cry, Colin had made his way upstairs and waited for a moment to make sure Darcy went into the nursery to care for his little girl.

Being so close, inhaling her fruity scent, seeing her handle Iris in such a loving, caring way, had had him questioning his sanity. They still had months to go and he was no closer to controlling his hormones than he was the moment he opened his door to her. But how could he kick her out when she and Iris were obviously the perfect pairing?

"That good, huh?" Stefan chuckled.

Colin gripped the phone, hating how his brother was across the globe and could still hone in on the truth.

"She's amazing with Iris," Colin stated. "I'm surprised how fast she's has taken to Darcy. Most times Iris prefers Darcy over me when we're playing a game. She climbs into her lap. It's like she's already choosing sides."

"And how have you taken to Darcy?" Stefan asked.

"She's the nanny. That's all."

Stefan's mocking chuckle filled the line. "Pretty defensive. I admit, I'm happy to hear it. I worried about you after Karina's death and then the backlash and speculation from the media. You closed in on yourself for a bit, but with this nanny, you sound a bit…agitated. You're showing signs of life again. You must like her on more than a professional level."

Colin watched out his office window as Darcy and Iris splashed around in the pool. Why did he torture himself by standing in here staring at her? Why did her faded, plain black one-piece do ridiculous things to his libido?

"That doesn't mean anything is going on with my nanny," he grumbled. Maybe he was so moody because nothing *was* going on with the nanny.

Darcy lifted Iris into her arms and climbed from the pool. With each step up, water sluiced off Darcy's curvy body. Watching as she bent to retrieve Iris's towel was pure hell. For several moments Colin took note of how Darcy cared for Iris, drying her off and making sure she was warm before focusing on herself.

And those few minutes were more than enough to have his body responding. He never should've gone so far the other night because now when he saw her, he could actually *feel* her. The combination was killing him.

"The ball is less than two weeks away," Stefan went on, oblivious to Colin's state. "If you're not here, the media will only try to crucify you more. Even though they won't be inside, they'll be hovering outside the palace to see who's here. Besides, word will get out and rumors will fly."

"I'm well aware of how the media would handle my absence."

Colin turned from the window. The last thing he wanted to think about was returning to Galini Isle for a ball hosting the monarchies from surrounding countries. The only bright light was that his best friend, Luc, would be in attendance, and since the man had recently gotten engaged Colin wanted to congratulate the happy couple in person.

But right now he wanted to forget all duties, all pressing issues that demanded his attention. Still, if he didn't go, Stefan was right, it would be like throwing gasoline on the proverbial fire. He just wished he weren't so confused. He was happy here, albeit sexually frustrated. He enjoyed living in California, but he also missed his brother. And being away from his duties had Colin wondering what his late parents would've thought of his actions. Would they support his decision if he chose to walk away? Would they be disappointed?

If he ended up going to the ball, he'd have to reveal his true identity to Darcy. Traveling back for the event would be tiring and he'd want her with him to help with Iris. A small sliver of him wanted her to know, he wanted to see how she'd treat him if she knew the truth. He liked to think she'd still be the same Darcy he'd come to respect and desire.

"I'll let you know what I decide," Colin stated as he headed down the hall and upstairs to his bedroom. "I'll give you a few days' notice for security."

"They're already on standby," Stefan confirmed. "They're ready to come to LA and hover over you. I had to tell them to stand down more than once."

"Keeping my identity a secret would be kind of hard with royal guards surrounding the perimeter of my home."

"Which is why I'm honoring your wishes and letting you have some privacy. But you'll have to make some decisions soon and I'm not just referring to the ball."

Colin closed his bedroom door and toed off his shoes. "You'll be the first to know what I decide. Right now I have more pressing matters to deal with."

Stefan chuckled. "I'm sure you do."

Colin disconnected the call, cutting off Stefan's mocking laugh. Quickly changing his clothes, Colin decided he was taking charge of everything in his personal life starting now. He was torn up over the decision involving his royal status, but he refused to have his libido all out of control, too. He was going to take what he wanted… and he wanted Darcy Cooper.

How would he know if whatever they were feeling was something real? Colin had told her he couldn't give her more, but those words had been spoken out of fear. He didn't want her to think he was using her, but he ached for her in ways he hadn't known possible.

Lust was something he remembered from his bachelor days, but Darcy was worth more than that shallow emotion and damn if it wasn't complicating everything right now.

He'd given her the space he promised. He'd watched her, kept his hands to himself and had not made any innuendos whatsoever. His self-control was choking him to death.

Their connection was obvious. Why couldn't they spend these next few months enjoying each other? Surely by the time he was ready to move on they'd be tired of each other.

Seduction would be the key to winning her over and he had every intention of pulling out all stops and making her just as achy and needy as he was. This entire plan was a risk because he knew he wanted to explore more, but what would happen if they reached the point of no return?

Iris wasn't acting sleepy at all after the swim and brief snack, so Darcy slipped back into the pool. Schedules were important for babies, but so was soaking up all the fun and memories they could. Delaying Iris's nap by half an hour wouldn't hurt. The other day the nap had been put off for too long, hence the mega tantrum, but Darcy had learned what Iris's nap meltdown threshold was.

Easing Iris into her baby raft with canopy, Darcy held onto the side and swished the float around in the water. Iris squealed and clapped her hands with each twist. Her little legs were working back and forth beneath the water. Darcy couldn't help but laugh as an immeasurable amount of joy filled her heart. There truly was nothing like a baby's sweet laugh. Darcy watched Iris's face as she led her further into the pool. Those bright eyes really sparkled in the sunlight…and reminded Darcy how much Iris looked like her daddy.

Dunking down lower to get her shoulders wet, Darcy tried her hardest to keep images of Colin from her mind. Of course the harder she fought, the more he kept creeping into her thoughts. It was so, so difficult to keep her professional feelings separate from her personal ones.

Darcy loved Iris, enjoyed every moment she got to spend with her. But she also thoroughly enjoyed Colin's company on a level that she hadn't expected. Her mind and her heart were in agreement for once, telling her that feeling anything for the man was a bad idea.

A flash of him doing chin-ups with one muscular arm, the memory of how he'd stared so intently into her eyes the instant before he claimed her mouth flooded her thoughts. Then there was the other side of him that also played through her mind. The man was an amazing father, always wanting to give Iris her bath, wanting to spend so much time alone with his little girl. The smile he gave Iris was unlike anything Darcy had ever seen. The man was truly in love with his daughter.

How could Darcy not be attracted to all facets of Colin? He may still be quite mysterious, and he still had that expensive SUV in the drive waiting for her to drive it, but he had her so torn up, she had no choice but to want to know more.

For the past three days he'd stayed away from her unless they were with Iris. Part of her hated the barrier she'd placed between them, but the other part knew the separation was the best thing for her. Between focusing on her business and reminding herself she needed to guard her heart, Darcy couldn't afford to fall into a fling no matter how she desired to do just that.

Memories of how amazing his weight had felt pressed against her as his mouth consumed her would just have to suffice. Unfortunately, right now, all the memories were doing was leaving her achier.

"How can I stay inside and work when there's so much fun going on out here?"

Darcy froze the same instant Iris squealed for her daddy.

No. No. No. She didn't want to turn around because if she did she knew she'd see Colin wearing some type of swimming trunks that only showcased his impressive set of abs and all of his other magnificent muscles.

She wanted to hide, to instantly be poolside and wrapped in a towel so he didn't have to see her get out of the water with her thighs jiggling and her rounded stomach that had stretched her "miracle suit" beyond the promised miracle.

From the corner of her eye, Darcy spotted a flash of black just as Colin dove headfirst into the pool. What was he thinking coming out here with her? Yes, Iris was present as they'd discussed, but he wasn't naive. He knew exactly what coming out here half naked would do to her. What type of game was he playing?

When Colin surfaced, much closer to her than she'd anticipated, he swiped the water back from his forehead and smiled at Iris.

"Hey, baby. Are you having fun?"

With Colin's hands on the raft, Darcy eased back. No way was she going to accidentally entangle her legs with his because she'd quite possibly start to whimper, which would completely override the speech she'd given him three days ago.

"I'll just let you two have some time alone."

Darcy made her way to the steps. There was no good way to get out without Colin seeing her ancient, thread-bare suit pasted against every dip and roll. Best to just get out, fake a confidence she didn't own and run like hell for the nearest towel.

"You don't have to get out because I'm here."

Darcy knew full well the man had his eyes on her, but she didn't turn to meet his gaze until she was properly wrapped like a terrycloth sausage.

"I'm not," she told him, lying through her smile.

Colin adjusted the canopy over Iris to keep her shaded. "Are you going to run every time you get uncomfortable?"

Gripping her towel at her breasts, Darcy straightened her shoulders. "I'm not running."

"But you're uncomfortable," he said with a smirk. "Your rules, Darcy. You can cancel them at any time and take what we both want for as long as we're here."

No, she couldn't.

"She'll need a nap soon," Darcy told him, dodging the obvious topic. "Just bring her in and I'll get her all dried off and ready. If you don't object, I plan on making almond-crusted chicken and grilled veggies for dinner."

"No objections here. At least not on dinner."

The man was so confusing. One minute he was moody and kissing her so she had to put on the brakes. The next minute he was agreeing to her terms and then he tried to muddle her mind by flashing that chest that should be enshrined in gold.

Darcy marched into the house, not in the mood to play whatever game he was offering. He had issues of his own, at least he said he did, and so did she. They had a temporary working relationship. Pursuing anything beyond that agreement would be wrong and settle so much awkwardness between them they'd never find their way out.

The last time she'd fallen hard for a man, she'd let him into her life, into her business because her grandmother thought he was perfect for Darcy. Darcy had trusted her hormones and ignored common sense for too long.

She'd let business and pleasure mix once before and she'd be paying for that mistake for the rest of her life.

Nine

Darcy may want him to give up, but until he quit seeing desire in her eyes each time she looked at him, he wasn't backing down. She'd been burned before and now Colin was paying for another man's sins.

She may have asked for space, and he wasn't one to go against a woman's wishes, but that didn't mean he still couldn't get what he wanted.

True, the house was huge so giving her space wasn't necessarily a problem. But their physical connection was so intense that the walls seemed to close in on them.

At first he'd fought the attraction, then he'd resigned himself to the fact it wasn't going away. Then he'd wondered if they could both heal by seeking comfort in each other. But as that thought ran through his mind, he couldn't help but wonder if there was something more building here.

He sounded like a woman thinking through all of his feelings and emotions, but Darcy was bringing out a side he hadn't known existed and he didn't want to cheapen whatever this was to a potential fling. They both deserved more than that, yet he couldn't help but want her and there was no point in trying to fight the tension anymore.

He'd failed in his attempt at seduction at the pool earlier today. He thought for sure spending time with her in a more relaxed setting with Iris would soften her. Now Darcy was up in her room and he was once again in the gym. He couldn't even come into this room anymore without seeing her pressed against the wall, flushed from arousal and looking up at him beneath heavy lids.

There had to be a way to break down the barrier she'd encompassed herself in. There were so many layers he'd yet to peel away. He wanted to know why she only wore three outfits and rotated them. He wanted to know why she was sewing things in her spare time and why she sneaked down to the gym early in the mornings before Iris woke when she thought he was still asleep. On a rare occasion he would catch her searching the internet for more recipes. Seems that cooking wasn't just a fun hobby for her as she'd stated, but a true passion.

Still, she'd made it apparent she didn't want to be alone with him so talking to her was damn near impossible, because when Iris was around he wanted to devote his time and attention to his daughter.

Colin pushed the bar back into locked position and sat up on the bench. Swiping a hand across his forehead, he cleared away the sweat as a brilliant plan entered his mind. He was going to have to get creative, to make sure there was no way she could run from what was happening between them. And something was happening whether she wanted to admit it or not.

Sliding his cell from his shorts pocket, Colin quickly did a search for the number he'd used when he'd first contacted her and placed the call. "Colin?" she answered, confusion lacing her tone.

He chuckled. "Yeah."

"Why are you calling my cell?"

A nugget of doubt slid through his mind, but he pressed on because he'd never backed away from a challenge.

"To talk."

Silence settled over the line. Maybe this was a mistake, but it was a risk he was willing to take. Hadn't he always been a daredevil? Hence his accident and recovery. "Darcy?"

"I'm here." She let out a sigh and a faint sound of sheets rustling filtered through the line. "What do you want to talk about? We're in the same house. You *are* in the house, right?"

He came to his feet and reached for a towel hanging over a weight machine. "I'm in the gym." Colin mopped off his face and neck, and flung the towel into the bin in the corner. "Did I wake you?"

"No. I had just turned off my light and crawled into bed."

Closing his eyes, he could easily picture her spread out on his guest bed, her dark, rich hair spilling over the crisp, white sheets. What did she wear to bed? A T-shirt? Something silky, perhaps? Nothing?

"Is everything okay?" she asked. "I'm a little confused as to why you're calling me."

"I want to hear your voice."

Colin shut off the light in the gym and headed toward his office. Only a small desk lamp lit the room. He knew he had to keep control of this conversation or she'd hang up.

"Tell me about your life before you came here."

Darcy laughed. "What about it? I work with kids and love to cook—that's about as exciting as I am."

She was so much more and he'd be the man to show her. Whoever she'd been with last was a jerk who hadn't realized what a treasure he had.

"You have friends, yes?" he asked.

"Yes. I was living with my best friend before I came here. What about you? You're from Greece, you're an amazing father, you keep simple working hours, but that's all I know."

"I'm not talking about me." He sank onto the leather sofa, leaned back and shut his eyes. He wanted to hear all about her, wanted her sultry, sleepy voice to wash over him. "We're talking about you."

"This Q and A can go both ways," she replied with a hint of a challenge. "How about we take turns? I'll go first. Why are you still trying to seduce me?"

"Wow. You sure you don't want to lead in with something lighter? My favorite color is red and my favorite sport is rock climbing."

"You're dodging the question," she stated. "You are the one who started this game."

"Fine. I want you." He shifted on the couch and propped his feet up on the cushions, then leaned back on the arm. "Why are you afraid to be alone with me?"

"Because you're sneaky and I wouldn't be able to resist you."

Colin smiled, settling a hand on his bare abs. "I'm not sneaky, I'm honest."

"That's debatable." She sighed and Colin imagined her upstairs in the dark, aching for him as much as he was for her. "It's my turn. How did you injure yourself?"

"I was rock climbing and made an error in judgment. Trusted the wrong rock."

Darcy's gasp had his own gut clenching. He was actually glad for the head trauma because he didn't remember the fall in any way. A minor blessing.

"You could've been killed," she cried.

"I nearly was. The doctors weren't so sure at first, but once they knew I would live, they told my wife I would never walk again."

"You're remarkable," she whispered.

As much as his ego loved her stroking it, Colin really didn't want her pity because of his accident. He wanted her, no question. But he understood she was burned in the past and he knew she was struggling for money, so she definitely had more at stake than he did.

"Tell me about the jerk who broke your heart."

Darcy groaned. "Why don't you ask something else?"

"Because my backup question is me wanting to know how fast I can be in your room with nothing between us but the darkness."

"You're not playing fair," she muttered.

Colin gritted his teeth. "Baby, I'm not playing at all. I'm tired of playing. We've danced around this attraction for too long and I'm going insane."

"Fine. We'll discuss the ex."

He didn't know if he wanted to laugh or cry at the reply.

Darcy's deep inhale had Colin eagerly waiting, but knowing he'd probably want to hunt this guy down and make him pay. Colin had no reason to be jealous, no reason to be so territorial...yet he was.

"My ex took every single dime I had to my name. I trusted him with more than my heart, he was my new business partner after my grandmother passed, and he betrayed me. Apparently he had another girlfriend and was using my money to buy her presents. And by presents I mean trips, a car, a condo." Darcy paused and Colin wasn't sure if there was more or if she was waiting for him to reply. After another soft sigh, she continued. "He not only ruined my business, he killed my dream of adopting a child."

Colin tamped down his anger. Whoever this bastard was, Colin loathed the man and wished for about five minutes alone with him. The fact he'd stolen all of her money was a sin in itself, but to know Darcy wanted to adopt was a morsel of information he was shocked she'd revealed.

Did she have a dream of adopting because she was compassionate toward kids and wanted to save them? Did she not plan on marrying? Or was there something medical that prevented her from having her own?

She'd answered one question and triggered a multitude of others.

But now he realized why Darcy had so little with her, why she was so upset over the new car and him having hers taken away without asking first. Her ex had thrown money around, albeit hers, and had used the funds to further his own desires. This woman was a fighter and she wasn't about to take handouts from the likes of Colin. How could he not admire how strong-willed she was?

Fortunately, he'd gotten her car back, now fixed, and it sat in one of the bays of his second garage behind the house. But even though he'd smoothed things over with Darcy, Colin didn't want to stop there. He was already in deep with her, so why not keep going to satisfy his curiosity?

"What's his name?" Colin asked.

"I'm sorry?"

Colin fisted his hand over his abs. "The lowlife who stole from you. I want his name."

"It's not your turn."

Her tone left no room for argument, so he waited for her to ask her question.

"You're a man of mystery. What's your profession?"

"I'm a CEO of sorts." Okay, there was no good way to answer, but he was a leader…for now. "I manage a large group back in Greece."

There. That sounded believable, didn't it? It was his turn to ask a question, but he wasn't wasting it on her ex's name. He could find that out later and take care of things. Right now, he wanted to dig deeper, to get to the point of his call. Priorities.

"What are you wearing?" he asked.

Darcy's soft laugh enveloped him as if she stood before him. Damn, he wanted to touch her, to kiss her, to feel her beneath him. He'd only known her several weeks and she all but consumed him. Obviously she had no clue the power she held over him.

"Are we playing that game now?" she all but mocked. "I'm wearing a black, silky chemise that leaves very little to the imagination."

Colin swallowed, the image now burned in his mind. "You're lying."

"You'll never know. What are you wearing?"

"Shorts and sweat. I just finished my workout where all I could do was see you pinned against the wall with your eyes closed, your mouth on mine and my hand up your shirt."

Darcy sighed. "What are you doing to me?" she whispered. "I can't keep up with how quick you turn me inside out."

"That goes both ways, *erastis*."

"What does that mean?"

"Come down to my office and I'll tell you." More like show her.

"I can't, Colin. You're making this so difficult for me. You have to understand that just because I want something, doesn't mean I can take it. Apparently you're used to getting what you want."

"I always get what I want."

"Sounds like a threat."

Colin smiled. "It's a promise."

"Tell me about your wife."

Colin eased up and shook his head. No way was he getting into how he'd let his wife down when he'd lived his reckless lifestyle and then pushed her away when he'd truly needed her most. He totally took the blame for their failed marriage because he'd been too proud, too stubborn to let her just help him through his rough time. Which was beyond ironic since he'd hired Darcy to assist him because he'd finally come to the realization he couldn't do it all.

Maybe it was time to break the cycle. To finally let someone in and keep his stubborn pride on the back burner. But, right now he had other, more pressing matters.

"Let's table that discussion for another time."

"Count on it," she said around a yawn.

"I'll let you go," he told her. "I need to hit the shower before I head to bed."

"I'll just be lying here in my chemise, dreaming."

Colin fisted his hand and came to his feet. "You're getting too good at this. Better watch what you say, you're playing with fire."

"You lit the match."

When she hung up, Colin stood in his office with a painful arousal and a ridiculous grin on his face. Yeah, he was used to getting what he wanted and he wanted Darcy in his bed.

And he would have her there. It was only a matter of time.

Darcy hadn't slept at all. Once Colin had started with the "what are you wearing" game her mind had formed so many fantasies, leaving her restless and aroused.

She hadn't lied when she said she was lying in her bed wearing a black chemise. She actually owned two. Sleeping in something so soft, so flawless gliding over her skin always made her feel more feminine. After dealing with children all day and spending most of her waking hours dealing with various problems and parents, she had to stay in touch with her femininity even if she wasn't sleeping with anyone.

Which was why last night's little chat with Colin left her aching in ways she'd never thought possible. She'd been with one man, and even during their intimacy Darcy had never felt an inkling of what she'd felt last night on the phone with Colin.

The man wasn't just chipping away at the defensive wall she'd erected, he was blasting through it with a sledgehammer. He'd started opening up just a touch over the past several weeks and he'd become playful, flirty and flat-out blatant regarding what he wanted.

Because she hadn't slept very well, she was awake even earlier than usual and in the gym. Of course, during her entire workout all she could picture was Colin down here last night. How long had he been sweating and working out while thinking of her? Did he regret calling her? Had he assumed she'd come running to him and they'd enter into this affair without giving the consequences another thought?

When she glanced at the time on her phone, she realized she'd been working out for over an hour. A great improvement over the first day. Granted, she'd had a hard time concentrating with Colin flexing his perfectly honed muscles all over the place.

If she could keep up this regime while she was here and continue eating healthily, she just may be on the fast track to getting her life back. In such a short time she already felt better about herself and had more energy.

More energy was something she would most definitely need if she was going to continue to battle Colin and his bold advances.

Darcy headed back upstairs, careful as always to be quiet while Iris and Colin slept. Grabbing a quick shower would give her time to get her thoughts in order before facing Colin. She knew the mutual desire would not go away. And as if fighting her urges wasn't enough, he wasn't playing fair. How could she keep putting up a strong front when he'd pretty much laid his cards on the table?

Lathering up her hair, she slid the strands through her fingers beneath the spray. She'd been worried about getting entangled with Colin after her last romance debacle, but Colin was so different from her ex. She only had to look at his interactions with Iris to see how loving he was. And he wasn't out to use her for anything because at this point he knew she had nothing to give.

Maybe he wanted her for no other reason than to satisfy his curiosity…just as she felt with him.

Darcy rinsed her body and shut off the water. Quickly she toweled off. She'd just pulled her hair into a messy topknot when fussy noises blared through the monitors.

Iris was crankier in the mornings than any other baby she'd dealt with. Of course, Darcy hadn't personally worked with a vast number of children under two, but Iris was certainly special. The toddler was happiest when she got her food. Darcy could totally relate.

Darcy wrestled her sports bra back on and yanked up her shorts; she didn't have time to find something else. When she turned the corner of her room and hit the doorway of the nursery, Colin was lifting Iris from her crib. That toned back with ink scrolling over his shoulder continued to mock her, because every time she saw it, she wanted to trace it…with her tongue.

The way he gently spoke to Iris, the way he held such a delicate little girl against his hard, strong body really hit

Darcy. Even rumpled from sleep, Colin Alexander was a man who demanded attention without saying a word.

When he turned and caught her gaze, his eyes did some evaluating of their own. Darcy was reminded she stood before him in only her sweaty sports bra and shorts. Not her best look, considering she wasn't perfectly proportioned or toned in any way.

"I just got out of the shower and threw on the closest thing," Darcy stated, keeping her eyes locked on Colin as he continued to close the gap between them. "Give me one minute to change and I can take her and feed her."

Colin's limp was a bit more pronounced this morning. Most likely he'd slept wrong. How had the man slept after that call? Maybe she was more revved up with this sexual tension than he was.

"You're flushed." His eyes traveled to the scoop in her bra and back up. "Looks good on you."

"Colin—"

"Go change," he urged. "I'll feed Iris and you better be fully dressed next time you're around me."

Darcy stared at him for another minute, which was a minute too long because he reached out, trailed a fingertip across her collarbone.

"Go, *erastis,* before I take what I want."

That was the second time he'd called her that and she wanted to know what it meant. She had a feeling it was a term of endearment or something sexy because his voice took on a whole other tone when he said it. She was drowning where this man was concerned and she knew it was just a matter of time before she succumbed to all of the desire and passion that kept swirling around them.

Darcy turned and all but ran into her adjoining bath. The man was killing her. She dug out a pair of jeans and her favorite pink T-shirt before heading back downstairs, praying she'd have control over her emotions. She should be praying Colin would have control over his.

She didn't see them in the kitchen, but the sound of the patio doors sliding open drew her attention. Through the wide window she spotted Colin with a banana in one hand and Iris holding onto the other as he led her out onto the stone patio. He'd just placed her on the settee when he lost his balance and went down. Darcy ran out the door and was crouched at his side in an instant.

Had he reinjured himself? Worry flooded her. How she would get him back up without hurting him further?

With a muttered curse in his native tongue, Colin pushed her away. "Don't. Just take her inside and feed her."

Darcy reached for him. "Let me help you up."

"Leave me be," he shouted, meeting and holding her gaze. "I'm not paying you to coddle me, I'm paying you to care for Iris."

Darcy jerked back and came to her feet. Iris started to climb off the chair and Darcy reached down, taking the little girl's hand.

"You're right," Darcy replied, swallowing the hurt. "I'll remember my place from now on."

Colin shifted and stood, wincing as he did so. Even though his jab sliced deep, Darcy waited until he got his bearings. Just as he opened his mouth to speak, Darcy turned.

"Come on, baby girl." Darcy swiped the banana from the ground where Colin had dropped it when he fell. "Let's get you some breakfast."

No way would Darcy make the mistake of trying to get close and help Colin again. If he wanted to run hot and cold with his emotions, he could do so with someone else. Darcy wasn't here as an outlet for his frustrations and anger over his accident.

Ten

Disgrace was a bitter, nasty pill to swallow.

After his spill that morning, Colin didn't know what he was angrier about, himself for falling and possibly hurting Iris or the fact that Darcy was there to witness his humiliation. He'd taken his anger and embarrassment out on her for no reason.

Hadn't he hired a nanny in case something like this happened? The real possibility that he would fall in the presence of, or God forbid, while holding Iris, had been his main concern. What he hadn't planned on was having his hormones thrown into the mix. And he hadn't been forthcoming with Darcy about his injury because he'd prayed there wouldn't be a mishap while she was here. He didn't want to be seen as weak or crippled.

Colin sneaked into the house through the back door after Darcy had taken Iris in for breakfast. After he'd showered and gotten his damn leg and back under control with some stretches his doctor and therapist had shown him, Colin felt somewhat human again.

This morning his goal had been to carry on the plan of seduction that he'd started on the phone last night. Then his past had come back to bite him when he'd fallen, completely erasing any impact he may have had on Darcy last night because of his inability to handle this entire situation like a mature adult. Wow, wasn't he just the king of all things sexy? Now instead of Darcy viewing him as a strong, confident man, she saw him as a cripple, as someone who couldn't even care for himself, let alone a child.

If the paparazzi back in Galini Isle ever caught a glimpse of his inability to stand on his own two feet at times, he'd be ridiculed, questioned and thrust into the limelight even more. They'd already speculated that he and Karina were falling apart, but since her death, they hadn't left him alone and he was sick of the pity, the way they portrayed him as helpless and lost.

He was an Alexander. They were strong men, determined and focused. Nothing would stand in the way of him getting everything he wanted.

Needing to get back on track and spend time with his daughter, Colin figured today would be a great day for a little outing. Darcy might not like men who threw their weight and money around, but he wanted to treat her. Out of every woman he'd ever known, Darcy most definitely deserved to be pampered, even if only for a few hours.

If she was working for him, then she was going to be treated like royalty.

Which reminded him, he needed to have a serious talk with her. He'd decided to attend the ball and he wanted Darcy to come with him. That conversation would have to take place at just the right time. He didn't want her to feel as if he'd lied to her…though he had by omission.

Just as Colin reached the bottom of the stairs, he heard

Darcy's laughter and Iris's sweet giggle. That combination slid a new emotion through him—one he wasn't sure he could identify and one he wasn't sure he wanted to.

When he found them on the floor in the living room, Colin stopped in the wide, arched doorway to take in the scene. Days ago the sight of freshly picked flowers, obviously from the landscaping, all over his floor would've had him enraged. But now, seeing those vibrant petals in Darcy's and Iris's hair had him smiling. These two were like kindred spirits and he could easily get wrapped up in watching them.

There he went again, sliding down that slippery slope even further toward Darcy. He had lost control somewhere between opening the door that first day and the first time she'd verbally matched him with her banter.

"Daddy!"

Iris squealed, scooped up all the flowers her little hands could hold and sprinkled them on top of Darcy's head.

"Deedee pitty," she exclaimed, clapping her hands.

Darcy glanced his way, but quickly darted away. "I'm Deedee. It's much easier for her to say."

Colin hated how Darcy wouldn't even look at him. He'd done that to her when he'd sworn he wouldn't hurt anyone again over this injury. Because of his inexcusable actions, he'd driven a wedge between them.

The fact his daughter had adopted a nickname for Darcy added another layer of bonding that was already wrapped so tightly around them. All part of the nanny-child relationship, nothing more—or at least that's what he needed to keep telling himself. Darcy wasn't part of this family; her presence was temporary.

"Darcy, go get yourself and Iris ready. We're going out for the day." He moved into the room and slid his hand over Iris's dark curls. "I'll work on cleaning this mess up."

Darcy came to her feet, catching the flowers as they

fell down her chest. "I'm sorry. We went for a little walk and picked some flowers from the gardens. I planned on cleaning—"

Colin held up a hand, cutting off her words, and offered a smile so she didn't think he was angry or a complete jerk after how he'd treated her earlier. "I've got it. Really. Go on."

"Okay." She bent down, lifted Iris into her arms and turned back to him. Finally, she met his eyes with a worry he didn't want. "Are you feeling all right?"

She didn't come out and ask about the fall, but he knew that's exactly what she was referring to.

He gave her a brief nod. "Do you want to know where we're going?" he asked.

Darcy's lids lowered. "My place isn't to ask questions. You're paying me to care for Iris, so I'm going to get us ready."

Colin absolutely loathed the words he'd spouted off to her earlier out of anger and humiliation. There was no taking them back now that they were out in the open. All he could do was show her he wasn't the ogre she thought he'd become.

Darcy left the room without another word. He needed to apologize, but words would only go so far. He would show her that he wasn't a terrible person. He'd make her see that she didn't have to work her butt off for nothing.

And by the time she left him at the end of her term, she'd never have to worry about her business or her finances again. If he did nothing else, he'd make damn sure of that.

He had to be kidding. That dress—as stunning as it was—cost more than an entire month's worth of groceries. Colin had talked her into shopping, but she'd had no idea he'd pull her into the most expensive store she'd ever seen in her entire life.

After working for him for several weeks now, one would think she'd have the courage to stand her ground and decline.

On the flipside, though, she'd discovered with each passing day that Colin was impossible to resist.

"At least try it on," he urged, holding up the elegant, one-shouldered, bright blue dress.

Darcy wasn't in the mood to be shopping, but Colin had claimed this was just another work incentive and he truly wanted her to have new clothes. After the morning they'd had, she really had no clue why they were here.

"I won't wear that dress," she told him, though she loved it. Being stubborn could go both ways.

On a sigh, he hung the dress back up and inched closer. "I already apologized, but I'll keep saying it until you realize I am honestly sorry for how I reacted. I know you were only trying to help, but my pride usually doesn't allow me to let others come to my rescue."

That she could understand. She, too, had her pride and he had come and apologized shortly after she'd completely ignored him.

"I just find it convenient you're getting me clothes today and calling them incentives," she shot back, talking quietly so the salesclerk didn't hear. Iris squealed and chewed on the baby doll in her stroller, oblivious to the turmoil.

"I'd planned on this anyway," he told her. "The timing is just wrong. If you're not in the mood, we can do this another day. I figured we could both use a break and to get out and do something fun."

Something fun? What man found shopping fun? Darcy chewed on her bottom lip as she considered how to approach this. She could be childish, the way he had been the other day, or she could accept the olive branch he was extending.

"Fine," she conceded.

With a wide smile, Colin lifted the dress back off the rack. "What size do you need?"

Darcy laughed, gripping the handle on the Cadillac of strollers. "Nice try, buddy. I'm not telling you my size. It's not in the single digits and I doubt that dress will look good on my frame."

His eyes scanned her body. "Your frame looks fine and you'll never know how it looks if you don't try it on."

Darcy shook her head and turned toward another rack. "Everything in here is so pricey. Why are we even here?"

Colin's hand came around, gripping hers over the handle. Darcy threw a glance over her shoulder and saw he was much closer than she'd thought.

"Pick out whatever you want." He held up a hand when she started to argue. "I'll take Iris to the toy store next door. Text me when you're done. The clerk has my credit card number."

Darcy closed her eyes. "There's nothing I need that will take me that long. Just give me a couple minutes."

"You may not need it, but you deserve it." His thumb stroked over her hand. "I'm not trying to buy you. I'm trying to put a smile on your face, to let you have whatever you want for the entire day. I'd bet my entire savings that you haven't bought anything for yourself for years."

Darcy glanced down to their hands. The contrast between his dark skin and her paleness was minor in comparison to their many differences.

"I'm not sleeping with you."

Colin jerked her around, his fingers digging into her shoulders. "I'm not offering this shopping trip as a bribe, Darcy. You going to bed with me has nothing to do with this. I'm here because I want to give you nice things while you're with me. If you want to leave everything when you go, then do that and I'll donate the clothes to charity. You were told up front you'd be getting bonuses along the way. Don't argue."

"Yet again, does anyone ever tell you no?" she asked.

A smirk flirted around the corners of his mouth. "You're the only one who keeps trying."

On a sigh, Darcy closed her eyes and nodded. "Fine. I'll pick out a couple of things. Seriously, though, we could find a cheaper store."

His eyes traveled over the racks, the displays and mannequins. "Do you not like this store?"

Darcy laughed. "Everything in here is gorgeous. I just think we could find one with smaller numbers on the price tags."

"Don't look at the price tag. Focus on how stunning you'll look, how beautiful you'll feel." Colin's intense gaze lasted a minute longer than she was comfortable with before he moved around her and gripped the stroller. "Take your time. I've got Miss Iris."

Darcy stared at his retreating back. He paused at the counter and spoke to the pretty female employee. Of course she batted her lashes and laughed at whatever Colin said before he slipped out the front door. The man seemed to have that effect on every female.

Colin was way too charming. Not only did he have that devastatingly handsome, sexy arrogance about him, he had a beautiful baby girl. All he had to do was be the loving, doting father he was and women's ovaries started weeping.

The burn in her throat had her swallowing. Colin and Iris were missing the female figure in their lives and Darcy was missing the family she'd always dreamed of having. Yet they could never mesh together because... well, just because.

She was his employee, she had goals of her own and right now she needed to get her business back up and running. Added to that, Colin made it clear he would probably be leaving in a few months to go back to Greece.

Darcy nearly laughed. She'd never have the chance to set foot on Colin's home turf. If he wanted to treat her like Cinderella today, she would let him. For once she would let someone else take care of her, do something nice for her.

By the time Darcy finished trying on clothes, she had way more in her want pile than in her "no" pile.

"Miss Cooper," the clerk called from the other side of the thick floor-to-ceiling curtain. "I have some shoes pulled and jewelry for you to look at once you're done. Can I get you any other sizes?"

Shoes? Jewelry? When had she ever purchased an entire outfit complete with head-to-toe accessories?

"My sizes are fine," she called back. "I'll be right out."

When Darcy stepped out of the dressing room, she resisted the urge to adjust her simple V-neck T-shirt. She didn't fit in this place and the clothes she'd tried on certainly wouldn't work for her daily activities relating to Iris's care. But if she left with nothing, she knew Colin would drag her somewhere else.

"What can I take to the counter for you?"

Darcy glanced to the perfectly polished clerk with her carefully applied makeup and elegantly coiffed hair. Darcy glanced back into the dressing room where she'd hung everything up.

"I'll take that blue dress for now," she told the clerk. "I need to think about everything else."

She hated to admit it, but the blue dress did hug her curves and made her feel beautiful. She didn't mind said curves or her figure so much, and with her workout sessions she was actually starting to see a difference in her body. The extra boost of confidence had her smiling.

Colin had liked the dress, so that's what she'd go with for now. And damn if he wasn't right. It had looked good on her, better than she'd ever imagined...not that she'd admit such a revelation to Colin.

"What size shoe are you? I was guessing a seven."

Amazing how the woman was dead-on, but Darcy shook her head. "Oh, I couldn't—"

"Mr. Alexander made me promise to add shoes and any jewelry you wanted to the outfits you chose." A soft smile spread across her face. "He also said not to argue and worry about the cost."

Darcy couldn't help but laugh. Colin thought he had all his bases covered. Biting her bottom lip, Darcy pondered what she should actually do versus what she wanted to do. She could go ahead and get the things Colin requested. If she didn't wear anything, he could return them and get his money back.

"I should also tell you, he also made me promise you'd leave with no less than three outfits." With her hands clasped in front of her bright pink capris and crisp white shirt, the clerk nodded toward the dress in Darcy's hand. "He also said you weren't leaving without that blue dress, so I'm glad you already chose that one."

Three outfits? The staggering cost of all that would be beyond ridiculous. Outfits, as well as accessories and shoes. What else did Colin have planned for her? Buying clothes and loaning her a brand-new car were both so personal. When he'd initially said bonuses, Darcy had assumed he'd meant the monetary kind. She really should've asked him for specifics, but she'd been too concerned about keeping her job and making it past the trial period.

"To be honest, I don't have a need for fancy clothes," she told the clerk. "I love everything in here, but I'm a nanny and caring for a child doesn't necessarily require bling and stilettos."

The clerk laughed, reached out and patted her arm. "Tell you what, let's look around and I'm sure we can find something to make you both happy. You can still be fashionable and comfortable while caring for that sweet baby."

An hour later the young worker, whom Darcy now knew as Carly, had delivered on her promise. New shorts, basic tops and adorable sandals were neatly wrapped in tissue paper and placed in two large bags…along with that blue dress Darcy would never have a use for. She had drawn the line at jewelry, though. There was no need for earrings or a necklace for Iris to tug on, not to mention Darcy wasn't preparing herself for a fashion show.

She shot Colin a text, telling him she was finished and she'd come to the toy store to meet him. After thanking Carly for all of her help, Darcy headed out the door. So much money spent for two bags worth of clothing, but he'd insisted, and to be honest she'd never let someone splurge on her before. Colin had been adamant he wanted to do this for her and she was done being stubborn.

Perhaps she was being selfish, but life had thrown so much crap at her, it was nice to have someone refreshing waltz into her life. She truly believed he wasn't buying her to get her into bed. If he'd pursued harder at home, she would have caved and they both knew it. Getting new clothes certainly didn't make her want to jump him. No, she'd wanted to do that from the second he'd opened his door and greeted her.

The bright sun warmed her face as soon as she stepped onto the sidewalk. A familiar scream of delight had Darcy turning her attention down the sidewalk to where Iris sat in her stroller, hugging a brand new elephant in one hand and a waving rather large lollipop in the other. Seeing the big, wide smile across her precious face, Darcy didn't know if she'd ever seen Iris happier.

Colin, on the other hand, looked as though he could use a stiff drink. His hair stood on end as if he'd run his fingers through it for the past hour, his lids were heavy and he appeared to be in a daze.

Darcy held back her laugh, but couldn't stop from smiling as he moved closer. "Looks like you had a good time at the toy store."

Colin's eyes snapped to hers as if he'd just realized she stood near him. "Do you know what they have in that place?"

"I'm assuming toys," Darcy stated.

"From floor to ceiling." He continued to stare as if he'd been traumatized. "But it's not just toys. There's candy. Everything lights up or sings or dances to get your attention. It's not even safe to walk through the line to check out. She was reaching for everything. It's like they don't even care about the parents."

Darcy did laugh now. "Surely this wasn't your first trip to a toy store with her."

Colin blinked, raking a hand over his face. "Actually, it was."

The statement shocked Darcy. Perhaps his late wife had always taken Iris toy shopping. Maybe they had another nanny where they'd lived before and she did all of that. Or maybe someone just delivered toys and they hadn't taken Iris to any stores yet.

"Why don't you take these bags and I'll push Iris." She didn't wait for him to answer as she thrust the sacks into his hands. "Let's head home and I'll start dinner. You look like you need to get back to safer territory. We can't have all those plush toys terrorizing you anymore."

Colin glared at her. "Now you're mocking me. We don't

need to go home. I just needed to escape that store with my life."

Darcy started pushing Iris down the sidewalk toward the SUV—the one he'd bought for her use. Yes, the man was used to getting what he wanted, in one sneaky way or another.

"I'm not mocking you," she told him. "I'm just stating a fact based on the evidence you presented to me." Colin grunted in response. Darcy smiled as she loaded Iris into the car seat. "What do you say we head over to the park and let Iris play while you recover? Then we can go home and I'll make dinner."

Colin seemed to think about the suggestion before a wide grin spread across his face. "That's a great idea. It's a beautiful day. We might as well spend it outside."

Elation pumped through Darcy. She was seriously having such an amazing day with them and it had nothing to do with her new purchases. Being out with Iris and Colin was just fun and broke up the monotony of being in the house. Darcy had been so dead set on not letting Colin buy things for her, yet here she was watching him load the new clothes he'd purchased into a vehicle that he'd also bought for her.

She was not a shallow woman and she certainly wasn't hung up on material objects. But, if she was going to be spending months with Colin and Iris, they would be leaving the house at various times and she couldn't very well keep going out in her ratty old clothes. Granted she didn't need thousands of dollars' worth of clothes, either, but she'd lost that fight. She also planned to leave them behind when her term was over because she didn't think it would be fair to keep them…not unless something deeper happened between her and Colin. And at the rate they were edging closer together emotionally, she wondered how they actually would end up at the end of the six-month term.

As they all settled into the car and Darcy climbed in behind the wheel, she realized the main problem. She was getting too comfortable with this family. Not comfortable the way she had on other nanny jobs, but comfortable as in she'd started envisioning this little family as hers. The thought alone was utterly ridiculous, but she couldn't stop the daydream any more than she could control her hormones around Colin. Everything about this family struck a chord so deep within her, she knew she'd carry them with her for the rest of her life.

Darcy was completely in love with Iris. The little girl could easily melt anyone's heart.

As for Colin…she knew she wasn't in love with the man, but she did have feelings for him. Feelings that had no place in her life or in this professional atmosphere.

Now if she could just keep telling herself that, maybe she'd believe it. But would she stop fantasizing about him?

Eleven

He had become a creature of habit at a young age, due in part to his royal status. Schedules were a normal part of his life and without them, the members of the palace's security team would not have been able to do their jobs efficiently.

And here in the United States he found he was no different. He was in the middle of his nightly workout, which meant he was sweaty, breathing hard and still aching for the woman who lately occupied his every blasted thought.

Today had been amazing and seeing Darcy's face light up was worth the sacrifice. He knew she wasn't easily bought and that was definitely not his intent.

He treated her just as he would any other employee. Colin and his brother were always quick to supply anything the members of their staff needed. Just because he was in the United States, away from the palace, didn't mean he wouldn't treat Darcy like any other member of his staff.

Except Darcy had become more than an employee the second he'd plastered her up against the wall and kissed the hell out of her.

Last night their phone conversation had stimulated him in ways he hadn't expected. Sleep had been a long time coming and he had a feeling he'd be in the same predicament tonight. For the next several months, in fact, if they didn't end up just giving in to their desires.

He needed to get his head on straight and figure out how to tell Darcy about this trip. He actually loved the thought of taking her to his home country. He could only hope she'd take the news of his royal status well and agree to go with him. Colin had just started doing squats with the weight bar across his shoulders when his cell chimed from the bench behind him. Of all his exercises, this was the one that nearly killed his back and leg so he welcomed the distraction.

Dropping the bar back into place, he turned and smiled when he saw the name on the screen. He should've expected this.

"Is this going to be a ritual?" he asked in lieu of saying hello.

Darcy's soft laugh greeted him. "I just wanted to tell you again how much I appreciate the clothes. You didn't have to do anything like that for me, and saying thanks seems so inadequate, but…thanks."

Colin gripped the phone, wishing she'd come down and thank him in person. From her soft tone, he knew she was feeling a bit insecure, most likely about the money, which meant absolutely nothing to him. He had an exorbitant amount of it, so why shouldn't he be able to spend it on people he cared about?

"You're more than welcome," he replied, playing it safe instead of telling her what he really wanted to say. "But you don't have to keep thanking me."

"Maybe I just wanted to hear your voice."

Colin froze as she tossed back the words he'd given her last night. "You hear my voice all day."

"It's not the same with Iris around."

Closing his eyes, Colin reached out and rested his arm on the cool bar. He dropped his head and contemplated how to approach this shaky ground, because each step could set off a series of events he either didn't want or wasn't ready for. "You can come to the gym if you want to hear my voice," he said, hoping she'd take him up on his offer.

"No. This is best. I just…this is so silly."

"What were you going to say?"

Her pause had him lifting his head, listening for the slightest noise in the background. Was she already in bed? Had she lain there and thought of him?

"When I talked to you on the phone last night it was as if we were alone, just without the pressure of being alone." She laughed, then let out a groan. "Forget it. I'm not making sense."

She made perfect sense. Everything about her and this crazy situation made sense to him at this point in his chaotic life.

"Maybe we should pretend we're alone and we don't have to have any boundaries," he stated, his mouth spouting off words before he could fully filter his thoughts. "What if you were here with me now? Or what if I was up there with you? If we were just two people who met and there was nothing holding us back from taking what we wanted, what would you do?"

Silence greeted him and he knew without a doubt images were flooding Darcy's mind because they sure as hell were playing through his.

"What would you do if I showed up at your bedroom door right now?" he whispered.

He knew he was torturing himself. Unfortunately, he fantasized about Darcy whether he was speaking the words aloud or keeping the thoughts to himself.

"If nothing stood in our way, I'd let you in."

Colin wasn't sure whether to be thrilled or angry at this torturous piece of information. At least she came right out and said the words, but words meant nothing without action.

"What would we do after I came in?" he asked.

Her soft laugh enveloped him. "I'm not having phone sex with you."

"I wasn't headed there." Though now that she'd put that thought in his mind, he wouldn't object to a little phone sex. "Tell me, Darcy. Once I came to your room and you let me in, what would happen?"

"Everything I've been dreaming about," she whispered. "But dreams aren't always meant to come true."

That sad tone of her voice said so much more than her actual words. He knew she'd been saving for an adoption. He wished he could be the man to give her what she wanted, but he was in no position to give anything unless it was financial or sexual. All superficial things, yes— anything involving his heart or too many emotions, hell no. He wasn't naive. He figured if things were different they may actually have a shot at something special, something more meaningful than intimacy. But how could they pursue anything beyond that when she had no idea who he was and he had no idea who he wanted to be?

A muffled sniff slid through the phone and Colin gripped the device tighter. "I'm coming up."

"No. Colin, you can't." Another sniff. "This is good, just talking. I haven't really talked about my feelings for a long time."

"You're crying."

He hated the thought of her lying up there upset, most

likely over a bad memory that had been triggered by what he'd said. Colin wanted her happy, wanted that light in her eyes he'd become familiar with and he wanted to break down every damn wall she'd erected between them.

"I'm fine," she assured him. "It's getting late and I need to get up early for my workout."

"You have a standing invitation to work out with me."

"I know."

She still wouldn't take the offer, but he had to remind her anyway. He wanted to be here for her, to give his support, and that thought scared the hell out of him. Taking on someone else's problems was not going to help him solve his own and would only push him deeper into Darcy's life…a place he couldn't allow himself to be.

"Good night, Darcy."

"'Night, Colin."

He disconnected the call and resisted the urge to throw the phone across the room. This was a dangerous game he was playing with her. Not only were her feelings obviously involved, he had a sense her heart was teetering on the brink, too. That wasn't his ego talking, either. He didn't know if he had it in him to give her his heart. He knew he wanted her on a primal level and he was fully aware that his emotional connection with her was stronger than he'd intended, but there were so many uncertainties.

On the other hand, he wasn't too keen on the idea of another man capturing her heart, either, which left him in quite a predicament.

He had some decisions to make in his personal life here and back on Galini Isle. No matter what path he chose, Colin feared he'd be making a mistake and now there were even more lives—and hearts—on the line.

Colin kicked a ball to Iris, and just as she went to raise her leg the ball rolled right by her, causing her to laugh hysterically just like the past seventeen times he'd purposely kicked it by her.

Darcy swallowed the lump in her throat. A child's laughter was the sweetest noise, and by the looks of Colin's little game, he thought so, too..

The day was too beautiful for them to eat inside so Darcy had decided to set up lunch in the outside eating area. The father-daughter duo was having so much fun, they hadn't spotted her yet and Darcy was enjoying the view. Colin epitomized what fatherhood was all about. Spending time with his child, putting work on hold and not caring if he was getting texts or emails.

Exactly what Darcy would want for the father of her child if she could've had children. But she had to wonder what profession allowed him to have such flexibility. He'd mentioned that he managed a large group back home. Maybe he delegated most of his tasks. She could totally see him in a position of power and authority.

After pouring fresh iced tea into two glasses and placing a sippy cup of juice on the table, Darcy stood back and double-checked to make sure she hadn't forgotten anything. She was trying out a new recipe on Colin and she hoped he'd like it. Finding healthy dishes that weren't an all-day task to prepare was proving to be more difficult than she'd thought.

Smoothing her hands down her new mint-green shorts, Darcy headed out into the yard. Blades of grass tickled her bare feet as she crossed the lawn. Shielding her eyes from the afternoon sun with her hand, she continued to take in the beautiful image of the sexiest man she'd ever met playing with the sweetest little girl she'd ever cared for.

To look at them right now, one would never know a piece of their life had been ripped away when his wife passed. On a positive note, Iris wouldn't remember the pain of losing her mother. But she wouldn't have any mother-daughter memories to cherish. Darcy's mother hadn't died, but she had abandoned her at a young age. Still, Darcy's grandmother had always been there and was an amazing role model.

Colin glanced up, catching her gaze and pulling her from her thoughts. "You come out to play?" he asked.

"I set up lunch on the patio," she replied, rushing to play on Iris's side. Darcy kicked the ball back to Colin. "I figured we could eat out here today."

Iris clapped as Colin sent the ball back. "Deedee kick it."

For the next couple minutes, Darcy and Colin carried on a game. Before she knew it, the competition had turned serious and she was all over the yard, rounding him with the ball, dodging any attempt he tried to get back control. Colin thought he could outmaneuver her. Wasn't he in for a surprise? She was no stranger to kicking a ball around.

Finally, Darcy had mercy on him and she kicked the ball hard, sending it soaring through the air. Colin jumped, his arms extended above his head, and caught it with his hands.

"I'm raising the white flag," he panted.

Darcy resisted the urge to bend at the waist and draw in some much-needed air. She'd gotten in her second work-out of the day, but she wasn't about to admit she was still out of shape and thrilled he'd called a halt to their impromptu game.

"How about we eat?" she suggested, reaching down to take Iris's hand. "I have fresh tea and I desperately need a drink."

Once they were all settled, Darcy sat next to Iris to help her with her food if necessary. Colin took a look at his plate and smiled.

"This looks great."

His verbal approval shouldn't have had her so excited.

She'd only grilled some pineapple and chicken and put a homemade glaze over it. Nothing too fancy.

"Were you an athlete in school?"

Darcy sipped her glass of tea, welcoming the cold, refreshing drink. "I played soccer, actually. My school was big, so we had our own girls' team."

"You were pretty quick out there."

Darcy shrugged, even though a bit of pride burst through her at his statement. "Not as quick as I used to be. After graduating and helping Gram full time, I lost most of my stamina. As I've said before, I'm pretty out of shape now."

"I've already told you, your shape is just fine."

Darcy expected to look up and find him staring at her, but he was cutting into his chicken. Apparently the comment he kept throwing her way didn't affect him the way it did her. He tossed the words out so matter-of-factly, yet they meant so much to her. More than he could ever know.

"Your new clothes look nice on you."

Iris kicked her little feet in the highchair, causing the whole thing to wiggle, sending her sippy cup to the ground. Darcy retrieved it and set it back on the tray.

"For what you spent, they better," she joked.

Silence settled in for a bit before Iris started gibbering. Darcy didn't mind the quiet meal. There was no awkwardness surrounding them, only the peaceful, bright sunshine and the beauty of the lush backyard. It was times like this that Darcy could imagine slipping into the role of something so much more than a nanny.

"Did you play any sports in school?" she asked, trying to distract herself from her wayward thoughts.

Colin's fork froze halfway to his mouth, a naughty smile flirted around his lips. "I pretty much concentrated on girls and defying my father."

Darcy could easily see that. "What about your mother?"

"She was killed in an auto accident when I was younger."

Darcy's heart ached for him. He'd lost his mother and his wife? How much could a man take in one lifetime? So much heartache, yet he still smiled, still pushed forward and created a wonderful life for his own daughter.

"I shouldn't have asked," Darcy stated, slicing into her pineapple. "That was rude."

"You can ask me anything you want," he told her. "There's no need to be sorry. You didn't do anything wrong."

"No, but I don't want to bring up bad memories."

With a slight shrug, Colin reached for his tea. "The memories are always there. Not talking about them won't make them disappear."

Once Iris was finished, Darcy tidied her up and wiped off the tray. After taking a load of dishes into the kitchen, she came back out. Colin had pretty much cleaned up the rest and had his own stack of dishes in hand.

"I would've gotten those," she told him. "Just set them inside and I'll clean up later."

He didn't say a word as he passed. Darcy pulled Iris from her highchair and took her back out into the yard to continue the game of ball before the toddler went in for her nap.

Running in the grass, laughing and playing with a little one may have been something Darcy had dodged for years, but honestly this was exactly what she needed.

But the way they'd settled in almost like a family terrified Darcy because falling for a baby was one thing, but falling for the baby's father was another problem altogether. Yet the more time she spent with Colin, the more she saw what an amazing, giving man he was and the more she wanted him.

She was done denying herself.

Twelve

For the past week, Darcy had spoken to Colin on the phone every night before bed. There was something soothing about hearing that low, sultry voice without having to look him in the eyes or be distracted by that hard body. She loved their talks, which ranged from joking to flirting to borderline naughty.

They'd also had some serious moments. Moments that probably wouldn't have happened in the light of day or face-to-face. For some reason saying personal things on the phone was relaxing—almost therapeutic. She'd shared memories of her grandmother and he'd shared stories about how he and his brother used to rock climb together.

Darcy shifted against the sheets, the satin of her chemise sliding over her heated skin. Her gaze traveled to the phone on her nightstand. They'd already hung up for the night, but she needed more.

Before she lost her nerve, Darcy picked up her phone and called him back.

"Forget something?" he answered.

Oh, the replies she could throw back.

"I wasn't ready for bed." At least not alone. "Mind talking a bit more?"

"Not at all. You're a welcome distraction from this office work."

Darcy slid from bed and padded down the hall, careful not to speak when she passed Iris's door. For once she was going to be spontaneous, she was going to take what she wanted and live for the moment because there was no way she would walk out of here with regrets when her term ended.

There was only so much a woman could take.

"Something specific on your mind?"

Easing down the stairs, guided by only the soft glow of the dimmed chandelier in the foyer, Darcy smiled. "Too many things to list."

Some shuffling and cursing in his native language had Darcy pausing, her hand on the banister at the base of the steps. "Everything okay?" she asked.

Colin laughed. "Yeah, just making a mess here."

Darcy knew that as soon as she hit the hallway he'd hear her talking, so she took a seat on the bottom step, curled her feet up onto the step below and looped her arms around her knees.

"If you wanted something more than anything in the world, but there were obstacles in your way, what would you do?"

"Are we going to pretend we aren't talking about you?" he asked.

"I'm pretending," she said with a smile, even though he couldn't see her. "You don't have to."

"Then pretend it's me," he told her. "When I want something, I find a way to claim it at any cost. I may not get it in the time frame I want, but eventually with enough patience, I make it mine."

Closing her eyes, Darcy let his strong words push through that wall of fear she'd tried so hard to hide behind.

"What if time isn't on your side?" she whispered.

"What is it you want, Darcy?"

His question, nearly a whisper, too, told her he knew exactly what she wanted…or whom she wanted.

"I started to come to you." She gripped the phone tighter as if she could somehow pull strength from him. "I'm afraid."

Admitting that really humbled her because she didn't want to be seen as weak or vulnerable. Colin was neither of those things and she didn't figure he'd find a woman who was so indecisive and fearful attractive.

"You think I'm not?"

That voice was in full surround sound. Darcy jerked her head up to see Colin standing before her, phone still to his ear. The glow from the light illuminated him, making him seem even larger than life.

Darcy laid her phone beside her on the step. "You're not scared," she countered, unsure of what else to say at this point.

Crouching down with a slight wince, Colin placed his phone next to hers before laying his hands over the arm that was still wrapped around her knee. "Just because I'm scared doesn't mean I'll let the fear control my emotions. I want you, and the second you said you were coming to me I had to meet you halfway."

The man truly didn't let anything get in his way, not fear, not worry for the unknown…absolutely nothing.

"Maybe—"

He cut her off as he claimed her mouth beneath his. His hands instantly cupped the side of her face and tipped her head for better access. Colin's body eased forward and

Darcy realized he'd placed his knees on the bottom step, so she spread her legs to accommodate him.

The moment her bare thighs slid against the side of his ribs, she groaned into his mouth. She'd never been this turned on, this ready for a man, and he'd only started kissing her. Granted, she'd only been with one man in her life, but there was absolutely no comparison between this passionate moment and anything she'd experienced before.

Breaking away, Colin peered down, stroked her bottom lip with his thumb and held her gaze. "Never hold back with me. I want it all."

At that firm command, he took her lips again. Shivers coursed through her as Colin trailed his hands down her bare arms then slid them around her waist. With only the silk of her chemise providing a barrier, the warmth of his hands seared her skin. Arching into him, she wanted more and she wanted it now.

In one swift move, Colin picked her up and changed their positions so he sat on the step and she straddled his thighs.

His eyes roamed over her body. "You really do sleep in a black chemise."

Without comment, Darcy did what she'd wanted to do since day one. She leaned forward and trailed her tongue across that ink scrolling over his shoulder and down to his pec. The muscles clenched beneath her touch and a low growl erupted from Colin. His hands came around to cup her backside, jerking her closer against his arousal.

Darcy trembled, clutching his shoulders. An ache even fiercer than before spread through her. There was nothing outside this moment. Not her financial issues, not her infertility, not the mystery surrounding Colin, because if she were honest, that only added to his allure. They were both taking what they wanted.

Colin moved one hand around, splaying it over her

upper thigh. His thumb teased just beneath the edge of the lacy trim on her panties, each stroke coming closer to the spot where she needed him the most.

Forgetting the torture of tasting his inked skin and chiseled muscles, Darcy dropped her head to his shoulder as he finally slid his thumb inside the material. Those slow strokes over her heated center were going to be the death of her. Darcy tipped her hips, silently demanding more. She'd denied herself this pleasure for so long, she simply couldn't take much more.

Her breath hitched as he eased inside her, her fingertips curled into his skin. He continued to torture her slowly, yet with so much control and power, Darcy was having a hard time getting her mind around the emotions tugging her in all different directions. But what if she wasn't enough for him? What if she disappointed him once they really got down to it?

She froze, not wanting this moment of blissful perfection to end, because it felt too good, too perfect. Too right.

"I told you not to hold back with me again," he growled in her ear. "Stop tensing up and let go."

With one hand still stroking her, he used the other to jerk down the top of her chemise. The strap snapped apart as his mouth settled over her breast. Darcy arched back, crying out as the full-on sexual encounter washed over her, sending her spiraling into the most intense climax of her entire life.

Before her tremors could cease, Colin was shifting beneath her and she realized he was working his shorts from side to side to get them down. Quickly she assisted him and found herself hovering right above a very naked, very aroused Colin. Then he slid his other hand between them and gave her chemise a tug, tearing apart the seam in the middle.

"I owe you another shopping trip," he muttered against her lips. "This time I'll be in the dressing room."

Oh, mercy. Shopping for lingerie with this man would be…heaven. They'd never make it out alive.

"I have protection in my office and in my room."

Darcy held his gaze, her mind trying to process the words because she was still in a euphoric state.

"I've been anticipating this moment so I was prepared." He nipped her lips, shifted his hips so his erection nudged her. "You have about two seconds to decide where this will happen."

"Whichever one we get to fastest."

Colin came to his feet, causing Darcy to stand on her not-so-steady legs. She didn't have to worry, though, because Colin lifted her once more, not in the romantic scoop she'd always read about or seen in movies, but hooking her legs around his waist, forcing her to wrap her entire body around him. Oh, yeah. This was the experience she wanted. Nothing mushy here, but full-out want, need and the snapping of the control they'd both been barely holding onto.

He moved down the wide, darkened hall toward his office. Only a small bronze desk lamp cast any light on the room. Still, with her wrapped all around him, Colin jerked open a drawer and tossed a foil package onto the glossy surface of the desk. Darcy nipped at his shoulder, earlobe and jawline. With protection taken care of, she wanted him. Now.

When he sat her on top of his desk, he eased back, taking her face in his hands. "You're sure?"

Darcy nodded. The intensity of his gaze and the way he held his lips firm told her he may have more to say, but instead he tore open the wrapper and covered himself before pulling her to the edge of the desk.

Darcy leaned back on her elbows, staring up at him

and watching as he gazed back down at her. Colin's hands gripped her hips as he slid into her. When he caught her gaze, a tick visible in his jaw, she smiled. "Don't worry about going slow."

Something must have snapped because the next thing she knew he wasn't holding back…in any way.

Darcy's head fell back as pleasure engulfed her, as Colin claimed her. She'd never experienced anything so perfect, so all-consuming in her entire life.

Their frantic pace sent something from the desk crashing to the floor, but she didn't care and the commotion didn't slow Colin down, either. She barely noticed papers shifting beneath her. With the way Colin's eyes were locked on hers, the way he held her waist with his strong hands and took her as if he owned her, Darcy didn't think she'd ever care about anything else again. He was completely ruining her for any other man.

Another wave crested over her and Darcy cried out, her legs tightening around Colin's waist. He jerked once more and stilled, his fingertips bruising her sides.

After they stopped trembling, Colin leaned over, his forehead resting against her shoulder.

"I haven't done that since before my accident," he muttered. "I was afraid I'd hurt you if I carried you and fell, but I had to try. I wanted you in my arms. I want to be the man you need."

He was that man and so much more. Darcy had wondered if her heart would get swept away with Colin because of his single-father status, but what she felt for him had nothing to do with his child, his finances or anything other than the fact that he alone turned her inside out and made her feel things she'd only ever fantasized about. He made her come alive in ways she never had before.

"If you give me a few minutes, I'll take you up to my

room." His lips cruised over her damp skin, causing her to already want him again. "I need you in my bed."

Darcy didn't say a word. She would follow him to his bed. She'd follow him anywhere he asked.

Darcy's hair tickled the side of his face, but there was no way he was moving. She fit perfectly against his side, tucked snugly into him, as if she was made to be there. But right now, after taking her on his desk, and pleasuring her again once they'd arrived in his room, Colin didn't want to think any deeper than this blissful, sated feeling. He couldn't, wouldn't dive into that black hole of thoughts where all of his worries and fears about committing to another woman lived.

For the first time in months, he let loose and enjoyed his time with a refreshing woman who pulled him back to basic life...exactly what he'd been searching for.

With Darcy's arm across his abdomen and her leg across his thigh, the woman was staking her own claim and he had to admit, he liked it. He liked her. To know she wasn't into one-night stands completely humbled him. She'd been brave to initiate the encounter.

"I have a trip I need to take in a few days." His words cut through the darkened silence. "I'd like you to accompany me."

Sliding her fingertips up and down his abs, she asked, "Where are we going?"

"I need to go back home for an event," he told her, unable to reveal the rest of the details. "We will only be gone a few days."

Darcy shifted, easing up on one elbow to look down at him. His eyes had adjusted to the dark, plus the soft glow from the security monitors offered a dim light.

"Do I need to pack anything in particular?" she asked with a smile. "I've never been out of the country before."

She'd need a passport if she didn't have one and that could be problematic unless his assistant pulled some strings. They'd be flying in the palace jet, but still there was customs. He'd have his staff figure out the details.

"That blue dress would be a nice start," he told her. "But just be yourself. That's all you need to do."

She didn't have to go, she could stay behind, but he wanted her there. Granted he had a whole host of people who could care for Iris—maids, butlers, assistants, his sister-in-law. The list truly was endless.

But he wanted Darcy on his turf, he wanted to see how she fit into his life.

Colin nearly gasped as a realization dawned on him. He was falling for this woman in his arms. He was falling so hard, so fast, but he couldn't admit it fully, because what if she rejected him?

"You mentioned your parents had passed. Do you have siblings other than the brother you've mentioned?"

Her question pulled him from his thoughts.

Being here with Darcy, going into public without guards or paparazzi snapping photos was so different, so refreshing and so damn freeing. But he still felt as if he was letting down not only his country but Stefan. His brother was all Colin had left and putting the entire future of Galini Isle on Stefan's shoulders wasn't fair.

"Just Stefan and his wife Victoria."

"And they live in Greece?"

"Yes," he replied, fully enjoying the way her fingers continued to travel over his exposed torso. "What about you? No siblings, I assume."

"No. It was just my Gram and me after my parents split town. Apparently they weren't into the whole parenting thing and my Gram wasn't about to let me go into the foster system. I lived with her, worked with her and learned everything I know from the most amazing woman in the world."

No wonder Darcy was such a fighter. She'd had one person to depend on her entire life…a life spent caring for others. Colin had a whole army of people he depended on back home and he was running from them.

"Did you once mention wanting to adopt a baby of your own?" he asked.

A soft sigh escaped her, tickling his shoulder. "I would love to adopt, but it's expensive and my business needs to get back on track again. I'm afraid by the time I get all settled financially and go through the process, I'll be too old."

"You're young enough."

Her fingertips traced his tattoo the same way her tongue had earlier. She'd damn near had his eyes rolling back in his head.

"I know, but given the experience I had with my ex… it just hurts." She settled her head back in the crook of his arm, but continued to run her hand over his chest and abs as if she couldn't get enough…which suited him just fine. "To know you share your dreams, open your heart to someone and have them lie and betray you like that. I'm not sure I'll ever get over that pain. My dreams were put on hold and I'm not sure I'll ever get them back."

Colin swallowed. He wasn't the same as this ex, so he shouldn't feel guilty about lying.

Still, he wanted to clear the air about something.

"The last woman I was with was my wife," he told her, hating this topic in bed, but needing to get it out. "I know I mentioned that before, but I wanted you to know I may have been reckless as a teen and into my early twenties, but between marrying, the accident and then Iris, I've calmed down. I didn't want you to think I was using you because you were here and convenient."

"I know you're not," she murmured. "I've only been with one man before you. I just don't take the time to date and a fling is not something I can do."

Colin laughed, earning him a smack. "Sorry," he chuckled.

"You know what I mean," she defended. "I'm going to be here several months, so I hope tonight wasn't a one-time thing. I mean, I guess that should've been discussed, but I assumed—"

Colin rolled over, pinning her beneath him and cutting off her words.

"I plan on having you as often as you'll allow me to," he told her. As he looked into her bright eyes, he knew he had to tell her the rest. "I need to tell you why we're going back home."

She stared up at him, her eyes locking directly onto his. "Let's not talk right now." She spread her legs so he could settle firmly between them. "I only want to think about right now, with you, in your bed."

The trip could wait.

Colin smoothed her hair away from her face, nipped at her lips. "Maybe I want you to just lay back, think of absolutely nothing but how good everything feels."

He didn't wait for her reply as he started kissing his way down her body. When Darcy clutched the sheets, he smiled as he continued his path.

The next few months were going to be amazing.

Thirteen

Darcy wore only Colin's T-shirt as she maneuvered around the kitchen getting breakfast ready. She'd skipped her early morning workout and opted to stay snuggled next to Colin's warm, strong body. Of course she'd gotten enough of a calorie burn last night, in the middle of the night and again this morning.

Not only had he ruined her for any other man, he'd ruined her for any other workout. Why exercise with some cold piece of machinery when she could get a thorough workout with a hunky man ready to meet her every need?

Iris sat in her high chair, tapping her spoon against the tray and babbling. Every now and then a coherent word would slip out, but she was mostly just entertaining herself while Darcy cooked up some pancakes.

Colin had wanted to shower early, so he should be joining them soon. Everything about the morning after wasn't at all uncomfortable the way she'd heard people say. If anything it was very…domestic and normal.

The chime at the gate jerked Darcy from stirring the pancake batter. Who on earth was trying to visit this early in the morning? As long as no one on the inside of the house buzzed the guest in, they wouldn't get beyond the gate, unless they had the code. Darcy wasn't allowing anyone to pass through because Colin hadn't mentioned he was expecting a guest and this wasn't her house.

A moment later Colin came down the steps wearing a pair of running shorts and nothing else but a tan and the tat. She'd explored that body, tasted and touched it, yet the sight of him still had her knees weakening. How had her life gone from being so bleak, so depressing, to something that sparked hope and new life?

"Was that the gate alarm?" he asked as he bent down to give Iris a kiss and ruffle her curly bedhead.

"Yeah. I didn't answer the call because I didn't know if you were expecting anybody or not."

Darcy went back to mixing, wondering how she should act this morning. The entire scene seemed so family-like, so perfect, and she feared she'd make a mistake and this dream would be over.

"I'm not. Wonder who wanted in this early in the morning?" he mumbled. "I take it you weren't expecting anyone."

Darcy laughed as she poured the batter for several pancakes onto the warm griddle. "Do you honestly think I've invited friends to come over?"

"You can, you know."

She glanced his way and rolled her eyes. "I may take you up on that. I've texted my friends, but I've just been too busy to entertain."

"You can entertain me anytime." He crossed the spacious kitchen, rounded the island and slid a hand up beneath the T-shirt she wore. "You look better in this shirt than I ever did."

How could she not get swept into the fantasy this whole scene represented? She had to keep everything separate— her attraction for Colin in one part of her heart, her love for Iris in another. And there was no room for this family bonding. Colin and Iris weren't her family no matter how much she wished they were. Being swept into a love affair was already uncharted territory, but allowing her heart to get caught up in this fantasy was only going to crush her in the end when she walked away alone.

The doorbell chimed, causing Darcy and Colin to freeze. His hand slid out of the shirt, leaving her cold where his warmth had been.

"Stay here. There's only one person who has this code besides us."

Colin didn't look happy. Who would have the code? They'd been here for two months and nobody had used it yet, so why now?

As soon as the front door opened, another male voice filled the home. She pulled the pancakes off the griddle and set them aside on a spare plate. After flicking the griddle off, Darcy cut up a half of a pancake for Iris. Raised voices from the foyer had Darcy plucking Iris from her highchair.

Who was here? Should she try to go out the back and get to a neighbor for help? Darcy cursed herself for only wearing a T-shirt. She scooted closer to the side of the kitchen that was closest to the foyer to see if she could hear better but not be seen since she was hardly dressed for company.

"Are you going to let me in?" an unfamiliar male voice asked. Whoever this man was, he had the same sexy accent as Colin.

Colin spoke vehemently, again in Greek—what sounded like a curse. Moments later the door closed. Whoever was here, Colin knew him but he was a stranger to Darcy.

Great. Her attire screamed that she'd just gotten out of bed…her lover's bed.

"Nice place," the other man commented. "But are you ready to come back and forget this notion of living in the States?"

"You should've called," Colin replied, his tone implying the guest still wouldn't have been welcome.

"We've talked nearly every single day. I wanted to surprise you."

Footsteps echoed, growing louder. Darcy moved toward the island and put Iris back into her high chair. She'd just taken her seat when a man who could be Colin's twin stepped into the room, Colin right on his heels.

"Stefan, this is Darcy."

She hadn't been able to hide behind the island in time and the man's eyes traveled over her, taking in her oversized T-shirt, the hem of the boxers peeking out from beneath it and her bare legs before going to Iris and then back to Colin.

"I'm sorry," he said, turning back toward Colin. "I didn't know…wait, is this your nanny?"

Darcy cringed and turned to concentrate on cutting up Iris's food. Whatever was going on with these two, she wanted no part of it. Clearly they had issues that didn't involve her. Well, maybe they did now.

"Stefan," Colin growled. "Not a word."

"I'm just trying to figure things out." Stefan shook his head and propped his hands on his hips. "Are you giving up your title, turning your back on your country and the throne for someone you barely know?"

Darcy froze. *Title? Throne?*

Slowly, she lifted her gaze to Colin. He stared back at her as if he was waiting to see her reaction, too.

"Shut the hell up, Stefan," Colin nearly shouted. "Apologize to Darcy. She has nothing to do with my decision and you know I'm taking the full six months to think this through."

"My apologies," Stefan said, turning and tipping his head toward Darcy. The worried look etched across his face told Darcy he was sincere. "I mean no disrespect to you. I was just taken aback. I've been waiting for my brother to come home, and I knew he'd found a reason to stay for now. I certainly didn't mean to take my shocked state out on you. Actually, Mikos has told me quite a bit about you and I want to thank you for being so kind to my niece."

"There's nothing to worry about with me," Colin cut in before Darcy could respond. "I'm still unclear on my decision."

"Mikos." The other man stepped closer to Colin. "Are you seriously that happy here that you're still confused? Have you not missed anything about Galini Isle or the people who love you?"

Darcy swallowed, terrified to ask, but needing to know. "Why is he calling you Mikos and what does he mean by throne and title?"

Colin's eyes closed on a sigh, but before he could answer, the other man turned to face her completely. "I'm calling him Mikos because that's his name and he's a prince from Galini Isle, a small country off the coast of Greece."

Darcy had no idea what to say, what to do. All those times they'd talked, every single day they'd shared together over the last two months and he couldn't find it in his heart to tell her any of that? Not even his real name?

Tears blurred her vision, but even through the hurt and confusion, she had a baby to care for. That was what he was paying her for, right?

Whatever game he was playing by seducing her, it was clear that she was pretty much just hired help. Had he ever seen her as anything more or had he been laughing at her this entire time?

"Darcy—"

With a jerk of her head and a glare, Darcy cut off whatever Colin, Mikos…whoever, had been about to say.

"You haven't told her?" the other man asked. "Classy, Mikos. Real classy."

Colin was seriously fighting the urge to punch his brother in the face. First of all, to show up unannounced was rude even for Stefan. Second, how the hell did he fix this with Darcy now? The last thing he wanted was for her to be hurt, for her to feel as though she'd been betrayed again.

But he'd lied because been so dead set on keeping his identities separate. He'd gotten so wrapped up in her, in this life, that he hadn't given much thought to consequences. He'd been thinking only of himself. Just as he had with Karina, and look how that had turned out.

"Let me feed her," Colin offered, stepping forward. "You go change."

Her hands shook with each bite she put in Iris's mouth, but Darcy didn't even turn to answer him.

"Darcy." Stefan also stepped forward. "I apologize for coming in like this and dropping a bomb on you. I'd assumed my brother would've told you about his status. Why don't you go change and I'll feed my niece? I haven't seen her for a long time."

Now Darcy lifted her head, gave a slight nod and headed out of the room, careful to go around the island to avoid getting too close Stefan and Colin. She didn't say a word, didn't look either of them in the eye.

Her pain lingered after she was gone. Colin would never forget the angst that had washed over her face right before she slid up that invisible wall and avoided looking at him. Good God, what had he done?

"I could kill you for that," Colin muttered.

Stefan leaned his hip against the island and forked up another bite for Iris. He made an airplane motion and some ridiculous noise to get her to open for him. Of course she clapped and kicked her feet, oblivious to the turmoil going on.

"Don't be angry with me that you kept the truth hidden. If you like the woman, and I have to assume you do because you're still here, then she deserved the truth."

Colin slammed his fist onto the counter. "You have no idea what has happened so don't even think about assuming you do." But Stefan was absolutely right. Why hadn't he seen this coming?

"It's about time you're showing emotion for someone else." A smile spread across Stefan's face. "I'm glad to see you're living again. Are you and Darcy serious?"

Colin rolled his eyes. This wasn't up for debate. He went to get a plate, but suddenly he wasn't hungry anymore. Right now Darcy was upstairs, most likely angry, hurt, maybe even crying, because he thought he could keep all the balls in the air and have control over every facet of his life.

"I don't know what we are," Colin defended himself. He thought he knew what he wanted, but would Darcy ever speak to him again? Did his wants even matter at this point?

Stefan paused, bite in midair. "She's wearing your shirt and whisker burn, cooking your breakfast and caring for your child. I'd say that's pretty serious. Yet you still lied to her. It makes me wonder why."

"I'm paying her to care for Iris."

Stefan glanced around the island, found a sippy cup and passed it to Iris before turning his focus back to Colin.

"And the rest? I know you're not paying her for that, and this is the first woman you've shown interest in since Karina."

"I don't give a damn what you think right now. I was planning on coming home for the ball, you didn't have to show up unannounced."

Stefan shrugged. "Last time we spoke you told me you weren't sure if you were coming back. I merely came to talk some sense into you. Victoria had to stay behind to get last minute things prepared for the event or she would've been right here with me."

Colin raked a hand over his still damp hair. "Watch Iris for me. I need to go upstairs and talk to Darcy. Stay down here and shut the hell up next time you see her. You've done enough damage."

Colin didn't wait for Stefan to confirm anything, he just turned and stormed from the room. His back was killing him, as was his leg after all the extra activities he'd participated in last night, but he was determined to march right into Darcy's room and set things straight.

He had nothing planned to say, had no clue what state he'd find her in or what was even going through her mind. He was about to enter unstable territory and it terrified him because he realized that what she thought was important.

Not only did he not want to be the one to hurt her, but he also wanted to be the one she counted on. So many people had turned away from her, betrayed her in one form or another.

And he'd just added his name to the list. Surely he could make this up to her somehow.

Yet he stood outside her bedroom door, staring at the barrier as if the inanimate object could offer insight. What a mess he'd made, all because he'd been too self-absorbed, too wrapped up in Darcy and his hormones to truly see the big picture. Not that he saw any clearer now, but he did know one thing, he still wanted Darcy and he'd make damn sure he would fix this disaster he'd caused.

Colin tapped his knuckles on the door. It hadn't latched completely so the weight of his hand eased it open just enough for him to see her standing across the room, her back to him, as she looked out onto the backyard.

"I know you want to be alone," he started, staying in her doorway. "But we need to talk."

Darcy's shoulders stiffened, the only sign she'd even heard him. Silence settled heavily between them, when only an hour ago they were lying side by side in his bed. At least she'd thrown on some pants so he didn't have to be tortured further by the sight of her bare legs. He could still feel them wrapped around him, entwined with his.

"I didn't set out to lie to you, even though that's how it looks." He had to keep talking. If she wasn't ordering him out, then he knew she was listening. "I have a lot going on back home, so much that I didn't want to talk about it with anyone. I wanted to separate myself from that part of my life for a while to get my head on straight. I had to put Iris's needs first and keeping our identity a secret was one of my top priorities."

He paused, giving her a chance to speak if she wanted. When she remained silent, he pushed on.

"I wish I could blame my brother for barging in here and dropping that bomb like that, but it's my fault you didn't know." Taking a risk, Colin stepped further into the room, raking a hand down his face as he carefully chose the right words. "You matter to me, Darcy. More than I want to admit and more than I thought someone could after Karina. I don't want this to come between us."

Darcy whirled around. The tear tracks on her cheeks crippling him in ways words never could.

"You mean you don't want your lies to keep me out

of your bed?" she threw back. "Because isn't that all we have between us? Our arrangement was never meant to be more than temporary. So, for once since I've known you, be honest."

Colin swallowed the fear, the anger. He'd brought it all upon himself. He had to stand here and take it like a man. He deserved every word, every bit of rage she wanted to fling at him.

"You're only up here because you want to continue what we started last night." Darcy shook her head and laughed, swiping at her damp face. "I was such a fool. You were probably laughing at me the entire—"

She gasped, her eyes darting to her closet before her face crumbled. Turning away, she let out a low moan as she hugged her arms around her midsection.

"You knew I had nothing and there you were, throwing your money around," she whispered.

Colin started to cross to her because he couldn't stand the anguish lacing her voice, but she spun to face him, holding him with her hurt-filled stare. He stopped only a few feet from her.

"Did you get a kick out of giving to the needy?" she asked, her tone nothing but mocking. "Did you enjoy knowing you had everything, while I had absolutely nothing? Money, power, control. You literally played me, never once thinking how this would affect me."

"I never played you," he corrected. "I wouldn't have told anyone I employed here about my life on Galini Isle. And I damn well did worry about you. Every single day we grew closer I worried how this would affect you, but I didn't know what to say or how to even approach it."

Her eyes narrowed. "Because you're a coward. Apparently running from the truth is what you do. You fled your home when you obviously didn't want to face responsibilities there."

How could she ever understand that he hadn't been strong enough to face his royal duties as a widowed father, trying to bring up a duchess? How could she ever grasp how much was involved in being a prince raising a child in the kingdom? What if Iris didn't want the title that came along with her prestigious family name?

At some point this getaway had turned from him finding himself to him deciding what was going to be best for the future of his daughter.

"I have to go back in a couple days," he told her, forcing himself to put up a strong front because the sight of her so broken was damn near crippling. "I still want you to come with me."

Pain-filled laughter erupted from Darcy. "You're insane. I'm not going anywhere with you. This isn't some fairy tale, Colin or Mikos or whatever the hell you want to be called. This is my life and I'm not just running to some island in Greece because you snap your fingers and expect me to."

"I want you to go to be with Iris," he explained, hoping she'd cave because he didn't realize how much he needed her to be there on his turf until this moment. "She's used to you, she's comfortable with you and I'd rather have you caring for her than any of my assistants."

Throwing her arms in the air, Darcy pivoted and moved around him to stand on the other side of the room. "You're something else. You probably have multiple people at your disposal, yet you continue to want to torture me. Why? Are you enjoying this power trip?"

Clenching his fists at his sides, he watched as she began to pace. "I'm not enjoying any part of this."

"You're using Iris as a bargaining tool." She stopped and propped her hands on her hips. "You're using her to get me to come with you."

"I'm being honest," he told her. "You wanted honesty,

I'm laying it out there. I tried to tell you this morning. I know that's a convenient thing to say considering the timing, but it's the truth. I want you to see my country. I want you to be the one to care for Iris while I'm home because I will be facing many challenges there."

He didn't want to get too far into everything that he was running away from. Darcy wasn't in the right frame of mind to hear it and he wasn't ready to admit how weak and vulnerable he truly was.

Darcy pursed her lips together, then nodded. "Fine, but if you want to throw that money around so much, then I want double my original pay for the entire six months. If I'm traveling, then I deserve to be compensated accordingly."

This was probably not the time to say he was proud of her for standing up for herself, for playing hardball and fighting for what she wanted. Most women would've packed their bags and left. He'd always known she was a fighter and she was coming back at him full force.

She was the only woman who'd ever challenged him. What would he do on Galini Isle without her by his side? He wasn't about to find out.

"Done," he said without second thought. "On one condition."

She quirked a brow. "What?"

"When we're at the palace, you have to do what I say. No questions."

"I don't think—"

"Do you want the money?"

Darcy stilled, and her nostrils flared as her cheeks reddened. "You're despicable."

No, he was desperate, but he'd never admit that aloud. "We'll leave Sunday evening and sleep on my jet."

"Of course you have a jet," she muttered before moving toward her door. "We're done here. I'll take care of

Iris, I'll do everything a hired nanny does and she will be my number one priority. That doesn't include sleeping with my boss. From now on our relationship is strictly professional."

Crossing the room, Colin kept his gaze locked onto hers. As he neared, her eyes widened but she never looked away. He stopped only a breath from her, then leaned down to whisper in her ear.

"I never set out to lie to you, Darcy. You have to believe me."

As he spoke, his lips caressed the side of her cheek. Just as she shivered, Colin eased back. Her hand came up to slap him, but he quickly gripped her wrist in midair.

"You're angry. Don't do something you'll regret later." Although he knew he deserved it.

Her eyes flared, filling with unshed tears. "I hate you."

He yanked her forward to fall against his chest. With one hand still holding onto her wrist, Colin hooked an arm around her waist. "There's a fine line between hate and passion," he said with a confidence he didn't quite feel.

Unable to resist temptation, Colin captured her lips, but let the brief kiss end for fear she'd bite him. He smiled down at her.

"Make sure to pack the blue dress for our trip."

He'd barely made it out her door before it slammed at his back.

Damn it. He had to do something. Somehow he had to make this up to her. Losing Darcy was not an option, but he'd messed up. He didn't deserve her forgiveness, but that wouldn't stop him from doing everything in his power to earn it.

Fourteen

Darcy could dwell on the fact that her parents had abandoned her at a young age. She could also hone in the fact that the man she'd thought she loved had stolen every last penny she had to her name. She could even focus on her most recent betrayal: Colin keeping the colossal truth that he was a freaking prince from her. But Darcy opted to go a different route.

From now on, she would choose anger, because if she even attempted to shut it out, all she'd have left to face would be soul-crushing hurt. There was no time for that because there was an innocent child in all of this…a child Darcy had been hired to care for.

As much as Darcy wanted to take the initial half of her pay and leave Colin, she wouldn't abandon Iris. Darcy couldn't walk away, not when she knew all too well the feeling of rejection. But what would Colin do at the end of the six months? Did he have other arrangements set up or was he going back home? Did he even know himself?

Darcy continued to stare out the window of the car that had been waiting for them when they'd arrived at the private airstrip on Galini Isle. Iris had been sitting, securely strapped in, between her and Colin, and since they'd left LA Darcy had barely spoken a word to him unless it involved the baby. Nothing else needed to be said at this point, the damage was done.

Iris continued to sleep, which was a blessing because the poor thing had cried a good bit of the flight. Most likely the pressure in her ears had been getting to her. Even though exhaustion threatened to consume Darcy, too, she was too angry to be tired.

Beyond the obvious anger toward Colin, she was furious with herself because of her reaction to his parting shot in her room about still wanting her. He'd known just what to say, exactly the right way to deliver the words for the most impact.

Colin may have been a different man when he was with her, a man he'd made up, yet she still wanted him. Nobody had ever made her feel more beautiful, more wanted than he did. He'd wrapped his arms around her and kissed her as if he had every right in the world.

But that was all part of his game. He'd created a new life in America and she was just another prop. More than anything she wished she could switch her emotions off to avoid the hurt, but she simply wasn't wired that way.

The chauffeur pulled into a drive. Darcy noted the gate, guards and white columns as the car made its way onto the estate grounds. What was she doing here? She was going to spend the next few days in a palace. *A palace.* Only a few months ago she'd had to sleep in her car because she'd lost her condo, and now she was going to be staying in a freaking mansion in another country. She'd never even set foot outside of California before.

When they came to a stop, Darcy started to open her

door, but Colin leaned a hand across where Iris slept and laid his other hand over Darcy's arm.

"They'll get your door," he told her.

Rolling her eyes, Darcy jerked from his grasp and opened her own damn door. Once she stepped out, she turned and reached in to gently unfasten and pull Iris from her seat. She slept on as Darcy cradled her against her shoulder.

"Ma'am." The driver held her door, tipping his head toward her. "I'll make sure your bags are brought in."

She nearly laughed. Her bag, singular, was still her ratty old suitcase that didn't suit palace living at all. Of course the clothes inside certainly did, considering they were purchased with royal money.

Ignoring Colin's attempt to put his hand on her and guide her, she stepped to the side and shot him a glare. "Just have someone show me where the nursery is and I'll take her in."

"I'll show you."

His tone left no room for argument. Whatever. She wasn't going to fight, not with sweet Iris in her arms. Darcy truly wanted the best for Iris, even if her father was a lying jerk.

The three-story mansion stretched along the grounds farther than any "home" Darcy had ever seen. Lush plants and vibrant flowers surrounded the palace, edged along the circular drive and flanked the steps leading up to the entrance. Guards in full military-looking uniforms stood at attention on either side of the door.

This world was definitely not hers. Everything about her life had been transformed the moment she'd met Colin. From the new clothes, her emotional state, her sexual experiences…every single aspect of her personal and professional life would never be the same.

Passing by guards, entering a grand home with a tiered

fountain inside the entryway—*inside* the entryway—was stunning. Darcy shook her head as she followed Colin closely. As they passed random people…maids, men in suits, servants? Darcy noted that Colin would nod in greeting while the others would slightly bow. People actually bowed to the man.

Yes, they were worlds apart in every sense of the term because Darcy was on the same level as these people bowing to the man she wanted to throttle.

Colin led her toward a grand staircase that would make the iconic home from *Gone with the Wind* seem miniscule.

Colin turned before ascending the steps. "Why don't you let me carry her up?"

"I've got her and your back has been bothering you."

The corner of his mouth tipped as if he were holding back a smile. "You know me so well. And you care."

Darcy moved around him, refusing to even look at that handsome, sexy grin, those mocking, alluring blue eyes. "I saw you cringe when you stepped off the plane and again getting out of the car. And I only care about Iris."

As she started up, she knew he was behind her, most likely eyeing her rear end. That was fine, she couldn't stop him from looking, but she could prevent him from touching.

She had to prevent him from touching because if the man even tried to come on to her, she'd have a hard time holding it together. She couldn't ignore her emotions or hormones, no matter how much she wished her body would stop betraying her.

Once she reached the second floor, she turned back to see Colin gripping the banister, taking the steps more slowly than she'd thought he would. An unwelcome tug on her heart revealed the anger still rolling through her.

With one arm securing the sleeping baby, Darcy eased down a step and reached out her free hand. Colin froze, glancing from her hand to her face. She thought for sure his stubborn pride would have him swatting her away, but he put his hand in hers and squeezed. He climbed the last few steps with her support, without comment.

Once he righted himself, he moved down the hallway and Darcy was relieved they weren't heading up to the next floor because she highly doubted Colin could make it. Being on the plane for so long had most likely agitated his injury. His limp was a bit more prominent as he moved down the wide hallway. She wanted to reach for him again, but...she couldn't. Focusing on following him, she took in the luxurious surroundings.

Gold sconces adorned each section of wall between each door. The ceiling had scrolling artwork that she would have to admire later because Colin had neared the end of the hall and was going into a bedroom.

Bedroom was seriously too loose a term. The area she entered was a condo all its own with a formal sitting area, open bedroom tucked away in the far corner and two sets of French doors that opened onto a balcony offering a breathtaking view of the ocean.

"This is the nursery?"

"This is your room. I've asked for Iris's stuff to be put in here so you can stay close to her and you won't have to be near me or anyone else."

The crib was nestled in the opposite corner along the same wall as the king-sized bed. Moving across the wide room, Darcy gently laid Iris in the crib, surprised when the little one nestled deeper into the mattress and let out a soft sigh.

Once Darcy was sure Iris was going to stay asleep, she turned and moved back to where Colin remained standing. His eyes were fixed on hers and, try as she might, she couldn't look away. She both hated this man and found herself drawn to him for unexplainable reasons.

"We'll be fine now." She hoped he'd take the hint and leave. "I'm assuming someone will bring our things to this room."

Colin stepped closer to her, closing the gap between them. Darcy had to tip her head back to look up and hold his gaze.

"The formal ball is tomorrow night," he told her. "I want you there. With me."

This fairy tale was really starting to get out of control. She only wanted to be here with Iris. Getting dressed up and playing any other role wouldn't be a smart move.

"I'm your child's nanny," she informed him, forcing herself to ignore the thread of arousal winding though her at his intense stare. "I'm not your date for hire or one of your assistants you can order around. Everything changed when you opted to keep the truth from me."

A smile spread across his face, showcasing that dimple she'd once found sexy…. His palms slid up her bare arms, curved over her shoulders and glided on up to frame her face.

"You forget you agreed to do what I want while we're here."

The reminder was the equivalent of cold water being thrown in her face.

"You can't use me like this," she whispered.

"I'm not using you," he replied, his face now hovering just above hers. "I'm simply taking what I want and I want you on my arm during the ball."

Another layer of anger slid through her. "Is that why you told me to pack the blue dress?"

"No. I don't want anyone else to see you in that dress." His thumb stroked her bottom lips, his gaze honed in on her mouth. "That dress is for my eyes only. You'll wear it for dinner tonight."

"I don't want dinner with you," she threw back, though

her voice wasn't as strong as she'd hoped it would be. "You said I didn't have to leave my room if I didn't want to."

That thumb kept sliding back and forth with just enough pressure to have Darcy nearly begging him to kiss her. Darn hormones betraying her common sense.

"You're not leaving your room," he stated. "Dinner will be delivered."

He stepped away, leaving her aching, wanting more and all he'd done was use that low, sultry voice and fondled her lips. How pathetic could she be?

"Be ready by seven."

With that he turned and walked out of the room. Darcy continued to stare at the door long after he'd left. How dare that man expect her to just be at his beck and call? If he wanted to have dinner with her, fine, but she had a surprise of her own for him and it sure as hell didn't involve that sexy blue dress.

Darcy was playing hide-and-seek with Iris—which was quite easy in a room of this size with the adjoining bath and colossal walk-in closet—when someone knocked on her door.

Iris squealed and ran to the door, standing on her tip-toes to try to reach the knob. Darcy laughed and eased Iris back so she could open the door.

Darcy was greeted by one of the most beautiful women she'd ever seen in her life. The stranger was holding a long, white garment bag.

"Hi, Darcy," the woman said with a wide, radiant smile. "I'm Victoria Alexander. I'm Stefan's wife. Would you mind if I came in for just a moment?"

Iris sneaked around Darcy and started reaching for Victoria.

"Hi, sweetheart." Victoria bent slightly, shifting the

bag to the side so she could give Iris a kiss on her head. "How's my big girl? I missed you so much."

Darcy stepped aside and let Victoria pass through. Victoria crossed the room and hung the garment bag over the door leading into the closet area.

When she turned back around, she scooped Iris into her arms and squeezed her. The instant burn to Darcy's eyes was unexpected. Iris obviously had so many people who loved her, who needed her. Darcy had to face the harsh reality that she was just a random employee of the prince passing through. The impact on Darcy was huge, life-altering, but Iris would never even remember her.

"First of all, let me tell you how sorry I am about this whole thing." Iris wiggled in Victoria's arms until she was let free. "Stefan explained everything to me and I am embarrassed that he dropped what I'm sure was shocking news when he visited. I'm even more embarrassed that my brother-in-law took it upon himself to lie to you by omission. The Alexander men can be infuriating and you were dealt a double dose."

Darcy clasped her hands in front of her, not quite sure how to take this woman, but from the looks of things, she could be an ally.

"I'm from LA, too, so I know this whole royalty thing can be overwhelming at times," Victoria went on, offering a sweet smile. "I just want you to know that while you're here, please feel free to let me know if you need anything. Stefan and Mikos can be quite…difficult to communicate with at times. They seem to have their minds set on certain agendas and tend to let nothing stand in their way."

Darcy laughed. "That's one way of putting it."

"Mikos really is an amazing man." Victoria's eyes darted to where Iris was running around the spacious room, dodging the chaise longue, weaving through the sheers by the patio doors. "He's a wonderful father and he's been through so much. Don't be so quick to judge him when he's clearly made a drastic mistake."

Darcy shook her head and sighed. "I'm just the nanny. It's not my place to judge."

"If you were just the nanny, I wouldn't have spent the last two days making a dress for you to wear at the ball tomorrow." Victoria pointed to the garment bag. "Once you try it on, let me know if it needs to be altered. Mikos was pretty specific in his instructions."

Darcy stared at Victoria, then to the bag. "What? You made a dress?"

"I'm a designer. It's what I do." Victoria shrugged. "Sounds silly, I know, considering I'm also the queen, but that's just a title. I was designing dresses before I ever married into the Alexander family and I didn't want to lose my identity."

A bit taken aback, Darcy made her way to the garment bag and slid the zipper down. Peeling away the protective plastic, she gasped at the shimmering, pale blue formal gown. With one shoulder open and the other covered in clear crystals that were heavy at the top and tapered off toward the ruched waistline, Darcy didn't know if she'd ever seen a more beautiful dress.

"You made this?" she asked as she stared over at Victoria. "In two days?"

Laughing, Victoria nodded. "I did and I have to say, I think you'll look stunning in it."

Darcy's eyes locked onto the dress. Colin had requested this for her? He'd not only requested it, he'd been specific about what he'd wanted.

Darcy swallowed, unable to even comprehend this world she was temporarily living in.

"Would you mind if I took Iris out for a walk?" Victoria asked. "Stefan and I were going to go down to the beach before the guests start arriving and things get crazy around here."

Still in a daze, Darcy turned back to Victoria. "Oh, sure. Of course."

Victoria lifted Iris into her arms and kissed her neck until the baby giggled. "Let's go get some sand between our toes."

"Thank you," Darcy said before Victoria cleared the doorway. "The dress is spectacular, so 'thank you' seems so inadequate."

Victoria nodded and grinned. "It was my pleasure. I'll bring Iris back shortly. You look like you could use some time to let all of this sink in."

Just as Victoria reached the doorway, she turned and glanced over her shoulder. "I know it isn't my place, but I can't let this go. Mikos left here because he couldn't face being a widowed father. Between all of the responsibilities and losing his wife, he was severely broken. He was only looking out for Iris when he left. She's always been his number one priority, so whatever he said or didn't say to you, was only to protect her in the long run."

Victoria slipped out the door, shutting it with a soft click. Iris's squeals could still be heard, but Darcy was stuck on Victoria's parting words.

A new plan started to form. Colin was coming for dinner and he expected her to wear the other blue dress.

What was it with him and blue? Apparently that was his favorite color.

She shook her head and focused on her plan. She'd wear the blue dress, but she was going to make him suffer. He might think he had control here, but they both knew she carried the power right now. She'd seen the vulnerability in him when she'd helped him up the steps and she'd seen how much he fought the weakness that continued to plague him.

But as far as their relationship went, she knew he still wanted her and most likely he'd planned dinner in her room as a way to seduce her. He may have started off lying to her, he may not have meant to hurt her, but he'd had ample opportunities to tell her the truth before taking her to bed.

If he wanted her for more than a romp, she wasn't going to give in so easily. She'd make him beg if she had to, because she was worth it.

Tonight she'd see what they both were made of.

Fifteen

Colin wanted to get to the room before the dinner arrived. He'd also asked Stefan and Victoria to keep Iris for a few hours this evening. He hated incorporating them into his plan, but he had to call for reinforcements because time was not on his side.

Taking a deep breath and willing his damn nerves to settle, Colin knocked on her door. He wanted time alone with Darcy, wanted to be able to let her into his life, his world because he'd come to realize she mattered more than he'd ever thought possible. At first the instant physical attraction had eaten at him, but he'd soon come to the conclusion that she was much more than someone he wanted to sleep with. Darcy was honest, invigorating and perfectly suited to him…someone he could spend the rest of his life with. The woman had woven her way into his world just when he wanted to be left alone the most. She'd awakened something fresh, something new inside of him he'd thought was long dead and gone.

When the knob turned and the door eased open, Colin's breath caught in his throat as his eyes traveled over the stunning image before him.

"I didn't think you'd actually wear it."

His eyes raked over the bright blue dress that wrapped over Darcy's breasts, dipping low enough for him to see the swell, then securing at her waist where her classy figure dipped in just above the flare of those hips that drove him insane with want and need.

She'd left her hair down, silky and straight. The barest of makeup made her seem so natural, so beautiful and so seamlessly matched to what he wanted but hadn't known he was looking for.

"Why wouldn't I?" she asked, gesturing for him to come on in. "You requested it. You are paying me, after all."

Cringing as he walked in, Colin hated that he'd thrown money in her face once again. He'd been so low as to dangle the very thing she needed and then relished his delight when he got his way.

He was no better than her ex and deserved nothing at all from the woman he'd found himself falling for.

Before he could say more, another knock sounded on the door and a member of the waitstaff rolled in a covered cart. He took it on out to the patio, bid them a good evening and was gone.

"Shall we?" she asked.

Not giving him a chance to answer, she headed toward the open doors that lead to the terrace. The ocean breeze slid through her room, bringing that familiar saltwater scent he'd taken for granted as a kid, but positively loved now. And he realized how much he'd missed the island now that he was back.

White table linens, gold candlesticks and a cluster of white roses adorned the table set for two. Darcy went to take the cover off of one of the dishes on the cart, but Colin stepped in front of her, blocking her action.

"You look beautiful," he told her, needing her to know how he felt, that he believed what he was saying. "You're more than I deserve right now."

She tipped her chin, leveling his gaze. "I'm your nanny, Colin. Or would you prefer Mikos? Perhaps Your Highness. What do your other servants call you?"

"You're not my damn servant." Colin gritted his teeth. She was mocking him. "You can call me Mikos or Colin. Either would be fine."

She bowed and something in him snapped. He gripped her shoulders and gave her a slight shake.

"Don't bow to me. Ever."

Her eyes widened as she ran her tongue over her plump, glossy lips. "I'm your employee, am I not?"

"You're more, damn it, and you know it."

She stiffened beneath his touch. "Do I? Because I assumed even friends were up front with each other. Employees and employers keep their private lives separate, so excuse me if I'm a little confused."

He needed some space to cool off and she needed to get used to the fact that he wasn't going to give up so easily.

Releasing her, he pulled out a chair. "Sit. I'll get your dinner."

Surprisingly, she obliged. Once he'd served the meal, they ate in strained silence. Thoughts, possible conversations played over and over in his mind. There was so much he wanted to say, needed to say. But would she hear him, would the words penetrate into her heart where he needed them to go?

Pushing away from the table, Colin came to his feet and moved to the rail of the terrace. Watching the water ebb and flow against the shoreline calmed him. He absolutely loved his home, loved this view he was blessed to wake up to every day. It was all the hype around his name, his title that he could live without. He wanted a simple family life and the ability to live without the media snapping photos of him and his daughter, splashing whatever headlines they chose.

Stefan and Victoria had managed to attain such a life. They were making it work with their titles and they always managed to find time to themselves, away from all the hype and press. Could he have that, too? Could he attend to his duties and actually have a family?

His heart clenched. He hadn't known how much he wanted a family...a family with Darcy and Iris.

"I stared at this view for hours after I came home from the hospital," he started as he kept his back to her.

He hadn't counted on talking, but he couldn't keep her shut out of his world...not if he truly wanted her to be a part of it. And now more than ever he knew what he wanted.

"I'd sit out on the balcony off the master suite and curse that damn wheelchair. Karina was pregnant and all I could think was what type of father I could be to our child when I couldn't even stand or put on my own pants."

Darcy's chair scooted against the tile, but Colin kept his back to her. He couldn't turn and look her in the eye, didn't want to see pity staring back at him.

"I gradually got stronger, but I was too busy working on myself to realize I had to keep working on my marriage. Karina went through the pregnancy pretty much alone because I devoted all of my time to my recovery. I was determined to be on my feet when our baby came."

From the corner of his eye he saw Darcy step up to the rail, but far enough away that she was just out of reach. Probably for the best. With his emotional state, if she touched him, if she offered compassion right now, he'd break down, and baring his heart was about all the vulnerability he could handle. No way in hell did he want to be that man who clung to a woman, sobbing...which is exactly what he feared would happen if he didn't concentrate on the words and not the feelings of the past.

"When Iris came my whole outlook on life changed," he went on as he watched a palace guard pass by below. "The media wanted pictures of her, wanted photos of the happy family. It was then I realized we weren't a family. Karina had started sleeping in another room, she started distancing herself more and more from me and I can't blame her."

"It takes two to make a marriage work," Darcy added, her soft voice hitting him square in the heart. "You can't take all the blame."

Risking a glance over his shoulder, Colin met her intense gaze. No pity lingered in her eyes, if anything he saw understanding.

"I abandoned her long before she decided to leave," he replied. "After she suddenly passed away, I couldn't handle the strain of my life here any longer. It's no secret to my family that I've never wanted to be Prince of Galini Isle. I didn't want that weight on my shoulders. Stefan took the lead as king, which was fine with me, but if anything happens to him, I have no choice as long as I retain my title."

The familiar twinge in his back started out dull, the way it always did before blowing up into something major, so Colin pushed off the rail and stood straight, twisting at the waist to keep the muscles warm.

"Are you okay?" she asked.

"Fine. Just needed to move."

She stared at him another minute before looking back out to the water. "I have no clue about the life you were running from. I see this place and I think you have it all. But then I hear the pain in your voice and I know you are torn. I know you don't take this for granted and you're seriously worried about what step to take next."

Turning to fully face her, Colin took a step closer. "I'm not only worried about the title, Darcy. I'm worried about us."

Shaking her head, her lids lowered as she bit her lip for a moment before speaking. "How can *us* even exist? There was one night. One amazing night, but it was built on lies."

He started forward again, but halted when she held out her hand. With a deep breath, she turned to face him. "You don't understand how deeply you hurt me. You can't imagine what it cost me to come to you that night. I kept avoiding you because you had everything I always thought I was looking for and I was terrified if I let my guard down, I would want too much. I would love too much."

Breath caught in Colin's throat. "Darcy—"

"No." She shifted, backing up a step as if she feared he'd reach for her. "Whatever I felt wasn't real because I developed feelings for a man who doesn't exist."

Swallowing hard, damning any risk he was about to take, he closed the distance between them and gripped her arms. She fell against his chest, her mouth opening in a gasp.

"Does this feel fake to you?" he demanded, holding on to her a little too tightly. "Every time I kissed you, touched you, did all of that feel like a lie?"

Her intense gaze held his as he continued to loom over her. She'd cracked open something deep within him, something he hadn't even known he was holding back. His heart was wide open for her and she just needed to walk through. Damn it, he needed her to.

"You were so brave, calling me, wanting to come to me." He softened his voice. "You realized what we had was worth putting yourself out there for and you were ready to take a chance. Don't back away now, Darcy. Don't make judgment calls until you really see the big picture."

With the way he stood over her, her body arched against his, Colin couldn't avoid temptation another second. Nipping his lips against hers, testing to see if she'd let him continue, he nearly wept with relief when she didn't pull away.

As he wrapped his arms around her, pulling her hips flush against his own, he covered her mouth completely and deepened the kiss. Darcy's hands remained at her sides, though her mouth opened, inviting him in. For a split second, she froze, as if her mind were starting to override her emotions.

"No," he murmured against her lips. "Don't think. Feel. I never lied about how I feel and you know that. Everything we shared with our bodies was real. Everything I ever told you about how I felt was real."

With her eyes closed, she licked her swollen lips. "I can't do this, Colin. I'm here for Iris."

"Well I'm here for you," he whispered.

Not giving her another chance to speak, he claimed her mouth once again and ran his hands around to the front of her dress. He gave each side of the material a yank to expose her lace-covered breasts. On a gasp, Darcy tore her mouth from his and he feared he'd gone too far, but she tipped her head back and groaned. Colin stole the chance to trail a path of kisses down her silky skin until he reached the edge of the lace bra.

Darcy's hands fisted in his hair as he turned and backed her up against the smooth stone next to the patio doors. The last thing he wanted was to stay close to the rail and have one of the guards look up. Darcy was his and sharing even a glimpse of her was not an option.

Colin reached down, bunched up the bottom of her dress and slid his hand over her heated center. She adjusted her stance as he tore away her lacy panties and he had no doubt they matched the bra he was about to remove.

With a flick of his fingers, the front closure sprang open. Colin feasted on her while his hand continued to pleasure her. Her heavy panting quickened as her body arched against the stone. This is how he wanted Darcy, delirious with passion, aching with a need only he could provide because he was the only man for her.

"I pictured this the moment I saw the dress," he murmured against her heated skin. "It was made for you, made to drive me insane with wanting you."

Her hands went from his hair to his shoulders. Fingertips dug into him, but he continued, ready to feel her release, to watch her come apart in his arms.

As her hips bucked against him, Colin lifted his head to see her face. When he glanced up, her eyes were on him. The intensity of her gaze flooded him with a hope he wasn't sure she even knew she was offering.

Within seconds she was flying apart, calling his name. Colin gritted his teeth, concentrating on making this moment all about Darcy, no matter the cost.

As her trembling ceased, Colin slid his lips against hers. "You're mine for the ball tomorrow."

When she started to speak, Colin laid a finger against her lips. His other hand smoothed down her skirt as he kept his eyes on hers.

"Whatever you may think of me, know that I want you and I don't just mean physically. Yes, I lied. I did it to protect Iris because in the beginning she was all that mattered. But now you matter, too, more than you could ever know, and I'm giving you the chance to see everything about me without any guard on my heart. I want you to take it all in before you decide anything."

With shaky hands, she refastened her bra, pulled her

dress back into place. "What about…you're not leaving now, are you?"

He smiled. "You mean why aren't we having sex? Is that what you want right now, Darcy?"

Her eyes held so much heat, so much desire. "I don't know what I want," she whispered. "I thought I did."

As much as it cost him, he took a step back. "I'm not staying and I'm not making love with you. Tonight was all about you. I wanted you in that blue dress because I knew you'd feel beautiful. I wanted you out here on the balcony for dinner because I know you normally eat fast to get back to taking care of children. And I wanted you to come apart in my arms without giving anything in return to me. From here on out, everything in my life will be centered around my daughter and you. Take all the time you need to think about what that means because I'm not going anywhere."

Her chin quivered. If she started crying, he'd have to hold her and he wasn't sure he was strong enough to wrap his arms around her and not take more than she was ready for at this point. Never in his life had he been this scared of losing it all. Even when he'd battled with his duties or being confined to a wheelchair, nothing had put fear in him as much as the thought of losing Darcy.

"Not all guys take everything, Darcy. Don't compare me with the jerk who shattered your dreams." He started toward the open French doors, but stopped at the threshold to look back at her. "I may just be the guy who can make your dreams come true if you'd take the time to look beyond the anger."

Oh, how he hoped she would do just that. Living without Darcy was simply a life that was unthinkable.

Sixteen

Colin swirled the amber liquid around in his glass, resisting the urge to throw it across the room. He hadn't heard a word from Darcy since leaving her room last night. The ball was in a few hours and he honestly had no idea if she was going to be there with him or not.

But right now he couldn't care less about the ball. He wanted to know where he stood with Darcy. He'd bared his soul to her, he'd passed all power over to her and now he had to wait. This was not how he lived his life…ever. Power and control were staples in his life, ingrained in him at a young age. But Darcy was worth giving all of that up for. She was worth every sacrifice.

"You're going to drive yourself mad and drinking won't help."

Colin didn't turn at the sound of his brother's useless advice. "If I want to drink, I will."

Standing on the balcony off his suite, Colin wasn't calmed by the water rushing the shore. For the first time in his life, he was consumed by emotions he had no control over: fear, frustration, worry.

"Luc just arrived." Stefan's shoes scuffed over the tile as he leaned against the rail beside Colin. "I told him you'd be down shortly."

Colin wanted to see his best friend, especially since he hadn't met Luc's fiancée yet. But he had to get his head on straight first. He couldn't go down to the ball with this much emotional baggage. Even if the media had not been permitted inside, he didn't want fellow dignitaries to see him so vulnerable.

"What have you decided?" Stefan asked.

Tilting back his glass, Colin welcomed the burn of the whiskey. "I haven't decided anything."

"Because of Darcy?"

Colin shifted, leaning one elbow on the rail as he stared at his brother. "You were a mess on your coronation day, if I recall. I know I was fresh from the hospital and in a wheelchair, but I remember how you were torn up over Victoria leaving you."

Stefan nodded. "She was my wife."

"Only because you needed her to be," Colin corrected. "You married her for one reason and fell in love with her later. It's no different with Darcy and me. She started out as Iris's nanny, but…"

Stefan's eyes widened. "Are you saying you're in love with her?"

Colin swallowed, afraid to say the words aloud. He merely nodded because the first time he admitted the truth verbally, it would be to Darcy, not his brother.

"And you're waiting to see what happens with you two before deciding whether to keep your title or not?"

Colin glanced out to the ocean, contemplating his next decision because no matter what he chose, the outcome would be life-altering.

"I'll remain on Galini Isle if Darcy stays with me." Colin pushed off the rail, began to pace in an attempt to release some tension. "I can't do this alone, Stefan. Raising Iris, helping you reign over this country. I won't leave Iris to be raised by staff, not when I have a woman I can't live without, and Iris loves her. I've realized that Iris is happy here or in LA but she is really attached to Darcy. And so am I."

Stefan smiled. "Then maybe you should tell her how you feel. I'm not the one you need to be selling this to."

Colin stopped in front of his brother. "You think she's a good fit for me?"

"I think Victoria is crazy about her and it's obvious Iris is, too." Stefan slapped a hand on Colin's shoulder. "And I've never seen you this torn up over a woman. I've also seen you face cliffs that would make even the most experienced climber cringe. Even after your accident you wanted to get back out there. You were angry the doctors wouldn't allow it. So the fact this woman has you in knots, yeah, I think she's a perfect fit."

"Then I need your help."

Colin laid out his plan, ready to fight for the woman he loved...the woman who completed his family.

The risk he was taking was huge, but the payoff would be substantial if every part of his plan fell into place.

Victoria had delivered Colin's message to Darcy that he wanted to meet her in the south hall, just outside the private entrance into the ballroom. Now he paced as Iris sat on the gleaming marble floor, playing with the simple doll Darcy had given her that first day.

He'd battled over whether or not to have Iris present for this moment; he didn't want Darcy to think he was using his child. But he needed Iris here because they were a package deal, they were a family.

The soft click of heels echoed behind him. Colin took in a deep breath, willed himself to be strong and prepared to fight for what he wanted.

"Deedee pitty!" Iris exclaimed before she jumped to her feet.

"You are beautiful." Darcy's upbeat voice gave him hope that she wasn't miserable, that she wasn't dreading tonight. "Your gold gown is so pretty, Iris. What a big girl you are tonight."

Pulling up a courage he'd never had to use before, Colin turned and was nearly brought to his knees. Darcy stared across the open space. She wore the gown he'd asked his sister-in-law to make, she'd pulled her hair back into something sleek and fit for a princess and she wore the diamond earrings that had been his mother's. Obviously Victoria had delivered those along with his message, but Colin hadn't expected her to wear them, though he was so glad she had.

Yet, as breathtaking as Darcy was right at this moment, it was the sight of her holding Iris's hand that stole his breath away. The two most important women in his life stared back at him, waiting for him to say something, but he was utterly speechless.

"Thank you for the dress." Darcy took a step forward, and Iris, still holding onto her hand moved with her. "I've never felt so…I don't know what the word is."

"Breathtaking," he murmured. "You're positively breathtaking."

Her eyes widened. "I could say the same for you. I've never seen you in something so formal."

The standard royal uniform of a black double-breasted jacket with gold buttons, his medals for various works and services and his signature blue sash meant nothing to him. His entire life on Galini Isle meant nothing without this woman by his side.

"Are you ready to go in?" she asked, smoothing her hand down her gown as if nerves were getting to her, too.

"Not just yet. I wanted a minute alone with you before we go inside."

Darcy glanced down at Iris before meeting his gaze again. "I actually wanted to talk to you, too."

No. He refused to hear her say she couldn't do this anymore. He needed to tell her everything he'd planned before she made any decisions.

"Let me start," he told her.

"Me, me, me." Iris let go of Darcy's hand and extended both arms up. "Deedee hold me."

Laughing, Darcy swung Iris up into her arms. Colin wanted to capture this mental picture of Darcy in that pale blue gown and Darcy in her gold dress with matching gold headband, both of them laughing and smiling at each other. The bond those two had formed had been instant.

Colin zeroed in on the doll Iris clutched. He'd frowned upon it at first, but realized now how much it represented. Life could be simple, he could still have a normal existence, as long as Darcy shared it with him. Every relationship took work and he was ready to put forth every effort to make sure Darcy was in his life and happier than she'd ever been…if she would have him.

"Colin." Her eyes held his as she stepped forward. "What did you want to say?"

"I love you."

Darcy jerked, her gasp audible in the nearly empty hall.

He cursed beneath his breath. "That's not how I wanted to tell you. I wanted to lead into it by telling you how you've changed my life, how you've brought out something in me I thought was dead."

Colin closed the last bit of space between them, placing a hand on her arm and another on Iris's back. "I wanted to tell you how being without you all day has nearly killed me and how going to sleep at night without hearing your voice has left me feeling empty. I needed you to know how much you mean to me, how much you mean to Iris before I told you how deeply I've fallen in love with you."

Unshed tears swam in Darcy's eyes. "You're going to make me ruin my makeup."

He gently swiped the moisture just beneath her lashes. "I want to be the man who ruins your makeup for all the right reasons. I want to bring tears of joy to your life, I want to lie by your side every night, knowing you're happy and that I've done everything in my power to give you all the love you deserve, all the happiness you can handle."

Darcy bit her lip and lowered her lids as Iris laid her head on Darcy's shoulder and cuddled in closer.

"I can't give you any more children," she whispered. "I know you'll want more heirs."

He shut her up with a soft kiss to her lips. "The only thing I want is you and Iris. You both will complete my family."

She glanced up at him, one tear trickling down her cheek. Colin swiped it away with the pad of his thumb and cupped the side of her face.

"We can adopt, too." He watched as her eyes widened, her breath hitched. "I'll adopt as many babies or children or teenagers as you want. I'm not above giving children a home. I love that you have such a strong will to help others and I know you'll make an amazing princess of Galini Isle."

"Colin," she whispered on a gasp. "What—"

"I want you to marry me."

Darcy wrapped her other arm around Iris and continued to hold his stare. Iris's eyes were slowly drifting closed, as this was her bedtime, but between the ball and Colin wanting her to be part of this monumental moment, he couldn't just leave her to sleep in her room.

"Have you thought about this?" she asked. "Have you thought about what having someone like me will do to the media you tried so hard to dodge so you could find the life you wanted?"

"I found the life I wanted," he told her, stroking her damp cheek. "I found you. I wasn't even sure what I was looking for, Darcy. I wanted to be alone, I wanted to figure things out, but you kept working your way deeper into my heart and I can't be without you now. No matter where we live, I want to be with you. Facing this country, standing by my brother's side is what I'm supposed to do. I just don't want to do it without you."

"I have a life in America, Colin. I have a business I'm trying to save because of a promise I made to my grandmother. I can't ignore who I am, I can't lose my identity."

Colin nodded. "I understand. You will restore Loving Hands to its former glory. I don't want you to lose your identity, either, because it's what made me fall in love with you to begin with. See what staff you can hire back and have someone manage the office while we are here. So much can be done online, but I'm assuming you have someone you'd trust to run the office?"

Darcy nodded, her eyes darting away as if she were already thinking through the plans that would need to be made.

"Tell me we can make this work," he pleaded. "We can even keep the home in LA to use when we go back."

"You'd come with me when I go to check in on Loving Hands?" she asked, her eyes wide, brimming anew with unshed tears.

Colin wrapped his arm around her waist, tucking her side against his so he didn't squeeze Iris too much now that she was sound asleep. So much for her taking part in his epic moment.

"I have to admit, I'm quite fond of those steps," he muttered against her mouth before he slid his lips across hers. "I think keeping that house is a great idea."

"I'm still under contract, you know. What happens at the end of my six-month term?"

"We can make it our wedding date, if you'll have me."

Darcy sighed into him, opening her mouth beneath his. Everything about her felt right, perfect. How did someone from a completely different world fit so effortlessly into his?

He eased back. "I should tell you, I allowed a trusted media source into the ballroom. If you agreed to stay with me, I wanted to be in control of who revealed our good news first."

She froze, her eyes searching his. "I thought you hated the media."

"I hate the stories they make up and how they were portraying Iris and me as broken. We're a strong force, and with you by our side we are even stronger."

Darcy smiled. "You're an amazing father. I love you, Colin."

He'd never tire of hearing those words. "What was it you wanted to talk to me about?"

Her smile widened. "I was going to tell you I wanted to give us another chance."

Shocked, Colin eased back. "You mean you let me go through all of that knowing you were giving me another chance?"

With a shrug, she shifted Iris a bit higher in her arms. "I wanted to know how far you'd go. I needed to see you grovel, just a bit."

Sliding a hand around her waist, Colin leaned in to whisper in her ear. "You want to see groveling? I still owe you a shopping trip and I plan on helping you in the dressing room. We'll see who's groveling then."

Before she could utter a word, Colin wrapped his arms

around his girls and ushered them out. After putting Iris in her bed with a staff member close by the nursery, Colin whisked his future princess into her first royal ball. The first of many royal gatherings they'd be attending as a family.

* * * * *

To Ms Bobbie Tate—many years ago, you became my grandmother through marriage. You became my friend through your sweet spirit and my Maw Maw through your love. I can't thank you enough for being such a treasured part of my life.

One

"Hello, beautiful."

KC Gatlin heard the bell of a store door as she walked past on the sidewalk, but it simply registered as background noise. That voice, on the other hand, landed like a grenade on her senses. She could still hear the same words, the same deep sigh as she opened her door to him for the first time. Only this time he sounded not just sexy, but surprised.

Turning slowly, she found herself face-to-face with a man she had hoped not to see for many long, long months. The expectation was unrealistic, she knew, considering she once again lived in the same town as his family. The town he came home to visit often. His appearance now marked the approach of sure disaster, even as it brought into sharp focus how much she'd craved a glimpse of his tall runner's build and the unique blend of blonds in his close-cropped hair.

"Jacob Blackstone," she said, stalling while her brain struggled to come up with the flirty, easy responses for which she was known. They made her great tips as a waitress and bartender. But now, when she needed flippancy the most, it remained scarce. "What're you doing here?"

Stupid. There was a very logical reason why he would

be here: to check on his invalid mother, Lily Blackstone, now that his grandfather was dead and his brother Aiden had moved home. KC had just hoped to catch a few months' breather before facing her past.

Facing her mistakes.

"I mean, what are you doing on this end of town?" At least that question made sense. After all, Blackstone Manor was on the other side of Black Hills. But her fears, along with the steady, sober gaze of her former lover, had her brains whisked around like scrambled eggs. She had to get a handle on the panic jangling along her nerves.

He held up a small shopping bag. "Bandages. I needed to pick some up on my way home from work."

"Are you hurt—wait, home from work?" She tilted her head back for a better view of Jacob's face. She'd loved his height when they were together; how it sheltered her, protected her. Too bad that feeling of security had been nothing but an illusion.

"Yes, from the mill." He didn't look away, his gorgeous amber eyes with their unusual swirl of dark chocolate boring into her. She wanted a break from his unrelenting stare…and paradoxically wished she could bask in his attention. While her reactions ricocheted inside her, he went on, "I guess you haven't been home long enough to hear the news?" His voice rose at the end in a question, along with his brow.

"I guess not. I just moved back this week." Her stomach slowly turned over. Once. Then again. Why had her family not told her before she came home? The answer was obvious: they wanted her here, with them. She might never have returned if she'd known Jacob was now a permanent resident of Black Hills again.

She and Jacob had met on a plane to Black Hills—she'd been coming home from visiting her aunt in Seattle and had made a connecting flight in Philadelphia, where Jacob had been flying from to check on his mother. They'd seen each other every time he'd come to town since. Then reality had caught up with her in the threats of Jacob's grandfather and she'd gone to live with her aunt. A world away from this fascinating man and what they'd shared together.

She'd thought returning to her family would be safe now that James Blackstone was dead and gone. His threats to take away the livelihood of three single women unable to defend themselves—and a lifetime of proof that he'd do it—would finally be over. She'd known she would have to handle Jacob eventually, but had hoped to have more time. Much more.

She had a feeling he was about to burst her bubble.

"I've moved back to Black Hills to help Aiden run the mill. He has to split his time between here and New York, and with all the problems at the mill, we wanted a full-time presence."

"Yes, I heard that there were some odd things happening over there," she murmured. *Full-time?* The Lord must be punishing her for the secrets she kept.

Speaking of secrets… She tilted her head to the side as unobtrusively as possible to get a glimpse of the sidewalk behind Jacob. Her mother and grandmother were due to come out of the general store any minute. While she knew she had to talk to Jacob soon, she would prefer not to do it on the sidewalk in front of Parson's Pharmacy with the whole town looking on.

At least she had one thing going for her: Main Street was lined with miniature Bradford pear trees that would keep any busybodies from getting a clear view from the surrounding stores. In late spring, they were packed with white blooms that afforded even more privacy. Maybe no one would see more than just two neighbors greeting each other.

If she caused a scene on the sidewalk, Jacob would probably have a conniption. Months of him not taking her anywhere in public in Black Hills had taught her that much.

In the year they'd dated, Jacob had never introduced her to his family, never taken her *out* on a date. They'd spent evenings at her house, cooking, watching movies and making love before he went home to Philadelphia. She'd gone to visit his apartment there once, hoping to learn more about the city he loved enough to leave his family behind. Maybe a little about his work as the head of a large manufacturing company. But they'd never made it out of the apartment. KC had craved a real love all her life, after being abandoned over and over again as a child. Jacob wasn't looking for love… Still, she'd wanted him, so she'd forced herself not to need more from him.

His actions had made it obvious he wasn't interested in a long-term relationship, so she'd ignored her secret yearning for more. She'd been too afraid of losing him to insist. Responsible, steady guys usually didn't look at her twice—after all, she worked in a bar. But it wasn't just his incredible looks, smart, confident attitude or how good he'd been at rocking her world. Until she'd disappeared, Jacob had been attentive, caring and sexy—everything she'd ever wanted. But never committed—which was the one thing she'd needed him to be.

"Waiting for someone?" Jacob asked, folding his arms across his chest.

Oh, how she remembered that stance. He mostly resorted to it when he was disapproving or uncertain and didn't want anyone to know it. She'd jokingly called it his Dom stance, though Jacob didn't need power games to keep the bedroom interesting. His tightened muscles and locked legs exuded a commanding aura that sent shivers down her spine. Jake had strength in spades, but she hadn't trusted him to use it *for* her, to keep her. Her childhood had taught her it wouldn't happen.

She must have gotten lost in her thoughts, because Jacob bent closer, looming over her. "A new man, perhaps?"

A man? She'd thought she could be happily done with

the whole species for quite a while, until today. Jacob Blackstone had jump-started her tingling all over again. That intense gaze sent her heart racing and mouth watering. "Um, actually, my mom is on her way. Just checking for her, that's all."

Wow, this was so far from her usual easy conversations that she felt as if her secret was screaming from her guilty heart. Still, she could use his assumptions to her advantage.

"But yes, I do have a new man in my life." Jacob didn't need to know in what capacity after all. Anything to keep him at arm's length as long as possible.

"Is that why you changed your number…after refusing to answer your phone for weeks?"

Whoa. Not the direction she'd anticipated. But then, Jacob Blackstone had never failed to surprise her. There were whole areas of his life she knew absolutely nothing about.

"Look, Jacob, I'm really sorry. That was very bad of me." But she'd been carrying a heavy load with no idea what direction to go. A reason, not an excuse. She'd finally run far away, only returning once James Blackstone was dead. If she'd known Jacob would return, too—but no. Keeping secrets from him forever wasn't fair. She simply needed time. Time that was now draining away with the speed of sand in an hourglass.

"I just want to know why," he said, toned shoulder muscles flexing beneath his dress shirt. How did a CEO maintain such incredible physique…and stamina? She had to remind herself that it hadn't been enough, that she needed a man who would fight for her, no matter what anyone else thought.

"Did you think I couldn't handle the news that you wanted to break it off?" he asked.

"I…" Across the street, KC noticed a group of familiar women strolling down the sidewalk. Black Hills was a relatively small town. Everyone knew most everyone else.

Standing on Main Street talking with Jacob was the equivalent of standing on a stage. She needed to escape before someone started paying attention—

Or her mother and grandmother made an appearance.

"I just… Well, I didn't know how to tell you I wasn't interested anymore, actually." Clunky, but the truth. Knowing she'd chosen the cowardly way out, she still forced herself to sidestep him, then back away. "And you never seemed to want to deal with any deeper stuff, so…really, Jake, I'm just, well, sorry."

Then she turned and walked away, praying she could sidetrack her mother and grandmother before they proceeded to parade her baby down Main Street. She couldn't let Jacob learn about his son that way. Because he'd take one look and realize the main reason why she'd disappeared, if not the whole truth. As much as his arm's-length attitude had confused her, he didn't deserve that.

Which meant instead of the months she'd convinced herself she had to introduce Jacob to his son, she only had a matter of days. And she probably needed to figure out how to do that sooner rather than later.

Jacob Blackstone was too good at reading people not to realize when someone was lying. KC Gatlin showed all the signs.

This afternoon she'd shifted from side to side, avoided answering directly and refused to look him in the eye. Much to his deep disappointment.

He'd anticipated that moment when their eyes would meet more than anything. He was still thinking about it as he sat with his brothers in a booth directly opposite the bar at Lola's, sharing a platter of man food—wings and cheesy bacon-covered French fries—and alcohol. Jacob's drink of choice had always been wine. His brothers ragged him about his caviar tastes, but Jacob refused to apologize for having the most refined sensibilities of the family.

KC was far from refined. She'd been the burn of whiskey his body had been waiting for. That was why he'd ached for her to look at him this morning. He remembered well the sparks that would explode inside him just from sharing her gaze. His long-dormant body craved another taste, like a kid craved Pop Rocks.

He'd never forget their first meeting. From the moment she'd taken the plane seat next to him, he'd been enamored. That first conversation had revealed intelligence and humor in a beguiling mix. When they'd landed at the airport an hour away from Black Hills, he'd offered to share a ride. From that moment on, whenever he'd been in town, he'd spent as much time at her place as Blackstone Manor, until she'd stopped answering his phone calls months later. When he'd come home for his grandfather's funeral, she'd been nowhere to be found. The little house they'd spent so many enjoyable hours in had been sealed up tight.

He didn't want to, was shocked that he couldn't stop, but he'd hungered for her since that very first plane ride together. Time and distance hadn't changed that, much to his disgust. Nothing about his obsession made sense. They lived in two different worlds. They had two very different personalities and approaches to life. Still, he wasn't ready to let her go.

She'd been as wild as he'd expected, but she'd also led him to more genuine fun than he'd had his entire adult life. Quiet nights at home with a movie, cooking for two and sleeping in—oddities in his workaholic routine. No woman had interested him in any way beyond the physical. KC had interested him in every way.

She still did.

"Excuse me, guys."

Leaving his brothers staring after him, he made his way around tables to cross the room. They'd been in their corner for an hour while KC tended bar, and she hadn't looked directly at him a single time. Every second without that connection had itched below his skin until he couldn't even concentrate on the conversation. He'd deliberately kept their relationship out of the local headlines, but Jacob was desperate enough to risk a little limelight right now.

Oh, boy. His attitude made him very afraid he might step into stalker mode now that the possibility of seeing her around was very, very real. Some days, thoughts of KC had made him feel as if he was losing his mind.

He braced himself for her special brand of sarcasm. Something that had been noticeably lacking this morning.

"Jake. What brings you in tonight?"

You. Jacob ground his teeth together. Not because the shortening of his name bothered him, but because hearing it said in KC Gatlin's husky voice reminded him of evenings being soothed by her presence after an upsetting day with his mom. Reminded him of long nights between the sheets.

Far too distant memories.

"Do I need a reason? Can't I just enjoy the opportunity to watch a beautiful woman work the crowd?"

For the better part of a year, such a simple comment would have had her eyes sparkling, those full, naturally red lips tilting into a luscious smile, her mouth ready and willing to talk back. But not tonight.

"You never came to watch me before," she said, then dropped her gaze to the bar and started scrubbing, leaving him bereft once more. *So she wasn't gonna make this easy.*

He settled on a bar stool, watching that compact body displayed to advantage in a tight T-shirt and jeans. She acknowledged the move with a quick flick of her lashes, then studiously avoided looking at him again.

Just the way she'd ignored his phone calls. For seven months. He should have moved on by now, but his obsession had only grown. Now this successful, accomplished businessman found himself hunting the woman he craved in the local honky-tonk, because, well…because the cravings had become unbearable.

It no longer mattered that he couldn't figure out how she would fit into his life plan without wreaking havoc on it. She was the woman he shouldn't want, but the one woman he couldn't forget.

So he sucked up the little pride he had left and leaned closer. "You never did say where you'd been, KC."

She paused, then dropped the towel and met his gaze head-on. One of the things that had long enticed him was the very moment those turbulent hazel eyes turned his way, letting him see the woman inside and her mood, based on the dominant color of the day. Blue for calm and sunny. Green for sultry and sexy. Brown for angry or sad.

On tonight's menu: swirling milk chocolate. Wonder what he'd done to piss her off.

He'd never had a clue. They'd hooked up every time he'd come home to see his mother or take care of some business for his grandfather, until he'd found himself making up excuses just to return to Black Hills so he could see her. Watch her face while he talked with her. Sleep wrapped around her sweet-scented body. Hell, he'd even flown her out to Philadelphia once when he'd had to cancel his trip to Black Hills because of business.

Man, that had been a weekend to remember.

But the blank look on her face told him she wasn't into reminiscing. How much of a glutton for punishment was he willing to be?

"Come on, KC. Even as a friend, don't I deserve an answer?"

"I thought silence was my answer."

Burn. "Right."

For just a moment, the blankness slipped, revealing a flash of emotion that he couldn't interpret before it disappeared. But it revealed one important clue: indifference wasn't the problem.

So what was she hiding?

The KC he'd known had been all on the outside, open

with her emotions and actions. This closed-off version made him curious…and angry.

What had stripped away her joy, her spontaneity? Whatever it was, her attitude seemed to be reserved solely for him. He'd been watching her flirt and smile with other customers for an hour. The minute he'd appeared in front of her—shutdown.

Funny thing was, her spontaneity was one of the main things that drew him—and the one thing that had always kept him distant. Just thinking about living with uncertainty brought the barriers up. Other people found that kind of living by the seat of your pants exciting. He had enough of the unexpected in his life dealing with his twin; he didn't need more on a permanent basis. Luke's need for speed was as far from Jacob's scheduled existence as one could be from the other. Not to mention that his high-risk career as a race-car driver worried Jacob a lot.

So again he had to ask: Why was he sitting here instead of celebrating his freedom from his own version of risk?

"Was it because of this mystery man? Did you move to be with him?" Though the thought of her finding someone else hurt, maybe it was for the best. He needed something to break this incredible, horrible addiction.

She leaned closer, bracing against the bar. With her petite frame, the edge hit her higher than her waist, which gave him a really good view of her breasts in her tight Lola's T-shirt.

He was only human. Of course he looked.

Wait, was he seeing things? Because she seemed curvier than he remembered.

"Jacob," she said, drawing his gaze upward to her expectant face. Luckily she didn't call him on where he'd been looking. "Look, let's not do this here, okay? Another time, maybe."

"Why?" And why was he continuing to push this? "Is he here?"

"No, Jacob, that's not it."

The sudden sound of a phone ringing didn't register at first. After all, the bar was full of music, laughter and talking from the Friday-evening crowd. But the ringtone was persistent, and gained volume until he couldn't miss it. KC pulled out her phone and took one look at the display before answering.

She turned away, taking a few steps down the bar while she talked. He would have thought she'd completely dismissed him, except for the quick glances she kept shooting his way. After a few words he couldn't hear, she disconnected. Then she simply walked away.

His body mourned. His sensibilities raged. What did he have to do to get a simple explanation? Something more than "I'm sorry." Was that really too much to ask?

Determined to get answers, he stood up and strode after her. He came around the far side of the bar to catch a quick glimpse of her slipping out the back door. He knew her mother and grandmother lived in a small house behind the bar, so that must be where she was heading. If he intercepted her on her way back in, he could confront her without an audience.

All the better.

He could just make out her figure in the darkness as he made his way outside. Her body was silhouetted in the porch light from her family's house. He slowed his long stride. As she mounted the steps, the door opened and a woman who looked enough like her to be her mother stepped out.

That was when he heard another noise. But what caught his attention in that moment was what the older woman was holding.

A crying baby.

Jacob's world narrowed to the child.

"Goodness, girl." The voice of KC's mother drifted to

where he stood in the darkness. "I can't get Carter to stop crying for nothing. He wants his mama and no one else."

Jacob's legs carried him closer, his brain on hold as he tried to comprehend what he was seeing.

KC reached for the baby with the ease of a woman familiar with the move. The crying stopped almost immediately as she snuggled the child close into the crook of her neck. So natural. So beautiful.

So his.

The knowledge exploded over him in a wave of heat. As she swayed in the porch light, Jacob couldn't look away from the unusual dark golden curls that covered the baby's head.

"My brother and I had those same kind of curls," he murmured inanely.

In the newfound silence, they must have heard. KC jerked around to face him. But it was her mother Jacob found himself watching as the older woman's rounded eyes confirmed the suspicions in Jacob's whirling brain.

"KC," she said sharply, then stepped back through the door into the house.

KC didn't look in his direction again. She disappeared through the yellow rectangle of light in the entrance before slamming the door behind her, leaving Jacob alone in the dark.

It took a moment to get his feet to obey. As if by remote control, they carried him back to his brothers. He sank into the seat without really feeling it, seeing any of it. The numbness kept him from thinking, from dealing with the reality of what he'd just seen.

The bubble burst as he looked across the booth at his twin brother. Instantly, images of photographs from their childhood flooded his brain. Two boys, both with that thick dark blond hair. Curls all over until they'd gotten old enough to tame them.

"Jacob?" Luke said, hunching forward into his line of vision. "Jacob, are you okay? Where'd you go?"

Reaching out, Jacob picked up his half-full glass of wine and lifted it to his lips to perform the ultimate wine drinker's depravity. He chugged until every single drop was gone.

Then he set the glass down carefully and lay his palm flat beside it, praying the solidity of the table would ground him in the spinning room.

Luke lay his own palm on the table, mirroring Jacob's. "You cool?" Their version of letting each other know they were there.

And just like that, the words came to him, along with the anger. "I think I'm a daddy."

Two

Twenty-four hours later, Jacob finally stopped seething enough to confront KC. When he'd imagined what it would be like to find out he was going to be a parent, he'd pictured being across the table from his wife at an intimate dinner or seated next to each other in a doctor's office. Instead, the most gorgeous woman in the world had made him a father—and failed to mention it for twelve months.

The numbness had melted into rage, keeping Jacob awake long into the night. He went over the figures time and again. They hadn't spoken for seven months—he was ashamed that he could remember it to the day. He didn't have a lot of experience, but he'd guess the baby to be three to four months old. So how long had she known she was pregnant before she left? Two months? Three? Either way, they'd definitely been together when she found out. And those curls proved the baby to be a Blackstone heir.

He knew better than to see her before he calmed down. He couldn't be responsible for his actions while struggling with the deepest emotions he'd ever known. Control was his drug of choice—being out of control was something he preferred to keep well hidden. So he waited until he had his reactions under lock and key, and then he got in the car and drove.

KC lived a little outside town in a tiny house. Though there were other houses around, it wasn't really a subdivision. More of a series of dwellings that had sprung up over time as family members and friends and even acquaintances bought land and started building. The result was individual, with plenty of space and large trees. Ideal starter homes. Just imagining the possibilities ignited his anger once more.

He knew she'd be there—familiarity with her schedule gave him an advantage.

Sure enough, the door opened before he even knocked. She didn't speak, but simply turned back into the house, leaving him to follow. His gaze tracked her, cataloging every inch as she walked to the far end of the living room. Yeah, that body had changed, all right.

If he'd known what he was looking for, he'd have noticed right away. He'd been too busy searching for a connection in her eyes. But drinking in the whole package in jeans and a tank top, he saw the more dramatic curve from her waist to her hips, the added fullness in her breasts and a touch of softness in her jawline.

He'd thought nothing could make her more beautiful, but somehow having his baby had. And he hadn't been allowed to be a part of it.

Irritation with his attraction only ramped up his intensity. Carefully shuttering every window to his soul, he faced off with her in true Blackstone fashion.

He jerked his head in the direction of the driveway. "Someone else here?" he asked, referring to the car parked behind hers. So help him, if there was a man living here, he just might explode. Had she moved on that quickly? Had she let another man care for Jacob's child?

"Mom," she said quietly, slightly dampening his fuse. "She's in the nursery with Carter."

His throat almost closed. "Carter, huh?"

"Yes. Jake Carter."

Jake. Her nickname for Jacob—spoken with laughter, with intensity, with passion. It seemed more personal to name the baby that than to give him Jacob's last name.

"So you admit that he's mine?"

"Of course," she said, as if it made perfect sense under the circumstances. How could anything she'd done make perfect sense?

He stalked closer. "Why would you do this, KC? Was I really so horrible to you that you refused to let me be a part of—this?"

"That was never the issue, Jacob—"

"Then what was?" A really deep breath helped him lower his voice. It kept rising without his permission. *Control.* He needed control. "What *was* the issue, KC? Because I can't imagine one big enough that you told yourself it was okay to deceive me. To keep my son a secret from me."

Her arms crossed over her ribs, pushing those delectable breasts higher in the tank top. Something he shouldn't notice right now. At all.

"I did not deceive you. I never lied. I was going to tell you. I just hadn't figured out how."

"So he's three months old?"

"Yes, a week ago."

"So at any time in the past twelve months you could have picked up the phone. Or hell, just answered the phone when I called."

"I was afraid to. Going away just seemed the safest thing until I was sure what to do."

Jacob was surprised by the low rumble of his voice. "Safe? How? What the hell would safety have to do with it? I would never hurt you."

"I know that, Jacob, but it wasn't—"

The emotional roller coaster of the night caught up with him, pushing him past reasonable thought. "Know what?

It doesn't matter. Fact is, you deprived me of three months of knowing my—son," he choked out. "Not a note, a card or a call. Hell, not even a text. *By the way, I'm pregnant.* That's all it would have taken, KC, but you didn't even have the decency to do that."

He'd made himself available, chased after her like a dog with no sense, and *this* was what he got for it.

He came even closer until he loomed over her petite frame. "So now, I'll have what I want."

He wished her deep breath didn't draw his gaze downward. The low-level buzz of desire beneath his anger made him want to curse. He should not be attracted to a woman who could betray him. But he couldn't help it.

"Jake, please let me explain."

He refused to look in those turbulent eyes again. "Too late. No talking. No thinking. Now I will act."

She straightened, bracing her spine, which was just as well.

"Carter will come home."

Her jaw clenched. "He is home."

"My home." Some sick part of him took pleasure in the panic creeping over her features. "He's a Blackstone. He should be with his family."

She swallowed hard. "Jacob, please don't do this."

"Mark my words, KC. I will make you regret what you've done. I promise."

As soon as he'd stormed out of her house, KC began to dread the moment Jacob would act on his threat. The longer she waited, the more her stomach hurt.

She knew she'd made a bad choice, but given the circumstances, she thought she'd done the best she could. Waiting until James Blackstone was dead to tell Jacob about Carter had seemed like the safest option for protecting her baby, along with her family. In the absence of a reliable husband or father, her mother had given her all to raising and providing for KC and her brother. KC had felt that pull of loyalties every day that she'd been away, but in the end, she'd chosen to take care of the women who had raised her. Her mother and grandmother would have no defense against James Blackstone if he'd retaliated by taking away their livelihood on a whim.

But Jacob didn't believe her, because he was acting on emotion, not facts.

How did she get him to listen to those facts now? She knew James's lawyer, Canton, could work all kinds of voodoo if he wanted. Was Jacob even now making arrangements to take her baby from her? The thought shook her deeper than any of the rest. Not just for the typical mommy reason: being away from her child for more than a day was more than she could handle right now. But Jacob was essentially an unknown as a parent.

Would he expose their child to the same rejection and abandonment she'd been subjected to as a child? In her experience, fathers didn't know the meaning of commitment. But she'd been luckier than her brother. Her father had hung around until she was eight. Her older brother had never really known his.

After stewing for the rest of the morning, she decided she couldn't wait for Jacob to make the first move. Jacob wasn't answering his cell, which scared her all the more. When she called Blackstone Manor directly, the old butler answered. She'd spoken to Nolen a few times before when she'd called to talk to her friend Christina, who'd married Jacob's brother. Nolen was helpful, telling her that Jacob had said something about going to Booties 'n' Bunting.

Panic and anger had surged in KC's gut. Booties 'n' Bunting was the only exclusive baby boutique in town. Jacob had the money to do all the things she couldn't. She'd bought all her baby furniture and clothes at Walmart. He'd have designer diapers and the best furniture, not to mention the best lawyer when it came down to a fight.

She'd made the mistake; now it was up to her to ensure that it didn't turn into a brawl.

KC's stomach twisted into knots as she drove across Black Hills. Whipping her little Honda into Booties 'n' Bunting's parking lot, she jumped out of the car and plowed down the sidewalk, not letting herself remember just how little she belonged in the boutique district, much less in a store selling fifty-dollar baby onesies. Jacob's Tahoe parked out front confirmed that he was here. No doubt arming himself with everything he needed to take her child away.

She let herself in with her head held high and tracked down her prey, standing next to the most gorgeous crib she'd ever seen.

"What do you think you're doing?"

Jacob faced her with surprise lightening his face. For a split second, KC saw the man she'd wanted more than anything. Then a mocking grin slid across his lips.

"Could you give us a minute, please?" Jacob asked the saleswoman. Until that moment, KC hadn't even noticed her on the other side of the crib. The woman turned quietly and walked to the back of the store before Jacob continued, "What does it look like, KC? I'm outfitting the nursery at Blackstone Manor."

Oh, no, he wasn't. "You don't need any of this stuff, Jacob, because Carter is *not* coming to live with you."

"And what makes you say that?"

"This isn't just about you, Jake. You need to think about what's best for Carter."

"I am. I have the means to provide my son with everything he needs. Unlike you."

Hurt streaked through her, but she pushed it deep down under her growing anger. "Really? Can you give him love? Can you comfort him? Can you guide him? Or are you planning on using your money to turn that job over to a nanny so you can go about your perfectly planned days?"

His narrowed eyes should have had her shaking, but

she refused to back down. Her son's future was at stake. She didn't want to hurt Jacob, but how else could she get through to him? "One thing I can say with certainty is that I can provide him those things. You, I'm not so sure about."

Not waiting to give him a chance to outthink her, she pushed forward. Crowding into Jacob's space, she said, "You want Carter to come live with you? I understand why you would. I don't blame you for that." Her breath caught for a moment. "And I don't blame you for not trusting me, but I'm not turning my son over to just anyone."

"Oh, you don't have to turn him over," Jacob said, his voice deepening as if he had gravel in his throat. "You can come, too. I'm sure I could find a…use…for you."

Strike number two. How many body shots did he plan to take? Because she sure didn't need the reminder that Jacob had wanted her for sex and only sex.

She wasn't sure how long she stood there with wide eyes before he looked away. But he wasn't backing down. "The fact is, you've had Carter to yourself for three months. Your time just ran out."

She'd guessed Jacob was a formidable businessman. But when he turned that laser-sharp stare on her, it sliced through what little armor she had and put every inner doubt on display.

"Jacob, I understand your anger," she said, trying to slow her panic with a deep breath. "I made a horrible miscalculation. So I want to do my part to make this work. But no lawyers. No fighting. You want Carter to be a part of your life? Prove it to me." *Please, please, let this work.*

"What do I need to prove? We knew each other for over a year. You know everything you need to know about me."

"I know everything about certain parts of you." If he wanted the truth, she could comply. "I know you're half-way decent in bed." That whopper of an understatement almost choked her. "How good you are at picking up girls on planes. That you enjoy being with me at home but don't want to be seen in public with me. That I'm good enough for sex but not allowed into any other part of your life. None of that tells me a damn thing about what kind of father you are."

"So you want me to prove I can change diapers?" His shocked expression would be a thing to savor later when she stopped being so afraid of him that she might wet her pants.

"I want to know that you're more than a sexual being, Jacob. Show me what kind of man you truly are. Can I trust your word? Can I believe you when you say you aren't bad-mouthing me to my child behind my back? Can I trust you to teach him morals and work ethic and decency? Because I won't let *my child* become a chip off James Blackstone's block."

Jacob stepped closer, literally towering over her. "What the hell are you talking about?"

Arching her neck to stare at him wasn't comfortable, but she wasn't going to concede with even a single step backward. "Since you didn't know about Carter, I'm going to guess and say you didn't know your grandfather came to see me right before he died."

"Aiden would have told me."

"Did Aiden know? He wasn't there."

"Who was?"

"That lawyer guy."

"Canton?"

"That's the one. They came to the house one morning. I'd only known I was pregnant for a week."

"How could he possibly know about that?"

KC shook her head. "I'm not sure. But he did know how long we'd been seeing each other. I wouldn't put it past either of them to spy on me somehow."

Jacob's Adam's apple shifted in his throat. KC was sorry to have to deliver her news.

"James knew you were pregnant with my child." The deadness in his voice reverberated through her. She'd often wondered how a man like his grandfather could have had a child. What kind of family did you create with manipulation and fear? No wonder Aiden Blackstone had run far, far away when he was younger.

Though Jacob had always seemed quite normal, she'd sensed a dark sadness underneath that excellent control of his. What games had James Blackstone played with his grandsons? What terror had he wreaked in their family before he died? Jacob had never even come close to sharing something that personal.

"That's the only reason I could think of that he would demand I leave town. And never come back."

Jacob seemed frozen; not a muscle moved. He gripped the crib rail with one hand. The knuckles turned white... and stayed white.

"But you didn't stay away."

"No. Once I found out he was dead, I thought the coast would be clear to come home." That might have been a mistake, too. "But he threatened my family's business—"

"How?" he asked, his eyes narrowing as if he suspected a lie.

"Jacob," she said, shaking her head at him, "your grandfather owned half the town. He'd rented us the land Lola's is on for my entire life but never would allow my mother or grandmother to buy it. I suspect it was so he could use it to his advantage if the opportunity arose."

She tried to breathe around the anger that rose at the memory. "He threatened to shut down the business. Everything my mother and grandmother own is tied up in Lola's. Not to mention that their house is on that land, too. So I agreed, and the men left. Then I cashed out some savings and used it to move away."

Jacob smirked. "Serves him right."

"When I heard about his death, I thought—well, we all thought—he couldn't hurt us anymore. I just hadn't figured out what to do about you yet."

"And you think this is the answer?"

"It's the only one I've got." Might as well be honest about that. "Let's face it, Jacob. You have money and a damn good lawyer. But James didn't own me, and neither do you. If you want to be part of Carter's life, stop throwing your weight around and work with me."

"Who put you in charge? You haven't exactly proved yourself trustworthy."

Unease rippled through her body. She knew she'd had good reasons for her choices, but when she looked at it from his point of view… "I'm not denying you access to Carter out of anger or revenge, Jacob. I simply want to know that he's in good hands. That you're willing to make a place for a baby in your life. Not hand him over to a well-paid nanny."

His eyes searched hers. "How can I be sure he's in good hands with you?"

"I— Well—" Words failed her for a moment.

"Face it, KC. You ran halfway across the country to hide my child from me. I'm not the only one with something to prove. The question is, how?"

Three

Jacob hadn't felt so out of control since the last time he'd had KC in a bed. Only, anger wasn't nearly as pleasurable. Still, he used the impetus to propel himself through the door to his brother Aiden's study at Blackstone Manor, knowing John Canton was there for a meeting.

This morning, Aiden had mentioned an appointment for the lawyer to drop off some paperwork for their grandfather's will. Canton still had control of the Blackstone inheritance, for now. There were some final hoops to jump through, then Jacob and his brothers would be free of James Blackstone and his minion.

"You bastard," Jacob growled, absorbing his brother's shocked look as he passed. But his focus was trained wholly on the lawyer.

The same lawyer who had assisted their grandfather in blackmailing Aiden into marrying Christina, their mother's nurse, terrorizing them with threats of compromising their mother's health and care if they didn't comply.

"I knew you would force two people to get married to suit James's purposes. Threaten, and bully, and even ruin an entire town on the whim of a dead man. But I seriously thought any decent human being would draw the line at cutting a child completely out of a man's life." He let his momentum carry him until he loomed over the smaller man. "Guess I thought wrong."

From behind the desk, Aiden asked, "Jacob, care to fill me in?"

Canton didn't even blink...or pretend not to understand what Jacob referred to. "I did as your grandfather ordered."

"Didn't you think I should have a say?"

Canton shrugged. "That was not for me to decide."

With a growl, Jacob reached forward, but arms made of steel were there to stop him. Slowly, Aiden inched him back until there was enough room for him to stand between Jacob and the man he felt like killing.

"I've obviously missed something," Aiden said. "Tell me now."

From the other side of the barrier Aiden provided, Canton spoke. *Brave man.* "I believe Jacob is referring to a conversation his grandfather had with Ms. Gatlin."

"What?" Aiden looked surprised.

Jacob turned away, relieving his brother of guard duty. At least not looking at his grandfather's lawyer would help him regain control. In thirty-three years, he'd never experienced this many emotional twists. He didn't like it. He needed stability. All the more reason to stay away from KC—but that wasn't an option anymore.

He turned back, focusing on his brother. "I went to see KC Gatlin."

Aiden gave a short nod. "So it's true? The baby is yours?"

"He's three months old." Jacob felt the need to clarify, now that he had more facts. "I met KC on one of my flights home and..." How did he put this without making it sound as if KC was simply a booty call? "Okay, I was sleeping at her place whenever I came to town." Why sugarcoat his selfishness?

Aiden's thick brows went up. "Wow, Jacob. I didn't know you had it in you."

"Not the time, Aiden."

"Really? You brought it up."

Jacob ignored the brotherly razzing and moved on. "The baby is definitely mine." That shut down his brother's grin. Real quick. "Dear ol' Grandpa threatened her until she skipped town, never telling me about it—my son."

Aiden narrowed his gaze on the lawyer. "How would Grandfather even find out KC was pregnant? Medical records are confidential. Was he rummaging through her trash for a pregnancy test?"

Jacob barely held his control as he waited for the answer.

Canton smirked. "Anything can be had for the right price. Turns out, one of the little nurses at KC's doctor has a serious cash-flow problem."

Jacob was rushing forward before he even thought. Only the barricade created by Aiden's body stopped his attack. His own heavy breathing sounded loud in Jacob's ears; his heart thudded as he realized the full magnitude of his grandfather's invasion of privacy. Jacob wanted to do bodily harm all over again.

"Easy," Aiden murmured against his ear. "Let's get our questions answered, and then he'll be gone. Forever this time."

Silence reigned as Jacob tried to gather the remnants of his self-control. His thoughts whirled, reminding him if he hadn't come home for good, he might never have found out he was a father. Pulling back, he announced, "It was only by accident I found out that KC had my child."

Canton spoke again from a safe distance across the room. "Then I don't understand the issue."

Jacob rounded on him but didn't move closer. He didn't trust himself. "The issue? You tried to separate me from my child."

"But by your own admission, we didn't succeed."

The guy simply didn't get it. "Would you ever have told me?"

"Your grandfather demanded complete loyalty. And discretion. Of course I wouldn't have." His weasel-like face didn't change expression. "And since Ms. Gatlin moved without contacting you and didn't come home during the remainder of your grandfather's lifetime, she'd fulfilled our terms. In which case, there was nothing to tell."

"I'm glad you think so. I guess that clears your conscience."

The man didn't bother to defend himself. "I don't have a conscience. I have a job."

"That's enough," Aiden interjected. "Canton, we're done for now. I'll reschedule with you *at your office* later and we will finish up the last of the paperwork for Grandfather's affairs."

The lawyer was smart enough to take an out when it was given to him. He scurried through the door without so much as a by-your-leave. But his departure ratcheted down Jacob's anger by a few notches.

"Man, I'll be glad to see the last of that guy," Aiden said as he straightened the papers on his desk.

"How much longer?"

Aiden had spent the year dealing with his grandfather's lawyer after James had blackmailed him into marrying Christina. Luckily, it had all worked out for the best, but the lawyer's presence was an annoying reminder of their grandfather's manipulations.

Aiden waved the papers at him. "This is the end of it. The year is almost up and we will be free from it all. Including Canton. I just wish there was a way to punish him for what he's done rather than be rewarded with the money Grandfather left him." Aiden settled back into his chair, looking every inch the sophisticated Manhattan art dealer, though he now lived in South Carolina instead of New York. "KC Gatlin, huh? Beautiful, but definitely dif-

ferent from your standard of socialites and fellow busi-
nesswomen."

"Tell me about it." Jacob started to pace, hoping to ex-
pend the energy thrumming beneath his skin. Hell, he just
might have to go for another jog, even though he'd done
five miles this morning. Especially as he thought about
KC's earlier accusations.

"Where do you want to go from here?" Aiden asked
after several moments.

More of that loaded silence.

Finally, Jacob said, "I would be lying if I said I didn't
want to see her again. Didn't wish we could pick up where
we left off when she disappeared. But—no." He glanced
over at his brother. "She's not right for me long-term."

"Why not?"

Good question. "Let's see. She doesn't fit in with
what I want in life, who I am. She's more like Luke—
unpredictable, headstrong." *And makes me feel just as unpredictable. Out of control.*

"She's gorgeous."

"She works in a bar."

"Ah, a hard worker."

Jacob stared hard at the bookshelves, cataloging the
shapes and colors of the books but not the titles. "She kept
my son a secret."

"So she panicked and made a mistake. You enjoyed
being with her before. What's the real problem?"

Could he let his guard down? Even a little? Jacob was
used to his brothers confiding in him, not the other way
around. "I just— Before, it was easy. But she's right. I kept
her compartmentalized so I wouldn't have any interference in my life." He ran his hand across his close-cropped
hair. "It had nothing to do with only wanting her for sex
and everything to do with making our relationship convenient for me."

"Relationships are anything but convenient. I'm learning to roll with it because the good far outweighs every-thing else."

Jacob felt a moment of envy. Inflexibility seemed to have been bred into him. Strict adherence to standards and procedures served him well in business, not so much in relationships. At least, the few he'd had. He rarely saw a woman more than a handful of times, since he wasn't ready for the long-term thing yet. Maybe not for several more years.

KC had taken him off guard. He could admit to himself that he'd kept her compartmentalized in his life because he'd been afraid—afraid of her taking over, afraid of losing control, afraid of being ruled by emotions instead of his brain.

I want another chance at that woman. No. "She's my son's mother. Better to stay close and know your enemy, right?"

Aiden's smirk took him by surprise. "Jacob, the last time I fell for that line, I ended up married to the woman who changed my life, my way of thinking, forever. For the better, but still…"

"Not me."

Aiden's expression screamed *famous last words*, but Jacob ignored it. Aiden had vowed at eighteen never to return to Blackstone Manor—now he was happily married and living here full-time, with frequent business trips to New York to manage his art import/export business.

Would Jacob end up the same? Moving home was definitely the right choice, especially since his son was now here. But married? Not to KC. As exciting as being with her was, he wanted peace, not unpredictability.

"Jacob."

The serious tone in Aiden's voice cut through Jacob's confusion. "Yeah?"

"What are you going to do about KC? About the baby?"

"Carter," he said, clearing his throat when it tried to

close. "Forcing her to give him to me would probably lead to a legal battle—and prove me to be a jackass. She might not have a lot of money, but she won't give him up without a fight." He frowned. "The bigger question is, what is she gonna do about me?"

Aiden thought for a moment. "Do you want her?"

"I do, but I told you, she's not right—"

"Sometimes things don't come the way we plan."

And Jacob had been planning his entire life. He didn't know if he could give that up.

"I can't walk away. He's my son." Deep down he cringed at the hypocrisy of speaking as if memories of those incredible nights together had no influence on Jacob's desire to see KC again.

"Then you need to be very careful…for you and for them."

Jacob glanced over. "What do you mean?"

"I mean what's going on at the mill. We still haven't figured out who's trying to sabotage our business, and until we do, nobody associated with us is safe. Delaying shipments and messing with customers' orders is annoying, but what happened to Christina last year could have killed her. She wasn't the target, but that doesn't change the result."

Jacob remembered all too well the night a group of thugs had set Aiden's studio on fire…with Christina inside. The incident was one of many suspicious events at the Blackstones' cotton mill, but it had escalated the game to a whole new level. "You think they might target my son?"

"Not on purpose, but then again…" Aiden leveled a look at him, sending unease running over Jacob's nerve endings. "It would be for the best to keep the connection quiet. For now."

"Right." *For now.* Jacob had a lot of experience keeping things quiet in this town.

"So get control, before someone else does."

Like KC. Jacob had been irritated and fascinated at the

baby store. Until she'd burst in and started making demands, he hadn't known what it would be like to have all that feistiness turned on him as a weapon. His whole body had lit up inside. At this rate, she'd have the upper hand in no time. Leading him about by the nose, or rather, another appendage he'd just as soon keep under control.

Jacob was grateful when Aiden moved on, pulling him back out of his convoluted thoughts.

"Back to business," Aiden said. "I had a call from Bateman at the mill right before Canton arrived."

Jacob had had a call, too, but he'd let it go to voice mail. He'd been too keyed up from his clash with KC to make sense of business.

A problem he never had.

Deflating like a balloon, Jacob dropped into one of the chairs facing the desk, grateful Aiden had replaced the old leather-and-wood chairs with cozy wing backs. His brother and sister-in-law were slowly updating things in Blackstone Manor—especially the study—inch by inch scraping away the depressive stench of their grandfather's manipulation to reveal the true beauty of a home that had stood for generations in the face of natural and man-made tribulations.

"I just don't know how to get a handle on the problems at the mill," Jacob said, reminding them both of the year they'd spent dealing with the saboteur. "We need to find another way of catching this guy. I mean, I'm there every day, but I'm in management. And no one's talking to me. We need someone on the floor, someone relatable. I think that's where the problem is."

"Definitely can't be either of us. See if Bateman can put you in touch with someone over there to help. He'll know who's trustworthy."

"Right." His foreman had already been very helpful. Because Jacob wasn't capable of judging anyone at the moment. Business would give him something to focus on besides KC, just as soon as they settled on some ground rules.

Start as you mean to go on, his mother had always said. For everyone involved, that was exactly what they needed to do.

As she faced off with Jake on her front porch, KC knew she was simply delaying the inevitable, but she couldn't stop herself from arguing just for the sake of it. "What if my mom wasn't here to watch Carter?"

KC spoke with no real hope of making a dent in Jacob's thinking but couldn't resist pointing out the inconvenience he was putting everyone through. Everyone but him. She hated the push-pull of her emotions. Wanting to keep him at arm's length, yet greedy for even a little bit of his attention. When he'd finally called after two days of silence, her heart had sped up, but she couldn't help being contrary about his sudden demand for her to take a Sunday drive with him.

"If we're going to do this, there will be ground rules," he said now as he waited impatiently on her doorstep. "That means we need to talk. Alone."

That take-charge tone shouldn't send shivers down her arms but it did. "Yes, we should," she conceded. "But you still could've given me a heads-up sooner."

She took her time walking back to the nursery. Not that she had anything important to do on Sunday mornings. Her mother usually came over before lunch for some downtime with Carter since Lola's wasn't open. Sometimes KC ran a few errands. Then they had family dinner with Grandma. Asking her mother to stay with Carter for a little while was really a formality, but it also wouldn't hurt Jacob to wait on her porch a few minutes, just for giggles and grins.

Her pokiness had her changing into jeans and pulling her hair into a ponytail, but she simply refused to hurry. He didn't comment when she finally came outside, just held the door for her to climb into his Tahoe and closed it with a firm hand.

The contained atmosphere of Jacob's SUV didn't settle her nerves. The interior smelled like him—spicy and dark. If she closed her eyes and breathed deep, she could almost remember what it felt like to have that scent all over her and wish she didn't ever have to wash it away. After all, she never knew when she might smell it again.

After she'd left, been away from him for a while, she realized how sad it was to need someone so badly and yet be relegated mostly to a physical relationship. They said men did it all the time—obviously Jake had—but KC had never felt more alone than when she was lying in his arms, wishing she was good enough for him to make her a true part of his life.

The door opened and Jacob slid into his seat with his phone pressed to his ear. "I'm on my way," he said as he reached for his seat belt. Without explanation he stowed the phone in the center console. Then he put the Tahoe in gear and pulled out of KC's driveway, all without telling her where they were going or what this was about.

"You said something about ground rules?" she prompted.

Jacob maintained a still silence for several minutes more, at odds with the hum of the tires on asphalt. "I've made it clear what I want—"

"Actually, you haven't."

He shot a glance at her.

"Well, you haven't," she insisted. "Are you trying to get Carter full-time? Not that I'd let you have custody, but still…do you want him part-time? Have you thought about how that will work, how it will affect him? Do you—?"

"Enough, KC."

His deep frown had her second-guessing her pushiness, but she wouldn't apologize for trying to protect her son.

"I started making demands because I was angry. Unlike you, I didn't get to think about this, plan for this, nothing. So I reacted out of emotion." The heavy sound of his breath was her clue to how much self-control he was exerting.

A part of her, the wounded part, wanted to push him. Make him acknowledge that she and Carter would have a big place in his life—something he hadn't found important enough to offer her before. Another part of her wanted to see that legendary control smashed to teeny-tiny pieces.

Just the way it had when they were in bed together. But as soon as the sex had been done, he'd been back in form— charming and attentive but perfectly capable of walking away.

"We have to do what's best for Carter," he said, staring straight out the windshield. "So how do we do that?"

"Let me get to know you."

"To what end? What are we striving for here, KC?" He ran a rough hand over his smooth chin. In the time she'd known him, she'd never once seen him with stubble. "Because if you think you can disappear with him if you don't like what you learn, that's not an option. I will always find you."

But for all the wrong reasons. "My family is here, Jacob," she countered. "It didn't take me long to realize that running is not a safe, long-term option. I made a mistake— one I won't repeat. But I'd better like what I see, because unlimited access to your son *is* on the line." She shifted against the leather seat, wondering if she could back up her big words with action.

"Look," she said. "I don't want us to spend our time trying to guard against each other. If this is truly about Carter—" she ignored Jake's look "—then we need to work together. I tried to do things your way before and got nowhere. So this really is all on you. Show me what you're like out of bed so I can see where Carter and—" *I. Carter and I.* She cleared her throat, grateful she hadn't finished that sentence out loud. "Where Carter fits. Prove to me that he's in good hands with you."

"So what is it I'm supposed to do to show you I'm a

good man? Hell, even I don't know if I'm a good father. I've never been one before. Is this a written exam? A field test?"

"Oh, it's a field test, all right. No more secrets, Jacob."

He shot her a quick glance. "Are you seriously saying you didn't learn anything about me in the months we were together? Why don't you tell me what you do know and I'll fill in the blanks."

All the memories of their time together flooded her mind—long nights, laughter and loving… No. Not loving. The thought created an urge to get under his skin in the only way she knew how.

She shifted as close to him as her seat belt would allow. "Well," she said, reaching out a fingertip. "I know you're sensitive here." She brushed gently back and forth along the outer edge of his ear, then down along his jawline. "I know you shave early and often because you don't like looking scruffy." The back of her hand rubbed down along his throat, then up along his collarbone. "I know your favorite sexual position is missionary because it gives you the most control—"

"What do you want to know?" Jacob interrupted, his voice deep and rough.

She leaned back in her seat, trying to cover her smile of satisfaction. Torturing him had always been fun. "What do you do—I mean, really do? What do you care about? Enjoy? Do you plan on staying here for longer than just the time it takes to get the mill on track?"

"What about you?" he asked, countering a question with a question.

"What do you mean?"

"The same questions apply to you," he said, turning the Tahoe into a nearby parking lot so he could face her. "This won't be a one-way street, KC."

Yes, her sins would haunt her forever. She should never have kept Carter from Jake.

His gaze held her immobile as he spoke. "I'm not the

only one paying for my mistakes," he said, leaning closer, crowding her until her heart fluttered in panic. "We're gonna be seeing a lot of each other."

"I'm sure," she said with a nod, trying to get a handle on her nerves.

His gaze dropped to her lips as she licked them, reminding her of things she was better off forgetting. The space around them closed in before he spoke. "The thing is, with your history, I'm now questioning every word from these pretty lips."

She had no warning when his thumb came up to rub back and forth across her mouth. It affected her more than she wanted to admit, and left her dreaming of more.

"Consequences, KC. Those are *my* terms."

Her lips firmed, and she had a feeling she'd adopted the stubborn look she was known to turn on disruptive customers. Jacob simply smiled, then pulled back and got them on the road again.

"Well," she said, a little stumped, "my life is pretty simple, as you saw before. My job, my time revolves around my family."

"They're supportive? Of you and Carter?"

Her heart jumped at the softening of his voice as he said their son's name. "Definitely. Our family is very close. And my grandmother, mother and brother love Carter unconditionally."

Even if their new connection to the Blackstone family scared her mother no end. KC rubbed her palms against her jean-covered thighs, searching for more words. "What about your family?" She swallowed hard, distracted by thoughts of her friend Christina, a true Blackstone now. She would be so mad when she realized KC had kept the truth about Carter from her. "Did you tell them?"

"I guess you'll see," Jacob said, then turned the truck abruptly into a construction area.

With a start, KC realized they were at the site of the new

playground Aiden Blackstone had raised money to build on the south end of town. The large field had been cleared and leveled, with concrete slabs laid in various areas to anchor the equipment. Current construction seemed to center around a two-story fort at the far end.

There, a group of people stood to one side while a handful of construction workers drilled to secure the platforms. "Do they know we're coming?" she asked.

"They knew I was coming," Jacob said. "You'll just be the bonus."

Yeah, right.

Jacob settled his palm on the door's handle, then spoke while staring straight ahead. "And for the record, my favorite position isn't missionary. It's you on top."

KC swallowed hard. That revelation held her in place for longer than she liked. Her mind wandered back to all the times—no. No time for that now.

She'd be better off remembering all the times he'd left her to go back to Philadelphia with rarely a call between trips. KC scrambled out of the car, ignoring Jacob's frown. He'd always liked to open the door for her, and she'd trained herself to wait for him. It had been hard for a girl who'd always taken care of herself, but she'd done it because it made him happy. And deep down, because it made her feel special. Letting him do it now would be too big of a reminder of those precious moments.

As she followed at a slight distance behind him across the open lot, KC wished there was at least one happy face in the crowd. She recognized the newlywed couple as they approached, and neither looked very welcoming.

Yep, the news of Carter's parentage had spread.

Jacob introduced her to his brother, but Christina stepped in before he could go further. "We know each other," she said quietly. "Hey, KC."

KC couldn't read her friend's tone or expression. They'd been very close before KC left, often hanging out in the same group of women. But she, Christina and their friend Avery Prescott had formed a tight bond through community work that hadn't been weakened by their different social statuses. KC had told them she was moving away for a job, and other than some chance encounters, she hadn't tried to renew her bond with the women since she'd returned.

All it would have taken was one of them to figure out who Carter's father was, and they all would have known. Living and working in Blackstone Manor—and now married to the Blackstone heir—Christina posed a danger to KC. She hadn't wanted to risk anything until she had all her ducks in a row.

Seeing Christina now reminded KC how much she'd given up in the past year, but keeping Carter safe had been worth it.

"KC, I'm sorry we've never met formally," Aiden said.

How should she respond? *Me, too?* Since she'd determined to stay as far away from the Blackstones as possible, that would be a complete lie.

He went on, apparently not expecting a response. "There's no point in beating around the bush," he said, earning an eye roll from his wife. "Jacob told us what happened, or rather, why you left town."

He glanced at his wife, and they shared a look of momentary communion. "If Christina and I understand anything, it's how manipulative my grandfather was, how he set out to twist the world into his own version of perfect. But for the record, we look forward to you and Carter joining our family."

KC shot a glance at Jacob, wondering how he felt about all this. His stoic look gave nothing away. "I'm not sure how this will work out yet…"

Aiden shook his head. "Doesn't matter. If you need us, we're here."

Then he turned to talk to Jacob as if he hadn't just dropped a bomb in the middle of the park.

"How's everything comin'?" Jacob asked, seeming un-fazed by his brother's words.

"Hartwell's doing a great job…"

KC watched as Aiden's hand cupped Christina's shoulder. He stroked up and down hypnotically, giving his wife his attention even while he talked to Jacob. The ache that bloomed deep in her gut didn't mean KC was jealous of the other couple. Not really.

Knowing that bridging this gap was up to her, KC wasn't willing to simply stand there while the men talked.

"Hey, Christina," she said, feeling awkwardly formal. If she was going to be around Jacob's family and regain her friendships, she would have to jump this hurdle. "How are you?"

"Good," her friend said. "Things are really good."

Drawing in a deep breath, Christina lifted dark, somber eyes. "Do you have any pictures of him? I haven't gotten to see Carter up close since you've been back."

KC tried not to wince. The implication hung in the air. It meant a lot to Christina that KC had cut her out of her life for the past year. Pulling her phone out of her back pocket, KC scrolled until she found the folder of Carter's pictures.

Then she held the phone out for Christina, hoping her willingness to share would start to repair the breach in their relationship.

"Oh, how sweet," the other woman breathed.

KC felt the motherly glow of pride she still wasn't quite used to spread over her. Then Jacob reached out and took the phone from Christina's hand. Turning the screen toward him, he started to scroll through the pictures. KC couldn't stand to look at him, the sadness in his eyes was so profound.

The guilt that had been growing over her decision to keep Carter from Jacob burrowed so deep inside she doubted she'd ever be rid of it. Yes, she'd been afraid. She'd been angry. She'd been pressured. But in the end, her choice to cave under James Blackstone's demands had deeply hurt Jacob. Now she got to live with the proof of that.

Finally he came to a single picture and stopped, simply staring at it. He didn't say anything, and the ache was made worse by his silence.

In an effort to escape, KC shifted her eyes, but found herself caught by Aiden Blackstone's hard stare. She'd heard he was a tough nut to crack, but the echo of his brother's pain she saw in Aiden's eyes told her she'd hurt not just Jacob but his family, too. A hard knot of self-disgust formed in her stomach.

"Let me show you what the construction crew is up to," Christina said, taking her arm to guide KC away.

Probably for the best. She might ruin her boundaries with Jacob by bursting into tears right there.

Not that being with Christina was much easier. She knew the minute her friend threw the first glance her way, then threw several more as they walked slowly away from the men toward the half-standing fort. The sound of electric nail drivers peppered the air. To the right, three men were securing a set of monkey bars into the ground.

"I really don't understand, KC," Christina finally said. "And I want to understand. I do."

"James threatened my family. I didn't know how to get out of that without hurting them."

"That part I get," Christina said "Trust me, I really do. My own experiences with James are numerous and traumatic."

KC could only imagine, living in Blackstone Manor with James while caring for his daughter, Lily, meant Christina had no way to avoid him. Lily required full-time care after a car accident had eventually led to a long-term coma. Christina's dedication to her patient and friend had put her at James's mercy. Then he'd forced Aiden and Christina to marry. Last year had been just as traumatic for her as for KC.

"What I don't understand," Christina said, "is why you

wouldn't come to me as your friend, ask for help, let me offer some kind of emotional support for you and Carter. Didn't you think I'd want to do that for you?"

KC stopped, afraid if she tried to walk and talk at the same time she might fall flat on her face. She wasn't prepared for this conversation, and sparring with Jacob took a lot out of her. "I am sorry, Christina. But I couldn't risk you putting two and two together."

"Putting two and two together? Honey, I had no idea you'd even met Jacob. How you managed to actually get pregnant by him is a mystery of biblical proportions."

KC had always appreciated that Christina got her point across in a ladylike but effective manner.

"Keeping our—" she swallowed hard "—affair a secret wasn't my choice. Only…afterward."

"Well, y'all did a damn fine job of it. I mean, I saw Jacob some when he was home all those times. I never had an inkling."

KC finally gathered the courage to meet Christina's questioning gaze head-on. "Which is not what I wanted. I never chose for our relationship to be this hidden thing. That was how Jacob wanted it, though I didn't realize it until after that first week. Somehow I knew, deep down, that Jacob wouldn't continue seeing me if we went public." So she'd bit her tongue and grasped at whatever crumb he'd thrown her, even though every secret encounter hurt more than the last.

"Why wouldn't Jacob want people to know about you?" Christina asked, shaking her head with the same confusion KC felt over it all.

"I suspect because he had no intention of our time together meaning any more than it did. When he came to visit, we would hang out and have, um, fun, but that's as far as it went. No invitations to dinner at a restaurant in town, no family dinners, nothing. If he wanted to go out, he drove me to Sheffield. What other message was I supposed to get from that, Christina?"

Her friend glanced back at the men over KC's shoulder. "I don't know," she murmured.

"It wasn't the type of relationship you bring something as permanent as a baby into." As much as KC wished it had been. "Not that I planned to keep Carter a secret permanently. I just hadn't figured out how to tell Jacob yet."

"But close friends are supposed to be there for each other. What about me? Avery? We could have helped you, KC."

"Asking you to keep this secret wouldn't have been fair to you. And James Blackstone would not have taken kindly to word getting back to Jacob. He made that very clear."

"Well, you weren't the first," Christina said with a grimace. "Thank goodness his days of manipulating others are over. Why didn't you come to Jacob as soon as you knew James was dead?"

Because I still wanted more than I could have. "It was kind of hard to figure out how to bring the subject up. Not that keeping it from him was ideal, either. But the important thing now is that Jacob and I learn how to work together for Carter."

She hoped her friend could see the sincerity she felt as she met her gaze head on. "And that you forgive me. Being without you and Avery these past months has been very lonely."

Christina hugged her, not holding back even though KC knew she still had to have reservations. After all, she was a Blackstone now. Who knew how this would all play out?

"I've missed you, too," Christina said.

KC closed her eyes and returned the hug. Her family had been there for her every step of the way. The aunt she'd gone to stay with had been helpful and loving. Really, KC had had a great deal of support. But she'd missed her friends. It hadn't been the same without them.

It hadn't been what she wanted. Sometimes, when she was pregnant, she would dream that Jacob was with her. Rubbing her back. Picking out names. Dreaming of the future. But she'd been too afraid to reach out for what she'd wanted.

She glanced back over her shoulder to see Jacob and Aiden still in an intense discussion. Jake's brows were drawn together, his eyes hooded. So far away from where she wanted him. She'd never have him now, not even the way she'd had him before.

Still, she'd make up for her mistakes with Jacob. Somehow.

Four

On the ride back to the house, Jacob sat in silence, wondering what Christina had said to KC. Their hug before they parted suggested it had been something good, but Jacob had been too caught up in his own emotions to track their conversation. He left KC to her thoughts as he tried to sort through the tangle in his own brain.

When they reached KC's house, there was a vehicle he didn't recognize parked in the driveway. This time, a Ford F150. Jacob felt jealousy make another appearance. Though plenty of women drove trucks in the South, it was usually a man's mode of transportation. What man would go into KC's house when she wasn't home?

They were barely inside before KC's mom appeared in the doorway from the kitchen. She watched him with wide eyes that made him ashamed of his threats to take Carter away. This woman was obviously afraid of his role in her grandson's life. Considering his grandfather's demands, Jacob could see why.

"Carter's asleep," she said, her voice hushed as if they were still in the baby's room.

"Thanks, Mom," KC said with a smile. "Did he give you any trouble? He's been a little fussy the past few days."

"As if that baby could be any trouble at all," her mother scoffed.

"That last time he got sick he screamed for hours," a man said, appearing in the doorway behind KC's mother. "Babies are cute, but trust me, they're trouble."

His mother glared. "Spoken like a true bachelor."

"Babies can't help it that their only form of communication is crying," KC said with dry humor.

The man in jeans didn't appear offended. Jacob studied him. He'd forgotten KC had a brother. Zachary, he thought was his name. Though his complexion was darker, his hair long and midnight black, those unusual hazel eyes were the same as KC's. After introductions, the men took each other's measure silently. From her brief mentions of him, Jacob remembered her brother worked hard to assist his mother and grandmother, full shifts at the mill, nights at Lola's and even extra gigs doing crop dusting for the cotton farmers around here. Hardworking and conscientious.

Ms. Gatlin eyed KC and Jacob both, as if wondering what they'd gotten up to while they were gone, then swung her gaze solely in Jacob's direction. The thorough inspection made him uneasy, but Jacob wasn't offering any explanations. Whatever KC wanted her mom to know, she'd tell her. Jacob just wished she would be on her way so he could finally meet his son.

Something he wasn't doing under the prying eyes of a crowd.

"Mom, I'm going to have to miss lunch this afternoon," KC said. "But we'll be there next week."

Her mother's look turned into a glare, but Jacob stayed silent. This was between KC and her family.

"Why would you do this, KC?" the older woman finally asked, turning her glare on her daughter. "Why would you give him full access to Carter?"

"Mom—"

"He's the enemy. Can't you see that?"

Offended, Jacob squared his shoulders, his back tightening. He felt as if he needed to jump to his own defense, to KC's defense, but the anguish in the older woman's voice held him back. He met the turbulent gaze of KC's brother as he placed an arm around his mother's shoulders. Jacob guessed her intensity had to do with more than just Jacob and the Blackstones. But he wasn't going to justify his right to see his son to anyone.

"Mother, he is Carter's father."

"Yes, and you ran far away rather than turn to him for help. What kind of father could he possibly be?"

Jacob wouldn't know until he was given a chance—

"I made a mistake," KC said. "It was wrong of me to keep Jacob from his son. I need to find a way to make that right. You knew he'd come into our lives when I moved back. Somehow."

"I can't believe you're just going to let him waltz in here and take Carter from us," she said, tears forming in her eyes, which were so like her children's.

Jacob couldn't stand it. "Ms. Gatlin, I'm not going to—"

"Why not? Old James sure did."

Yes, and Jacob was getting very tired of the reminder. "I realize my grandfather was a selfish man, a bully who had to get his own way. In his mind, threatening her, driving her away, meant he could control who became a true Blackstone." His conscience twinged as he realized he'd inherited some of that need for control himself. Still, Jacob stood a little taller. "But I'm not James Blackstone. The last thing I want is for Carter to disappear."

It was clear from her face that he hadn't made her feel better about him. "Then I guess it's a good thing she didn't take the money to abort him, isn't it?"

Jacob choked, heat flushing up his neck to his face. "What?"

Her eyes widened as Ms. Gatlin realized she'd gone too

far. She looked to KC, her mouth opening but no sound coming out.

With a resigned look, KC murmured, "I was offered a check. I could have had the money if I'd been willing to get rid of Carter for good. But I couldn't."

"And he just let you walk away?" Apparently there were a few things Canton had left out.

KC shrugged as if it didn't matter, but her face told a different story. "As long as I abided by the rules and didn't contact you, he let me go and my family didn't have to suffer. He said, well, he said I was a rare find."

"Why?"

"He called me an honest woman who knew her limitations. Coming from someone who'd just threatened the livelihood of three single women, it wasn't really a compliment, though in his twisted way he probably meant it as one."

Jacob could see how James would feel that way. He would have wished for her to take the permanent option, but as evil as James was, he would admire someone who held on to her integrity, even while he was crushing her will under his demands.

"So you're not your grandfather," Ms. Gatlin said, not willing to completely let go. "But I saw how you treated KC before. And you're still a hotshot businessman, right? Always looking at the bottom line, aren't you? How do we know you won't take Carter and try to destroy us because we stood in your way?"

"You don't. You simply have to trust me."

"Men aren't usually trustworthy."

Jacob could see the shadow of pain in all three pairs of eyes. It was obvious the distrust ran far deeper than their treatment at the hands of James Blackstone. He glanced over at KC, seeing shades of despair on her beautiful features. Having lived in the same town as the Gatlins all his life, he should know this story. Sadly, he didn't. And the fact that he had never asked drove home his own failings in his time with KC.

"Ms. Gatlin," he said, the fear in the older woman's eyes making it impossible for him to keep silent. "I assure you, KC and I are going to work this out in the best possible way *for Carter*. That is the goal here."

KC's mom looked skeptical, almost militant, but Jacob wasn't fazed. He only had to prove himself to KC. The rest would work itself out later.

"Fine, KC," her mother conceded, though she still sounded skeptical. "What about tomorrow?"

"Same schedule as usual," KC said with a quick glance his way. "I'll see you around noon."

Schedules. Another thing they'd work out later.

With that assurance, KC's mother and brother were on their way. Jacob remained rooted where he was while KC walked them outside. A deep breath in, then out, cleared away his tension from the meeting with KC's family. The silence seeped into him until he thought he could almost hear the whispering breaths of his son as he slept. Fiction, he knew. A product of his strain to connect with the son he hadn't known existed. Yet he couldn't move. Couldn't make himself walk down that hallway.

He could do this. He might not have prepared to have children yet, but it was like any kink in the manufacturing schedule. A good manager evaluated the situation, decided on the best approach and followed through. Right now, that situation entailed seeing his son up close for the first time.

KC stood talking to her mom out by her car. Turning away, Jacob took one step, then two, until he was in the short hall that connected the rooms in KC's tiny house. Having been in the house before today, Jacob easily guessed which room was Carter's. Sure enough, a little plaque adorned with pictures of painted tools, baseball bats and soccer balls was hung on the door.

Easing it open, Jacob peered through the dim light to

the white crib at the far side. His heart pounded as he registered the white noise of a small fan, the green walls and the mobile of stuffed dinosaurs in bright colors over the crib.

Despite the adrenaline rushing through his veins, Jacob forced himself across the small space. His first peek over the crib railings revealed an incredibly small…person. Splayed on his back, Carter slept with arms sprawled and legs kicked out at crazy angles. Jacob smiled. KC slept the same way. They'd never done the traditional spooning thing for longer than it took for her to fall asleep. After that, she needed her space. He wondered if Carter was just as grumpy in the mornings.

Carter's cheeks were round and chubby, his lips the same full bow shape as KC's. Those dark golden curls covered his head, prompting Jacob to reach out and slip his finger inside one with careful precision. His son. His *son*.

Though he hadn't heard her come in, he felt KC as she approached his side. He couldn't turn to face her, afraid the unexpected emotions swirling through him in this moment would be plain to see on his face.

"You can pick him up if you want to hold him," KC whispered. "He's still in the stage where he sleeps through a lot."

Jacob hadn't even known there was such a stage. He knew absolutely nothing about babies. His brothers had never had kids. His colleagues who had children didn't talk about them much; their existence was marked by no more than the requisite picture on their desks. Seeing Carter lie there, so innocent, so alive, showed him just how wrong that was.

But how did he do the fatherhood thing differently? He'd have to dig deep to remember his own father, those early years before their time together was stolen by James Blackstone.

His hand tightened on the railing of the crib, but he couldn't bring himself to move. Carter looked too small;

surely he needed special handling. Jacob didn't even know where to start.

As if she could read his body language, even in the gloom, KC reached over and scooped Carter up. Nothing more than a twitch of his mouth showed that he was aware. Not giving Jacob a choice, KC lifted Carter's small body to rest against his chest.

"Let his head rest in the crook of your arm," she said.

Jacob felt himself follow her instructions, easing the baby into position. He supported Carter's head with his elbow and placed his arm along the back of the child's spine. His hand cupped a diapered rump. As the warm weight settled against him, Jacob's other arm came around to hug his son close.

As he stared down, conscious of Carter's weight and fragility, something deep inside him sighed. He might be daunted by the task in front of him, but in that moment, he knew he wouldn't stop until he'd done the best he possibly could for the child lying so trustingly in his arms. This was no longer just a wrestling match about who would have custody of Carter.

Raising his gaze to the woman who had brought about such a miracle, despite all the circumstances, Jacob couldn't hold back the words. "Thank you."

As her answering smile doubled the emotion he was holding inside, he knew a moment of panic. Because if this new feeling he had was any indication, he wasn't going anywhere for a long, long time.

All the emotions and discoveries of the past few days had jumbled up inside of Jacob, creating a desperate need for activity. He'd chosen a doozy. Jacob pulled into the driveway leading to Blackstone Manor just a few feet ahead of the furniture truck from Booties 'n' Bunting. Good. He hadn't wanted to miss the delivery.

By the time Aiden showed up, Jacob had supervised the

unloading of all the furniture into the third-floor nursery. Jacob was there, surrounded by the parts of the sleigh-style crib he'd chosen, when his brother found him.

"Why is that the only piece of furniture that didn't come assembled? You know they have people for that, right?" Aiden picked up a railing and twirled it, testing the weight.

Jacob immediately stole it back. "*I* wanted to do this part."

His brother considered the room and all its new contents for a moment before turning back to Jacob. "This baby stuff has really gotten to you," he said.

Jacob didn't bother to answer. The evidence lay all around him.

"What about the woman? She get to you, too?"

Jacob really didn't want to talk about that—or the lack of consensus over the care of their son, though he hoped to remedy that soon. But the few moments he'd spent with Carter—perfection.

Aiden crouched nearby, watching as Jacob finished sorting the parts and then started to assemble the crib. When he spoke again, it was in a more serious tone. "What's it really like, Jacob?"

Jacob looked up, ready to throw out his usual flippant reply, until he caught sight of Aiden's intensely curious gaze. A lot had changed about his brother since his forced marriage…or maybe Jacob was just getting to see more of the real Aiden. Either way, there'd been more moments like these in the past year than there'd been their entire lives.

"You mean with Carter?"

Aiden nodded.

"Scary," he admitted as he tightened a screw. "Exhilarating, fun, messy…" He torqued another.

"Sounds a lot like marriage," Aiden said with a grin, dropping to the carpet on the other side of the pile of crib parts.

Jacob thought of KC—how exciting it had been to be

with her, addictive but unsettling, because she kept him so off balance. Not neat and tidy the way he'd set his life up to be. He'd thought he was the only man who felt that way. "I wouldn't know," Jacob said.

"Did I really just hear a man admit that he didn't have all the answers?" Christina teased as she walked into the room. "Surely that's a sign of the end times or something."

She bent over to kiss Aiden, her wealth of deep brown hair sweeping forward. Then she straightened and looked around the room. Jacob followed her gaze, wondering if the medium green walls, light wood furniture and race-car theme would meet with a woman's approval. His answer came with her smile.

"This is really beautiful, Jacob," she said. "I'll admit I couldn't resist a peek when the painters were here. But this furniture—it all blends so well together."

Aiden put in his two cents'. "That's female speak for it matches."

He ducked away from Christina's swat, rolling across the soft new carpet with a laugh. Jacob couldn't help but smile. He'd never seen two people so happy—especially not in this house. Miracles did indeed happen.

He thought he might just want a miracle of his own.

"So when is KC moving in?" Christina asked.

And that stopped the fun right in its tracks. "So far, she's not."

Christina and Aiden glanced at each other, sending a jolt through Jacob as he recognized that same form of unspoken communication he and KC were developing. Then Christina waved her hand around the room. "I don't understand. What's all this for if she and the baby aren't going to live here? Is she refusing to give you a chance?"

When Jacob didn't answer quickly enough, Christina gasped. "Jacob, you aren't going to try to separate them, are you?"

He didn't like the thread of panic in her voice any more

than the panic rising in his own throat. Especially since he wasn't sure whether it originated in thoughts of losing KC...or keeping her.

"We haven't decided what we're doing in the future," he said, trying to smooth things over.

"Obviously *you* have," she insisted, "or preparing this nursery would be completely pointless."

"Christina, don't interfere," Aiden warned.

"How can I not?" she asked, trembling in her distress. "KC is my friend. I realize she made a tough choice, a wrong choice, but separating her from Carter wouldn't fix that."

"I'm not trying to punish KC. Or permanently take Carter from his mother." Jacob glanced around the room, not able to put his thoughts into coherent words. Commitment with KC wasn't even on the horizon, but already his love for his son had solidified. At least he could have this special place to start building his own family, even if he didn't get the girl. "I'm not really sure what I'm doing here. I just...need this. And so will Carter, regardless of whether or not KC and I are together."

Christina had a warning for him, though. "That may be all it is, Jacob. You may have no intention of doing any harm. You probably don't want my advice, but there's something your two testosterone-soaked brains need to realize," she said, glancing at Aiden. "If KC sees this room, and it doesn't come with some form of commitment to her, too, she'll think one thing and one thing only. That her trust in letting you into her life with Carter was sadly misplaced because you planned to take her baby from her all along."

Five

KC stood near the guard shack leading to the mill factory grounds, waiting for Jacob to make an appearance. It had been a week, and they still hadn't come to a conclusion about custody arrangements. This couldn't be put off any longer. While she dreaded the outcome, the wait was killing her. She couldn't sleep for worry, and the last thing she needed with a baby and full-time job was no sleep.

That could make things very emotional, very messy.

Finally Jacob walked through the gates toward his Tahoe. The frown on his face spoke of deep thought, until he spotted her leaning against a tree near his vehicle. Then his stride turned determined, purposeful. Within a minute or two, he had pulled KC out of sight of the guard shack and urged her into the Tahoe's front seat. Her door closed just as the bell rang for change of shift.

"Still ashamed of being seen with me?" she asked.

Jacob paused before putting the key in the ignition. "Do you want our former relationship to go public like this?"

Technically, he hadn't answered her question, but she didn't argue because he was right. She didn't want whatever was between them to become public in a rush of twisted gossip. But she couldn't wait any longer to ease the churning in her stomach. She wouldn't admit to herself that his use of the word *former* made it churn that much more.

She didn't speak as he started to drive. She just fidgeted in the seat of the Tahoe, watching as raindrops started to hit the window as he gained speed.

"What's wrong?" he asked.

She forced herself to quit moving and speak her fears aloud. "Are you going to sic that lawyer on me?"

"You mean Canton?" He shook his head, his jaw tightening over his thoughts—whatever those might be. "No, KC. If he's never near my son again, it will be too soon."

That was promising, at least. "Another lawyer, then?"

"Why? Are you anxious to get it all in writing?"

Fear dried her mouth, postponing her response. After a moment, Jacob pulled over and turned to face her. The distance between them felt like miles instead of a few inches.

"Look. We can do this two ways." That no-nonsense look on Jake's face scared her even more. "We can decide between us. Or we can involve a judge and a lawyer."

And who would lose in that fight? She had a feeling she couldn't afford the same caliber of lawyer as Jacob.

"Like your mom said, I'm a businessman. I'm used to covering my ass with a contract." Despite his words, he reached out to push her hair back with his long fingers. The touch disconcerted her, bringing back feelings she'd rather leave buried.

His tone softened. "But this isn't a company we're talking about. It's a person. You've already proved that you value Carter more than money."

Startled, she met his inscrutable eyes.

"You could have had a lot of money and no hassle, but you chose to give birth to my son instead. I don't agree with how you did it. I'm just grateful that you did."

Her breath caught in her throat, but she finally murmured, "Thank you."

For long moments the magic of communion whispered

between them. KC's heart ached for more, but anything more with Jake was just a dream. A dream she should have woken up from long ago.

Finally he turned back to look out the windshield; rain pounded heavily on the glass. "To keep this amicable, I think we can come up with a schedule between the two of us and each have our own time. Don't you think?"

His words chased the intimacy away like wind against fog. "Wait. What?" she asked, shaking her head. "You want unsupervised visits?"

"No." He drew the word out. "I want Carter to live with me."

"Um, no."

Jacob didn't show a hint of anger, his face remaining blank. "Why not?"

She hated that he was so calm while she felt white-hot and shaky. "I've told you why, Jacob. I don't know what kind of dad you'll be."

"How am I supposed to find out if you won't let me?"

"We'll find out first, then talk about you having Carter all alone." She almost choked on that last bit, but forced it out. "Until then, you can see him at my house. We both can. That way I'll know he's okay." *And exactly where I want him to be.* But she needed to speak logically, not basing her argument on emotions. "Besides, I have everything a baby needs at my house. You don't."

"Are you sure about that?"

Fear trickled over her as she pictured him standing over the beautifully carved crib at Booties 'n' Bunting. He sounded way too certain. What kind of plans had he been making while she'd been wallowing in fear?

"Well, Carter and I are a package deal right now. And I'm not moving." This fight wasn't one she was going to lose. So much of what she wanted had disappeared, but not Carter. Never Carter.

"Then I'll come to you."

That didn't sound as good as she'd hoped. "What do you mean?" Oh, heck. Was she really starting to fidget again?

"I mean, I'm not settling for a three-hour visit once a week. I want to be with my son 24/7. If I'm not at work or in the shower, we'll be stuck together like glue."

She could feel her eyes widen. Seeing Jacob every couple of days was one thing. But constantly? "I don't think this is the answer."

He crouched closer, invading her space. "You're lucky I don't drag you and Carter to work with me. We are a family. It's about time we started acting like one." His eyes were dead serious. "It's time to decide, KC. One way or the other. I'm either with him or calling a lawyer. Your choice."

KC washed down the tables during the midafternoon lull. The bar was open for lunch on Saturday and did a pretty brisk business. She had a few short hours to get caught up on all the cleaning before the wildness of the evening began.

If only all the activity would drown out the worries over Jacob's ultimatum. He'd given her twenty-four hours to decide. She knew what she wanted—Jake at her house, in her bed, becoming the true family she'd fantasized about. But that wasn't what he was offering. And moving to Blackstone Manor...

The doorbell chimed as someone came into the bar. KC looked up, surprised to see Christina walking toward her.

KC's classy friend had looked out of place the few times she'd been here. But she was friendly and always welcome. KC couldn't think of a single person who didn't love Christina. She epitomized the picture KC had of a true lady.

Their eyes met, and Christina sent a tentative smile across the distance between them. At least one thing seemed to be working out. If she could just figure out this situation with Jake...

"Hey, girl," KC said. "You want something to eat or just a drink to cool off?"

"A drink would be nice. Thank you."

Christina slid onto a bar stool with ease despite her pencil skirt. KC's mom stayed and chatted for a minute before going back to washing dishes. KC poured up a tall sweet tea, knowing her friend didn't usually drink alcohol.

"Jacob says you're in a deadlock," Christina said after a long swallow.

"Did he?"

That shouldn't surprise her, but it did. Jacob didn't seem the type to do the confiding thing.

Christina grinned, looking more than a little sheepish. "Actually, I overheard him telling Aiden, who was grilling him." Her grin quickly faded. "Why don't you want Carter at Blackstone Manor?"

"It's not about keeping him from there, or keeping him from you. It's about—"

She couldn't force the words past her lips. This was about her heart, and not being able to trust Jacob with it. Which made it even harder to trust him with their son. The men who'd been a part of her life hadn't cared a thing about her heart when they'd walked out the door. Would Jacob do the same to Carter once the novelty of being a father wore off?

She looked down to find Christina's hand covering her own.

"I know," her friend whispered. "Trust me. I know."

Christina probably did. From what she'd told KC, she and Aiden had been through their own rough times before deciding they loved each other and wanted to stay married. KC was a little jealous of her friend's happily-ever-after. Because she had to face reality instead.

"He's not taking my child."

KC wished she sounded strong and sure, but knew her voice was a little bit weepy, a little bit pained.

"And why should he?" her mother said, working her way back down the counter to the two of them. "I still say men aren't to be trusted."

Christina winced. "Ms. Gatlin, I don't think Jacob wants to take Carter away. He simply wants a chance to get to know his son." She spread her fingers wide, studying the ring on her left hand for long moments before looking back up. "Listen, I don't know Jacob well, but I've seen him in action. He's hands-on with his mother and has been for years. Most men can't or won't do that. Not even for family."

She locked gazes with KC, her sincerity reflected in her expression. "I really think you can trust him."

With Carter? Or with her heart? What was she thinking? Jacob had already taught her not to trust him with her heart. But Christina was right. All those visits home hadn't been for KC. They'd been to visit Jacob's mom, sometimes for doctor's appointments, because she was sick or just to check in on her. Jacob cared about his family. And he knew how to take care of them. Shouldn't she give Carter the chance to know his dad that her brother never got? That she'd barely had?

"I can't risk coming to Blackstone Manor."

"Why?" Christina asked.

KC threw a sidelong glance at her mother, then turned her gaze down to the bar top. "It would just be uncomfortable. I mean, he would never take me there before. Going there now? It would feel like—"

Her mother leaned in. "Turning into his mistress?"

"Mom!"

Her mother picked up Christina's empty glass. "Well, that's what it would look like to everyone else."

She had a point. "Well, he can come to my house."

But her mother wasn't done. "So you're just going to take him back in your house, in your bed? Hasn't our life

taught you better than that? Don't you remember how easy
it is for them to walk away?"

"No, Mom. I haven't forgotten. And don't worry about
the bed thing." She forced the words out, even though she
almost choked. "I don't think I'll be ready for that in a million years." *Please don't let me make a liar out of myself.*
"But it could be fun to watch him squirm on the couch."

Six

Jacob finished up a conversation with one of the line supervisors, then strode across a portion of the production floor that was down for maintenance. This company grew on him every day. Not because he had a passion for textiles, but because of the hardworking people. Some he'd known for years; some were part of a whole new generation coming to work at Blackstone Mills. For the most part, they were a dedicated bunch of locals who took pride in their product. Getting to know them better had been a privilege and a pleasure.

Now the question haunted him: Who would want to ruin all this?

Not far from him, a tall figure stepped out from a side aisle. Jacob had been so lost in thought, it took him a moment to recognize KC's brother, Zachary. Jacob halted abruptly, bringing him within inches of the other man. They were about the same height, and Jacob met his challenging stare head-on. Great. Another family supporter. *Not.*

Jacob didn't move, standing his ground with a level look. Since he'd moved into KC's little house two days ago, her family hadn't come around. Was this his official "talkin' to"? Zachary studied him with those hazel eyes, so much like KC's. Just as Jacob thought the tension might crackle in the air, the other man stepped back with a small nod. "Jacob," he acknowledged.

"Zachary." Jacob extended his hand for a firm shake. Neither he nor Zachary tried to assert too tight a grip. Just a simple acknowledgment of each other as equals. This might work out better than Jacob had hoped.

"You don't have to eye me like that, boss. I'm not here for the whole 'keep your hands off my sister' talk."

Jacob felt his eyebrows rise, and wished he could tell the other man keeping his hands to himself wasn't an option. At least, that was what he hoped. KC had called two hours before the deadline with her choice: he would stay at her house. Somehow it came across as her doing him a favor, as if control had been snatched away from him with those simple words.

As if getting settled in her house had deflated some of the uneasiness between them, he and KC had moved back into their more natural state of flirting with each other, skirting around the sexual tension that built every second they were together. It reminded Jacob of their first date, played over and over in slow motion. The surprising part was, he enjoyed the anticipation.

But KC hadn't made clear where they stood—hope still simmered despite the fact that he'd slept on her couch last night.

Zachary wasn't done. "Besides, it's a little late for that talk. Considering Carter and all."

"Yes, I'd say so," Jacob said, keeping his grin inside. "But I meant what I said at KC's house the other day. I want to do what's best for Carter. That doesn't include backing down or letting your sister off the hook."

To Jacob's surprise, Zachary smirked. "Oh, I think you're up to the challenge. Just keep your eyes open with that one."

"She can be a handful."

Zachary nodded, an understanding look in his hazel eyes. "The two of you did a good job keeping this a secret. Even I didn't realize what was happening for a long time."

"I guess Carter was a pretty big giveaway."

"For the family, yeah. I knew a couple of months before that," Zachary said.

That surprised Jacob. "Guess it was a shock."

"Yes, but I respect my sister too much to butt into her life."

That was a concept Jacob didn't run into very often these days. Most people were more than happy to meddle. He cocked his head at Zachary in question.

"KC is a self-sufficient, capable woman," the other man said. "With our family history, she's had to be. Why she would want to be relegated to the shadows, I don't know. But I assumed she had her reasons."

She hadn't wanted it—Jacob knew that now. She'd viewed the clandestine part of their relationship in a whole different way than he had. He'd anticipated each moment with her and could only focus on her when they were alone. He knew now it was a possessive attitude. Not only did he not want the complications of other people, he'd wanted KC to himself.

Just the thought had his heart pumping.

"That being said—" Zachary continued.

Here it comes. The brotherly rebuke was clear in Zachary's voice.

"I'll stand behind KC…however she needs me to."

Jacob nodded to the other man with respect. It took guts to go against his employer in support of his family. Openly and without apology. Without the stereotypical "I'll hunt you down with my shotgun" diatribe. Because Zachary was more worried about his sister and her needs than asserting his manhood.

"Good," Jacob said. "Family should stand together."

Lord knew his family had its crazy moments, but he and

his brothers were there for each other every step of the way. So why had he not included them in his relationship with KC until he was forced? Not even his twin brother, Luke.

The answer to that lay in a part of his psyche Jacob wasn't sure he wanted to explore further.

"Do you enjoy working here, Zachary?"

The other man crossed his arms over his chest. "Why? Am I about to lose my job?"

"Far from it." Jacob gathered his thoughts for a moment, glancing around the area to ensure they were still alone. He was taking a risk here, but his gut told him it was the right one. Lowering his voice, he asked, "What do you think about all the problems around the plant?"

Once again Zachary studied him, thinking before he spoke. Jacob's respect for him grew.

"Why would you trust what I have to say?" Zachary asked.

Jacob answered with a challenge of his own. "Should I not?"

Zachary nodded slowly, as if coming to a decision. "We've got some sneaky mischief going on. It's pretty hard to go incognito with this many people around."

"Are you speaking from experience?"

"Ex-military. Air force."

Hmm… That could come in handy. "Any ideas how it's happening?"

"It wasn't really my place to look into it."

"What if it was?"

Before his possible new ally could answer, footsteps sounded from down a nearby aisle. Unlike the normal rubber-soled work boot, this was the *clip-clip* of dress shoes. That meant management. Zachary fell back a step while Jacob stretched his shoulders, loosening the tension that was gathering there.

A familiar face appeared a little farther down. Mark Zabinski had gone to high school with Jacob. They'd attended the only private high school in Black Hills, where they'd both been prominent in Future Leaders of America and student government. A business management degree had gotten Mark hired as one of the daytime line supervisors. He'd moved up through the ranks to manage the accounting department, but hadn't been able to get any further than that. Jacob couldn't help thinking his enthusiasm for the return of the Blackstone brothers was a little too forced.

"Hey, guys," Mark said, eyeing Jacob and Zachary in turn. "Everything okay?"

Zachary didn't rush back to his station like an employee who'd been caught loafing. Instead, he held his stance, looking down on Mark from his superior height without a word.

Jacob watched with interest but also refused to rush away. "Yes, Mark," he said. "Everything's fine. Zachary was just explaining to me how some of the equipment worked."

Mark nodded with enough enthusiasm to shake his longish, eighties-style blond hair and started describing how the surrounding machines worked, causing Zachary to quirk the corner of his mouth in a look of almost condescending amusement. Mark didn't seem to notice, but Jacob did. He agreed with Zachary more than he could admit in front of an audience.

As soon as the other man took a moment to breathe, Zachary jumped in. "I'd better get a move on. Day shift is almost over and I need to shut down."

Mark nodded, his look of supreme approval hinting that the idea had been all his.

Zachary shook hands with each man in turn, but his gaze caught Jacob's. "If I can help with anything else, just let me know."

Oh, Jacob would be calling. A man on the floor was just what he needed, and Zachary's position and history made him perfect. He'd check with Bateman, just to be sure there wasn't anything else he needed to know about KC's brother.

Mark watched the taller man's retreat, then turned back to Jacob with an ingratiating smile that scraped along Jacob's nerves. The man insisted on kissing up when Jacob would be happier if they just treated each other as equals. "You sure everything is okay?" Mark asked.

"Sure." Jacob wasn't about to reveal what the last part of his conversation with Zachary had been about—or the first part, for that matter. Though he hated how much it reminded him of his earlier attempts to keep KC under wraps, he and Aiden had decided it was safer to keep the relationship quiet for now. "What're you doing down here, Mark?"

"Oh, just checking in. You know, sometimes you have to stay on top of people, make sure their work is up to par."

Jacob couldn't decide whether to question that statement or mention that Mark didn't belong in this part of the plant anymore. "Well, we're good down here. Let's get shift change taken care of, shall we?"

Because Jacob had a woman to get home to…

Seven

Jacob wished he could ignore his eager lead foot on the drive out to Lola's. As scenery flew by, he reflected on how KC was at work and Carter was at her mother's. There wasn't any need for him to be there. The fact that he'd promised her 24/7 wasn't a really good reason for him to be speeding down the road toward the bar.

His body knew only one thing: get to KC. He wasn't even sure why. His body wasn't going to get what it wanted, regardless of how fast he drove.

Still, he obeyed.

Luckily he didn't get pulled over by a cop before he reached his destination. Lola's was sparsely populated on a Wednesday, but patrons were trickling in after getting off work. Jacob joined them, waving a few hellos, and decided he'd find a table somewhere KC could see him. It couldn't hurt for her to know he meant business about their mock-family togetherness.

He wasn't being stalkerish. *Not at all.*

Shaking his head at how messed up his mind was, Jacob crossed the room. He let his gaze sweep the bartending area, not wanting to appear obvious. Until he noticed KC wasn't there. Instead, her mother straightened bottles behind the bar. That stopped him in his tracks. Unsure now, he waited a few minutes. He knew KC would walk out of the back room any time now.

Seconds ticked by… Nothing.

Letting go of caution, Jacob strode over until he stood front and center. "Ms. Gatlin?" he said.

She raised wary eyes to meet his, though she didn't straighten from her task of refilling the bottles under the counter. A stubborn squint had replaced her earlier look of fear. "Yes, *Mr.* Blackstone?"

Cheeky. "It's Jacob. Where is KC this evening? I thought she was working."

"She was. Now she's not."

He raised his eyebrows at that cryptic answer. Definite carryover of animosity from the previous day. "May I ask where she is?" he said, pulling out his phone for a quick glance to make sure he hadn't missed a call from her.

"Not here," she said, her tone even tighter than before.

Jacob stood, frozen in a quandary. He had a feeling that, as was the case with KC, throwing his weight around would get him nowhere. At least with KC, the arguing was part of the fun. That didn't apply here. Could he appeal to reason? Probably not. Ms. Gatlin was a mother, with a mother's emotions. What should he do?

"Ma'am—" he started, not even sure where he was going with the sentence. Then Zachary stepped around the corner of the bar.

KC's brother held up his phone, displaying the text message screen. He was a little too far away for Jacob to read the words, but he got the point. "She's at home," Zachary said, ignoring his mother's glare. "Looks as though Carter started running a fever around noon. She's taking care of him tonight instead of working."

Torn between his irritation at KC's mother for keeping that information from him and anger at KC for not letting him know, Jacob locked his emotions down tight. "Thanks, Zachary," he said.

He turned back to the door, his mind now on getting to KC's house, when Ms. Gatlin finally spoke. "Why don't you take some food."

He half twisted back, eyeing her over his shoulder. Part of him couldn't help wondering if she'd poison his portion—if she even gave him a portion.

She refused to meet his gaze but continued speaking. "Sick babies don't leave a lot of time for cooking."

She headed off to the kitchen, and the men shared a knowing look. Ms. Gatlin wasn't about to offer Jacob anything, but she wasn't a heartless woman.

Twenty minutes later, Jacob was finally on the road with his lead foot and a fried-chicken dinner for two. When he arrived, he could hear Carter crying from the porch, which gave him pause.

Then he shrugged. He could play the big bad man too macho to handle crying babies, or he could play the man big enough to step in where he was needed. Even if he didn't know what he was doing. Pride be damned.

Walking through that door was a tough step, but he did it. When he crossed into the living room, what he saw gave him pause.

He couldn't believe that a woman holding a sick, crying baby could be so darn cute. In pink sweatpants and a tank top, her hair haphazardly pulled up in one of those clip things, she looked frazzled and concerned. She bounced Carter gently in one arm and patted him on the back. He would have smiled and kissed her if she didn't look on the verge of tears as Carter paused in his crying to cough.

Spotting him in the doorway, she glared as if he was the cause of all the ruckus. So fussing at her for not calling him wasn't an option right now, either. They'd come back to it later. The noise pulled his gaze down to Carter, whose chubby cheeks were now flushed. The rims of his eyes were red, too, but Jacob didn't see any tears.

KC raised her voice as her eyes narrowed on him. "If you want to throw your weight around, I'm not in the mood, Jacob."

He could feel the frown forming between his brows and struggled to maintain his mask of calm. How could one child produce such a racket? "Actually, I'm here because I thought that's what we committed to. When I say 24/7, that's what I mean."

She opened her mouth, but he plowed forward before she could argue.

"What do you need?" It might be better to head this discussion off at the pass.

He saw a sheen of tears forming in her muddled hazel eyes. "Um." She swallowed hard, turning away for a moment.

Jacob gave her the chance to regain her composure. He took the food into the kitchen and lay the containers out on the table. Then he returned, grateful the cries had subsided to whimpers interspersed with snuffles. Who knew a baby's distress could shake a man's firmest foundations?

"What do you need, sweetheart?" Jacob repeated, keeping his voice as gentle as possible. "Do you need me to hold him?"

"No. He wants me," she said, patting and bouncing the baby in a set rhythm. "But he needs to eat. Could you make a bottle?"

As Jacob made up the formula, he knew he'd have to take this situation in hand. From what Zachary had said, KC had been with the baby since a little after noon. It was now a quarter past six. Her disheveled appearance and quick tears, unusual for her, spoke to her exhaustion, yet she still tried to maintain her superwoman front. He wasn't going to let her run herself into the ground and catch Carter's fever. She'd pushed him to the periphery of

Carter's care since he'd moved in, but today he'd be jumping in feetfirst.

Returning with the bottle, he helped KC settle into the overstuffed chair she and Carter usually cuddled in. A relieved look swept over her face as the baby took the offering without protest. "Good. I think the medicine the doctor gave me is helping. This is the first time I've been able to get him to eat with any appetite. His other bottle sat out too long, and I didn't have enough hands to fix more."

He let her talk out her frustrations. There wasn't anything for him to add. The tension relaxed around her eyes, and she took on the peaceful expression that entranced him as she watched Carter eat.

How on earth could he feel this attraction and need when her focus wasn't even on him? Where was the crying when he needed a distraction? "He's not the only one who needs to eat."

"Well, you'll have to cook for yourself," she said with a frown. "I've got my hands full."

Boy, cranky babies sure created cranky moms. Though it was probably like any bad day on a job with grumpy customers, only worse because the care was hands-on with no quittin' time. "I meant you," he said, leaning closer to catch her gaze. "I brought home food from Lola's. Your mom wanted to make sure you ate." He'd keep her mother's attitude to himself.

Her eyes widened for a moment, then she gave a tired grin. "You know what? I didn't even notice you bring that in." She ran her fingers over Carter's hair. "Sorry."

"No problem." Surprisingly, it wasn't. Her attitude didn't make him mad or eager to walk back out the door. An urge to face the challenge she presented rose within him. He would do this. Whether she wanted him to or not.

They sat in silence for long moments. Almost as soon as the bottle was empty, Carter drifted off to sleep. KC, too. Her long lashes rested against the purple circles under her eyes. She looked so fragile, awakening Jacob's protective urge once more. One he wasn't comfortable with but refused to ignore.

He carefully lifted Carter from her arms, stilling her with a firm look when she jerked up. "Let's get you something to eat," he said as he settled the baby in the bassinet that she'd moved into the living room.

"Yes," she agreed, though her eyes stayed glued to the sleeping child. "I should eat while he's out."

Jacob led her to the kitchen table with a firm hand. "He'll be fine. We're right here."

She dug into the food with muted gusto. Had she eaten at all today? Or had her entire focus been on Carter? As soon as she stood to clean up, Jacob was on his feet, too. "Time for your own bed, sweetheart."

"I can't go to bed," she protested. "Carter might need me."

"That's what I'm here for. You've had him all day. You rest." He led her into the dim back bedroom, where he could see the bed that had been the stage for so many hot nights with her. But tonight, it was for her alone. "I'll come get you if we need you."

"But what if he starts crying?"

"What about it?" His confidence was built on shaky ground, but she'd never know.

"You won't know what to do."

She was right, but that wasn't the point. "I'll manage. Now, into bed."

As if to show her defiance, she strutted into the bathroom and shut the door with a firm click. He wasn't about to leave, because sure enough she'd be back in the living room if he left the path unguarded. So he crossed the room to confiscate the baby monitor on the bedside table, then took up residence in the doorway so he could hear Carter if he woke.

When she returned, she had a vulnerable look on her

face and wore soft, comfy clothes, which inspired him to hold her close. Then he remembered the reason he was here had nothing to do with their previous closeness, and locked his knees just in time. But he wanted to—boy, did he want to—with an ache that dug into his gut.

"Promise me you'll come get me if he needs me," she said.

He met her worried gaze, shadowed with fear and exhaustion. "I promise if we need you, I won't hesitate. Now rest."

She crawled into the side of the bed he knew she preferred, and snuggled beneath the dusky-purple comforter that had kept their body heat cocooned so many nights before. He swallowed, his body and his mind wishing he could join her just one more time.

Then he turned away, closing the door behind him. Returning to the living room, he gazed down at his son, praying he could live up to his words.

"It's just you and me, kid," he said. "I told your mom I could handle this. Don't make a liar out of me, okay?"

KC shot straight up in bed, her heart racing as if she'd just run a marathon. What was wrong? Something was off. What—

Carter!

Barely noticing the dark outside the windows, she rushed down the hallway. Only as she skidded to a stop in the living room did she notice the most telling clue to her long sleep—silence. A single soft lamp kept the lighting dim. Jacob sprawled in her comfy chair, his legs splayed before him, his big body overflowing the space. But it was the baby sleeping on his bare chest that made the breath catch in her throat.

She stepped closer, noting the natural flush of Carter's chubby cheeks. The red of his earlier fever was gone. Jacob had changed him into a baby gown. As her hand rested on

Carter's upturned cheek, she didn't detect any fever. His sleeping face was turned up to his daddy's; his arm spread across Jacob's chest with his fingers curled into the light sprinkling of hair.

She couldn't resist the temptation. Certain that Jacob was asleep, she let her eyes wander over the muscled pecs that were usually hidden beneath his button-down dress shirts. He'd discarded his belt along with his shirt, but he still had on his navy dress pants, creating a dark contrast against his lightly tanned skin and Carter's creamy-yellow gown. Jacob's feet were now bare, prompting KC to smile. She'd learned that the one primitive habit Jacob had was stripping off his shoes and socks the minute he was behind closed doors. Unfortunately, his long, lean feet were as sexy as the rest of him.

A sudden wave of emotion hit her. Dreams from her pregnancy flashed through her mind. Dreams of a real family, of Jacob being with them, being devoted to them. Two days into his challenge, and already her fears of him abandoning Carter were dissolving like sugar in water. Which only opened up a new set of fears—after all, children were forever. Romantic partners were a whole lot more disposable. History had taught her that long before she knew what romance meant.

Yet one long look at the surprisingly sexy picture of her ex-lover and her son tempted her to forget her worries and take the plunge. Then she noticed Carter's lips pucker as if searching for a bottle. His little body squirmed. A feeding was about to be on the agenda. Her heart melted as Jacob's hand came up; he patted the baby's back without opening his eyes. Bittersweet as it was, the picture before her assured her Jacob wanted to be a part of Carter's life. He'd be a good dad, even if he wouldn't let himself be husband material.

Slowly Jacob's hand moved up to lightly brush Carter's forehead, a move KC recognized as her own in checking

Carter's temperature. She smiled, then looked up to meet Jacob's unexpectedly open eyes. For a moment she froze, held by the intensity of the emotions swirling there.

Anxious to hide her own feelings as her awareness of him soared, she mouthed, "When did he eat?"

With barely a jiggle, Jacob reached for his phone and checked the time. "A little over four hours ago," he whispered.

Suddenly eager to get away, she hurried back into the kitchen. An open laptop caught her attention. The geometric shapes of the screen saver floated back and forth. She shouldn't look, wasn't even sure why she wanted to, but she couldn't resist. A single swipe of her finger across the touch pad and the screen cleared.

Her heart contracted. Jacob had appeared confident and ready for the challenge of being left with Carter as he'd bullied her into bed. But the internet search on the screen suggested otherwise. *How to soothe a crying baby.* Bless his bachelor heart.

Well, whatever he'd found, it worked. She hadn't heard Carter all night. The clock now said 3:00 a.m. About time for Carter's middle-of-the-night feeding, if he was still on his usual schedule.

No wonder she'd felt dazed. She hadn't slept eight hours straight since Carter had been born. Of course, she'd have slept like a baby on that chest, too.

She'd just gotten the bottle heated when Carter woke in earnest. While she settled down in a kitchen chair to feed him, Jacob headed to the fridge. With his back turned, she didn't have to avert her eyes from the long line of his spine or the subtle ripple of muscle as he moved. The upper edge of a tattoo peeked from the waistband of his pants. Discovering that yin-yang symbol, which he'd attributed to his connection with his twin brother, had been quite a shock. A sexy shock. Conservative businessman Jacob hadn't struck her as the tattoo type.

Turning her thoughts from the ways she'd shown Jacob her appreciation of his body art, she tried to focus on the present. When it came to cooking, Jacob had only one specialty: omelets. She'd imagined him as having nothing more than eggs and cheese in his apartment refrigerator back in Philadelphia. She hadn't been far from right. Now he pulled out all the ingredients and arranged them on the counter.

"Why are you cooking at 3:00 a.m.?" she asked, even as the smell of bacon browning in the pan made her stomach growl.

And why couldn't the man put a shirt on? Hunger hit her hard, in more ways than one. Amazing how a full night's sleep could make her feel like a new woman.

"No point in me going back to sleep," Jacob said. "I have to be at the mill early for a management meeting. Might as well feed us before I get ready."

"Thank you."

He nodded absently, continuing to crack eggs into a bowl.

"Jake," she said, her husky voice catching his attention. "I mean it. Thank you for your help."

His gaze held hers, and awareness shivered across her skin. Then, in that wicked tone of voice she'd only heard when he was lost in the depths of arousal, he said, "My pleasure."

If she hadn't been awake before, she sure was now. Relief that Carter felt better distracted her from the temptation of the half-dressed man cooking in her kitchen. Having gotten a good sleep himself, Carter was ready to socialize. For once, his eyes weren't only for mama. The occasional noise drew his gaze across the room, searching for the man who had bonded with him during the long hours of the night.

That was what she'd wanted. Wasn't it?

The question haunted her as she ate. Finally, KC ran a hand across her son's sticky curls. At some point during the night, he'd sweat, then it had dried, leaving his hair thickened and clumpy. "Since we're awake, I think it's time for a bath, sweetie."

Jacob watched as she readied the sink, setting up the baby bath and starting the water. "What's that?" he asked.

"It just makes it easier to give them a bath when they're this little and you can't safely put them in the tub."

She deftly got Carter stripped and settled. He immediately started to pat at the water and kick his little legs. Standing next to the sink, she let him play for a few minutes.

"Wow, someone's feeling better," Jacob said.

She smiled in his direction, trying to regain control over the seesaw of her emotions. Sharing moments like this with Jake was both a blessing and a curse. It was necessary to establish the relationship she wanted him to have with Carter, but a poor substitute for what she really wanted— for them to be a family.

"He loves me to give him a bath," she said, adjusting the water so she could wet a washcloth.

With just a couple of steps Jacob closed in, his heat blanketing her side as he spoke softly in her ear. "If I remember correctly, so do I."

His words sparked images in her brain: Jacob undressing her, leading her into the shower, bodies soapy and slick. She shook her head before the temptation could pull her under. Without missing a beat, she pointed the spray nozzle in Jacob's direction, the water catching him by surprise.

"Down, boy," she warned as satisfaction spread through her, along with laughter at his yelp.

A few feet away, Jacob froze, his eyes wide. Her little joke just made the temptation worse. She couldn't pull her gaze away from the river of droplets chasing down Jake's bare skin. As if he could read her mind, Jacob chased one rivulet down his chest with his thumb.

"Well, then," he said, his gaze zeroing in on her smile. "If I'd known you wanted me all wet..."

Her heart skipped a beat. *Please don't go there.* She wasn't sure she'd be able to resist.

"I think I'll take a shower now, too," he finally finished.

She knew better than to open her mouth, because anything she said would be provocative, not productive. She focused on soaping Carter down, but Jacob didn't leave. Finally, she asked, "What time do you have to be at work?"

"I've got to call Bateman to find out exactly when he wants to get started. I left yesterday before he knew, and I wanted to see you—check on you and Carter. I told him I'd be in touch later."

Yes, but did you tell him why? Or were she and Carter still the best-kept secret in Black Hills?

Eight

Jacob had faced down corporate sharks who worried him less than KC's grandmother. Not because of size or strength, but the sheer tenacity with which she held on to her dislike of him.

She was like a Chihuahua, pint-size with sharp teeth, and determined to hold him accountable for missing some standard that he didn't quite understand. When KC insisted he call her Nana, because that was what everyone called her, he simply couldn't picture it.

And KC's mother—well, she had gone back from angry to afraid. The family gathered every Sunday for an early supper. Twenty-four/seven meant Jacob had tagged along. Every time he reached for Carter, Ms. Gatlin flinched as if he would whisk the baby away, with no thought to how it would affect anyone but him.

He refused to let their reactions stop him from holding his son, something he'd gotten much more comfortable with over the past week of nightly baths, diaper changes and bottle feedings. At first, KC had tried to edge him out, but he'd shown her that he wasn't one of those men who wanted to hand everything over to the *little woman*. If she'd let him, he'd have been with her every step of the way—pregnancy, labor and delivery. Despite the successful night he'd spent with Carter when he'd gotten sick, Jacob hadn't gotten her to the point where she'd let him care for Carter unsupervised, but they'd get there.

One way or another.

He'd insinuated himself into KC's and Carter's lives with a seamlessness that surprised even him. Still, they were living their lives as if they were skimming the surface of a deep lake, and Jacob was surprised to find himself dissatisfied. Something momentous called to him from the depths, but he still hesitated to dip his head beneath the calm to find the answers.

Although he'd sure appreciate not sleeping on the couch, which he had a feeling KC found secretly amusing.

As they settled down to a casual but hearty meal dished up straight from the stove, Jacob was grateful for Zachary. Another man helped bridge the estrogen river in the room. Too many women, not enough excuses. A little work talk helped create balance, though by unspoken agreement they kept themselves on general topics. Before they left, though, Jacob would need to talk to Zachary about a little industrial-reconnaissance mission. Fingers crossed he'd come on board.

Jacob had feared the timing of this meal, and sure enough, Carter started to whimper. Not a full-blown cry. His afternoon nap was the hardest to get him settled for—most other times he slid into sleep with ease. Something for which Jacob, inexperienced as he was, thanked his lucky stars.

When rocking the baby seat with her foot no longer worked, KC abandoned her plate to soothe Carter. The other women and Zachary continued to eat as if this was a regular occurrence. Jacob couldn't. Shoving in his last bite of Ms. Gatlin's incredible homemade peanut-butter cookies, he stood up and crossed to take the baby from KC's arms.

"Sit down and eat," he said. She'd barely had time to make a dent in her food.

"I'll eat in a little bit after I get him settled," she protested.

Jacob was having none of that. He repeated, "Eat," this time accompanied by a stern look. He lifted the baby from her arms before she could protest. Situating Carter snugly into the crook of his arm, stomach to stomach, Jacob supported Carter's legs with his other arm. He'd learned quickly that his son would wiggle those little legs enough to drive himself and Jacob crazy. So he tucked his son close, his hand covering most of Carter's back. A now-familiar rhythm of patting immediately took over.

Back and forth, Jacob took them on a stroll for a few minutes until Carter finally relaxed and slid into a light sleep. Then Jacob settled back into his chair at the solidly built table that showed a lifetime's worth of wear and tear. As the baby snuggled against him—one of the best feelings in the world, though Jacob would never admit it out loud—he looked up to meet KC's grateful gaze.

Spending a lot of time with a sleeping baby meant they'd started communicating with a type of telepathic speech. All Jacob had to do was make eye contact, and he'd be able to tell what she was thinking from the look on her face. No words had to be spoken. It was the most intimate thing Jacob had ever experienced with another human being. Even more intimate than sex. And right now, that hazel gaze told him he'd be moving from sleeping on the couch sooner than he'd thought.

"That's quite the touch you have there," Zachary said.

Glancing at the others, Jacob was disconcerted to see he'd become the evening's entertainment. Varying degrees of disbelief, suspicion and approval registered on the faces of KC's family members. Which left him feeling both disconcerted and, yes, a little smug.

Jacob smiled down at Carter. "Well, practice makes perfect."

A grumpy huff drew his gaze back up again. "The big question is," KC's grandmother said with disbelief in her voice, "does he have any staying power?"

Jacob had to admire a woman who wasn't afraid to speak her mind, wasn't intimidated by Jacob's money or status. Her only concern was her family, as it should be. Jacob's own concerns were now wrapped up in KC and Carter. Sometimes more than he felt comfortable with, especially in such a short amount of time, but he was adjusting. Mostly. He just had to stay in control.

"Nana!" Apparently KC wasn't as approving of her grandmother's candor. "Don't be rude to Jacob."

The older woman stared down the table at her granddaughter. "Are you telling me you haven't thought it? After all the women in this family have been through? Divorce and abandonment. Abuse and neglect. The only thing more important than a man who will stick with you is one who'll treat ya right."

Jacob could tell by her expression that she *had* thought about it. Had he given her any reasons to think otherwise?

Zachary broke in before KC could respond. "You make it sound like y'all are antimen," he joked, his expression clearly saying *what about me*.

Nana graced her grandson with a crooked smile. "You're the exception, boy. Not the norm."

"Nana," KC broke in again. "You can't judge all men by a few. There are good ones out there."

What about in here?

The hope in KC's eyes, which he could see even though she refused to look in his direction, made his chest ache. He looked down at Carter and thought about what kind of man he hoped his son would grow into. How would he want Carter to behave if he found himself in the same situation as Jacob? The idea blew his mind.

"That attitude will get you into trouble," Nana went on. "One man might just be an example, or even two. But four between us? The pattern is there." She waved her hand at each of the kids in turn. "Zachary's dad and his wandering ways. Your dad got tired of responsibility. My husband, David, and his drinking. So I thought a boyfriend would work better, and ended up having to take a fryin' pan to him after he dared raise his hand to me." She shook her head. "I think I'm justified in my opinions."

Maybe so. They did seem to have the worst luck. Or was it really poor choices? As Nana turned her knowing eyes his way, Jacob was again reminded of a toothful shark…or maybe a barracuda. Who could blame her after a lifetime of being left to take care of herself and her children, all alone?

"So what have you got to say for yourself, boy?" she demanded.

Jacob looked around at the faces of the Gatlin women— strong women who persevered despite being repeatedly abandoned—and admired them. They reminded him of Christina. His sister-in-law had an incredible talent for blooming where she was planted, despite all the odds against her.

"I don't."

The women met his refusal to defend himself with wide-eyed surprise. Zachary hung his head as if Jacob was doomed.

"Nothing I say will convince you I'm any different, Nana," he said, soft but sure. "Nor you, Ms. Gatlin. I'm sure all those men had plenty of flattering words that they used to get what they wanted from you, but I'm not a man of charm. My portion went to my twin brother, Luke. But I *am* a man of action—I'll let my deeds prove my worth for me."

The look of approval in KC's eyes, mixed with something fiery, told him he'd scored more than a few points with his words.

Still, the uneasy current in the room continued until after the table was cleared. Figuring the women needed some time to discuss him, Jacob followed Zachary out back. An unusually large garage occupied substantial real estate behind the house. As soon as he stepped inside, Jacob could understand why.

He let out a low whistle as he eyed the old-school Camaro on blocks in the middle of the room. "Nice. You do the work yourself?"

Zachary nodded. "It's relaxing."

"You'd get along really well with my brother Luke."

"I've never had the pleasure of being formally introduced to our resident celebrity, though I've seen him some in Lola's. I'd love to take a look at his racing car."

"He has a mechanic for his stock car, but he does a lot of work on it himself, too. Says it's soothing."

Zachary smirked. "I agree. But somehow I suspect you didn't come out here to talk to me about restoring cars."

Jacob gave a half grin. "Caught me." He paced a semicircle around the front of the car, letting the open hood and engine beneath distract him. "So how bad was it? What do I need to know about KC's childhood?"

"Why haven't you asked her?"

Jacob didn't need to turn around to see the condemnation on Zachary's face. He could hear it in his voice. "No, I haven't. Or I didn't, before. Now…" He shrugged. "I'm not sure we're ready for that kind of conversation."

"When you're sure, KC should be the one to tell you."

But conversations like that were easier to have while staring at cars instead of facing a woman's vulnerable eyes. Which was why he'd asked Zachary instead of KC.

Remembering the other reason he'd come out here, Jacob glanced over his shoulder. Zachary stood near the tool bench, twirling a wrench between his fingers. "Have you thought any more about our conversation at the mill?"

"Oh, yeah, I've thought about it a lot. Hard not to. I'm keeping my ears and eyes open. You'd be surprised how little attention people pay to Maintenance."

"No, I wouldn't. When I spoke to him, Bateman said you have a great track record. He doesn't understand, with your outstanding military career, why you chose to come home."

"And be just another man who couldn't stick around to help my family? The military gave me a chance for an education I couldn't have afforded otherwise. Now I have a decent job close to home and can be here to take care of my family on a daily basis. Something they've never really had."

Which made Jacob all the more anxious to prove to KC that he could be there on a daily basis, too. And not just for Carter—heaven help him.

Time to get off this subject before his guts got any more twisted. "So you'll help us?"

"I don't really see it as helping you and your brother, or even Bateman. I'm worried about the safety of the people who work there, the security of this town. I think the more vigilant security team has helped shut down some of the problems, but I want to know how the saboteurs are getting onto the mill floor and tampering with the equipment."

Jacob nodded knowingly. "So I'm giving you an excuse to do something you already wanted to do."

Zachary grinned. "I'll never tell, boss."

Zachary may be helping them, but he was as cautious as his sister, and Jacob had a feeling the other man wouldn't have hesitated to brush him off if he hadn't already wanted to get involved. He was his own man, and didn't apologize for his choices. Which made him a good brother for KC, and a good role model for Carter—

Jacob hoped Zachary didn't end up being the only role model in Carter's life. Could Jacob possibly live up to Zachary's example?

* * *

What to do with a man you would alternately kiss or smack silly? KC could feel the conflict pulling her in two different directions.

"Thank you for letting us babysit," Christina said softly, as if she could read the unease vibrating along KC's nerves when she handed over her baby.

Christina snuggled a sleeping Carter closer, the move reassuring KC. She'd never left him with anyone other than family. And the fact that she'd only found out about this little trip an hour ago hadn't given her time to prepare her emotions.

Or pack her stuff.

"I hope I remembered everything," she said, sliding the overstuffed diaper bag off her shoulder and putting it next to the travel bassinet Jacob was setting up. "Carter usually stays with my mom while I'm working. It was easier to just outfit her house with everything he would need since he spends so much time over there." She couldn't hide a frown at the man who had sprung this idea on her without notice. "Jacob didn't give me much time to prepare…"

The scoundrel had the audacity to glance up at her with an unapologetic grin. What was he so happy about? He used to hate any kind of spontaneous decisions, unless they could be carried out in the privacy of her house. She'd be scared, if he didn't seem so pleased with himself. This was like a date…which she'd never truly had with him.

He'd even gone to the trouble of getting a sitter for it. Her married friends often complained about their husbands not doing that. She should be grateful, excited.

She kept telling herself not to let this mean anything, but her hopes rose without her permission. The past few days they'd shared many heated glances and deliberately accidental touches. But she'd been afraid to make the first move, to invite him back into her bed without an understanding of what he was really looking for here.

Instead, she waited. Where was all her spunk when she really needed it?

Aiden chimed in. "Oh, whatever we don't have I'm sure we can find up—"

Christina's sharp movement, seen out of the corner of her eye, pulled KC out of her distraction. "What?" KC asked.

Her friend simply tucked her arm securely back around the baby. "Aiden was saying we'll find it if we don't have it." She threw a wary glance in Jacob's direction. "After all, we'll need to learn what we're doing soon enough. We've recently started trying for a baby of our own."

Shock held her still for a moment, then KC rushed over. Smiling her excitement, she hugged her friend carefully around Carter. "That's wonderful, Christina. I'm so happy for you." Happy, and maybe a little jealous. Christina's world would be real, not the make-believe one she and Jacob had created.

"What about all the travel y'all will be doing between here and New York?" Jacob asked from behind her.

Aiden shrugged with a nonchalance that KC hadn't known any of the Blackstone brothers to possess. "Christina says we'll manage."

"I have no doubt she will," KC said with a smile for her friend.

Christina was one of the most capable women KC had ever met outside of her own family. She cared full-time for Lily Blackstone, the men's comatose mother, ran the household and was highly involved in the community. Now she was building a life with her new husband.

If KC had based her opinion solely on Jacob, she'd have thought inflexibility had been bred into the Blackstone brothers. Strict adherence to standards and procedures served him well in business, but not so much in relationships. On the other hand, Aiden was a successful art import/export dealer, now running his business in New

York from Blackstone Manor in South Carolina. Even with trips to New York, it wasn't an easy task. Had he learned to adapt on his own, or with Christina's help?

Of course, with a nickname like Renegade, Jacob's twin, Lucas, was a whole different animal. After all, it took a special kind of daredevil to take on stock-car racing as a career.

The conversation whirling around her finally came to a halt and Jacob ushered her toward the door. "He'll be ready to eat when he wakes up," he said, surprising her with the same last-minute instructions she'd been about to give. "Make sure Aiden gets diaper duty. It's the ultimate test of manhood."

Then they were out the door and walking to Jacob's SUV. "Are you going to tell me where we're going now?" she asked as he helped her into her seat.

"Nope." Stubborn man.

His grin reawakened the ache in her chest. He was so beautiful with the sun glinting off the dark gold of his hair. For a moment, time stood still as he leaned against the side of the car watching her settle into her seat. She could reach out and touch him, pull him close if she wanted to, but fear of risk kept her still.

Then the moment passed and he headed around to his side of the Tahoe. He belted in, then they started forward instead of back down the driveway as she'd expected. "Come on, where could we possibly be going back here?"

Without answering, Jacob drove around the impressive manor with its landscaped back lawn and down a rutted road carved out of the surrounding fields of tall grass. They meandered down along the fence line until they passed a cabin that looked as if it was under construction, then turned into some dense woods on the opposite side of Blackstone Manor from the mill. She'd never been on this side of Blackstone land. Their families obviously ran in different circles, so all her hiking and partying experiences with her friends were in the forest south of town.

"I wanted to give you a surprise," Jacob finally said, throwing her a teasing glance she felt all the way to her toes.

"I thought you hated those," she retorted. He did. She could tell by the small frown that formed between his brows whenever she threw him off balance. He'd often overcompensated when she'd do anything not according to his plan, reestablishing control over every situation. Not that she had a problem with him being in control; it was simply fun to throw a wrench in his works every once in a while.

He paused the SUV, glancing over at her with a look that threw her even more off balance. It was a look of lust and mischief with an intensity she hadn't seen in a long time. "Surprises might not be my favorite," he said, "but you love them. Don't you?"

Normally she did. Thrills like surprise birthday parties and unexpected gifts peppered her life because her family knew she loved them. Most of her friends knew it. She never thought Jake had wanted to acknowledge it.

Only this time the thrill was combined with nerves. Not because this didn't make her happy but because she didn't have the one answer she really wanted. Why was he doing this?

"You surprise me all the time," he said. "You work hard every day *and* night. I thought you deserved something special."

There was no escaping the sexy intent in his gaze. They'd been skirting around this issue for days. But if this was an attempt to take their relationship back to where it had been before Carter, was she willing to accept that?

Obviously nothing had changed since their affair, except the fact that they were living together and their families knew. He came into Lola's most nights while she was working, but they had only the most casual of interactions while they were in public. Barely any conversation. Nothing other people could construe as a *relationship*. But his eyes rarely left her unless one of his brothers was present.

Nine

"You're not eating much," Jacob said as he watched KC pick at the potato salad on her plate. "Marie's a great cook. I thought you'd enjoy this."

KC had been behaving oddly ever since they'd left Blackstone Manor. He'd understood her nerves in taking the baby over there. After all, she'd never left Carter with anyone but family. But he was confident Christina would take good care of him, and thought KC would be more comfortable with someone she knew than with him hiring a sitter.

He simply hadn't been able to wait any longer for time alone with his former lover.

But KC didn't seem to be enjoying herself. She set down her drink and turned her turbulent hazel eyes his way. "I just—don't understand, Jacob. I mean, this feels like a date." She shook her head, her thick tumble of hair catching the sunlight. "Is it supposed to be? Because I honestly don't know how to respond."

Jacob aimed to keep it light. The last thing he wanted was to pressure her. "How else was I supposed to signal that I wanted to take what we have to the next level? I thought putting the moves on you over spit-up duty wouldn't be quite appropriate."

Her grin was just what he'd been aiming for. "What's the matter, Jake? Getting tired of the couch?"

He met her smile with one of his own. "Oh, a long time ago, believe me."

When she shook her head at him, he decided it was time to push just a little. "What? Wouldn't you be? Can you blame me for trying? After all, we are living together." *At the moment*. He shook the thought away.

"No, Jake, I don't blame you," she said, sobering. "It's just so like you to ask me. Most men would have let the heat of the moment take care of that for them."

"Considering everything that's gone before?" He shrugged. "That doesn't seem right. Besides, I couldn't get through life without a plan."

She nodded, a slight smile forming on her lush lips. "You're right. Having a plan is *so* you, Jake."

He couldn't stop himself from reaching out to trace the curve of her jaw with his fingertips. "You deserve the best, KC." And she did. After thinking about everything her family had been through, Jacob had been doubly ashamed of letting her believe she wasn't worth acknowledging. Especially since the whole purpose of keeping her a secret had been to keep his own life simple and uncomplicated.

Or had it? Going public would have meant exposing her to James Blackstone months before the confrontation that had sent her away. Would Jacob have lost those days with her if she hadn't been able to handle the pressure? And what about the community? Would they have been able to accept the differences between the two of them? Or would they have looked down on her as a woman who made herself conveniently available to him when he was in town? As accurate as that sounded, the truth had been a beautiful thing for him.

Suddenly he couldn't wait to get to his big reveal. "KC,

I need to take a trip." He gave her soft skin one more stroke before he pulled back. "I want you to come with me."

"The whole 24/7 thing?"

He shook his head, already picturing how that was about to change. "Nothing to do with that. I'm ready for more than just being your co-parent, KC. This trip—it would be just you and me."

She swallowed hard. "Where? When?"

"I need to go back to Philly for a fund-raiser, a ball for a charity I've been involved in helping for a long time. I'd love for you to accompany me."

Instead of the happy acceptance he'd been expecting, KC pulled back with a frown. "You want me to go to Philadelphia again?"

"Yes." He drew the word out, uncertain now. His memories of their one weekend in Philly were some of the best of his life. Weren't they for her?

"I don't think that's a good idea." She rose, pacing across the thick carpet of clover.

He watched her for long moments, not sure how to respond. Coming to his feet, he asked, "Why not?" Why did he have to choose a complicated woman to become involved with? Nothing was simple with KC.

"What's the point, Jacob?" She faced off with him, squaring her stance opposite his. "Nothing's really going to change, is it? I thought I could accept that, I really want to. But I think that might do more damage than I'm willing to accept."

What? "I'm confused," he said.

"I mean, a weekend in Philly for sex and a fund-raiser. I doubt you want to show me off to your high-class friends, but I'm guessing you'd feel guilty about taking another date. While here at home, I'm still only good enough to be kept like a hidden mistress." She hugged her arms around her waist. "I thought I could live with that, but—no thanks, Jacob."

As he took in KC's obvious distress, Jacob winced.

"I'm sorry, KC," he said, swallowing past the lump in his throat. He closed in, wrapping his arms loosely around her. He needed to touch her, for her to feel him, but he still wanted to look into those hazel eyes as he told her the truth. Hopefully, she'd believe him.

"I'm really sorry for not realizing how much this was like, well…" He swallowed again when she raised her eyebrows. "How this was exactly like before. But that wasn't my intention. I'm trying to keep you and Carter safe."

"What?" she asked, tilting her head as if she hadn't heard him right.

"I forgot you weren't here when Christina was hurt."

Surprise stiffened her body. "Hurt? What happened?"

"There was a fire. Aiden's studio at the back of the property. The one that's now being rebuilt. Some guys set it on fire, not realizing she was inside. They were trying to strike out at Aiden, but she got caught in the cross fire. She could have been seriously injured if Aiden hadn't gotten there in time to get her out."

"Oh, my goodness. I didn't even realize."

Jacob could read the regret on her face. Christina had told him that the two of them had been estranged since KC's return. Which was also his fault, since KC had been afraid of telling Christina the truth and putting her in an uncomfortable situation.

"Aiden and I talked right after I found out about the baby. He mentioned that, since things were still unsettled at the mill and I'm a prominent figure over there, I might want to keep my connection to you quiet for now. That way you and Carter won't become a target if someone is upset with the way I'm handling things."

"So you think we'd be in danger?"

"I don't want to think so, but I also don't want to take that chance."

She paced away, leaving him feeling empty and cold.

KC had never been predictable, so he should have known she'd come back with something he wasn't prepared for. It wasn't long before she said, "So you talked about this with Aiden?"

"Yes."

"And when were you going to talk about it with me?"

Working with the public, and drunk people in particular, KC had become pretty good at reading between the lines. And the surprise on Jacob's face gave him away.

He wasn't going to discuss it with me. It hadn't even occurred to him.

At least, not until he was sure he wanted this relationship to be about the two of them, not just about Carter. Although, he hadn't lied about it. That much was good. KC's dad had been a chronic liar, hurting them all time and again before he left.

"Jake, you can't expect to make decisions that involve me or Carter without my input. Regardless of what happens between us as a couple, we're going to be working together as Carter's parents for many years. If we're in this together, as a couple or not, you have to be open with me. Leaving me in the dark doesn't build trust."

He moved close, rubbing his hands up and down her arms. "I didn't think about it that way. I didn't really think of it at all, to be honest. I'm sorry."

"And how can I be diligent and protect my son if I'm not aware of the danger?"

His slow blink of surprise told her that had never occurred to Jacob, either.

"As much as we've labeled this 24/7, you can't be with us all the time, Jake. I need to know what's going on." She couldn't stop herself from taking a step back, then another until his arms dropped to his sides. "I'm not a doll to be moved around at will. I spent a lot of years dependent on other people's bad decisions. I will not have that for my son...or for me."

"You deserve better than that, KC," he said. "I know that now."

When he turned away, she didn't know what to expect. From the way he rubbed the back of his neck, she knew he was thinking hard. She'd watched him do that so many times, her heart ached. She knew, deep down, Jacob was a good man. But was he the type of man she could depend on?

When he turned back, his expression was more open than she'd seen anytime outside of a bed. "I want you, KC," he said, his voice gaining strength as he went on, "I want to take this to the next level. But I also want to protect both you and Carter until this situation at the mill is resolved. People knowing that I'm living at your house doesn't make you safe. So for now, I'd like to keep it just like we've been doing, with only family and close friends who know just how involved we really are."

A sinking feeling hollowed out her chest, but she kept still. Her response would determine where they went from here. Could she make the right decision—for Carter *and* for herself?

"But only for now," he added. "Do you agree?"

Was it what she wanted? *No.* Could she argue with his desire to keep her and their son safe? *No.*

"Yes, Jacob," she said, smiling as she thought over the past thirty minutes. Most men would have simply taken her to bed and left the rest up in the air. At least with Jacob, she knew there was a plan even if she wasn't sure what it was yet. "I'll go to Philadelphia with you."

His relief was almost palpable. He rubbed his hands together, obviously wanting to reach for her. Instead, he motioned to the food. "Shall we finish eating?"

That little streak of mischief resurfaced, and she couldn't help giving it free rein. "Actually, I thought we would celebrate." After all, they'd just made a pretty big decision. Why hadn't he reached for her yet? Didn't he realize she wanted him?

"What do you mean?"

Bless his heart. This man desperately needed to let loose every so often. Luckily, KC knew the perfect way to tempt him.

"Jacob, we're in a secluded spot and alone. No baby. No audience. What do you think I mean?"

Just one look from Jacob turned KC to jelly. But she wasn't giving him the upper hand yet. As he stalked closer, she whipped her T-shirt over her head. Jake slid his tongue across his lips in anticipation.

He stopped just out of her reach, watching the show, his body tense and ready.

She unbuttoned her shorts, pushing them over the curve of her hips while she slid out of her shoes. Jake's gaze followed her every move. Next, she whisked away the tank she was wearing under her shirt. She watched as Jacob made a long, slow perusal of all her new curves.

The need that filled his eyes whenever he took her was the most naked emotion she'd ever seen in him, and she'd ached to see it again. There it was. Before, these had been the only moments she'd felt she was seeing the real Jacob. Since her return, she'd only seen him show unguarded emotion when he held Carter.

She'd missed this, missed him. Turning away, she shucked off her bra, releasing her breasts, which were much rounder since she'd given birth. She threw the garment over her shoulder and made for the stream nearby. On her way, she tossed her best come-hither look his way, marveling at how his gaze was glued to her backside.

Her first step into the cool water felt good in the early-summer heat. The chill traveled up her skin as she waded into the stream. Her arousal rose along with it. The liquid surrounding her soaked into the silk of her panties, which she knew would color them transparent. Her nipples peaked, and she covered them with her arms, protecting them from the cold and from Jacob's gaze.

When the water was finally waist high, she turned back toward the shore. She took in the dirt beach with its tangle of tree roots, then Jacob's bare feet in the clover, then his gaze as he devoured her from his higher vantage point. "Aren't you going to join me, big boy?" Her mouth watered at the thought of those clothes coming off.

He shook his head. "You are crazy."

"Maybe," she teased. Then she let her arms ease down until nothing was left to the imagination. "But I'm fun. Don't you remember how to walk on the wild side?"

She hoped so, because she was desperate for him to walk with her once more.

To her intense delight, he grabbed the hem of his T-shirt, easing it up and over his shoulders. When clothed, Jacob seemed to have an average build. But underneath all the fabric were beautifully sculpted muscles that made her heart pound and her core ache. He was all leashed power... until he loosened the reins.

From her vantage point, she got to see every sleek line, every flex of muscle. The ripple of his biceps as his hands gripped his waistband. The bulge of his pecs as he opened his fly, then pushed his pants and briefs down to the ground. The chill of the water and the magical surroundings receded as memories of his body flooded her brain. Powerful hips. Muscled legs. And the hardness jutting from the cradle of his hips, the part he used to drive her over the edge into insanity.

He stood unashamedly in the dappled sunlight, and she wanted to weep for the brief time she'd likely have him. She had no doubt that one day he would leave her, but she'd savor him while she could.

For now, he was all hers.

Ten

Jacob barely noticed the temperature of the water as he stalked toward the naked angel before him. Heck, he was surprised steam didn't rise from the surface, considering the fire burning beneath his skin.

Before, he'd only known sexy KC. Whenever he'd seen her, the dark temptations beneath her surface called to him on every level. So much so that the pull had remained even after she'd left.

Living with her, seeing her with their son, highlighted a whole other side only hinted at before—the angelic woman who went out of her way to love those around her, do whatever she could for them and help with any needs she saw. That was KC, too.

One part angel, one part danger...wrapped up in the body of both. It was a combination he couldn't walk away from again, but he'd worry about that another time. For now, he was eager to learn that body all over again. Leave the emotions for later.

As he got close, she ducked to the side, evading him as her laughter tickled the air around them. With a grin, he gave chase. He'd never had so much fun as with KC—not even with his brothers. It seemed right now, that was exactly what she wanted.

They played tag for a few minutes, forging against the water in a strategic game of Keep Away. Jacob had never enjoyed another view as much as the water parting around KC's waist, her naked breasts swaying with her movements. All too soon, watching wasn't enough. His hands burned for a touch.

With a heavy lunge, he grabbed her. Dragging her body up against his, he clamped down on his urge to emit a primitive howl. Heat instantly sparked between them. Jacob caught the laughing look in KC's hazel eyes. Her long lashes sparkled with water droplets.

His body automatically reacted to hers, even while his hands cataloged all the changes since the last time he'd held her like this. Her waist, slightly thicker. Barely there stretch marks beneath his thumbs from carrying Carter. A rounder curve to her hips that matched the rounder curve of her breasts.

"Like what you see, Jake?" she asked, her look turning mischievous.

Ah, the temptress was here, all right.

"Oh, I like what I see," he said, letting his gaze slowly inventory all the sweet flesh down to where she was pressed against him. "But does it taste as good as I remember?"

She squealed as he lifted her in his arms, carrying her to the shore with quick strides. His body wouldn't wait much longer. Her arms tightened on his shoulders as he climbed the bank, then strode across the carpet of clover. Now his angel sparkled all over as the filtered sunlight highlighted the water droplets decorating her body.

He spread her out on the blanket, then sat back on his heels for a longer look. His breath hissed through clenched teeth. *Gorgeous.* She released her hair from the clasp, and it spilled around her head in waves of blond. Her firm, shapely legs tempted him closer. Her perky little toes with nails painted pink made him smile.

She was the incredible mother he'd come to know. The sexy temptress he ached for. All his. Right now.

She lifted her arms toward him, and his eyes met hers. He saw the vulnerable streak of emotion there, as if she, too, could sense that they trembled on the brink of something new. She opened her arms, hiding nothing.

Jacob crowded over her, his legs firmly straddling one of hers. His erection was pressed against her thigh, causing him to suck in his breath. So sensitive, as if too much pressure would end their encounter too soon—a worry he hadn't had since high school. Unwilling to lose the moment, Jacob started in on her plump, succulent lips.

He took his time with the kiss, tracing the outline of her mouth before their tongues tangled. Then his hips surged forward, and he couldn't hold back his groan.

Her hands found his shoulders, pulling him down. Sucking him under as their bodies met and melded. He heard the catch in her breath, followed by a soft whimper, and his brain swirled with all the times he'd heard that same sound before.

He ached to jump ahead but forced himself to slowly reacquaint himself with all his favorite places. Only this time, his heart beat faster, her scent made him dizzier and his need pounded higher than ever before. Because this was KC.

And everything about her captivated him.

His heart should have stalled at the revelation, but his need wouldn't allow it. Instead, he slipped on a condom and eased his body into hers, savoring every inch. She'd been partly right: this was one of his favorite positions. Because he could take in every nuance of her expression while his body drove them both wild.

He pulled back slowly, then drove in hard. Her cries filled the sun-heated air around them—a sound Jacob knew he'd never forget. Over and over, he teased them both while his tongue traveled from nipple to nipple. He savored her taste, her sound, her passion. And finally her ecstasy as her body clamped down on his.

Letting himself lose control, he pounded into her until only one thought remained. This was more than simple lust, but could he break past the fear and admit what it truly was?

In the week since their picnic, KC had more than enjoyed reacquainting herself with Jacob. She'd treasured every second they were together. He was everything she remembered and more, as if the long months without each other had only heightened his appetite. They had definitely heightened hers.

But intimacy with a baby in the house was a lot different than when she was a single woman, so KC was pretty sure Jacob had planned on enjoying a free-for-all during their weekend in Philadelphia. Starting as soon as they crossed the threshold.

He had another think coming.

They were barely through the door of the hotel suite and he was already marching her across the tiled floor with his signature heated look. She wanted to give in, truly she did. But they needed to start off on the right foot, so she put up a figurative roadblock. "Where should we shop for my dress?"

Jacob's look was incredulous. "We have baby-free time and you want to shop?"

Men. Everything had to revolve around sex. "I didn't have time before we left town, and you promised…" She deliberately drew out the word, paired with a look of wide-eyed innocence.

He studied her, giving her the impression he could divine every thought. "You. Are. Serious."

You bet your booty, buster. The ache in her core betrayed her, but she refused to give in. "I told you, this trip wouldn't be like the last time."

"I don't see what the problem was, honestly." He leaned back against the wall with his arms crossed over that wide chest. *And here we go again with the Dom stance.* "I thought we had a wonderful time."

"We did have a wonderful time. At your apartment. Having sex. The only time we left the house was to get to and from the airport."

She could see the revelation steal over him, but still he tried to bluff his way out of it. "And that was a problem because…?"

"Depends." Standing her ground, she faced off with his seeming nonchalance. "Do you want me here just for sex? Or for something else?" She couldn't make him prove his commitment at home, not so long as she and Carter could be hurt by taking the relationship public. But here in Philadelphia, she could take a stand.

She wasn't backing down.

His disappointment was almost palpable, and she found an echo in her own body. Maybe she should tell him he'd definitely be getting lucky, just not this instant? She quickly tossed aside the idea. She wasn't sure whether she was just being mischievous, or whether she really wanted him to pay. Either way, it wouldn't hurt to let him suffer for a little while.

"The ball is tonight," she reminded him as they took the elevator to the lobby. "I don't have a dress. And you said we had plans for this afternoon, so…"

He hailed a cab, then held the door open for her. "Will it take all morning to find a dress?"

"There're only two hours left in this morning, but we'll have to see…"

His poor-puppy-dog expression was so very cute, but he'd live. Even if he didn't think so.

The cab dropped them off at a side street filled with

adorable little boutiques. KC wandered for a bit, peeking into window after window, unwilling to admit to Jacob that the high-priced surroundings made her feel inadequate. The only time she'd ever shopped for a formal had been for her junior and senior proms—she had found both dresses at consignment stores. Somehow she thought this would be a whole different experience.

Pausing before a window display of beautiful dresses, each decked out with a unique flare, KC knew she'd found the right place. She turned to Jacob. "I'm going to go in here and look around. I'll be out in a while."

He frowned. "I can't go in with you?"

Poor thing. Nothing about today was going according to his plan. "Nope. I want my dress to be a surprise."

"But I'm planning on paying for it." His satisfied expression said he'd hit on the perfect workaround. "That's kind of hard to do from out here."

"No need. I'll handle the bill myself—"

"No." If she didn't know Jacob very well, his scowl would have had her stepping back. "This trip was my idea. I want you to buy whatever you find that you love and not worry about the cost."

Her spirit rose up in protest, but he held up a hand. "No arguments, KC. Pick out what you want, have the saleslady ring it up, then come and get me. I'll take care of the rest."

Blinking, KC didn't know how to respond. Not only was he going to pay for her to have a dress, but he wasn't pushing his way inside when he could have. She swallowed hard. "Thank you, Jake."

He shot her a grin. "You're welcome. Besides, I'm building up brownie points."

I bet. She moved to the door, only to look back over her shoulder when he said, "Shoes and a bag, too. No arguments. Don't make me ask for an itemized statement as proof."

"Yes, sir," she said with as much cheek as she dared, then headed inside.

Contrary to her concerns about being treated as an inferior, the two women in the store were more than helpful, taking it upon themselves to find her the perfect dress for the ball. Both had heard about the event, so they knew exactly what she needed. After a couple of tries, KC found something that had her grinning like a buffoon at herself in the mirror. "Oh, yes, this is it."

"I agree," one of the salesladies said from behind her.

The black dress was anything but ordinary. A flesh-colored silky layer was overlaid with a transparent black lace appliquéd with black roses, showcasing glimpses of the flesh tones underneath. The bodice had a deceptive plunging neckline that cupped her abundant curves and provided support at the same time, the décolletage formed by the uneven edges of rose petals and vines entwined throughout the intricate layer of lace. The neckline was echoed in the low scoop in the back, and the hem fell to the fullest part of her calf. Here again the material's uneven edge gave the dress a uniquely strong, sexy look that KC found flatteringly feminine. Jake would love it as much as she.

Twenty minutes later, she had shoes, stockings and a small clutch to match, along with a filmy shawl to protect against the cooler evening air. The saleswoman added everything up and stowed the dress in a garment bag before Jacob was led into the store. Without a single question, he handed over a credit card, his cooperation earning matching smiles from his audience.

"You're gonna love it," the saleslady assured him.

Reaching around KC's waist and pulling her snug against his side, Jacob placed a light kiss on her neck, just below her ear where he knew she was sensitive and the touch would bring on chills. While she was still recovering, he said, "I'd love anything on her."

"Yeah," she joked, unsettled by this public display of affection. "He even loves my T-shirts covered in baby spit."

"Men love anything that highlights your, well, cleavage," the redhead said with a wink.

KC's heart melted when Jacob blushed. Yeah, she knew exactly how he felt about her boobs.

The brunette grinned at them before adding, "Nah, accepting you no matter what you look like is a sign of true love."

As they walked away, KC wondered with a touch of panic how right she was.

Eleven

Jacob's breath stuttered to a stop as KC breached the doorway from the bedroom. She hadn't been kidding when she'd said her dress would be well worth the anticipation.

Boy, had he anticipated.

The saleswoman's comments had kick-started his libido, making him wish for X-ray vision to see through the garment bag. Then, from the dress shop, they'd gone to a nearby lingerie store for the proper undergarments, which consisted of a smooth satin corset and matching panties. Was she trying to kill him? Then they had a late lunch; all throughout, KC's sexy persona was turned up high.

Just when he thought he couldn't take any more, he found himself pacing the suite and ignoring his work while she had her nails done in the hotel salon. It hadn't been how he'd pictured their first day in Philly, but now...now his body and mind slipped into overdrive as he soaked in her beauty.

If anything could capture his dual vision of KC as both angel and sex goddess, this dress was it: black flowery lace and flesh-colored fabric gave the illusion of lingerie, yet she was technically covered from chest to midcalf. Of course, knowing what she had on underneath tipped the scales in a dangerous direction. But the steamy look in her eyes—now turned a deep green—warned him that was part of her plan.

Her inner and outer beauty stole his breath. The intensity of his need sparked a touch of fear, but he quickly brushed it away.

He was tempted to persuade her to stay in—skip the reason they were here and give him a chance to peel her out of that dress and the lingerie he knew was hidden underneath. But one look at the tentative excitement on her face shut down his desires without a word.

I'm good enough for sex but not allowed into any other part of your life. Back in Black Hills, he couldn't openly acknowledge his relationship with her and Carter without endangering them. But here, he could take her out in public with pride.

He was ashamed that she had believed he viewed her only as a sex object. He would never demean her like that again.

"You are incredible," he said simply. "I couldn't be more proud than to have you on my arm tonight."

The faint uncertainty in her expression fled, and she glowed under his praise. But soon enough that saucy look returned. "I do believe you'll be rewarded for your kind words, sir…later."

Her husky promise sent him back into overheated territory. He hustled her out of the suite and away from the bed before he proved himself a liar.

Never had the dichotomy in KC's personality been more evident to Jacob than in the crowded ballroom, where they were surrounded by men and women Jacob had been doing business with for years. The lights sparkled off tiny jewels embedded in each flower on her dress, and she shone like the star she was as she conversed with an ease that shouldn't have surprised him. After all, he'd seen her calm the most ruffled of feathers at Lola's. Here she was an angel, but Jacob could read the latent sensuality in the graceful movement of her body and the continual meeting of their eyes. Hers held a promise. Which turned to surprise when his name was called from the stage.

"We are happy to honor all the board members for their hard work for a charity that goes above and beyond in caring for children and their families as they receive the medical treatment they need. Jacob Blackstone, our chairman, would you please make the presentation tonight?"

Jacob cursed in his mind. He should have remembered this part and prepared KC. He'd been more focused on having her here than on the presentation he'd made numerous times.

After announcing how much money the event had raised for the charity, and giving the usual plea for continued generosity, Jacob returned to KC's side. Only there was no time to explain as one person after another came up to talk.

Finally Jacob swept her to the dance floor, taking advantage of a few moments of privacy. Of course, he was fooling himself if he didn't admit he was eager to hold her close once more, even if he couldn't take what his body was begging for. Still, his fingers savored the bare skin of her back in the dim lighting.

KC, with her usual no-nonsense attitude, went straight to the point. "That was a surprise. I guess I should have done a Google search of you before we dated, found out how important you were everywhere, not just in Black Hills…"

"I'm sorry, KC. I should have made it clearer that I was the chairman when I asked you to come with me. I just wasn't thinking—"

"About more than getting into my pants?"

He choked back a laugh but couldn't help the big grin that split across his face. "Guilty."

It was a much more rewarding subject of conversation, in his opinion. "Have I told you how beautiful you are tonight?" *And every night?*

He savored her upturned face, that gorgeous hair swept to the top of her head, giving him a view of the vulnerable parts of her neck where he knew a simple kiss would have shivers running along her body. They moved in time to a classic slow dance, their bodies barely brushing against each other.

Good thing. Jacob didn't want to embarrass himself.

"This is incredible," KC said, her wide-eyed gaze taking in the crystal chandeliers suspended from the ceiling and the glittering decor that sparkled in the strategically dim light. "Way better than the Under the Sea theme from my senior prom."

They shared a grin.

"Yeah, the committee goes out of its way to create a very special night. We have a wonderful coordinator, and she makes it well worth the amount the donors give."

"You've made a big jump from executive with all the perks to running the mill. Are you really ready to leave all this behind?"

He looked around the room, seeing so many people he knew, so much from the life he'd built away from Blackstone Manor. "My family, brothers, Carter—" *You.* "Sometimes life is where you're needed. Besides, I won't be giving it up completely."

He felt her stiffen beneath his fingers. "What do you mean?" she asked, her voice calm despite her body's message.

"I've enjoyed working with this children's charity for a good many years. While I won't be located in the city, I will be visiting regularly and remain on the board to help keep it viable." He smiled down at her. "I think we'll have plenty of opportunities for glamour, because I'd sure hate to never see you in this dress again."

Her husky laugh tingled along his nerves. "You are such a man," she said.

He couldn't resist this time. His hips pressed briefly

against her before he returned to a polite distance. "Yes, ma'am, I certainly am."

She tightened her grip as if she would pull him back to her, but she, too, continued the proper dance moves. The decorum of their public display only emphasized to him exactly what was lurking beneath the surface. Fire and need that burned so much hotter for their restraint. He struggled to concentrate.

"I've thought of establishing some kind of foundation in Black Hills," he said, his shaky control letting his private thoughts free. "I simply haven't found a cause that's spoken to me quite yet."

"It should be one you feel passionate about," she said, licking her lips in such a way that he knew she was talking about something else, something far more private.

"I know," he said, struggling to rein in his control. Since he couldn't have her body, he let his mind wander and kept talking. "Here, a job is a job. In Black Hills, my job is about more—it's about keeping a community alive and protecting a way of life. Not as a monument to my grandfather but to something—" Jacob wasn't sure how to articulate the emotions swirling through him.

"What?" KC asked, her voice husky, her eyes searching for the truth.

He couldn't help giving it to her. "Something that means more than a dollar amount, something my son—" he swallowed hard "—and you can be proud of."

He felt her hands clutch against him once more, but she didn't speak for a moment. "Having a kid changes a lot about your perspective, doesn't it?"

"Uncomfortably so," Jacob admitted with a quiet laugh, grateful for a break in the emotional tension building between them. "But all these charity events have taught me one thing," he added, pulling her just a touch closer so his body took control of the dance in an elemental way.

"What's that?"

"I dance a heck of a lot better than I did in high school." And he swirled her around the floor, expertly leading her around other couples to end with a flourish as the music crescendoed. He tipped her back, savoring the slide of her hips against his as he pulled her gently up into his arms. This time he didn't hold back. Despite the crowded room, he let his lips find hers and do the rest of the talking.

"Let's leave," KC murmured against his lips. Her body couldn't seem to break the contact. "I've waited long enough."

Even in the dim light KC could see the *yes* that leaped to Jacob's face, though he managed to maintain a strained outer decorum. He immediately ushered her across the crowded room toward the exit. Laughter bubbled up at his quick pace, but she wasn't about to argue. The door was just in sight when a man stepped into their path.

He stuck out his hand with a grin, completely unaware of his unwelcome intrusion. "Jacob, wonderful event. I hope there will be many more, despite you leaving us…"

To anyone else, Jacob's switch to consummate gentleman would have appeared seamless. Only KC noticed the tightness of his stance and the tick of the muscle in his cheek as he introduced Robert and his wife, Vanessa. The Williamsons had been to many of these events with Jacob, since Robert also served on the board of the charity.

As they chatted around her, KC almost felt bad about knowingly pushing Jacob past his limits today in an attempt to make her point. But she had a feeling the wait would be worth it. She shivered, drawing Jacob's arm around her bare shoulders as he spoke. Today had been a day outside of her normal experience with men, or even with Jacob. Funny, serious, sexy, emotional. If this kept up, she'd be treading some dangerous waters.

The men chatted about some project they had worked on together, giving KC a clue that this could take a few minutes. So she turned to Vanessa. "How are you tonight?" she asked politely.

Vanessa's smile was slightly off-kilter, just a little too wide to be completely natural. "Oh, just fine," she said with a heavy Southern drawl. "Where are you from?"

KC relaxed a little. "I'm from Black Hills, South Carolina."

"So Jacob finally got him a down-home girl. Guess that's what's keeping him entertained in the back of beyond."

KC raised her brows, a little taken aback, even though the woman's tone hadn't been ugly. She was even more surprised as Vanessa looped her arm through hers. "Let's have a little chat and a drink. I could most definitely use another."

Of coffee. KC had dealt with enough drinkers to know that Vanessa was a couple of drinks away from having to be carried home. Or embarrassing herself and her husband.

They settled at the bar, and Vanessa ordered a martini. "Sparkling water with lemon for me," KC said.

Vanessa didn't seem to notice. They chatted about the party for a moment—the gorgeous decorations, delicious desserts and cool little band—before Vanessa asked, "So what do you do?"

It seemed that KC didn't have the appearance of a woman of leisure. "I'm a bartender."

Vanessa looked at her with surprise, and then their bartender set their drinks in front of them. Without missing a beat, KC switched the glasses, setting the water firmly in front of Vanessa.

"Hey, that's mine," she said with a frown.

"You don't really need it, do you?"

Vanessa stiffened. "I'm not drunk."

As all tipsy people insisted… "I didn't say you were," KC said, adopting the reasonable tone she knew would work with someone of Vanessa's personality. "But do you really want to end the night puking on those fabulous Jimmy Choo shoes?"

Vanessa blinked at her for a moment, then her eyes watered. She quickly glanced down at her shoes. "You have a point."

Good. Vanessa seemed nice, straightforward and interested in her as a person, not just as Jacob's date. KC would hate to see her move into obnoxious territory. Besides, her people radar made her wonder if there was something else going on here.

Vanessa tipped her water glass at KC before taking a long drink. Then she gave a half smile. "Well, I'm betting you're a good bartender," she conceded. "Is that how you met Jacob? In the bar?"

"Nope. I met him on a plane. I'm not the best flyer."

"That's a shame," Vanessa said.

Confused, KC asked, "Why?"

"Because being in a bar would mean Jacob was having some fun. He needs to have a good time every once in a while. He's so serious, as if he has something to prove all the time."

"Yes. He does seem that way..." Except in bed. Then his only goal was how many times he could make her explode.

As if she was echoing KC's thoughts, Vanessa leaned closer and asked, "Is he that focused in bed? Bet he would view each woman as a challenge to be solved."

Um... "I hope that's the alcohol talking."

"Nope," Vanessa said with a saucy grin, the alcoholic haze starting to fade from her movements. "I'm just too curious for my own good—especially about hunks all hidden under the perfect business suit."

KC had dealt with a lot of unexpected conversations, but this one truly caught her off guard. At least Vanessa was still curious, which meant she didn't know for sure. Still, KC wasn't comfortable engaging in traditional girl talk with a stranger. Not that she was ready to talk about

Jake at all in that capacity—it was too new, too intimate, too complicated...

"Not gonna say? I don't blame you," Vanessa conceded. She shook her empty glass at the bartender for a refill. "I'm happy for him. Although having him move permanently because he's finally found something to take his mind off work will deplete the eye candy around Philadelphia."

KC just raised her brows. Vanessa had obviously said what she wanted; maybe that was just the alcohol. But at least she was up-front and friendly about it.

And she wasn't done. "You're lucky," Vanessa said with a frown into her now-full glass of lemon water. "My husband has hardly looked at me all night."

Ah, now this situation was making more sense. KC jumped in headfirst, since Vanessa seemed the type to appreciate straight talk. "Have you made him look at you instead of wasting your time drinking?"

Vanessa stilled for a moment.

"I know we just met, but you don't seem like a woman who takes no for an answer," KC said, spotting the men approaching over Vanessa's shoulder. "So don't give him the chance to ignore you. You deserve better."

"Everything okay, ladies?" Robert asked as he reached his wife's side. He studied her glass for a moment.

"We're good," Vanessa said, winking in KC's direction. "But I'm in serious need of a dance with my husband."

Robert nodded, but his attention had already been snagged by a passing suit. "Yes, dear, I just need to see—"

"No, Robert," Vanessa interrupted as she regained her feet. Not a wobble in sight, despite her four-inch heels. "You can talk *after*. This sexy getup shouldn't go to waste." She paused, giving her husband a chance to look for himself—and he did.

KC suppressed a grin. Sometimes changing a man's focus was way too easy.

Without further interruption, Vanessa led her husband

to the dance floor, Robert's focus definitely where it should be. Vanessa threw a wink KC's way as she slid confidently into his arms.

Jacob glanced between them suspiciously, then shook his head with a grin. "I don't want to know," he said.

He pressed a kiss to her neck, eliciting a shiver. Then he whispered, "Where were we?"

He had her out the door and hailing a cab before she could answer. Not that she complained. The anticipation of the day had set her senses on high alert. Now she would cap off this romantic night in the perfect way with the man she loved.

KC's stomach dropped as if she'd jump-started an elevator. She'd known she was infatuated with Jacob, but she thought she'd been able to wall off all those tender feelings, leaving only the attraction. Seeing so many different sides to him over the past month had only deepened her desire for something more, some permanent attachment to this strong, steady man.

She had no doubt he would never turn away from Carter, but his son was his blood. He'd turned his life upside down in recent months to help his family. But she wasn't family… She was expendable.

The one thing she'd always feared.

She had been determined to be the strong one, the one who could walk away. And she had, but she couldn't stay gone. Would she survive if he chose to leave her?

KC forced herself to shut down her thoughts as Jacob led her into the bedroom of their suite. The moonlight streaming through the gauzy curtains glinted off his blond hair as he peeled himself out of the black jacket of his tux. He unbuttoned his dress shirt, revealing his muscled chest a few inches at a time.

He pulled the ends of the shirt from his pants, leaving it to hang open as he stalked closer to her. Half sophisticate, half primal male. KC's heart fluttered in feminine awareness. She backed slowly away.

Jake kept coming, his intense stare telling her everything he would enjoy doing to her. But first…

"I've been dreaming about what's underneath this dress since this afternoon, KC," he said, his deep voice brushing along her senses with the skill of a master musician. "Now I will see it for myself."

She smiled up at him. "That was the plan."

Reaching to the side, Jacob eased her zipper down until the unique creation slid to the floor, leaving her more vulnerable and exposed than she'd ever been. Not because the corset left little to the imagination with its mesh panels, but because the man before her wasn't looking for a good time—he was intent on consuming her.

And she would let him.

His palms traced the boning from her hips up to her waist, then around to her plump breasts beneath the satin cups. The flesh swelled, threatening to overflow its bounds. "KC," Jake said, sounding a little strangled. "White satin. Couldn't be more appropriate for my angel."

She didn't know why he was comparing her to a heavenly being, but she'd savor the reverence in his voice, his touch. He continued to explore, running his hands back down to the garters attached to her stockings, then up the back to the completely unprotected roundness of her backside. With a firm grip, he pulled her against him. The friction of his tuxedo pants and the stockings on her legs sent her head spinning. Her hands dipped beneath his shirttails, meeting warm flesh just above his belt. Part of her ached for more; part of her reveled in the joyous miracle of having Jake in full flesh before her.

Only this close could she feel the slight tremble in his muscles, feel the sheer sheen of sweat over his skin.

"KC," he said with a groan. "I wanted to wait, honey. To make it last. But I can't."

"Then take me, Jake," she whispered against his skin. "Take all of me."

Two steps and he had her balanced on the edge of the dresser, knees spread wide to accommodate him. His touch was rough this time as he dragged the cups of the bustier down to give him full access to the treasure he sought.

Her heart raced into overdrive as his mouth teased her nipples. Then he gave a soft pull that strengthened the pulse that beat between her thighs. She needed him…needed him…

He didn't disappoint.

Seconds later he was pushing inside her, filling her in the best way imaginable. Physically, emotionally. Stretching her to accept him. Overwhelming her protests. Completing her in a way she'd never thought possible.

His mouth settled at her neck, sucking along her skin. His thumb pressed against that most precious of spots as she panted out her need. All the while, the hard strokes from his body drove her insane until all the sensations coalesced into a crescendo of heat that detonated in a single blinding second. Jake's hoarse cries in her ear pulled her back from heavenly nothingness to the precious gift of his own release.

They drifted back to reality together, aftershocks rocking them for long, long moments. Then he tried to pull away—and stumbled. Shocked, she clutched at him.

Beneath her fingers, a rumble started, then grew into laughter. Jake's laughter was that much more precious for being so rare. "What's so funny?" she asked.

"My pants are still around my ankles," he confessed.

She couldn't help it. She had to laugh, too. "Well, let's get you properly undressed before you fall and we have to spend the evening in the emergency room rather than the bedroom."

He was already stripping himself down. "Yes, ma'am. That sounds like a perfect plan to me."

Twelve

The ringing of the phone roused KC from the deepest sleep she'd ever had. At least, it felt that way. Maybe because she'd so rarely gotten a full night's sleep since Carter was born—

Carter!

KC was standing next to the bed before she even realized she'd moved. Her vision blurred for a moment before she blinked, her body swaying in confusion. Who was she kidding? It was always hard to wake up.

With deliberate focus, she found Jacob sitting on the bed with his back to her, phone to his ear. Had his movement woken her or the phone? Confusion once more clouded her mind for a moment until he stood and ended the call.

"Get dressed," Jacob said, clipped and to the point. "We need to go."

Carter?

Concentration was hard to come by, but KC forced herself to snap to it. By then, the passionate, compelling lover of last night had been replaced by a man in full action mode. Jacob was already dressed in cargo pants and a casual polo for traveling. He swept out the bedroom door with his phone, leaving her on her own.

With the urgency of a worried mother, she quickly followed him. "Is Carter all right?"

Jacob didn't answer. She moved around the couch to see his phone in his hands, his fingers speeding across the screen.

"Jacob, what's wrong?"

Still no answer. Anger swept through her this time. His focus was so intent that she got close without him even noticing. She reached out her hand and covered the phone so he couldn't see it.

He glanced up, frowning in her direction.

"Is Carter okay?" she asked, enunciating each word.

He blinked, and she could almost see the realization steal into his eyes. *Yes, dear, you left something out.* "I'm sorry, KC. Yes, Carter is perfectly fine."

"Then what's wrong?"

"Just something out at the mill," he said, but his normally straightforward gaze slid away. He stepped back, dropping the phone to his side. "But I really need to be on the next flight home."

What was going on? Why was Jacob avoiding the issue with her? Or was he so focused on what was happening back home that his mind had already traveled there, leaving her behind? She returned to the bedroom to dress and pack, but her thoughts lingered on the man who was already back furiously texting once more. After last night, she would have described them as being closer than ever.

So why had he pulled away?

As they left the hotel, her heart mourned the short duration of their time alone together. They were supposed to have been here for two more days, but whatever was going on at the mill was important enough to cut their visit short. The delicious ache between her thighs reminded her just what she was forfeiting. But it had to be bad for Jacob to need to be home so quickly, didn't it? Hopefully everyone was all right.

Not that Jacob was talking. She finally closed her eyes on the plane and attempted to make up for the lack of sleep the previous night. Jacob's restlessness beside her kept her from more than dozing, but at least she got some rest and felt better able to handle an afternoon alone with Carter. Obviously Jacob wouldn't be there to help.

"I'll take you to your mother's to get Carter, then I'll need to head out for a while," he said as they collected the car from long-term parking. "There are some things I need to check into with Aiden."

Not wanting to pry but hating the timidness of her question, she asked, "Is there anything I can do to help?"

A sharp shake of his head was the only answer. His silence frustrated her, but she refused to beg. So she backed off after that, spending the rest of the ride to town in silence. As long as her son was okay, she could handle anything else.

Or so she thought.

As they neared Lola's, the space between the bar's parking lot and her mother's small house was occupied with a couple of city police cars and a whole crowd of people. Fear pounded inside KC's chest as if she was having a heart attack. Instead of stopping, Jacob accelerated past the building.

"What? Wait!"

Confusion and panic had her twisting in her seat. Jacob parked on the side of the road a little way down. "I thought you said Carter was okay," KC gasped. Jacob barely had time to stop the car before she had her door open and was running for the house.

It wasn't until she started pushing through the crowd that she realized Jacob wasn't with her. She glanced back over her shoulder and saw him slowly approaching, but then she broke through to the other side of the crowd and her thoughts were only for her family.

As she mounted the first step to the porch, the door

opened and a few of the local deputies she recognized from
the bar came out. Surprise jolted through her as her brother
appeared between them. Faces grim, they all crossed the
porch together and filed down the steps. Murmuring from
the crowd behind her swelled, but she only had eyes for
Zachary. One of the officers had his hands on Zachary's
arm, which told her he wasn't just going for a joyride.

"Zachary?" she called, but somehow Jacob was there,
holding her out of the way of the approaching party.

The deputy escorting her brother paused, giving her a
better look. No handcuffs. "Zachary," she whispered, fear
double-timing her pulse.

"It's okay, KC," her brother said, his face carefully un-
concerned. "Everything will be fine."

But she didn't believe him. Especially when they escorted him to a cop car and into the backseat. Jacob remained silent the whole time. Behind her, the screen door
banged. Turning, KC found her mother on the porch.
"Mom?" KC's voice broke as she rushed up the steps, Jacob
finally letting her go.

"They said something about some crops he dusted last
week," her mother murmured, her eyes glued to the cop
cars backing out of the driveway. "Said they're dying or
something. They had lots of questions for him."

KC turned accusing eyes on Jacob. She could read his
knowledge of the situation in his body language. He'd
known. And hadn't told her.

As if he could read her body language, too, Jacob said,
"KC, I'm sorry. I didn't know they'd be here. I thought
they'd pick him up at his apartment."

"He was here helping me fix the sink," KC's mom said.
"It was clogged. I guess his landlord told them where to
find him."

"What's going to happen?" KC asked.

Jacob slowly shook his head, his eyes once more
guarded. He glanced at the people behind him. The crowd

was diminishing, but those remaining seemed very interested in KC and Jacob's presence. "Let's get you and Carter home. Quietly. You can rest while I look into it."

But he knew more than he was saying. More than he would share. Which proved to KC that there was something important going on—but he wasn't going to include her.

"Don't bother," she said, taking a step back up toward the porch. "Mom will get me home."

Even though she wanted to believe he had a reason for his actions, nothing hurt worse than his turning and walking away—without a word.

"Your sister is going to come after me with a cast-iron skillet if I don't come home with the right answers soon," Jacob said to the man sitting across from him in the local police station's tiny interrogation room.

Not to mention that I'll be back to sleeping on the couch tonight.

Zachary smirked as if he could read Jacob's mind. "Well, you're the one who played mute. Why didn't you just tell her what was going on? Trust me, KC can take it."

Obviously a lot better than Jacob. He hadn't known what to say or how to say it, so he'd said nothing. He'd let his business mode take over, oblivious to KC's need to know.

Plus, the crowd had made him nervous. Who knew if the saboteur was watching, enjoying the drama, waiting for Zachary to be charged with a crime he didn't commit? At least intentionally. Or had he?

This situation was majorly screwed up. So Jacob had remained silent. Something he just knew KC would make him pay for, with relish.

"Just tell me again what happened," he said, hoping to block that out for a few more minutes.

Luckily the local police knew Jacob, had been working with him and Aiden and management to try to catch whoever was sabotaging things at the mill. He also saw the sheriff a couple of times a month at the local country club, so they'd let him in to see Zachary, who wasn't technically under arrest…yet.

"After my army gig, I missed flying, so I bought a little Cessna to do some crop-dusting work during the growing and harvest seasons. People like me because I do good work and am reasonably priced, so almost ninety percent of the farmers around here use me."

Zachary rubbed his hand over his shaggy black hair. "A few days ago I took the plane out to dust pesticides over a lot of the cotton crops in the area. Did the rest of my customers the next day. Well, apparently those crops have started dying. All of them."

Jacob sucked in a breath and held it for a moment, then let it out in a rush. "How bad?"

Zachary's green-brown eyes, so like his sister's, met Jacob's. "If all of them die…? We're talking total devastation for this community. I think all of those farms sell to the mill, so you'll have practically no raw material come harvesttime." Zachary's fists clenched. "Not to mention the number of families who no longer have cash for their crops this year. How could somebody do this?"

"So you didn't do it?"

Once more Zachary's gaze met his. "Oh, I did it. I flew the plane. But I have no idea how I could have dumped something that would kill the plants. When I loaded, those tanks were marked for common pesticides."

"Tell me what happened from the moment you arrived at the airfield."

He knew Zachary had to be tired of repeating the story, but Jacob had to be sure the man was telling the truth. For himself and the company. But most of all for KC.

But Zachary didn't falter as he related step by step how he checked in, confirmed and loaded the tanks and prepared for takeoff. Behind him, the deputy nodded. Seemed as if Zachary was telling the truth.

"Why would someone want to do this?" Zachary demanded. "And why through me? I hate that."

Jacob sympathized with Zachary's anger. And admired his calm. After all, he was sitting in a police station. The deputy had said, depending on what happened, he could be facing destruction-of-property charges for every family that had been harmed. That was a lot of charges.

Hopefully, Jacob could prevent that.

"What do you think was used?"

Zachary shrugged, his palms opening in a "how should I know" gesture. "Honestly, I haven't seen any of the plants, so I'm not sure. The chemical tests will tell them what they need to know."

The door opened and the local police chief walked in with Aiden. The police chief spoke first, confirming that they'd been listening through the speakers. "We've sent samples off, but it will take a while for them to come back."

"I loaded the right tanks," Zachary insisted. "I double-checked myself."

Aiden jumped in, his narrowed gaze not leaving Zachary for a second. "Look, I don't know anything about farming. That's not a secret. But something wiped out those plants, and a lot of livelihoods with it."

"One of the deputies on the scene confirmed that the tanks are marked and were checked into inventory as pesticides," the police chief said. "Not that it would stop someone from putting something else inside them."

Jacob found himself defending Zachary, even though Aiden was clearly suspicious. "Why would he kill plants and his own income with them?" he asked.

Zachary snorted. "Damn straight. Shut down the mill, the farmers and my own earnings in the process."

Aiden nodded. "Makes sense."

Jacob could see his brother mulling it over as he started to pace. It did make sense as a defense. But would it be enough?

"Although," Aiden continued, flashing a concerned look in Jacob's direction, "if you were paid to do this, it would be a lot more than the income you normally make."

Zachary dropped his head into his hands.

The chief answered his phone, spoke quietly for a few moments, then ended the call. "After examining a sample of the crops, the consensus seems to be they were sprayed with defoliant."

Silence reigned for a moment. Zachary's head dropped into his hands. "At this early stage, that means death for all those plants."

The deputy nodded. "Most likely."

"Jeez."

Jacob shared a look with Aiden. Not good. But then Aiden surprised him. "How accessible are the tanks to somebody besides yourself?"

"I guess someone could get to them," Zachary said with a frown, "even though they're locked up. And of course, some of the airport security personnel have the key."

"It's a small facility," the policeman said, "and a lot of locals hang out there. Especially the older men. So a good bunch of people come and go without much notice. Someone dropping by wouldn't stand out too much."

Zachary's eyes met Jacob's, letting him know their thoughts matched. Their saboteur had expanded his reach.

"How long does he need to stay here?" Jacob asked.

"A few hours," the chief said. "Then he can go. For now."

Zachary groaned.

The chief shot him a sympathetic look. "Sorry, son, but I can't make any guarantees until I get to the bottom of this. Which we will. I promise."

Zachary looked more defeated than he had since Jacob had arrived. Not that he could blame him. After all, he had sprayed the plants. But did that mean he was responsible for the destruction if he'd sprayed the defoliant unknowingly?

"Look at it this way," Jacob said in a lighter tone.

"Wouldn't you rather be here than having to explain this to your sister? Like I'm going to have to do?"

Because Jacob had no doubt his girl would be ready for a come-to-Jesus meeting when he got home. He'd better have some answers, or his head would be on a skewer.

Thirteen

Jacob opened the door quietly, anxious not to wake Carter. It was long past the time he should have been home. Worried about Zachary and how what had happened would affect the town, he'd hung around until Zachary was released. Then he, Zachary and Aiden had spent some time going over all the information they had. Jacob had texted KC when Zachary had left jail, but hadn't talked to her since then.

One look at KC's face and he realized it was a whole lot worse than he'd anticipated. She gently jiggled and rocked the restless baby in her arms, but her red-rimmed eyes and flushed cheeks attested to how upset she was. And to Jacob's guilt. He still found her disheveled look cute, but he knew better than to say so.

Carter seemed to sense his mother's unhappiness. There was no full-blown crying this time, just a restless stirring of arms and legs to keep himself awake. Without a word, Jacob lifted Carter from her arms and tucked him into his own special hold. His son looked up at him long and hard, then blinked slowly. Once. Then again. And started his slow slide into sleep as Jacob swayed him back and forth.

As those incredible eyes closed for a final time, Jacob

smiled. "He seems to have grown in just the small amount of time we've been gone."

KC nodded, though she kept her face averted after his one quick glimpse. "Yeah, incredible, huh?"

He winced at her scratchy voice, feeling himself falling into unknown depths. The KC he knew was strong, independent, sexy. He'd never seen her cry. That was something he truly didn't know how to handle. To escape, he carried Carter down the hall to his room and settled him into bed. Staring into the crib, he took several deep breaths before going back down the hallway.

Jacob couldn't leave her hurting. The woman he cared for deserved better than that. So he found her at the sink, washing bottles. He suspected it was simply an excuse to hide her face from him, but he would allow her that modicum of privacy. It was the least he could do after telling her nothing, rushing her home and then leaving her with Carter by herself all night.

"I waited until they released him, just in case. Then he, Aiden and I went over everything together. I didn't mean to be so long."

"Do you suspect him?"

"Zachary? Once I heard all the facts? No."

She turned to face him, her stare demanding in its own right. "Tell me the truth, Jacob."

"KC, Zach is not the saboteur." He held her gaze, intent on conveying his belief. "I know because I've asked him to help me catch whoever is doing all this."

Her face completely blanked for a moment. "What?"

"Your brother works maintenance at the mill. He's all over the floor, sometimes at odd hours, and no one thinks anything of him being there. He's been keeping his eyes and ears open for me. That may be why he was targeted this way."

With deliberate intent, he stepped closer. "That's why I didn't say anything while the police were picking him up at your mother's. I wasn't sure who might be watching, listening in that crowd, and I certainly didn't want your mother to think I'd put Zach in this position."

"I—"

He'd never seen her this much at a loss for words.

"Jacob, I don't even know what to say."

"Zachary will be fine."

"This isn't about Zachary." Her voice gained volume until Jacob worried about waking Carter. "I can't believe you don't see that. This has nothing to do with my brother, and everything to do with you not keeping me in the loop."

Jacob stared for a moment. She was right—he hadn't seen that as the real problem, more as a sideline. Jacob proceeded with caution. "I didn't think you cared about the day-to-day stuff at the mill."

"This isn't a daily occurrence, is it? You said you were worried about my and Carter's safety, but you don't even let me know you've put my brother in a position that could get him hurt, or even just fired?"

Well, no. That was definitely not the right answer. "I thought I was approaching the situation logically. I needed help—"

"A spy."

"—and your brother agreed to help me. It's business, not personal."

"When it involves my family, I consider everything personal."

Huh. Jacob wasn't even sure how to respond to that. He knew KC approached things emotionally, but he hadn't thought this would ever come up. He had never imagined the saboteur would use Zachary to hurt the mill.

She didn't comment on his silence. "Why is it okay to keep us in the dark and let us think he's going to jail for something we know he would never do? My mother has been calling me, worried sick. I've been worried. When you don't let me know what's going on, what am I supposed to think?"

"I told you I'd take care of him. Zach won't go to jail. I promise. We've got a plan."

She turned that heartbreaking gaze on him full force. "But I'm not part of it, am I?"

No. It had never occurred to him that she'd want to be, even though he knew how much she loved her family. He felt like such an idiot.

"I don't expect you to hire me so I can watch my brother at work. Or text me a minute-by-minute update. But I'm not some old-fashioned maiden who sits home by the fire while you do all the work. I thought you knew me better than that. It has to be more than just a text here and there. If we're—if we are going to be partners, I need you to include me, accept me as part of the plan. Keep me informed ahead of time, not after the fact. That's what partners do."

Jacob wasn't sure if he could promise that. He cared about her. He knew that. But he'd been doing this on his own for so long. He didn't know if he could open himself up to the idea of partners, especially one that operated so differently from him.

He wanted KC to trust him. Even now, he could see the fear cloud her eyes. But working on his own terms was what he knew. Could he change that?

"I need you to decide, Jacob. Are we working together, or are you strictly solo?"

His only answer was to pull her close and hold on tight. He couldn't bring himself to lie, so he kept his fears locked inside. The only truth he knew was that the man he was now would die if she left him all alone.

Zachary let out a low whistle as Jacob led him into the breezeway at the heart of Blackstone Manor. "Wow. And I thought this place was impressive from the outside."

Jacob let him look his fill around the central corridor

and the staircase, which gave visitors an unobstructed view of the elaborate railings on the landings of the two upper floors.

"At least now it's seeing some true happiness," a feminine voice said.

Jacob smiled up at his sister-in-law, Christina, as she descended from the second floor. Her lilac scrubs contrasted with the dark waves of hair falling to her shoulders. "How's Mother?" he asked.

Christina gave a sad little smile. "The same. Today's a pretty good day for her." She turned to the other visitor. "Hey, Zachary. How are you?"

"Good for now," he returned with a grin. "The police confirmed that there's no proof I added the defoliant to the tank, which was marked pesticide. But the two working security cameras were turned off that night, so I'm still the primary suspect, mostly because I'm the *only* suspect. But my guess is, they're also waiting to see if any money turns up."

Jacob watched as the two chatted. He'd known Christina and KC were friends but didn't realize Christina knew Zach. It shouldn't surprise him, though. Christina had a knack for connecting with people that Jacob had always envied.

"How is KC?" Christina asked. "I haven't seen her in several days."

"She's been subdued when I've seen her at Lola's," Zachary said. "Hovering over me like I might disappear at any moment, though they've been keeping me mostly in the back to discourage any retaliation. She's worried about the farmers."

So was Jacob, but he hadn't figured out what to do yet. "She's quiet at home, too."

Another situation Jacob didn't know how to fix. Jacob knew he hadn't convinced her of his loyalty, or his desire to be equal partners. Taking the steps to truly include her in every part of his life had his control-freak side, well, freaking out. So they danced around each other, keeping every conversation light, not delving too deep into things that might be tricky to navigate. Then at night, after Carter was asleep, their bodies talked intimately in a whole different language.

"Oh, Jacob's got that 'worried about my woman' look," Christina said with a grin. "I think he's doomed. What do you think, Zachary?"

"I'm pretty sure you're right." Zachary gave him a speculative once-over, but in the end nodded his approval. "She could do worse."

Jacob did not want to get into this. He looked expectantly at Christina. "Aiden?"

Her smirk told him she knew his avoidance tactics well, but she let him slide. "He's in the study."

Jacob led the way around the staircase and halfway down the breezeway until he came to his grandfather's former study. Zachary's expression said *wow* as he took in the floor-to-ceiling scrollwork bookcases and masculine furnishings.

Aiden greeted them with a distracted nod. "He's gone off campus again."

Jacob shook his head at Zachary. "For some reason, he thinks we can read his mind. Do you mean the saboteur, Aiden?"

His brother frowned. "You know I do, Jacob."

"The fact that he's hitting places away from the plant worries me," Jacob said. "It makes him—or them— dangerous."

"And unpredictable," Zachary added.

"Messing with things around the mill itself is annoying and a concern. But no one has been hurt on mill property. But showing that he's willing to expand his targets outside the mill itself? This convinces me that whoever was behind this incident was behind the group who set fire to my studio," Aiden said, his steely gaze meeting Jacob's.

His heart skipped a beat. That meant KC could still become a target…or an innocent bystander who got in the way. "I'm doing what I can to keep them safe."

Always observant, Zachary didn't miss the subtext. "Is this why you're still keeping your attachment to my sister on the down low?"

KC's brother deserved the truth, and giving him the information would mean that there'd be one more person to watch over Jacob's new family. "It's not the only reason, but yes, I don't want KC and Carter to become targets, so we're being careful to keep things casual in public."

The look Zachary threw his way made Jacob think he wanted to know the other reasons, but Jacob didn't want to talk about the deal he'd forced Zachary's sister into playing out.

"Zachary," Aiden said, averting his attention from Jacob, "what are you hearing at the plant?"

"Well, there's lots to hear," he said with a slow shake of his head. "Rumblings all over the floor. Low level up to management. And I mean a lot. Mostly upset over whoever did this, but—"

He paused, his face taking on an uncomfortable look.

"What is it?" Jacob asked.

"There're also people talking down on management for not putting a stop to the sabotage by now. People worried they'll be the next target. Or simply get in the way and get hurt." He steeled his hands against his hips. "A lot of people know those farmers, their relatives, friends. I can see the situation escalating. Soon. But I'll never know about anything before it happens."

"Why?" Jacob asked.

"I'm persona non grata right now. By association, you know."

"How hard is this hitting the farmers?" Aiden asked.

"Some of them have day jobs, so that helps, but without a crop to harvest, that guaranteed income won't be there. They'll lose their investment. Some years, their income might fluctuate if the season is too wet or too dry, but this is a complete wipeout. Bad is an understatement."

Jacob was ready for action. "What do they need? Money? Food? What would be best?"

"It's probably different for different people," Aiden said. "Let's think on it. Zachary, you get back to us if you find out more."

"I already know one thing you're gonna need."

"What's that?" Aiden asked.

"Cotton." Zachary paused a moment, as if letting that soak in. "We've got to find a cotton dealer—soon. KC might can help you with that. She's got a good friend who's a cotton dealer. Works with some of the farmers around here, too."

Involve KC? Jacob's first instinct was to keep her out of this. There were people at the plant who could handle it. But Jacob felt a personal responsibility for the farmers and the people at the mill, and wanted to fix things himself. And this just might be his chance to prove to KC that he was willing to include her in this decision. That they were in this together.

Fourteen

Jacob watched KC finish washing up behind the bar. Normally, when it was past closing time, he would have already left, taken Carter home and put him to bed so she didn't have to do that after a long shift on her feet. But her mother had asked if Carter could spend the night. Jacob's standing with her was still precarious; she'd given him a stern look before nodding in her daughter's direction, as if to say *fix this*.

KC had been unnaturally subdued since the police had interviewed Zachary. He wasn't used to this. Normally, her every movement, no matter how quiet, was filled with life. Now she seemed to spend her days on Pause, as if her spirit were holding its breath, waiting to see what was going to happen next.

An even bigger problem: Jacob wasn't sure if she was worried about Zachary…or the two of them.

Tonight, he needed a chance to reconnect with her. Not just sexually. KC was open to his touch, but even there he could feel her holding herself away from him. Not losing herself quite as fully as she normally did in their passion. Which hurt. Ms. Gatlin's offer to take Carter for the night provided the perfect opportunity to fix things.

KC's mother left with Carter, who was already falling asleep in her arms. Still, KC kept scrubbing.

Jacob moved to a spot directly across the bar from her, but she didn't look up. Finally he reached out and stilled her hand with his own. "KC, I need your help."

Now he had her attention. *Such a mama bear.* "What's wrong?"

"The farmers and their families are going to need support to get back on their feet. I'm trying to figure out the best way to do that."

"Another fund-raiser?"

Jacob shook his head. "No, I was thinking something more personal. First, I need a cotton dealer, or a lot of people are gonna be out of a job come September. Zachary said you could help."

She paused in her scrubbing, those turbulent eyes suddenly lighting up. "Easy peasy."

Was she being glib? "Really?"

"Yep. I know exactly who to contact." She grinned, her first genuine smile in days. "A guy I met when he first started working with the farmers out here about five years ago. He doesn't buy in Black Hills every year, but he keeps track of sales around here." She dropped her rag into the dishwater, giving Jacob her full attention. "What else?"

"A lot of people lost their immediate livelihood. They're going to have some tangible needs. Remember me telling you that I wanted to invest in a charity that spoke to me?"

KC nodded, her eyes sparking green deep inside the brown.

"This is it, but I want to start off right. I have some ideas, but I'm used to how charities work in a big city." Which was totally true. More than that, he wanted her involved. Soliciting her ideas was the best way to get her on board. "I don't want some anonymous charity run by a big impersonal board. This would be a hands-on project. But I don't have time to run it. Any ideas?"

She propped her elbows on the bar. Resting her chin in her hands gave him a distracting view of her cleavage, but he maintained his focus. Barely. KC appeared oblivious as she said, "Better to be effective than to just do something for the sake of doing it."

Exactly. "I want a hardship fund to provide a variety of things to families and workers in need. But the community as a whole still views me as an outsider, I think. I'm not familiar with the people here nearly enough. And they probably wouldn't feel comfortable with me, either."

He smiled as he continued, "We need someone to administer the fund who is familiar with the townspeople on a grassroots level. That's why I wanted to ask if you would be willing to help me. You know these people. You know this place. Will you do this for them?"

Shock widened her eyes. Her mouth shaped the word *me*, but no sound escaped. A few heartbeats later, she cleared her throat. "Jacob, I don't know anything about coordinating a big charity. I mean, I do know a lot of people—"

"And you know about handling them, evaluating what they need with dignity and respect. Sounds perfect to me. I can manage the boring parts of it—the money and paperwork and all."

She stood quietly for a moment. "What about the saboteur? Do we need to worry about him retaliating against me?"

"For helping the community? I doubt it. He seems more concerned with things that directly affect the mill. The goal has been accomplished—kill the cotton. Helping the people left behind shouldn't endanger you. Now, Aiden and I bringing in cotton could be a trigger."

She squirmed, the light in her eyes dimming a little.

"Don't worry. As long as we're careful to keep our public interactions nonromantic, you and Carter should be fine."

"Maybe." She studied him for a long moment. "You

know people will eventually find out you're living at my house?"

"As I said, we're being careful."

"Yes, and they've stopped questioning your presence here. And the neighbors don't notice your car parked in the back shed. And we're careful not to go anywhere out together. But how long will you be happy with that?"

Her tone told him she wasn't happy, but she was probably too afraid for Carter to push the issue. He wasn't sure how he felt about going public, but he couldn't force himself to leave her—them. One day he might have to, to protect them both. But for now, staying was his only desire. He gave her a short nod, keeping his thoughts to himself. "We'll deal with that when we get there. For now, what about the charity?"

"Um, okay. I mean, yes," she said, then laughed as he nodded his approval.

Now they were on track—and seeing her so excited had an incredibly stimulating effect on his libido. "Any ideas for what we could do?"

"Maybe we could raise money for care packages, get donated gift cards for clothes and groceries, or even money to help pay essential bills."

"Baby, you've got some great ideas in that head of yours."

Resorting to her sexy persona, Miss Mischievous winked at him. "Sure you don't want a fund-raiser? I could open a kissing booth."

Unable to stop himself, he grasped her hand. "I don't think so, woman," he said, the deeply possessive note betraying him, but he didn't care. "The only man kissing you will be me."

"Ooh, territorial." The heat filling her eyes belied her light tone.

He rubbed his thumb back and forth over the delicate bones in her hand. "You like?"

"Definitely." Her eyes, green in the dim light, were tentative and fearful as they met his. How could he resist her? As he marched around the bar, her breathing sped up, light and fast.

Jacob used his height to trap her between him and the bar. Need rose like a tsunami, threatening to overwhelm him. "What about this?"

The dilation of her pupils gave him his answer, but he waited for her words. Her permission. "Oh, yeah."

Then he crowded in close, grateful the doors were closed and locked, the lights low or off. Her body felt incredible—muscled legs against his, soft belly cradling his need, full breasts against his ribs. So delectable. So *his*.

He brooked no argument as he pulled her Lola's T-shirt from her jeans and over her head. The low lights glittered off the shimmery satin of the pale pink bra that did a fine job of displaying her womanhood. Unwilling to wait, he lifted her to sit on the counter.

Her squeal of surprise echoed around the empty room, bringing a smile to his lips. *That's right.* He had a few tricks up his sleeve, too. Then he lost himself in the plump upper curve of her silky flesh, kissing his way across the hills and nuzzling into the valley between. He lifted her breasts upward for the return journey, squeezing a little as he dipped his tongue beneath the edge of her bra for a lingering taste of her oh-so-sensitive nipples.

She squirmed and a little whimper escaped her. *Yes, that's what you like.* The way her body went wild under his mouth confirmed it. Her hands clutched at his shoulders, seemingly desperate to drag his clothes off, too, but he wasn't giving in that easy. Instead, he released the clasp that held her bra in place. His hands eased it down her arms to encircle her wrists, then inexorably guided her back until her spine met cold, polished wood. She hissed as she arched up, then moaned once more.

But she wasn't getting away. Control was his. Making her feel him was his only goal.

He palmed his way down her ribs to her waist, then applied his nails to the denim along the inside of her thighs. Her hips lifted, telling him she was willing and ready. Anchoring her hips with his hands, he kissed and nipped lightly, making his way down her body, closer and closer to her core.

"Jake, please," she pleaded, the sound shooting straight to his groin.

"Please what?"

When she didn't answer, he opted for more torture. Reaching under her, he squeezed the ass that had tempted him all evening as she worked the bar, then kissed the bare skin right above the waistband of her jeans.

"Please, Jake," she repeated, her hips lifting for more.

Please what, baby? Jacob waited her out, needing her desperate, aching for him and only him. Sliding his hands up and around, he grasped her waistband and pulled downward as if to remove her jeans.

"Yes," she cried.

"When I say," he growled against her skin, deliberately letting go. She was so beautiful, spread out before him, wanting him. Just as he wanted her.

Her breath panted out, ragged and choppy. Turning the tables, KC dug her fingers into his hair before pulling lightly, eliciting a groan from him. He glanced up and caught the smile stretching her lips. If he'd paid attention to history, he'd have known she wouldn't remain passive for long.

With hands grasping her hips, he pulled her toward him, almost completely shifting her rear off the bar. Her hands slapped against the edge, the sound sharp in the air, as she struggled to keep her balance. He lifted her legs higher, resting them on his shoulders so he could savor the feast before him.

She squeezed, searching for a tighter grip on his shoulders. Her hips lifted higher. Jacob licked his lips, anxious for more, but forced himself to hold back. With sure fingers he unsnapped her jeans. He lingered on the small amount of newly exposed skin for a moment before moving on. This time to the zipper, bringing it down, oh, so slowly.

She moaned her frustration, but he grinned. She was so much fun to play with. His body and mind stilled in surprise for a moment. But yes, he and KC were playing. Not a plan in sight, and it was glorious.

Anxious himself now, he peeled the fabric from her, using her position to keep her helpless and himself in control. Finally, shoes and jeans and panties hit the floor. This time he retraced his journey to her center with sucking kisses and searching tongue.

Before long he couldn't wait himself. He knew to be prepared every second with KC, so he dug the condom out of his pocket and readied himself ASAP. He didn't care that he was almost completely dressed. He needed her now before his body exploded without her.

Together. *Always.*

Jacob couldn't linger on the thought. If he did, he might panic. Lifting her again, he turned and pressed her back against the wall. His weight held her steady while he joined them, her greedy flesh and gasping breaths driving him higher than high. He guided her legs around him and supported her with a hand under each thigh. He started slow, aching to savor, but his body wasn't about to cooperate.

"Jake," she gasped. "Take me, please."

There was his girl. His hips moved with steady purpose, until her breath caught in that familiar way. He leaned down, his head resting against the side of hers. They were so close he could almost hear her heart pound. Only then did he let the emotions take him.

So he shouldn't have been surprised to hear himself whisper the words "I love you" as the world narrowed to the two of them and the ecstasy they found together. KC didn't give any indication that she'd heard him over her gasping cries, but he'd heard. Now he had to decide what to do about it.

When KC said she knew whom to call, she wasn't kidding. Two days after her conversation with Jacob, the cotton agent she had in mind walked into Lola's for a friendly little drink. She'd convinced Jacob to meet him here in a casual atmosphere, rather than having the formal business meeting he'd suggested.

She knew she was right. *Jacob* just didn't know it yet.

"Hey, Toby," she said, grinning at the agent as he slid onto a stool. "How's it going?"

"Always better when I can see your pretty face."

KC laughed at Jacob's glare; he'd approached in time to hear Toby's compliment. Jacob smoothed out his expression as he settled himself onto the stool next to Toby.

"Aw, you're too sweet." She winked, and then motioned to Jacob. "Toby, this is a friend of mine, Jacob Blackstone."

Toby turned an impressed face toward Jacob. "One of the infamous Blackstones? Cool to meet ya, man. I may not have grown up in Black Hills, but everyone in this part of South Carolina has heard of your family."

She could read the minuscule release of tension in Jacob's shoulders as he shook hands with Toby. *Told ya he was cool.* But she just grinned and leaned against the bar.

"I appreciate you dropping by, Toby."

Jacob's gaze dipped down to her chest, reminding her of his attentions on this very bar just a few nights ago. KC quickly straightened up again with a blush.

"Am I gonna get a cherry cola for my trouble?" Toby asked.

"Of course. Want some nachos with that?"

She busied herself making the drink while the guys yakked and got to know each other. Jacob asked about

Toby's hometown, his family, letting him do the talking…
and giving KC a chance to watch.

She often watched Jacob surreptitiously while she was
working, but today she ached to just soak in his blond good
looks. His thick hair feathered back in perfectly clipped
waves. Which only made her want to muss them up. She
could watch his mouth all day, that tempting curve that gave
away all the emotions he tried to keep hidden. Like now. He
might be smiling, but she could see the touch of firmness in
his lower lip. He was worried about something—probably
how this deal would work out. But he'd never let her know.

It was one of so many things he kept from her, though
she knew he was trying to change that.

Being a bartender had honed her timing. She returned
during the perfect lull in their conversation, setting the soft
drink in front of Toby, who got one every time he came.
"You may have heard about the trouble around here," she
said to him.

"Oh, yeah. There're some pretty crazy rumors floating around."

Toby wasn't the type to go for a bunch of half-truths
or white lies. So she gave Jacob credit for not pulling any
punches. "Well, some of them are probably true," he said.

"You lost most of your cotton crop?" Toby asked, eyeing him over the rim of his glass.

KC stepped in, wanting to add a human element to the
issues. Luckily, Toby was familiar with her family. He came
here to eat or hang out just about every time he was in town.
"It's really bad, Toby. Zach was the one who sprayed what
he thought was pesticide, so he feels really responsible. You
know how he is about that kind of stuff." Her brother's history of military service had desensitized him in many ways,
but he'd become a quiet crusader for people in need, as his
offer to help Jacob find the saboteur had shown.

"Wow," Toby said, glancing back and forth between
them. "How'd that happen?"

KC didn't think Jacob was ready to be that forthcoming yet. Sure enough, he gave a generic "We still don't know. The important question is, how do we fix it?"

Toby was already shaking his head. "I've promised most of my crop out already. We're halfway to harvesttime. I've got orders to fill."

KC noted Jacob's restless shifting on the bar stool but ignored it. Instead, she turned on the charm with a look of feminine pleading. "Come on, Toby. We're talking about the livelihood of an entire town here. Couldn't you try to hunt us down *something* to help?" Hell, she'd even lean against the bar again if she had to.

"How much we talking about?" Toby said with an exaggerated sigh.

Sucker!

At that point, the conversation dissolved into a bunch of logistics that had KC's eyes glazing over. She was a people person, not a numbers person. And in the end, Toby was frowning.

"Please, Toby," she begged. Man, did she need to bat some eyelashes? "Isn't there anything you can do?"

His good ol' boy smile made an appearance. "Let me make some calls. You know I love ya, doll, but this is a tall order."

"We realize that," Jacob said, standing up. "But KC says if anyone can make it happen, you can."

Toby glanced her way, eliciting a grin of her own. "Did you really? I knew you were sweet on me."

KC could tell Jacob did not like that at all. "Like a brother, maybe," he said.

Ooh, possessive male glowering. Interesting. She raised a brow. "You'll have to overlook him, Toby. He's too serious for his own good."

Toby laughed. "Honey, the looks he's been shooting your way told me the whole story. You could at least give him a chance."

"Oh, he's had a chance," she confirmed, going full tease. "Now he thinks he's big stuff."

Jacob stepped closer, the intense look in his eyes speeding up her heartbeat. "I don't hear you complaining," he said.

Toby sputtered. "Wow, I never thought I'd see the day somebody tamed this kitty. I'll definitely see what I can do for ya."

What? Ignoring her squeal of outrage, Jacob handed over a business card.

Toby was barely on his way before KC was putting out a glare of her own. "What was that?" she demanded.

"You said I needed to have more fun," he said, but she wasn't buying that innocent look for a second. "Besides, all that teasing got us some cotton, didn't it?"

"I'm pretty sure it will," she said, a small glow of pride lighting inside her. She'd done it. If they could get even half the amount of cotton Toby had mentioned, the mill wouldn't have to go through layoffs and the town would be more secure. She'd already been in touch with Christina and Avery about the hardship fund.

Boy, it felt good to know she was making a difference.

But Jake wasn't through with her yet. "Still, we need to have a talk about your methods." He glanced down at her chest, reminding her of her tight T-shirt and accidental overexposure.

"Really?" Men had astounding audacity.

"Yes, really," he said, his voice deepening in that telltale way. He was so easy to read when he was aroused.

This time she deliberately leaned on the counter. Like clockwork, his gaze slid down. She chuckled. "We'll talk when you can keep your eyes on my face, dear."

Fifteen

KC struggled through the door to her house lugging Carter's car carrier—occupied by a crying Carter—his diaper bag, her purse, a grocery sack and box of diapers. She could have made two trips, but walking that many more steps through the pouring rain just wasn't in her plan for the day.

"Jake?" she called.

His SUV was outside, but the house sounded empty. At least from what she could hear over the wail of her child.

Dropping everything else to land wherever it would, she crossed to the coffee table to set Carter down. Those tearful eyes begging her to get him out while she maneuvered the straps were both pitiful and amusing. Boy, could he get to her. You'd think her leaving him in his car carrier this long was the end of the world.

Lifting him up against her shoulder, she crossed to the kitchen. Empty. Then she walked down the hall to her bedroom. Also empty. It wasn't until she was about to turn away that she registered the room itself. The drawers she'd emptied out for Jacob to use hadn't been closed completely, leaving the dresser with a slightly snaggletoothed look.

Moving around the bed, she saw a couple of T-shirts on

the floor. The dress clothes Jacob had worn to work this morning were tossed haphazardly over the small chaise occupying one corner. She lay Carter down in the center of the bed. With a trembling hand, she slid one of the drawers open to find clothes shoved about, instead of the neat little rows Jacob usually maintained. It was the same in his pants drawer.

Returning to her son, KC held him close. To other people, clothes on the floor might be an everyday occurrence, but Jacob was as obsessive about his environment as he was his schedule. Her house had never been cleaner. Jacob picked up after himself, and her, and Carter as he went through his day. It was something she thought he actually did unconsciously. He was just that neat of a person.

For the clothes to be askew? He'd been upset about something.

Back in the living room, she snatched up her purse as best she could with Carter in her arms and dug out her cell phone. Her heart skipped a beat when she saw a missed call, but it was just a girlfriend. A few swipes and she'd dialed Jacob. While she waited for him to answer, she jiggled Carter, who was starting to snuffle against her shirt—his precursor to demanding food.

Voice mail. *Dang it*. Should she leave a message? Call again? Carter started to wiggle, so she simply hung up and set the phone down so she could pat his back. "Okay, buddy," she said. "Let's get you some dinner, then we can track down Daddy."

Only, the longer she waited, the more time she had to think. About what could be wrong. About why he hadn't called. About where he was right now.

She and Carter had been settled in the chair with a bottle for about ten minutes when the doorbell rang. The baby startled, his eyes glancing toward the door, before returning to his dinner.

Jacob?

Of course not. Jacob had a key. Juggling the baby and bottle, KC went to the door and answered it. "Christina, thank goodness."

Christina might at least have some answers. Except Christina's tear-streaked face didn't do KC's sense of panic any good.

"Where's Jacob? What's wrong?"

"He and Aiden left midafternoon to go to North Carolina," Christina said as she came through the door and dripped on the carpet. KC was alarmed to see her friend didn't even have a raincoat or umbrella. "It's Luke. He had a car accident during a practice round." She glanced around as if unsure where she was or how she'd gotten here, turning almost in a circle before plopping onto the couch and letting her head fall into her hands. "I haven't heard an update since they got to the medical center in Charlotte, but his crew chief says it's pretty bad."

"Why didn't Jacob call and tell me?" *I'm simply a phone call away. Is that too hard?*

Christina was already shaking her head. "I'm sorry, KC. He was in total twin mode. That's why I figured I should come over here and tell you in person."

Twin mode. Oddly enough, she knew just what Christina meant. Jacob and Luke talked at least every other evening on the phone—and that was just what she saw here at home. She suspected they talked during the day, too. Or his phone would ring and Jacob would say, "That's Lucas," without even looking at the screen.

He had a connection to his brother she couldn't understand but did recognize. Had he thought she wouldn't?

Did that connection mean there wasn't room for her? Leaving town without even a simple text screamed she wasn't important enough to be told. She was simply a convenience, an obligation that came with his son.

In that moment, she knew she didn't want to be. She ached to mean enough to him to warrant that phone call.

To be truly needed. To be worthy of him sticking around—
for her, not just for Carter.

Silence settled in the room as KC finished feeding
Carter his bottle. The force of the wind spraying the rain
against the windows added to KC's uneasiness.

Christina didn't seem to mind the silence. She simply
sat there, probably not wanting to be alone. KC couldn't
blame her.

Then the phone rang. From the ringtone, KC realized
it was Christina's.

"Aiden," Christina said, relief raising her voice.

KC watched her as she settled Carter in his bouncy seat
so he could kick his legs and reach for the little toys attached to it now that his tummy was full and he was happy.

Christina nodded several times as Aiden spoke, then
closed her eyes in what looked like a painful squeeze. "Oh,
Aiden," she breathed.

KC's heart pounded. *Please, let Luke be okay.*

Christina turned teary eyes in her direction and nodded.
"Yes, I'm at her place now. Okay," she said, leaving KC
frustrated with the one-sided conversation. If Aiden could
talk to his wife, surely Jacob could call her, too.

Christina said her touching goodbyes to her husband
and hung up without any word about KC. Obviously, Jacob
hadn't asked for her.

"Aiden said the doctors are talking about more surgery
tomorrow. He's gonna be okay eventually. But his legs are
in pretty bad shape." Christina hugged herself and rocked
a little. KC took a seat next to her and rubbed her back.
Christina had always been friends with Luke. KC tried to
remember that and how much her friend needed someone to
comfort her with her husband a couple hundred miles away.

Not how that loathsome feeling of abandonment was
once again spreading through her own mind and heart.

"But he's out of danger now?" KC asked quietly.

Christina nodded, a tear slipping down her cheek. Then

Carter blew a raspberry and the women laughed, breaking the tension.

"Come on," KC said as she stood. "Let's fix some dinner."

They were halfway through eating before KC trusted herself to ask without sounding needy, "Are they all okay?"

"They made it across the state line just before the storm hit, which worried me, since they were driving Aiden's car," Christina said. Then her eyes met KC's and the realization of what KC was asking dawned. "The doctors let Jacob stay in recovery with Lucas, but Aiden said he's hanging in there."

But Jacob couldn't step outside to update her personally? Even for a few minutes?

No. She wouldn't think like that. She simply nodded and moved on.

Not long after dinner, the local television station broke off programming for the announcement of Luke's accident.

KC wanted to ignore it, but she couldn't look away. Aiden and Jacob stood together behind a podium, forming a united front in stylish suits. But Jacob did the talking.

Across the bottom of the screen scrolled the words Local Celebrity Car Racer Severely Injured in Practice Accident. KC shivered as Jacob greeted the crowds of reporters. In their small-town life, it was easy to forget that all the Blackstone brothers had made names for themselves away from here.

"Good evening. I'm Jacob Blackstone." His calm, cultured voice washed over her, ramping up her need to be with him. *Beside him.* "Thank you for joining us today. Our family is deeply grateful for your concern over our brother, Luke 'Renegade' Blackstone."

She caught a barely perceptible shift from one foot to the other as Jacob paused. His face, usually a calm mask, had added stress lines across his forehead and a tightness around his mouth she wished she could ease with a gentle kiss.

He looked so tired, so worried, that guilt crept over her. Here he was in a life-or-death situation with his brother, and she was thinking only of herself. Still, that desire to comfort him wouldn't go away.

"Luke has suffered extensive damage to his legs," Jacob was saying, "along with broken ribs and other injuries. They are not life threatening, but we suspect he will be in recovery for a while."

Christina gasped, even though they'd already heard the news. Tears overflowed onto her pale cheeks.

"We ask that you bear with us as we learn more about Luke's medical needs and recovery. We will release more information as it becomes available. I'm sure, as much as he loves the spotlight, Luke will be happy to talk to y'all as soon as he's able."

A light round of laughter swept across the audience.

"Please respect our family's desire for privacy as we adjust. Thank you."

The men didn't stay for questions. Instead, they moved to a side door, where they exited with Luke's crew chief. The door closed behind them, leaving the reporters clamoring for more answers. KC felt left out in the cold, too.

After long moments of silence, Christina rose to her feet. "Are you sure you don't want to come stay at the manor with me?" she asked.

As much as KC wanted to comfort Christina, tonight's emotional roller coaster and the realization of her true feelings just as Jacob proved how shallow his were, meant she needed time alone. "I'm sorry, but it'll be easier to get Carter to sleep here. And I don't want to cart all his stuff over in the rain."

Christina's lips parted as if to speak, then her gaze slid away. "No problem. I completely understand."

KC really hoped so. She didn't want Christina to feel

as if she was abandoning her. "I'll call in the morning and check in, okay?"

But as Christina pulled out of the driveway, anger sparked in KC's heart. She could reach out, do the sympathetic, caring thing for her friend. But she couldn't do the same for Jacob because he'd cut off her access to him. And he refused to offer her the same consideration.

Yeah, she wouldn't be offering any sappy declarations of "luv" anytime soon. If ever… Instead, she piled in the chair, cuddling Carter in her arms. This was where she belonged…where she was loved. This was where she should stay.

Shouldn't she?

Jacob's back ached from his hours-long slump in the chair in the corner of his brother's hospital room. He'd heard nothing but the beep of the heart monitor and his own breathing for what seemed like forever. His gaze was trained in his brother's direction, but he was so tired he wasn't really seeing anything anymore. Still, he couldn't leave.

Since they were kids, Luke had been the reckless one, the one to take all the chances. It usually got him in trouble, but Jacob was always there to pick up the pieces. That was his role. He took care of his brother.

Even if all he could do was sit by his side in the hospital.

"What are you thinking?"

A minute or more passed before Jacob realized the voice was real and not a figment of his imagination. It was the husky, battered quality that convinced him his brother had actually spoken for the first time since his accident. Jerking to his feet, he crossed the space between them in seconds. "You're awake."

"What were you thinking?" Luke repeated.

Words Luke probably couldn't afford to waste, considering his current physical state.

Jacob grimaced. His thoughts had centered around only two things since they'd gotten into this room: Luke and KC. How Jacob wished she were here. Making him smile. Soothing him with her touch so his brain wouldn't run away with scenarios of his brother never walking again. But he couldn't say any of that to Luke. So he kept it bottled up and ached for her in silence.

"Just wondering whether you'd ever stop sleepin' the day away," he said instead.

Luke's half smile released the tension deep in Jacob's gut. "We can't all be boring, clock-watching suits like you."

It was an old argument between them. But there was a new undertone, slightly hazy from the painkillers.

Suddenly Aiden spoke from the doorway. "Good to finally see those peepers, brother."

As he walked toward the bed, Jacob noted that Aiden's spiky hair now spiked in a few different directions. He'd probably run his hands through his hair dozens of times last night. They'd both been worried, even after they moved Luke out of ICU.

"I just got off the phone with Christina," Aiden said. "Everyone at the manor is good. Not much damage from the storm. And I just saw your doctor down the hall, so she should be in soon."

Jacob's heart sped up. "Was KC with her?" He'd told Aiden to have Christina invite her to the manor. He worried about her and Carter being alone in her older house with a thunderstorm raging outside.

Aiden shook his head. "No, she didn't go home with Christina last night." He hesitated a moment, raising Jacob's suspicions.

"What?" he demanded.

"Christina says KC was pretty upset when she went over there. You really should have called her." Aiden looked down at Jacob's hand, then cocked his head in inquiry.

Jacob knew what was there: the cell phone he'd had in

his hand for hours. He'd picked it up with the intention of calling home, then thought about what he wanted to say, needed to say, and couldn't make himself dial the number.

He'd meant to call her sooner, but at first there'd been no thought for anything but Luke. This twin thing didn't come out often, but when it did, it was no joke. The feelings of responsibility that came with it were all consuming. Only later did Jacob let the outer world break through...

By then, his heart had been running scared. Acknowledging the words he'd said to her in the bar had been tough enough, though they hadn't discussed it. But Jacob knew they were true. He did love her. With an intensity as deep as his love for his brothers.

Now he stood in the hospital room of the brother he'd almost lost. His entire world had spiraled out of his control with the news that Luke had been in an accident. It had been like his father's death all over again.

Jacob wanted—no, needed—his control. Tight and locked down. But if he called KC, he'd be begging her to come to him, aching for her comfort and ultimately giving his control over to someone outside of himself.

"I'll talk to her, explain," he said, though he had no clue what he'd say.

"Dude." Luke's weak voice barely topped the monitors, but he kept going. "You'd better grovel."

Jacob knew his brother was right, but he couldn't act in the face of his fear. His fear and selfish actions had landed him in deep trouble.

Luke's doctor walked into the room, taking Jacob's mind off the looming disaster back home. She moved directly to the bed, zeroing in on her patient. After a quick examination and a few questions, she addressed the elephant in the room. "Luke, I'm not going to lie to you, this is going to be a long recovery," she said.

Luke blinked slowly at the doctor, as if he couldn't quite take in what was being said.

"You will recover. Eventually. But with compound fractures this bad, in both legs, you'll need time to heal, then lots of work to rebuild your muscle strength and ability to walk. And that's not even addressing your other injuries."

Jacob looked at his brother, his leanly muscled body so still for once, and knew exactly what was going through his mind. Luke wouldn't care about pain, or rebuilding his strength—he'd only care about one thing. "His racing?" Jacob asked, feeling his throat close around the words.

She shook her head. "I don't know. The physical requirements of the sport might end up being too much, especially on his feet. It all depends on how he heals." She grinned at the prone man. "Which means you have to *take orders* and do the work."

"Oh, I'm used to work," Luke teased, though his smile was a mere stretch of tight lips. Jacob could feel the ache of Luke's sadness echo inside his own chest. "But I'm not takin' orders from nobody."

And wasn't that the truth? His brother could be as stubborn as they come—he was a Blackstone after all.

But the doctor smiled, probably as happy as Jacob to see Luke even attempt a joke at this devastating setback. "I guess that's the best I can hope for. We're gonna keep you here for now. See if there needs to be one more surgery, and make sure no infection sets into the places where the bone broke through your skin."

Jacob winced inwardly but maintained as much outward calm as he could manage. Normally, that was easy. Today, not so much.

"I'll let y'all know how things look tomorrow and give you a better time line for what's gonna happen. Just rest and let the antibiotics do their job."

Luke nodded, his eyes already drifting closed again.

Jacob and Aiden followed the doctor to the door, where she paused to look back at her patient. "Jacob, your twin is going to need you a lot, especially over the next few months. I understand that you live in South Carolina?"

"Yes," Jacob confirmed. "Down on the coastal side. Farther away than I'd like."

"I would consider finding him rehab options closer to home. I think he'll weather the upcoming difficulties much better surrounded by his family. Let me look into what's available in your area."

"Thank you, Doctor," Aiden said, then escorted her out into the hall. Leaving Jacob once more alone with Luke.

He pulled his cell phone out of his pocket once more, staring at the screen for long moments. He felt shaky, off guard. The past six months had been one change after another. Moving home. His job. Carter. This new, different relationship with KC.

He knew he needed her to steady his world and keep him strong. But he was supposed to be the strong one. He wasn't supposed to lean on someone else. And that was exactly what he wanted to do.

His hands started to shake, forcing him to tighten them into fists. His cell phone case dug into the edges of his palm.

So this was why he'd kept his relationship with KC simple and below the radar. Giving up his heart meant giving up control. Hell, he wasn't even sure he was capable of doing that.

He'd lost his dad. He'd almost lost Luke. Was he seriously considering adding another ticking time bomb to his life?

I love you. Immediately his mind recalled the warmth of KC's body cuddled against his in the dead of night. The spike of joy in his chest the first time Carter had smiled at him. The ache of need that grew with every minute he was away from them both.

Well, damn. It looked as if it was a little too late to fight this one off. "Wow," he heard from the bed. "That's some pretty intense stuff going on in that brain of yours. If you need someone to talk to, I can listen."

Jacob glanced over to find Luke's eyes open once more. "I know." Luke might offer to listen, but he had enough on his plate at the moment.

"I have nothing better to do. And I'll be asleep half the time anyway, so there's no need to be embarrassed. Just get it off your chest, dude."

Why not? His brother's drug-induced haziness made things a little easier to say. Maybe after, Luke wouldn't remember Jacob being so weak. "I screwed up, leaving her like that."

"You sure did."

All he'd been able to think about was getting to Luke. His logical brain had reasoned that KC couldn't travel on such short notice because of Carter, but it had all been excuses.

"I'm such an idiot," he said. How could he have convinced himself it would be better for KC to hear the news about Luke from anyone but him? He'd been worried about maintaining his gold-star control by keeping her at arm's length, worried he might toss aside his pride and beg her to come to him. Had he once thought about how all of this affected her?

"I've told you that a lot but you never listen," Luke said in an almost singsong voice, suggesting to Jacob that another dose of pain meds must have been delivered through the IV.

"I know, brother," Jacob murmured as Luke's eyes drifted closed. "This time, ignoring you isn't gonna work."

"Call her," Luke murmured. Then his eyes were shut tight, and that intangible connection between them broke.

Heart pounding, though he'd never admit it, Jacob slipped out the door and found Aiden in the hall. "Could you sit with Luke for a few minutes?"

Aiden's brows jumped toward his hairline. "Why would you even have to ask?"

Because taking care of Luke was *his* responsibility. "Right." He cleared his throat. "Can I use your phone?"

"Why?" Aiden asked with a frown.

"My battery is dead."

"Of course," Aiden said, handing it over. Jacob ignored Aiden's knowing look and headed for the stairs with the phone. Two minutes later, he was outside, staring across the dark alleyway behind the hospital as he listened to the ring on the other end of the line. He couldn't go out front— there were too many reporters hanging around. The staff had said this little area was secure if they needed to smoke or anything.

"Hello?"

KC's tentative voice caused emotion to tighten his throat, forcing him to clear it. "KC?" Then he remembered he wasn't on his own phone. "It's me. Jacob."

For a minute, he thought she wouldn't answer. When her soft "Hey" came across the line, sweet relief ran through his veins. Maybe just a moment too soon, because that was all she said.

Struggling to fill the silence, Jacob relayed the doctor's findings. But when he paused to draw a breath, KC broke in, "I know. I saw you on television."

"Right." Had she been all alone? Or had Christina still been there? "The press have been crazy here. Camped out all over the hospital grounds, trying to get in the doors... One even sneaked in through the emergency room then tried to grill a nurse for information on Luke." He grinned at the memory of their night nurse telling an animated version of the story. "Luke might start to think he's hot stuff."

"I bet he will." She spoke the words, but there was no life in them. He was definitely in the doghouse.

Not only was she quiet, but it sounded as if the house

was, too. His voice softened at the thought of his son. "Carter asleep?"

"Yes."

"Did the storm keep him up last night?"

"Some."

What about you? he wanted to ask. *Did it keep you awake? Did you wish I was there? Because I wish you were here.* Did he have the courage to say it? "The house okay?"

"Yes. It's stood for fifty years. It'll stand for fifty more."

This awkward conversation was not going the way he wanted, but he had no one but himself to blame.

"Listen, Jacob, I need to go to bed. It's been a long day, and like I said, we didn't sleep very well last night."

"Neither did I." He drew in a deep breath. *Time to suck it up, big man.* "Without you."

"I'm sure," she murmured.

"KC?"

"Yes?"

I'm sorry I'm such an idiot? No. Probably the wrong approach. "I love you, and wish you could be here with me."

She didn't ask the obvious: *So why didn't you give me the chance?* Instead, she whispered, "Thank you," and hung up the phone.

Sixteen

Aiden stepped into the room the next day right after the lunch lady cleaned up Luke's tray. If one could call broth "lunch." "You have a visitor," he said.

"I don't think he's up to it yet," Jacob said, noting Luke's groggy stare trained on his brother.

"Not him, dummy. You," Aiden said.

Who could possibly be here to see him?

"She was just gonna drop off your stuff and go," Aiden said, "but I told her to wait."

Stuff. KC was here? Jacob was through the door in the fastest move he'd executed since his mad dash to reach Luke. Stepping into the hall was easier this time than all the times before because his connection with his brother no longer pulled like a taut rubber band between them. As Luke's pain diminished, the wound on the twin brothers' psyches was beginning to heal, as well. For Jacob, it was now a barely noticeable twinge.

It would be a much longer road for Luke.

A few steps brought her into view. He'd expected a display of anger or even rejection. Instead, her face was an impassive mask, not really telling him anything.

He didn't know where to start, except with the obvious. "What're you doing here?"

A flash of uncertainty broke through the mask for a single second, but just as quickly disappeared. "I know you left in a hurry," she said, the words rushing from those perfectly shaped lips. "Too quickly to get your stuff. So I brought your travel bag." She gestured to his black bag on the floor next to her feet. "Some clothes, those protein bars you like for breakfast..."

Wow, fresh clothes. Jacob's outfit was rumpled, and he reeked after sleeping in a chair for three days. He'd already rotated through the two outfits he'd grabbed to bring with him. He simply didn't have it in him to leave the hospital, much less go to a store for something.

Her hard swallow drew his gaze to her throat. This seemed as difficult for her to say as it was for him to listen. "When you're ready to leave the hospital, Aiden will have a suitcase for you at his hotel room. Including your laptop. He put it in his car for you."

Holy smokes. She'd thought of everything. But then again, this was KC. Had he thought she'd do anything less?

"And I thought you might eventually need this." She pulled a gray cord out of her pocket—his phone charger. "You left it beside the bed."

"KC, thank you. This...this is very thoughtful. Did you drive up?" Man, that would have been hard for her. Crack of dawn was not something KC did well.

She shook her head. "No, Zachary flew me up. Just a quick trip."

"You flew?" His mind automatically went back to the day they'd met...and just how scared she was of flying. Which made her presence now even more incredible. "I don't know what to say." Especially since he'd left her behind without a word. Literally.

The difficulty of having this conversation and speaking to her after what he'd said on the phone...

Jacob hated this. They were so stiff with each other—avoiding eye contact, talking but not really saying anything. All his fault. All of it.

"There's nothing to say," she said, though her gaze was a bit too solemn for his liking. "We're partners. I just want to help any way I can." She gestured to the bag. "This I knew I could do."

What impressed him wasn't her words, but her tone. She could have called him out for ignoring her, for leaving town without notifying her or even for not calling personally for over twenty-four hours. But she didn't.

He could do no less. "I'm sorry, KC. I didn't have time to prepare."

"And we all know you like to be prepared, Jake," she said with a smirk, but her gaze still wouldn't lift to his.

That was probably why all this had thrown him for a loop in the first place. The plan was all-important to him. Now he needed to set that aside and he wasn't even sure how.

"KC, I know this is going to sound cowardly, but when I get home, can we talk?" This time those beautiful hazel eyes peeked from beneath her lashes. As their gazes met, he could see the same awareness that he'd heard permeating every word between them on their phone call. "There are some things, more things I need to say, starting with I'm sorry. But you deserve better than a rushed apology in a hospital hallway."

To his surprise, a sheen of tears graced her eyes. "I'd like that," she murmured.

"Thank you," he said simply, and then tried to get the conversation off more emotional topics before he pulled her close and refused to let her go. "Your mom got a handle on things with Carter?"

She swiped her fingers across each eye before nodding. "Yes, but that reminds me." Reaching into her own oversize tote bag, she pulled out a white paper sack. "She sent these because she said none of you should be forced to live on hospital food." She held it out like a white truce flag.

Jacob opened it, only to be seduced by the sweet aroma of a couple dozen peanut-butter cookies. "Wow," he said, not wasting any time shoving a whole one in his mouth. As the creamy, crunchy treat dissolved on his tongue, he couldn't hold back a moan.

"I'll take that to mean the cookies are appreciated," she said with a wistful smile. "I'll be sure to let Mom know."

"I must be weakening her barriers against me." This time, he actually got KC to share his grin.

"Jacob, the doctor is here," Aiden called from across the hall.

Jacob nodded before turning back to KC. "I need to go." He'd tried to be present for every update, worried about these first few steps of healing. But now he was pulled in the opposite direction.

He wanted her with him, even if it was only for a little longer. "Could you... Would you come with me?"

The surprise on her face reminded him of all he'd kept to himself. Everything she'd never been a part of. He'd claimed it was to keep her and Carter safe, but was it really? Had he been protecting her or himself?

He'd demanded they behave like a family—24/7—yet he'd failed to mingle the two most important halves of his life.

Gently taking her hand in his, he led her across the hallway and into Luke's room. The doctor was already speaking with Aiden and Luke about the additional surgery he'd be having the next morning. Resignation strained Luke's already pale features. He remained silent while his brothers asked all the pertinent questions.

Luke's sadness crept over Jacob, and he squeezed KC's hand tight. He simply couldn't let go. Even when the doctor extended her hand before she left, Jacob moved KC's hand into his other one so he could shake.

"Doctor, this is KC Gatlin."

After a quick glance at their joined hands, the doctor gave him an understanding look. "Don't worry," she told them both. "He will get through this."

Whether she meant Luke or himself, Jacob wasn't completely sure.

As she left, he felt KC's thumb rub along his. The fact that she would offer him comfort humbled him. After all he'd done, she still stood here with him. He led her forward to Luke's bedside.

Luke adopted a semblance of his trademark grin. "Wow, is this what I have to do to get pretty visitors?"

Jacob groaned. "Stop flirting with my woman, you egomaniac."

KC grinned, bumping her side against Jacob's. "Don't give your brother a hard time." She reached out to brush her free hand over Luke's. "I'm very sorry, Luke. If there's anything I can do for you..."

"Oh, just make sure I get to meet that cute little nephew of mine when I come back into town." His grin was a short-lived flash of brilliance. "Gives me something to look forward to."

Jacob heard her quick catch of breath, but no tears this time. "I sure will," she said. "But for now, I'll let you rest. I really need to get back to the airport. My brother is waiting to take me home."

Jacob was once again reminded of how scared to death she must have been in that little bitty plane, but she'd still flown all the way here—just to bring him what she thought he would need. KC was a giving person, but this was something more.

And he had to make sure he was worthy of it.

"I'll be back after I get her safely on her way," Jacob said. Aiden acknowledged him with an understanding nod, and then Jacob led KC out the door.

There were complications to visiting here. Paparazzi

were everywhere. If she was seen arriving or leaving the hospital with him, word would spread quickly. The vultures would hunt down her story in seconds, and he refused to leave her unprotected.

One of the nurses called a cab for them. Jacob walked KC down to a back corridor where security guarded an outside entrance. This way he could ensure her safe departure without interference from unwanted visitors. After only a few short minutes of waiting, Jacob gave into his need and wrapped his arms around her. He guided her head to rest against his chest, stroking his hand along her silky hair in an effort to soothe her.

Looking down at her guarded face, he knew she was still worried he'd walk away—indeed, he had without a word. But she made no demands. Gave no ultimatums. "I just don't know what to say. You could have really dug into me for behaving like an—" He stopped when she shook her head.

"I was angry. I've had too many men walk away in my life not to be."

The reminder of her childhood made him feel even lower.

"But then I realized something. The question isn't whether or not you go without me, Jacob. Life happens. I understand that. What really matters is whether or not I'm part of the decision. Part of the plan. That's what's important. And totally up to you. I will not be an obligation to you, Jacob. This is something you have to decide for yourself."

She was trusting him. He refused to disappoint her.

"Jacob, now," Aiden said as he slipped back into Luke's room.

"I'll call," Jacob murmured against her hair.

All too soon the cab arrived. She gave him a quick kiss, then started to walk away. She seemed completely unaware he was shaking inside from her gesture.

Her actions drove home exactly how deep he was in this relationship, because he wanted to meet her expectations, not just his obligations toward their son.

With just a few quick strides he was once again by her side. He cupped her face between his hands, guiding it up so he could brush his lips over hers. Once for the hello he'd failed to give. Once for the goodbye he hated to say. And once more as a promise. "I'll be home soon."

As he headed back into his brother's room, Jacob made a decision. As soon as he was sure Luke was stable, it was time to go home to his new family and win KC back.

In the way she truly deserved.

Jacob stood outside the door to Lola's, listening to the sounds of a busy Friday night. The parking lot was packed with cars. It should have been like any other Friday when he left work and had dinner with Aiden in the corner booth, watching his woman from across the room as she worked the bar.

Not tonight, he thought with a leap in his stomach. Tonight, he would finally make it official.

He'd stayed in Charlotte another few days after KC's surprise visit, long enough to make sure that Luke was well on his way to recovery. It would take time, but his brother would get back on his feet.

But he was sidelined from racing for the foreseeable future. Jacob didn't want to consider the emotional implications of that prognosis. Luke took every lick with a smile and a laugh, much the way he had when they were kids. But Jacob could see the shadows behind the laughter. His heart ached for his brother. But Jacob had come to a point of desperation: he had to get home to KC and Carter. Sure, they'd talked a few times on the phone after she'd left Charlotte—mostly about the baby. And KC never asked when Jacob was coming home or complained about him not being there.

Most men would be thrilled, but not Jacob. He hated that she didn't feel worthy of placing those demands on him. But with her family history, he understood why she didn't. It was up to him to show her those demands were her right. That she shouldn't let men take advantage of her—even him.

But the things Jake wanted to say, well, they shouldn't be said over the phone.

Jacob had finally acknowledged that he needed KC with him. But when Luke moved home soon, Jacob had to be with him, too. Once Luke's doctor released him, they were going to move him back to Blackstone Manor and do his physical therapy here. Luke was gonna need help, which meant things had to change. Jacob couldn't be in two places at once, and there was no room at KC's place for his brother. Jacob had a choice to make. His brother was an obligation he couldn't—no, wouldn't—turn his back on. But leaving KC and Carter alone put them in danger, and wasn't even an option anyway. The past few days had shown him he didn't want to be just a part-time dad…or a part-time lover.

So he'd made his choice. Would KC make the same one?

"You gonna go through that door or just stare at it all night?"

Jacob threw a dirty look at Zachary over his shoulder. As usual, it didn't faze KC's brother.

"Sis know you're back in town?"

Jacob turned back to the door. "No. I just got here."

"Okay," Zachary drew the word out. "So seriously. Why are you hovering outside the door like a mother hen?"

"I'm not, you goof. I'm just trying to decide what to say…"

"Yeah, laying your heart bare can be a little difficult. I'd hesitate, too."

Jacob threw a sidelong glance at the other man. He was awfully chipper for a guy the police still considered a prime suspect in a major felony case. "She said she trusted me to come back to her."

"Finally figured it out, didn't ya?"

"You know, I've had money all my life, but her trust in me? That's one of the most precious gifts I've ever been given."

Zachary nodded.

"I'd better be damn sure not to break it," Jacob concluded.

"Bingo. I think you've got this figured out." Zachary spread his hands wide. "My work here is done." Then he looked Jacob straight in the eye. "Did you hear? KC's been doing a great job getting the charity started. And Toby secured us some cotton, thanks to KCs skills as a negotiator. We're good to go for fall."

"Thank goodness. I knew putting her in charge was the right move."

"Trust me, putting Sis in charge is always the right move." As Zachary walked away, he said over his shoulder, "Hope you made sure the ring was spectacular."

Damn, that man was a mind reader. Jacob did have a ring, but that wasn't the most important thing he was offering tonight.

Determined now, he marched through the door and made his way straight to the bar, not looking left or right. Only KC, dead ahead in his sights, mattered. His heart tried to crawl up his throat before he reached her.

Man, was she beautiful. He watched as she pulled a beer with naturally confident moves, smiling at the customer with graciousness and a hint of flirtation. He wanted to growl out that she was his, but she wasn't—not so long as he chose to keep her a secret, as if she wasn't important enough to be an acknowledged part of his life.

That was about to change.

She saw him and smiled her casual smile, sticking to

the routine of the past months. Only the slight widening of her eyes gave away her surprise.

"We need to talk," he said, nodding toward an unoccupied corner of the bar.

He could tell from her slow steps that she wasn't sure she wanted to follow him. But it seemed that she couldn't stop herself. "Jacob, you don't have to—" she said from behind him.

"Yes," he said, cutting her off. "You may not need the words, but I do. I need to explain what happened while I was away."

Her eyes widened. He'd given her no reason to expect this, no reason to anticipate him doing anything more than waltzing back home as if nothing had changed. But it had. He had.

He came around the bar into the forbidden bartender zone, not caring who was watching. "I'll be honest. I don't know if this is the right thing to say. I know it's not the most romantic or charming. It wasn't until I got to the hospital that I realized, if I called you, the only thing I'd ask was for you to come. To be there with me."

She shook her head. "Why didn't you? Why didn't you ask me to stay?"

"Uprooting you, disrupting Carter's schedule... It made no logical sense."

"But I would do it because I love you. That's what people do. Not shove the people who love them away because they aren't convenient for them."

"You're right. You aren't convenient."

Her wince told him that stung a little. But his point wasn't a soft one.

"Neither is how I feel about you. Or Carter. I want everything to fit in its little compartment and you don't... Which is a good thing."

"I *really* don't understand."

Her welling eyes made him feel like such a jackass.

"I'm rigid in my own ways, sort of like my grandfather. I like consistency. Logic. Rules. You are none of those things. And I want you more than anything." Shaking his head, he couldn't hold back an unexpected grin.

"I left. I didn't call. I had reasons—my battery died, I couldn't leave Luke's bedside, there were paparazzi everywhere and things to take care of. But I figured out they were just excuses...and not even good ones."

He moved in closer, anxious to feel her body heat against his. She threw a glance to the side, looking over the crowd, but for once he couldn't care less who was watching.

"I screwed up, KC. The truth is, I was afraid. If I had called you, I'd have dissolved into a blubbering mess begging you to join me."

Now he had her full attention. "But I still don't understand why that's a bad thing," she said, reaching up to rub the curve of his jaw.

"It's just a thing I'm not used to. Something I don't know how to handle." His laugh was dry. Half-angry. "Aiden, Luke and I—we've stood on our own since our father died. Not relying on anyone else. I don't know how to change that. But I have to try, because these feelings aren't going away."

He ducked his head to nuzzle her soft hand. "I know I won't handle things the way you want me to. Emotions and life and fear. But I will always come back to you and Carter. Always. Not because I have to, because I want to."

Her expression was wide-eyed and wondrous. Was it happiness...or fear?

Or both?

As she took a tentative step toward him, the DJ took a break. Perfect timing.

The music faded from the room, leaving the sound of people making their way to the bar for another drink. But she had eyes only for him. Out of his peripheral vision, he saw her brother serving the patrons lining up at the bar. Then a mischievous grin spread across her lips.

"So what is it I can get you, Jacob Blackstone?"

Her sexy confidence, mixed with carefully cloaked need, melted every last ounce of resistance inside him. "You, KC Gatlin."

He spoke loud enough for the words to carry to those behind them. After that, the speed of gossip in a small town took over. By the time she asked, "What?" he had the attention of half the bar.

"KC, I only need one thing," he said with a small grin. He let his palms flatten on the smooth counter behind her to ground himself, ground them. "Would you and Carter come live with me at Blackstone Manor?"

She joined in the collective gasp, her big eyes even rounder now. She glanced at the crowd. "Jacob, what are you saying?"

"I'm saying my mother needs me at home. My brother will need me there very soon. But in the midst of all of that, I want to give you what *you* need. Please come with me. Don't make me go alone."

"But I don't belong—"

He stopped her protest with a kiss. "You're the best thing that could have happened to me. I'm just sorry it took me so long to do something about it."

The whispers rippled across the room. Heavy footsteps sounded behind him. "Come on, KC," Aiden said. "Put us all out of our misery and accept the poor guy. His moping is driving me crazy."

Jacob glanced over to Zachary. "Zachary, may I?" Jacob asked, garnering permission in more ways than one.

KC's brother gave a short nod and a smile. "Be my guest."

In seconds, Jacob had the ring in his hand.

"I thought you didn't like public displays," she said, examining the princess-cut emerald that matched the green that was flashing in her eyes.

He tilted her chin up with his finger to get a look at the real thing. "Sweetheart, with you, I'll take you any way I can have you. And I'd rather the world know you were mine than risk for a moment the chance of being without you."

"But what about…" She glanced around at their audience, then leaned closer and whispered, "The mill, the crazy person threatening people? You said it wasn't safe."

"I promise you now, I will not let him ever harm you or Carter, no matter what it takes." He pulled her closer, now whispering in her ear, "KC, I love what we've built together. But I need you with me, in every part of my life. Will you marry me? Please?"

"Jacob, don't you know I'd follow you anywhere? All you had to do was ask me."

As the cheers erupted around them, he let his lips speak his gratitude against hers.

Seventeen

Later that night—long after all the excitement had died down, Jacob had bought a few rounds and Zachary had offered to close up for the night—KC finally had Jacob to herself. He opted for a long, hot shower to wash off his travel fatigue. When he came out of the bathroom, KC was in bed, staring at her new ring.

"Is Carter asleep?" he asked.

"Yes, I just got him back down." Her little man's excitement at seeing his daddy again had simply added to the night's joy.

Jacob reached for her hand, rubbing over her fingers right above the band. "I realized something while I was in the shower."

"What's that?"

"I didn't tell you the most important part."

Yep, KC's heart was definitely gonna explode.

"I told you I was too logical." He grinned in a self-deprecating way that warmed her, because Jake was usually the confident one. "I do love you, KC. You've changed me, you and Carter both. For the better, I hope."

I believe you. The words trembled on her lips. She wanted to say them so badly, but all she could think about was her daddy leaving for the store one day and never coming back. Logically, she knew it wasn't the same. But her woman's heart wouldn't give up the fear.

"KC, do you remember what I told your mother and grandmother?"

She looked over at him sitting on the corner of their bed. She felt like a kid who'd been given permission to go crazy in the candy store but was afraid the sugar might kill her. "When?"

"That first Sunday dinner? Your grandmother asked me how she could know that I was trustworthy."

Oh, right. She nodded, afraid to speak as his words brought a lifetime of thoughts rushing to the surface.

"I told her then and I'll tell you now—me promising to always be here, to put you and Carter first is all well and good. But they're just words. Instead, I'll have to prove it to you through my actions."

"Like taking our relationship public in a major way?"

"Oh, yes. But in my defense, your brother egged me on."

"What?"

He grinned, reaching out to hold her hand, turning it so that her engagement ring caught the light. "He's really sneaky, that one. But seriously, it will take time, and I may make mistakes, but I'll prove it to you and Carter. Every day."

Jacob was looking at her as if all her secrets were already known. As if he knew he couldn't force a response, he changed tactics. "Would you come to bed with me?"

Oh, boy. She should be more than ready to jump into bed with the man who'd just asked her to marry him. But her emotions were all over the place, her thoughts racing... "I don't know." Why did she feel as if she was being put through an endurance test?

"Not for sex," Jacob said, surprising her. His sincerity shone from his amber eyes. "Right now, I need something more."

More? She'd always thought men saw sex as the ultimate expression of their emotions. And in a way, it would be easier to go back to that sexual focus. But she needed more—and she wanted to give Jacob the opportunity to prove himself to her in a way no man had bothered to do before now.

"I love you, KC, and after everything that's happened between us, I can't think of anything better than to spend a few hours just lying in your arms." His voice deepened, his face twisting with emotion. "I need you."

Minutes later, as she sank against him in their bed, no longer alone and abandoned, she knew she could let go of the fear. "I love you, too," she whispered.

Less than a week later, KC took the one step she'd resisted since Jake's return to her life. Fear and excitement settled in a tingly mass in the pit of her stomach as she stood before the elaborately carved entrance to Blackstone Manor. Even the lion door knocker intimidated her, which was saying a lot. Usually she was pretty hard to rattle.

Standing confidently by her side, Jacob said, "Welcome home."

She clung to the happiness in Jake's eyes as if it was her own personal life preserver. She wasn't used to this kind of wealth; most of her life, she'd had an average amount of money, though she had vague memories of some financial struggles after her dad hit the road.

But a house this size, the luxurious grounds, someone to cook, to clean… She was totally out of her element.

Even Christina's welcoming smile didn't calm KC's nerves about fitting in. Holding a sleeping Carter in her arms like a shield, she let Jacob escort her inside, despite a deep-rooted desire to return to her little house on the other end of town.

But it wasn't long before the residents were welcoming her as if she were a long-lost daughter. Nolen smiled as he greeted her. The look in his faded blue eyes was sincere as he encouraged her to let him know if she needed a hand with anything. Marie didn't have any of the older man's reserve. She embraced KC and Carter together, then oohed and aahed over the baby.

Jacob grinned. "Now, I don't wanna start a rivalry, so I won't comment on your mom's peanut-butter cookies in front of Marie…"

The cook frowned in his direction.

"But Marie's chocolate-chip cookies are the best I've ever tasted. If you smell them baking, better get to the kitchen. They go fast."

Leaving the beaming cook behind, Jacob showed KC where everything was on the first floor. With a mysterious intensity, he said, "Do you want to see our suite?"

She looked up the elegant, sweeping staircase to the second floor. "Actually, don't you think it's time I met your mother?"

His gaze sobering, Jacob led her up the staircase and to the right. KC paused and nodded toward the opposite side of the hall. An open set of double doors revealed a room under construction. "What's that?"

"That used to be my grandfather's suite." He squeezed her shoulder. "We're renovating it for Luke because it's closest to the elevator."

She met his look, seeing all the worry and exhaustion over his brother's injuries, emotions Jake kept well hidden—except in the darkest hours of the night when he held her close.

Then Jacob led them into a feminine suite decorated in shades of lavender. Lily Blackstone lay as still as a frozen angel, her only movement the lift of her chest as she breathed.

As they approached the bed, Jacob said, "KC, this is my mom, Lily."

His hushed voice held respect and tenderness. KC

watched the comatose woman in silence for long moments, thinking about her own mother and her love for Carter. With a small smile, she left the warmth of Jacob's arms and crossed to the side of the bed opposite all the medical equipment. "Ms. Blackstone," she said. "This is your grandson, Carter."

Then she slipped her son into the gap between Lily's arm and her side, cradling his head against his grandmother's warm body.

Carter continued to sleep soundly as KC talked. "He looks a lot like Jacob and Luke. Jacob says they both had these same blond curls when they were babies. He has Jake's feet, too—long and a little narrow—"

After a few more minutes by Lily's side, KC felt Jacob's presence behind her. Though she twisted his way, he didn't give her the chance to glimpse his face. Instead, he buried his head into the crook of her shoulder, his arms drawing her close.

He stood like that for a long time—silent, shaking—until he finally pulled back. It was reminiscent of the night he'd asked her to marry him, long after they'd lain down in bed together. Finally looking down, his amber eyes were dry but glowing with emotion.

"Thank you." Two simple words—it was amazing how much they meant to her.

Then he kissed his mother's cheek and scooped Carter back into his arms. Their son's eyes peeked open for a minute, then closed once more after he'd reassured himself that Daddy was there.

"I've got something to show you," Jacob said, taking her hand to lead her back down the hallway and up two more flights of stairs.

"I can see I've got my work cut out for me," she teased, huffing a little at the climb.

Jacob paused. "I should have taken you to the elevator."

"Are you kidding? My legs are gonna look great after a month of this."

He grinned, stepping close to brush his lips across hers. "No, KC, it's hard to improve on perfection."

She loved that he would let himself tease and be teased now. "Flattery will get you everywhere, Mr. Blackstone... So will hefting the baby up these stairs for me."

They continued to the third floor, this time turning left at the top of the stairs. "We'll be close to the elevator, too. I'm just used to taking the stairs unless I have my hands full," Jacob said, adjusting Carter in his arms.

She ran an appreciative eye over the main room, decorated in various shades of green. Then Jacob led her through a door on the other side. "We have a good chunk of this floor," he said as he led her through what looked like a walk-in closet. "There's a single bedroom on the other side that Aiden uses for storage, since the room he shares with Christina isn't very big. And another empty room."

"And what else?" KC asked, mentally adding up all the square footage on the floor and marveling at the size of the place.

"This."

Jacob opened the door onto a baby boy's wonderland nursery. Walls painted a green shade to match the other room. A race-car theme, which made KC smile. Everything a baby and mama could need, including a snuggle chair built similarly to the one in her living room. "Wow, Jacob. This is beautiful. Did Christina do this for you?"

He raised his brows in mock offense. "Heck, no. I did this myself. Even assembled the crib."

He'd done it all himself... Jacob had been gone for a while, and there hadn't been enough time for him to do it since his return. So that meant... "You started this as soon as you knew," she breathed.

"I did, KC." He moved over to the crib and settled Carter inside. When he turned back, his gorgeous eyes were clouded over, bringing out their brown highlights. "I want you to know I didn't do this to show off or outdo you. I guess…I hoped you'd see that I was invested—in him, in us, something other than work."

"I'm glad," she said, the beauty around her feeling right. It wasn't pretentious, didn't have the cold look of someone trying to show off. But each color, each item spoke of love for a baby and his comfort. "It's perfect."

Sliding into his arms felt just as right.

"I love you, KC. I'll never leave either of you again. You can trust me."

"I'll never leave you, either," she said, and knew deep down how very true her words were. "Family sticks together, right?"

"Right." He granted her a beautiful smile. "That sounds like the perfect plan to me."

* * * * *